Rasha Adly is an Egyptian writer, born in Cairo in 1972. She is a researcher and freelance lecturer in the history of art, and Cairo correspondent for the Emirates Culture magazine. She is the author of six novels, and *The Girl with Braided Hair* was longlisted for the International Prize for Arabic Fiction (the "Arabic Booker") in 2018.

Sarah Enany is a literary translator and a professor in the English Department of Cairo University.

The Girl with Braided Hair

Rasha Adly

Translated by
Sarah Enany

hoopoe
AN IMPRINT OF AUC PRESS

First published in 2020 by
Hoopoe
113 Sharia Kasr el Aini, Cairo, Egypt
One Rockefeller Plaza, 10th floor, New York, NY 10020
www.hoopoefiction.com

Hoopoe is an imprint of the American University in Cairo Press
www.aucpress.com

Dar el Kutub No. 25913/19
ISBN 978 977 416 987 8

Dar el Kutub Cataloging-in-Publication Data

Adly, Rasha
    The Girl with Braided Hair / Rasha Adly.— Cairo: The American
University in Cairo Press, 2020.
        p.   cm.
        ISBN 978 977 416 9 987 8
        1. English fiction
        823

1 2 3 4 5   24 23 22 21 20

Designed by Adam el-Sehemy
Printed in the United Kingdom

To everyone who has been defeated by life or had their dreams broken.

1

Cairo: Winter 2012

YASMINE ARRIVED AT WORK AND headed straight for the Conservation Department. She put on a smock over her clothing, gloves and a mask, and sat down to continue with the painting that she had started work on a few days ago. She reached for it with great care, as it was ancient and all but falling apart. Watching her was Jean Simon, director of conservation at the Louvre, who had been appointed by the ministry especially to oversee and restore the priceless books damaged in the fire that had swept the Egyptian Scientific Institute in 2011. Noticing how nervous and careful she was being, he approached. "A true artist," he observed. "What a shame that the painting has no identifying information."

"Yes," she responded. "There are a lot of portraits out there of Egyptian faces, but there's something about this one that's different."

The director gazed thoughtfully at the painting. "I believe it is the first time I have come across a work by this particular painter. I don't recognize his style or the characteristics of his brushstrokes." He took a breath. "When an artist studies under a great master, frequently their brushstrokes will be similar, but this doesn't resemble anyone else's, not even any of the contemporary masters." He smiled. "In any case, don't worry. When you're done with the preliminary conservation, we can do an infrared examination, and it may yield something."

As he left the room, her phone pinged with a message. She picked it up hurriedly. *2, Left Bank. I'll be there.* Smiling, she put the device back in her pocket.

2

SHERIF DIDN'T EXPECT HER TO text him back, no *I'm on the way* or *Sorry, I can't make it.* He would just let her know where he was. Sometimes she came; sometimes she didn't.

They had met at a conference on architecture. He was an architect who owned his own company, a firm that specialized in building luxury hotels and mansions for the wealthy; she was a professor of art history who specialized in Renaissance, Baroque, and Neo-Baroque art, well-known in architectural circles as a consultant to major construction firms. She had been recommended to him by a consulting architect he usually worked with, who had been forced by illness to excuse himself from working on a project. She had received a phone call from Sherif some days later, asking her to oversee the plans for a new construction project in the Baroque style.

Their romance had lasted a year; he had loved her passionately, and she had whispered "I love you" into his ear a few times. Suddenly, like a light switch flipping off, her love had winked out, all her passion and desire for him gone. His eyes had always held a question; she always avoided answering it. One time he asked her straight out, "Why did your feelings for me change?"

She was truthful and cruel: "There's someone else."

Strangely enough, he did not argue or blame her, but nodded and left. He knew that it was no use talking: he was experienced enough to know how labyrinthine and changeable the paths of human affection are. He also knew that he was not a skilled lover; he did not string together honeyed words, nor did he purchase gifts and flowers.

They met less frequently; the silence between phone calls stretched longer and longer. Tedium crept into their time together, and her feelings toward him cooled even further. Without realizing it, she had fallen in love with someone else. Oddly, that man did not return her love; he was, however, adept at the art of romance. The question remained, as it always does: should we stay with the one who loves us genuinely, though they be an inept romantic; or be with a master of romance, although they do not truly love us?

She had thought that love—and love only—makes puppets of us all, pulling our strings to take us where it will. However, with the other man, she had discovered that it was not necessary to love in order to woo someone. From the first, he had been honest with her: he told her he knew nothing of love, and could never tie himself down to one woman for the sake of something as worthy as love. Still, she pressed on, swept away by her feelings for him. Something about him attracted her, something charming and magnetic. She never did manage to put a name to it. Then she came to herself, as though slapped awake from a dream, when he told her he had found someone new, his voice ringing in her ears: "I never promised you anything."

She went back to Sherif and cried on his shoulder. Generously, chivalrously, he listened. "Don't ever blame yourself," he told her, "if you genuinely loved him. Emotions are the most beautiful thing one can possess." He told her, "It's enough that he lit the fire of love in you, even if he didn't intend it. Such feelings are rare. This is why we must be grateful to anyone who makes us feel them, ever. There are people who live out their lives in the illusion of eternal love, deliberately forgetting that love is the result of complex and changeable chemical reactions." What he said made sense to her—after all, she had loved him once, and it was over. Wasn't it?

3

THE MEMORY WAS REPLAYING IN Sherif's head when she walked in; she found him lost in thought, in another world. "What are you thinking of?" she asked.

He jerked up, finding her already in the seat opposite his. He smiled, "You."

"Oh? And what were you thinking?"

He did not reply; she did not press him. From the way his eyes lit up at the sight of her, and the unsteadiness in his voice when he spoke her name, she could not doubt that he still loved her. It would have been cruel to twist the knife. They had not spoken of the subject since the last time they talked, when they sat facing each other at a café on a rainy winter day. Back then, he had asked her, "Why have you changed so much?"

"It's because of you," she had responded truthfully.

"How?"

"The way you love me," she explained, "it's . . . the spark is gone. You're cold, and the cold is in us now, too. It's too long between calls and between dates. We meet at the same places, say the same words, order the same things. The logs in a fireplace need to be stirred up every once in a while so the flame will burn bright, but you've let the fire go out."

"It's funny," he had said, "that you say 'the way you love me.' Isn't it enough that I love you?"

"No," she'd replied, "it's not."

Back then, he had not argued with her. Maybe, as she said, he was not adept enough at the ways of love, perhaps he didn't know how to keep his woman's heart aflame. When they parted that day, he had meant it to be for always; but she'd called him weeks later, telling him she missed him and wanted to see him. Before she hung up, she had said, "Sherif, I think my life was meant to have you in it." It wasn't about romance: their relationship had deepened to the point where her life was unimaginable without him. There was nothing in it for him but to fold his passions inside and play the part of the shoulder to cry on, the person to talk to. We all have someone like that in our life; sometimes we don't quite know what they are to us.

He ordered two espressos. When they arrived, he asked her how she'd been. Her eyes glistened: he knew there was something important. "I'm working on an unsigned painting by an extraordinarily talented artist. What's strange is that the painting was never a success. It isn't well-known or famous at all, although it belongs in a top-tier art museum."

"What I think," he said, "is that the chance for success comes once in a lifetime. If you let it slip by, it's lost forever." He took a sip of his espresso. "Be sure of it: opportunity comes once in a lifetime."

She appeared to catch his meaning, and so did not contradict him. Instead, she gave him the innocent smile he liked so much, the one that revealed her inner child. Was it only her smile he was fond of? He loved everything about her, from her large eyes and thick brows to her plump lips, loose, wavy hair, and shining bronzed skin. He loved the expressions on her face when she talked: her eyes had a way of widening and then narrowing, and unlike any woman he had known, her beauty came from her simplicity and her allure from her ingenuous nature.

They were used to sitting in comfortable silence; he enjoyed reading the language of her eyes, and she could read his body language in a nod or a lift of his eyebrows or the way he steepled his hands; so what need had they of talk? Eventually, he looked at his watch. "It's 3:30. What do you have planned?"

"Nothing," she said easily, "I'll just go home."

"I need to get back to the office," he said. "I've an important meeting at four." They rose to go. She wrapped her scarf around her neck while he put on his coat. "Where's your car?" he asked as they walked outside.

"I thought I'd walk today," she said, "I could use the exercise."

"Do you want a lift?" he asked. "It's kind of windy."

"Let's see where it blows me."

He ran his hand over her hair by way of goodbye, and left.

4

HER EYES FOLLOWED HIM AS he crossed the road to his car. He walked straight and erect, striding confidently across the street. No woman could resist him, from the soft, pleasant huskiness in his voice to his deep, piercing eyes that seemed to see into you. But for all that, he'd let the flame burn out.

Her phone rang in her coat pocket. "Grandma!"

Her grandmother's voice was breathy and halting, but commanding as usual. "Don't forget the cat food!"

Her grandmother was ninety and suffered from senile dementia: the only things that kept her alive were her cats and whatever fugitive scraps of memory she had left. Whenever Yasmine looked at her, her conviction increased that time was a tyrant. Could this, she wondered, be her fate? An old woman who forgot more than she remembered, whose hair had all fallen out except for two white tufts on the right and left, her face furrowed and lined with wrinkles, her eyes dulled and pale, peeing into diapers like a child? Heavens, what a fate. And yet, her grandmother was lucky: she had a loving granddaughter who cared for her and her cats. Many people that age had no one to take care of them. Yasmine had once thought of putting her into an old people's home, especially because she traveled a lot to exhibitions and conferences, but every time it occurred to her, she pushed the thought away and hired a nurse instead. And every time, she would come back to a torrent of complaints from the nurse about her grandmother, "that old woman who's always screaming and never stops giving orders."

Yasmine knew that her grandmother liked to run a tight ship, and nothing was ever good enough for her; she was used to it by now, and excused her grandmother's foibles as the failings of old age. The one thing that upset and saddened her was when she picked up the phone and entered into long one-sided conversations with people long dead, telling them about the events of her day. The doctor had told Yasmine that it was to be expected. "But she can't remember recent events," she'd said to him worriedly, "and these old numbers are still stuck in her memory, and things that happened all those years ago."

"Long-term memories are easy to access," the doctor said, "if they are bright in the mind."

Yasmine accepted reality. It became routine to hear her grandmother dialing a number at four in the morning and launching into a long conversation with a long-departed friend, recounting the events of a day in her life that had taken place years ago, and telling her how her husband and children had loved the special meal she had cooked.

She turned left onto a long, narrow downhill street that sloped toward the Nile. Every step seemed to propel you downward, shoving you into the face of the river. On either side were beautiful old buildings and villas, most of them deserted. It was strange not to see a single modern building all down the street, as though this was a place that refused to be touched by wrecking balls. Since Zamalek was built, when Khedive Ismail had divided up its land among that era's elite on condition that they erect structures in fine artistic taste, its buildings had remained untouched. Their opulence and history struck her anew every time she passed them: a strange feeling came over her, as if she could hear the footsteps of the people who had lived here walking through time. Even the supermarket on the street was one in name only, and was more of an old-time grocery store. Everything in it evoked a bygone era: the floor-to-ceiling wooden shelves on the walls, the sausages hanging by cords from the rafters, the incessantly rotating ceiling fan—even the goods on sale seemed on their way to extinction, brands that were hard to find anywhere else. The owner, seated on a wooden stool, tallied up your purchases with pen and paper and handed you a handwritten receipt. On the top of the paper was printed, "Abdel-Aziz Nakhla & Co., Grocers—Founded 1930." She found it quite natural, in that place with its contents, to be transported to another time.

She needed to find a real supermarket to buy cat food. Stepping into the supermarket was like coming back into the present: the gleaming display, the shopping carts, and the register with its credit card machine.

5

WHEN YASMINE TURNED THE KEY in the lock, her grandmother was screaming as usual, praying to the Lord to deliver her from her suffering. Dumping her purchases on the kitchen table, Yasmine went straight to her. "What's the matter, Grandma? What happened? What suffering?"

"Let me scream in peace!" her grandmother snapped. "My diaper hasn't been changed since this morning! And what do you call that? Isn't that what you might properly call suffering?"

Although they had a maid who also cooked, and would have been happy to change the diaper, her grandmother refused to let the woman see her naked. She insisted that Yasmine change her, bathe her, and do her hair as well. This was one of the things that made Yasmine periodically think that putting her grandmother in a home would be an excellent idea, and decide to do it; but moments later, she would find herself shaking her head violently, as if to throw the idea out of it. *No, no, I couldn't.*

The diaper changed and the table set, dinner was dished out. The two of them sat facing each other at the kitchen table. "In that white shirt, you look a lot like your mother," said her grandmother.

Yasmine smiled, chewing, but said nothing. She had no desire to get into that subject, as it always led to painful memories and strong disagreements.

Clearly, though, her grandmother had decided to upset her today. "If she were alive, poor thing, she'd have been sixty-five. But she chose to leave at forty-five. What a woman she was, so vibrant!"

"Grandma, please, let's talk about something else."

"But that bastard of a father of yours," she plowed on as though she hadn't heard, "it was all his fault! It was him who drove her to suicide, it was, and as if that wasn't enough, he didn't even have the decency to stick around! Ran off like the worthless coward he is."

"I told you a hundred times, she was depressed. That was why. Nobody *makes* anyone kill themselves. It was just . . . a thing that happened."

"And who was it who made her depressed, eh? Wasn't it him? Lousy womanizer! With her best friend, yet. It's enough to make any woman kill herself."

"She could have gotten treatment and started fresh. You just said it yourself—she was beautiful, attractive, full of life. She could have made a new life, she could have tried to forget. It was her choice to close every door."

Her grandmother sighed. "I can't believe it either, that such a beauty, such a success, would end her life for that Casanova. But he was the love of her life. Ever since her first year in university, she was his girlfriend. Do you even know what that means? And she married him the minute she graduated—she'd never known another man!" Her grandmother chewed her food, lost in thought. "From the first, there was something about him that set me on edge. Eyes like a fox, he had, cunning and wily."

"Why not blame the woman who made him do it?" Yasmine sighed. "You said it yourself—she was her best friend. That's low, if you ask me."

"But it was your father's fault more than anyone. He knew how your mother adored him. He should have cherished that love, cherished his family." She set down her fork on her

14

empty plate. "And her best friend, of all women! Couldn't he find someone else? Did it have to be her best friend?"

Yasmine pushed back her chair with a clatter and started to stack the empty plates. "It was Mom's fault they got that close." She carried the dishes over to the sink. "She was the one who let her into her home and let her get close to her family. She shared all her secrets with her, everything she did, everyone she met, what happened, what was going to happen—all the details of her relationship with Dad, and the rough time she was having with him." Clattering, she stacked the plates, then started on the glasses. "She let her spend time alone with Dad whenever she came to visit—sitting and talking to him while Mom was in the kitchen cooking. And she even insisted that Dad drive her home! She practically put out a welcome mat for them to have an affair."

"Whatever the temptation," her grandmother insisted, "if you're loyal by nature, you don't give in."

Yasmine's hands stilled on the dishes, lost in a faraway corner of memory. She could still remember that Jezebel—skimpy clothes, bright red lipstick, overpowering perfume, and throaty, silky voice. Mom was just the opposite—she dressed modestly and everything about her was soft—her prettiness, her voice. How hard would it have been for Mom to recognize that that woman was doing her best to get close to Dad and entrap him? They tried to hide what was going on, never suspecting that a ten-year-old could recognize the gestures and glances that went between them, the whispers that gave it all away.

Poor Mom, making dinner for them in the kitchen while they flirted. God, could they have let her down any worse? What kind of pain must she have felt? What a dagger through the heart. No wonder she couldn't stand to go on living.

As usual, talking about it brought nothing but pain. The whole thing was like a wound covered in ointments and bandages to stop the bleeding until such time as it might heal—only it never did. Every time she recalled it, the bleeding would start again. Yasmine went into her room, slamming the door.

"There are faithful men! You must know it!" Her grandmother's yell came through the door. "Don't let it turn your heart against them all!"

"Don't worry," Yasmine muttered with a sad smile, not caring whether or not her grandmother heard. "You don't need to worry about that."

6

THE NEXT MORNING, SHE HEADED for the office of her former art history professor, Mahmoud Anwar. A good-looking man in his fifties, he had a smattering of white hairs at his temples and unparalleled expertise in the history of art. He was forever researching and seeking out new knowledge. She told him about the painting, and he promised to help. "I'll come by the lab after classes," he promised, "and take a look at it."

Afterward, she went to the lecture hall to teach a class. "Art history," she began as she had many times before, "is not only a matter of taking an interest in the piece of art itself or its provenance, its date of creation or the life history of the artist who made it. It is everything that surrounds a work of art: the political, economic, and social factors that eventually led to its production. You can be sure that your research into the history of a painting will lead you down many exciting avenues you had no idea even existed."

After class, hard at work in the lab, she startled to find Professor Anwar standing right behind her. "Let's take a look at this priceless treasure of yours," he said.

With a smile, she rose to show him. He was always like that, with his own way of speaking that sometimes drew the mockery of his students. Carefully, she placed it on the easel.

He slid on his spectacles and crouched close, scrutinizing it first with, then without his glasses. He seemed to be looking for something. Finally, he shrugged. "To tell the truth, I don't see anything inspiring or absorbing about this painting," he admitted. "It's the same as a hundred other paintings of Egyptian female subjects painted in the nineteenth century, the 'golden age' of Orientalism. They were mad about drawing women with 'Oriental' features and clothing they saw as exotic."

"Yes," Yasmine shook her head, "but there's something different about this one. Look at the girl's clothes. They're a mix of Oriental and Western. She's wearing a *gallabiya* with vertical stripes, but that thing on her shoulder is a lace scarf. Egyptian women weren't wearing those kind of fabrics in that era—they were unavailable in Egypt. And there's no signature or date on it."

"What's so odd about that? Maybe the artist wanted to do something unconventional, so he made her clothing a cross between East and West. He could have just imagined the lace scarf." The professor straightened. "As far as the signature goes, he may have forgotten to sign it. Or perhaps he was unknown and saw no point in signing his work, as it would have gone unrecognized one way or the other."

Yasmine gestured to the background of the painting of the girl, which depicted several houses with wood-carved meshrabiyeh windows. "You can't tell what neighborhood this was painted in. Islamic architecture was everywhere in that era, and they used meshrabiyehs as a motif. It could be anywhere."

Anwar leaned in again, peering at the image of the girl. "Was she that lovely in real life?" he sighed. "In any case, you can do an infrared examination, it might help."

It was the same thing Professor Simon had said. Changing the subject, Yasmine began to speak of work and study, after which they made an appointment for the infrared examination.

After Professor Anwar left, Yasmine sat at the painting alone, working, wondering why she was so preoccupied with the girl in the picture. Anwar was right: she was no different from a hundred portraits of Eastern women painted in that era, the product of Orientalists' boundless fascination with Eastern women and a world they saw as exotic. A dark-skinned girl with kohl-rimmed eyes and long, black braids lying gently across her shoulders: what was so special about her?

She went back to work on the painting, scraping off a fleck of the black of the braids that had faded from damage. Gently, she scraped off the faded area. It was odd: this part was thicker than the others, as though the artist had mixed it with another medium. Suddenly, something strange appeared beneath the color.

She touched it with her fingertips. It felt like human hair.

Yasmine drew in her breath sharply. "What the . . . am I going crazy?" she said aloud. She fumbled for her magnifying glass and peered through it at the exposed fleck. It was indeed real hair.

With exceeding gentleness, she scraped the color off the braid. Then she touched it again. It was human hair, hidden by the artist under a hard layer of something carefully mixed with his black pigment. A smile of renewed confidence formed on her lips as she thought, *I knew my feeling was right.* From the first glance, she had known there was something unusual about this painting and this girl.

Cairo: July 1798

A girl, slender like a stalk of rattan, her skin an unusual color, not white and not dark, but the color of saffron dust. Lips red as cherries, hair black and thick like a waterfall, a spring in her step like a leaping deer. Her gestures, smooth as a butterfly's. She wore a *gallabiya* of vertically striped silk, her hoop earrings echoing the curves of her body, which indicated she was just coming into adulthood. She was in that awkward stage between a child and a woman: too old to run and play with the children, but as yet unwelcome among grown women; she was lost between two worlds, the world of childhood she had not yet left behind, and the world of womanhood she was yet to enter.

Her mother bent with a straw broom to sweep the dust off the tiles of her floor, dusting the couch with the wooden arms and replacing the bolsters stuffed with good Egyptian cotton. She wiped the round wooden table and polished the brass tray on top. Finally, she lit incense to perfume the room, then, satisfied that she had prepared the seating area adequately for her husband Sheikh al-Bakri and his friends and fellow Azharite clerics, she went out and closed the door.

Still absorbed in housework, she noticed Zeinab standing in the center of the house, a small mirror in hand, plucking her eyebrows. "What are you doing, girl?" she snapped, startled. "Do you want tongues to wag about you? Would you have people say that the daughter of Sheikh Hassan al-Bakri plucks her brows like a harlot or a belly dancer?"

Zeinab smiled, her small mouth revealing rows of pearly white teeth, her cheeks dimpling charmingly. The smile did little to calm her mother. She grabbed the girl by one of her black braids that were long enough to sit on. "Stop doing that and come and help me with the housework! Girls your age are already married with husbands and children to care for!"

"All you do is sweeping and mopping!" Zeinab huffed. "You could spend the whole day cleaning house, like the only thing you were made for in this life is cleaning!"

"Well, whoever marries you is going to have his hands full, I can tell you that, girl. Quickly, put the firewood in the oven. Your father's almost home and we haven't even started the baking yet."

Zeinab walked away with soft, indolent steps. She watched her mother clean and polish, with every ounce of strength she possessed, the Constantinople mules that her father wore on his feet, laying them carefully on the floor by the couch where he sat. "As if we were only brought into this world to sweep and clean," she muttered rebelliously.

Around the spacious central courtyard of the house, the rooms were set in rows. There were stalls for cattle and donkeys and others for birds, and a large storehouse for grain and coal: ever since they had first heard of Napoleon's campaign in Egypt, most households had prepared themselves to be self-sufficient. Wells had been dug; chickens were raised; gardens were planted in every home to provide what vegetables were needed, and carpenters had been employed to fit bolts to every wooden door. Zeinab ordered Halima, their black slave, to fill a pot with clean water from their cistern, which the water carrier had filled this morning. Zeinab took up the censer and walked around the space, perfuming the air with incense. "That's all you're good for," her mother snapped.

After the sunset call to prayer, Zeinab heard the sound of horses' hooves pounding the gravel entrance way, and stopping outside their gate. Finally, her father was permitted to ride a horse, after many years of being forbidden from riding: horseback had been reserved for the upper echelons of Mamluk rulers, while the rest of the populace were restricted to donkeys and mules. Her father had picked out a noble Arabian stallion, and decorated its bridle with gold and silver.

Her father's horse neighed when Rostom, the groom, put him in the stable, letting everyone know he was home. The regular consternation reigned whenever he arrived at the house: slave women rushing to the kitchen, girls scurrying to their rooms, boys adjusting their turbans on their forcibly clean-shaven heads, thanks to the scorching August heat.

A slave girl placed the dishes on the round brass table: mutton soup with jute-leaf *mulukhiya, aseedah* creamed wheat, rice, fried duck and stuffed pigeon, and baked oxtail. Murmurs and whispers filled the courtyard as the men walked through it. Zeinab caught a glimpse of them from behind the meshrabiyeh of her room, and realized that something important had happened: the group included several men of great importance, including Sheikh Sharkawi, Suleiman al-Fayumi, al-Sawi, and al-Sirsawi. These men coming together in a single meeting at her father's house meant something was afoot, and it must be urgent: but what concern was it of hers? The Damascene fabrics that the Levantine saleswoman had brought her today were all she could think about, especially the length of Damascene brocade embroidered with glass beads and pearls. She took to thinking of a new design, something good enough for the fabric, and for her. She was tired of the same old cut that her seamstress always made for her, the same one all the women wore. The meshrabiyeh of one of her friends' houses overlooked Beit al-Alfi, the house of a nobleman named al-Alfi Bey. Al-Alfi had fled the country as soon as the French Campaign had entered Egypt, and Napoleon Bonaparte had taken over the mansion as his quarters. She had stood at the window one day and watched a ball held in the garden of Beit al-Alfi: the foreign women, with their ravishing ball gowns, puffed up and embroidered with beads that glittered when the light played upon them. How she wished for a dress like one of those.

She was consumed with curiosity about those women and their appearance: how did they endure such garments in such cruel heat? What need was there for such big hats, adorned with fur, under which the head and neck surely groaned? Could the fans made of feathers they held in their hands cool the heat? Perhaps the glasses carried around on trays by the servants could, or rather, the drink that glittered inside the crystal glasses in their delicate hands. It couldn't possibly be like the crude liquor her father drank in secret, some mix of burgundy and brandy. She could still taste it in her mouth from the time she was emboldened, and driven by curiosity, to sample the bottle her father hid in his closet. She had found it by accident one day as she was putting his clean clothes inside; opening it, she had smelled a pungent odor, and taken a sip which she quickly spat out. It was bitter as gall.

No, the wine those women drank must surely be different. They drank it down in one gulp, and enjoyed it. She and her friend watched for hours through the tiny openings in the meshrabiyeh, looking out onto a wider world. It was all new to them: different faces, a strange language, bizarre clothes, lights and music and banqueting tables, glasses making the rounds, beautiful women, and handsome gentlemen. One look at that world was enough to realize the misery of their own dismal lot, not even allowed to take off the veils that covered their faces.

"It's her!" cried one of the girls. "Look! Look!"

The girls pushed up the meshrabiyeh and clustered around it, watching the foreign woman with her puffy dress. She had taken off her hat and removed the pin that held her hair back, and was running her fingers through it to let it flow loose around her shoulders.

"Heavens, what a beauty she is!"

"Her dress is breathtaking!"

"Look at the color of her skin!"

"Her hair is *blond*!"

"Be quiet!" Zeinab yelled at them. "I don't see anything pretty about her! She's pale as the dead and her face is like a loaf of dry bread. She's built like a boy!" And she furiously undid her braids and pulled her *gallabiya* taut around her waist. "Look! I'm prettier and more woman than she is!"

The girls exchanged glances, then burst into giggles. "If she was as plain as you say, Bonaparte would not have taken her as his mistress!"

"Bonaparte's mistress?" Zeinab retorted. "How do you know?"

"Everyone in Egypt is talking about it."

"I don't think," Zeinab tossed her head, "that Bonaparte likes that type of woman."

The other girls stared at her. "Maybe he likes *your* type!" one girl said.

"Wake up and take a look at yourself in the mirror," another jeered, "and look at your color."

"You're just jealous," Zeinab shot back at her, "because you know I'm prettier than you."

That insult could not go unpunished: soon there was a fight, with much screaming and exchanging of blows. Once the other girls pulled them apart, Zeinab wrapped her scarf around her head haughtily. Covering her face, she turned to leave. "You'll soon see!" she growled as she stormed off. As she left, the echo of the others' laughter rang in her ears.

Outside, a cool breeze greeted her, laden with the soft scent of night-blooming jasmine. Several French officers in uniform were walking in the streets, tanned from the relentless sun. They looked at her with lascivious eyes: it was rare to see a girl or woman walking alone in the streets, for they were accustomed to seeing them either on donkey-back or riding by in a cart in a flash of black-clad, a blur from head to toe, like passing ghosts. But now they saw a girl walking slowly, with a sway in her step, bronze anklets jingling and gold bracelets jangling with her every step. They could see her face through the thin chiffon veil: she let it slip, and fixed them with big, black, bold eyes. Delicately, she picked up the edge of her garment from the mud of the path, revealing her slippers, embroidered with gold thread and beads, curved up at the toe in the Moroccan style. One of them approached her and said in French, "What is your name, beautiful girl?"

She stepped back. Another man came up beside him, clearly not a military man although he wore French clothing, and pulled him away. "Leave her alone! You're frightening her." With a smile, he gestured to her to continue on her way. "Please accept my apologies for his behavior."

They were still speaking French, so she had no idea what was being said; but she guessed his meaning and thanked the man who had cleared her path with a smile, which he returned. As she walked on, the men's raised voices echoed after her, and she realized that she was the reason for their altercation.

In a language Zeinab could not understand, the first man was saying, "Have you lost your mind? Stepping in the path of women in a public street and scaring them? Haven't we injured them enough?"

"How do you know she's not a prostitute who would have been happy to talk?"

"Prostitutes wear revealing clothing and stand in the street without shame, and they're the ones who make the first move. Didn't you see how you scared the girl when you walked up to her? Was that the behavior of a prostitute?"

That evening, in a house on the other side of Cairo, Zeinab's mother, Fatima, was sitting in the central courtyard of the house. It was a beautiful evening, the moon hiding behind wispy clouds only to come out again and light up the night, then hide, then come out again, and so on and so forth. In her hand was an amber rosary, the beads of which she was shoving nervously through her forefinger, middle finger, and thumb, whispering, "Praise the Lord, praise the Lord." All around was calm and still except for gentle snores from the upper floor, where her boys slept next to one another on a reed mat. The tallow candles cast a soft light.

Her head jerked up at the sound of a distinctive knock on the door, Zeinab's knock. She leapt up and rushed to the door, almost upsetting the flowerpot. "Why are you so late?" she hissed. "Haven't you heard about the kidnappings and the murders that are happening everywhere these days?"

"I lost track of time," said Zeinab, lifting her veil off her sweaty face.

"Well, don't do it again! I want you home early from now on."

Zeinab went straight to her room. She stood before the mirror and took off her clothes and undid her braids, then lifted up the edge of the cotton mattress and took out a tin box. She painted her lips with its contents, dried powdered deer's blood, and reddened her cheeks with it. Then she dipped a pigeon-feather into the silver kohl bottle, and painted her eyes with kohl. She stood admiring herself in the mirror for a long time, turning left and right and smiling confidently. She imagined her girlfriends standing around her gazing enviously at her beauty, and stuck her tongue out at them in the mirror. Then she remembered his smile, and it took her to another world.

Cairo: August 1798

The Nile waters had risen. Everyone went out early to celebrate the flooding of the Nile. For days, preparations had been underway for this day. Every family was standing outdoors in front of their house: the streets had been sprayed down with water to keep down the dust, decorations hung up in the streets, and lamps filled with oil. A week previously, the water-carriers had put on their new clothing and perfumed their gourds of water with flowers and jasmine oil, and walked through the streets and alleyways, giving water to drink to anyone who was thirsty in the street, and to every house, without recompense. They rattled their brass cups against one another with a joyous clang. The women vied with each other to see who could make the best sweets: *sadd hanak, basbousa,* and *luqmat al-qadi,* and the children went out laden with trays on their heads, handing out sweets to the passersby in the street. And in a tradition thousands of years old, several strong men gathered at Fom al-Khalig, "the water's mouth," to build a dam of sand weak enough for the gushing of the Nile's waters to demolish. When it fell, that was the signal for everyone to cheer and celebrate.

That day, Zeinab stood at her mirror longer than usual. She painted her eyes with kohl and reddened her cheeks, and let a few locks of her hair hang loose across her forehead. Then she put on her embroidered head veil, and went out with the young girls and children of the neighborhood, all in new clothes, and they cried out, "The waters have risen! The river is full!" beating loudly on drums and tooting horns. She joined the throng and sang and made noise with them.

All along the banks of the Nile, boats were decorated with colorful ribbons, carrying gaudily dressed revelers, floating through the narrow canal that separates Roda Island from the bank of the Nile. Crowds gathered around conjurers performing their acts, while bands of musicians roamed the crowds, playing joyfully. It was as if everyone who lived in Egypt had come out to celebrate. Crowds thronged the banks of the Nile, and some even put up tents. Like a cloying drink, people poured into the streets and every corner of the earth seemed filled to the brim with them, and when the street would not hold them, some climbed trees and stood on the rooftops. There were merchants, fat wallets concealed under ample turbans; women carrying their children on their shoulders and muttering prayers; dervishes with rosaries hung around their necks; beggars with tin plates; and French folk in odd raiment looking all around.

On a high hill, a huge marquee had been erected, its walls made up of *khayyamiya*, a thick cotton fabric embroidered with colorful Arabesque designs. The inside was covered with brightly colored and embroidered Persian rugs, and dotted around with wooden couches covered in red velvet and large cushions embroidered with gold thread. A long table ran down the middle, covered in plates of delicious-looking fruit and nuts, the Egyptian and French flags erected above it side by side. Bonaparte stood at the center of the assembly in full regalia, medals and decorations glinting at the breast and shoulders of his uniform in the sunshine, surrounded by several of his high-ranking officers. Next to them stood the imams of al-Azhar and the elite of Egypt. At a distance, everyone could see the flamingo feather in Sheikh al-Bakri's imposing turban, waving in the wind. His shoulders were draped with his golden-yellow cloak. Zeinab saw him and pointed with a finger, saying proudly, "Look! That's my father sitting at Bonaparte's side!"

"Shame on him to sit next to him," muttered one of her friends.

"Why? Isn't he here to rid us of the Mamluks' brutish rule? Didn't he promise to make things better for our country? It's enough that he commanded that the houses be cleaned and the refuse removed from the streets and—"

"But he's an infidel!" the girl interrupted.

"Our Prophet says," Zeinab challenged, " 'You have your religion, and I have mine.'"

The cries of the revelers grew louder, making conversation impossible. The pounding on the tins and drums increased to a deafening pitch. Suddenly, the water burst forth, breaking down the false dam, and the canal filled up until it was on the same level as the river. The mayor threw some shiny *bara* coins into the water, newly minted specially for the occasion in keeping with the tradition that new money brings the Nile flooding. The young men and boys leapt into the water to catch them. Zeinab, seeing that everyone was preoccupied with cheering for the men and boys and encouraging them to dive for the coins, slipped away from her friends toward the marquee where her father sat with Bonaparte. She crept past the guards watching the commotion and went straight to her father. She bent to kiss his hand, whereupon the guards finally noticed her and crowded around. Sheikh al-Bakri whispered into Napoleon's ear, "It is only my daughter, Zeinab," and Napoleon commanded them to let her be.

Her father nodded to her, hinting that she should pay her respects. She bowed her head low, smiling behind her chiffon veil, showing off her dimples. Napoleon, charmed, smiled back.

He was a small man indeed! But he sat proudly, all puffed out, his jacket encrusted with gold medals. She felt small beside him, not in size, but in status. He was fully aware that he ruled over all he surveyed. Out of the corner of her eye she watched him. His face was white, with a few freckles here and there. His eyes were small and the color of honey, full of cunning. His mouth was small, too, and enticing behind his sparse mustache. His features betrayed nothing of his cruel nature: if he took off his regalia and dressed in civilian clothes, she thought, and walked among regular folk, he might be taken for an Azharite sheikh or the scribe who sits outside court-houses to help the illiterate write down their complaints.

At noon, the sun was high in the sky, the day at its hottest. A gentle breeze sprang up, easing the sweltering heat. From the marquee high on the hill, Zeinab was entranced by the sight. She could see the domes of the mosques and churches, and the pyramids seemed small at this distance. A military parade passed by, rows and rows of officers and soldiers, to the tune of a military band. Yells and cries broke out when the traditional 'Bride of the Nile' statue was thrown into the water, and several women threw scraps of their clothing or locks of their hair in after her. The boats that had been in a long race since daybreak began to arrive, and Bonaparte himself handed out the medals to the winners. Then he began to give out gifts and largesse of golden *bara*s to the public, and there was a general pushing and shoving to get some. He motioned to Zeinab with the tip of one finger: with shy, hesitant steps she went to him. When she drew level to Bonaparte, he took her small hand and placed several *bara*s into it, then closed her hand firmly around them. With difficulty, she managed to squeak out, "Thank you." She looked straight up into his eyes. There was something unreadable in them. She ran back, a child running like the wind in joy at the gift of the 'Emperor of the East.' She asked herself: had he pressed her hand a little longer than strictly necessary? Or had she only imagined it?

The diamond in Napoleon's ring glittered as he motioned to an officer, who came running. He whispered something into his ear and the man hurried out. Moments later, he came back, bearing a caftan of pure silk, trimmed with fur and adorned with diamonds. Bonaparte placed the caftan onto the shoulders of Sheikh al-Bakri and announced that he was to be the new Naqib al-Ashraf, the Head of the Prophet's Descendants, replacing Sheikh Omar Makram, to the cheering and blessings of the crowd. The judges, merchants, and other important men clustered around Sheikh al-Bakri, congratulating him. He returned their congratulations with pride and pleasure. Napoleon took his leave, surrounded by his military procession, but not before telling Sheikh al-Bakri that he would await him the next day to discuss the responsibilities of his new position. What was truly strange, however, was that he asked him to bring his daughter.

7

Cairo: Autumn 2012

HER ALARM WOKE HER FROM a dream. The hands of the clock read a quarter to seven. She had a class at 8:30. Sluggishly, she pushed the covers off herself and yawned and stretched like a lazy Persian cat. Sleepy-eyed, she padded to the kitchen, flicked the electric kettle on, and shoved a cheese sandwich into the toaster. She was exhausted; the discovery she had made the previous day filled her with so many questions that she hadn't slept all night. She had to find answers.

Quickly, she dressed in something suitable for work. She disliked formal attire, much preferring jeans, a T-shirt, and some sneakers, but a university professor must appear conservative. Therefore she followed the Egyptian proverb, "Eat what you please, and wear what pleases others."

She looked into her grandmother's room with a cheery "Good morning." Receiving no reply, she watched her chest to make sure it was still rising and falling. She was always haunted by the fear that the old woman would have a heart attack and die in her sleep. Relieved, she packed some papers into her briefcase, swallowed down her sandwich, and went out, travel mug in hand. As Yasmine was waiting for the elevator, Fatima, the Nubian-Egyptian maid, came out of the service entrance as she had been doing for more than a quarter of a century since she started working for them; she refused to use any other door, although the service staircase was long

31

deserted and inhabited only by stray cats. Even the newspaper man and the milkman used the elevator: only Fatima insisted on using the service stairs. She was continuing the journey her mother had started half a century before, when she had first gone into service with Yasmine's grandmother. She used to take her up the service stairs with her as a little girl, and thus she never used any other. She belonged to the 'servant class' that used to exist in bygone days, the people who bowed when serving the coffee, and used 'Sir' or 'Madam.'

The weather was crisp with spring, encouraging her to walk to the Faculty of Fine Arts, only a few streets away from her house. She needed time to collect her thoughts and exercise in accordance with Nietzsche's maxim, "Great ideas come to us while walking," but she was only preoccupied with one idea, one painting, one girl, one artist.

In class, she stood distracted at the slide projector, hardly able to see the painting before her for her mental image of the girl. They merged in her mind, although they were completely different. "Look at her thick black braids," she said, pointing to the hair of the model in the painting.

"What?" The students murmured loudly.

Yasmine blinked. There were no black braids; the painting was of a blond with her hair up and a hat on her head. "Excuse me," she said, shaking her head. "I meant, look at the way her hair is arranged and the design of the hat, a look popular in nineteenth-century France."

As soon as the lecture was over, she went straight to the Conservation Department. She sat a few meters away from the painting and tried to view it with the eye of an ordinary viewer. The girl's features combined innocence with seduction: there was a promise of *something* in her eyes. The gold hoops in her ears indicated that she was from a wealthy family. Her lace scarf was draped around her shoulders, her black braids peeking from underneath it. That fabric was unknown to Egyptian women of the era. Her *gallabiya* was black, with vertical stripes of red, gold, and blue. The artist had paid attention to all of these small details, to the features that mingled innocence and seduction, good and evil. Which of them did he mean to portray?

The voice of Professor Anwar jolted her out of her thoughts. "Still staring at that painting? Is it really that much on your mind?"

"Yes," she responded.

"Tomorrow we'll take it down to the infrared lab."

She smiled at him gratefully.

After class that day, she wrapped the painting carefully, obtained a permit to remove it from the premises from the head of the Conservation Department, and took it home.

Fatima knocked on the door to her room. "I've done the housework, fed Madam, your grandmother, and given her medicine."

"Thank you," said Yasmine. "I don't know what I'd do without you." The compliment was by no means an exaggeration: Fatima relieved her of a burden she was incapable of shouldering.

At six, he called to invite her out to dinner, "unless you have plans tonight."

"I don't have any plans."

"How would you feel about going out for pizza?"

"Pizza?" she repeated slyly.

She was well aware that since their breakup, he would never say he wanted to see her, and would never call to tell her "I miss you" or "I need to see you." All he would say was "I'll be there at such and such a time, if you want to join me," and give her the freedom to come or not as she chose. There had been a time when the relationship they shared gave him the right to demand her company. Now he had no excuse. She knew perfectly well what he was thinking. "No, I don't feel like pizza tonight. I'll come by the restaurant at nine and we can take a walk together. That's what I really need."

"I'll be waiting."

She pulled on something from her closet, a short wool dress, and put on a coat over it, leaving her hair loose and only putting on some kohl and lip gloss. That was all she needed when she went out to see him, for with him, she could be herself. That was the best thing about this relationship, to feel this close. She never felt the need to put on a mask to meet him, or pretend when talking to him.

Pizza Thomas was a few streets away from her home in Zamalek, and had been there since the 1950s. Its owner had preserved it perfectly in its original vintage style. The kitchen was open onto the dining area: you could watch the pizza cooks rolling the dough and pressing it into the dishes, then putting the ingredients on top of it and sliding it into the oven. It gave the place a perpetually warm and delicious smell. She approached the glass front of the store through which the tables and customers were visible. She saw him at his usual seat, and waved at him to come out.

Outside, he put an arm around her and they walked together: sidewalk followed sidewalk and street followed street. Each street had its own smell; each path sounded different as feet displaced tiny stones. Now they were face-to-face with the Nile. He sat on a bench facing the river and lit a cigarette. "Something on your mind?" he asked.

"Yes," she replied. "You remember the girl I was talking to you about?"

"What girl?"

"The girl in the picture."

He let loose a hearty chuckle. She had always loved his laugh: he threw his head back and looked up and laughed long and loud, making it impossible not to share in his merriment. "What are you laughing at?"

"This!" He pointed to her head. "This head of yours!"

"Oh?" she said coolly.

"You leave the here and now and go running after the past." He let out another laugh. "My dear, it's just a face in a painting, and you're spinning tall tales about it! She's just another Egyptian girl, like any other girl. The artist saw her, and fancied her, and painted her. There's nothing more to it." He took a deep breath. "You've got your life ahead of you, clear, transparent, waiting. Why do you run away down the corridors of the past?"

"Well," she retorted, "If she's just a regular girl, why would the artist weave locks of her hair, human hair, into the pigment he mixed with the color for her braids? Tell me there isn't a secret behind that girl. Why would he do that?"

Sherif sobered. "True. Why would he do something like that?"

"I've got the painting at home. Come," she said eagerly, "let me show you."

"Now?" he protested, looking at his watch.

"Yes, now."

Yasmine took his hand and they walked to her building. When he saw it, the architect let out a long, low whistle in admiration of its Baroque architecture with the double entrance, one leading onto the main road, and the other into a side street. She smiled, knowing how much he liked it. On the inside, it was even more like an ancient castle: the stairs were polished marble, the banister wrought-iron. He refused to take the elevator, choosing instead to walk up the stairs: "I don't trust elevators. They make me claustrophobic."

"Me too."

The echo of their footfall on the marble staircase was loud in the silence; it seemed wrong to speak in such an atmosphere. Many of the older apartments in the building were uninhabited thanks to the outdated rent-control laws that plagued Zamalek and other quarters full of historic buildings. As a result, walking through the building was like entering a place where time had stopped—locked into the old, empty apartments.

The sound of a television reached them from behind Yasmine's door: her grandmother was used to turning it up loud.

When they went inside, she hung up her coat on the rack and asked him to wait in the entryway. He could see that the apartment was a lot like her, plain and simple. It was easy to tell that an artist lived there from the paintings hanging on the wall and the artwork on the tables. Everything was quiet, except for the din from the television. Her grandmother ignored her: she was watching a televised black-and-white recording of an old play and guffawing loudly. Yasmine picked up the remote and turned down the sound, bending to speak in her ear. "Grandma, we've got company. A colleague, here to see a painting."

The old woman's face filled with astonishment. "Well, do let him come in—no, wait! Do I look presentable?"

"Yes, Grandma."

The old woman wrapped her shawl around her shoulders tightly and touched her braids to make sure they were straight. "This is Sherif, he's an architect, Grandma."

He bent to shake her hand: she peered at him with the unabashed curiosity of old age, scrutinizing him from head to toe. Yasmine went to the kitchen and came back with a glass of orange juice. "Here you are."

Her grandmother looked disapproving. "Go and put on a nice dress and some makeup!"

"There's no need."

"But your fiancé shouldn't see you like that!"

"My fiancé?"

They exchanged a smile while the old woman went on. "You're over thirty! And you, young man, how old are you? You look over thirty too. What are you waiting for? In our time, folks your age had grandchildren."

He smiled. "I'm quite happy to go ahead right now, but Yasmine is otherwise occupied. When she's free, we can decide on a wedding date."

"I'm taking our guest to my room," said Yasmine, having had enough of this, "to look at the painting."

Her grandmother didn't look too pleased at the idea of her granddaughter taking a strange man into her room, even her future husband, but finally agreed.

Yasmine walked ahead of Sherif, heels clicking tensely on the wooden floor, down the long corridor that led to her room. "Why did you tell her that?"

"Tell her what?"

"That we were going to get married."

"Because she wouldn't have listened to anything else."

Yasmine opened the door and stood facing him. "You don't know Grandma. Starting this minute, she'll be planning the wedding. And she's not going to stop asking me about you, day after day after day."

"You can just tell her anything. . . ."

"Anything like what?"

"Uh, that you found out I was a lowlife. That I dumped you and left the country. Or found another woman. Or told you it wouldn't work out between us."

She could see what he was getting at, so she cut off the conversation so as not to start a fight; she had quite enough going on. Standing directly opposite the painting, she gestured to it. "Here, look."

He looked at it for a few minutes. "It's quite unremarkable," he said, "if you look at it like a regular viewer. One of the Orientalist paintings they left behind to show they were here. A girl, like hundreds of girls." After a moment, he added, "Maybe a touch of something . . . in her eyes. Like a glow. Makes you feel she's still alive and looking back at you."

Yasmine listened to him, nodding, certain that what he said was true: there was nothing about the portrait that would strike the fancy of an ordinary viewer. Just a girl in a black *gallabiya* with vertical stripes, a lace scarf covering the front of her head and shoulders, braids emerging from beneath, hands folded over her midriff.

Sherif stepped closer to the painting and reached out to touch the girl's braid. "If it wasn't for that lock of hair," he murmured, "I would have said you were imagining things."

"The minute I saw that painting," Yasmine nodded, "something told me there was a secret behind it."

She was still gazing at the portrait, while Sherif looked around him. Her room was different from the others in the house, a thing apart: everything in it seemed to belong to a girl of fourteen. The white furniture, the patterned wallpaper, the pink curtains, the giant dolls, everything was as cheerful as she could possibly make it. Nothing about the room said 'Art History Professor.' Still, it was the other face of her, the child inside.

He reached out and picked up a photograph from the bedside table. It was a picture of Yasmine with her family when she was about ten years old. Next to her stood her sister Shaza, the height difference making it clear that the latter was several years older. Behind them, their parents stood, her father's arm around their mother, both smiling. "You look a lot like your mother," said Sherif. She said nothing, but gave him a wan smile. "Your eyes are the same, and you have the same smile." He replaced the photograph. "You never talk about your family."

"You know all there is to know," she snapped. "My mother died years ago. My father left to go work abroad not long after. Shaza went to study in England and eventually found work there. Is that enough or do you want more?"

"Well . . ."

She rounded on him. "Let me tell you." She stomped over to the picture and snatched it from him. "To see him like this," she stabbed a finger at her father, "his arm around her like that, you'd say they were the perfect couple. To see her smiling like that, you'd say she was the happiest woman in the world. And you'd call me and Shaza lucky girls with a bright future ahead of us. That's always what the pictures tell you." He opened his mouth, but she plowed on. "The reality isn't quite like the photos. That man in the photo," she gestured violently, "made that woman kill herself. He made her slit her wrists with a razor because he cheated on her with her best friend. She died. He left. These two girls were left with nothing but grief. One of them couldn't stand to live in this country any longer, so she packed up and left for somewhere far away where she knows nobody and nobody knows her. The other is . . . as you can see."

He stood there, speechless. He knew that all the words in the universe could not take away her grief or console her. He felt an overpowering urge to hold her close and make it up to her, all the years of unhappiness. Taking the photograph from her hand, he gently replaced it. Then he put his arms around her. Her body was warm and fragile, her heart beating an anxious tattoo. She stayed in his arms for a while, trembling as he tried to comfort her. Then, with a quick kiss on the cheek, he left.

Cairo: August 1798

Zeinab could hardly believe it. Had she been sitting next to Bonaparte himself? The man whose very name made the strongest men quake in their boots? Had she been sitting side by side with him? Had the man himself taken her hand and closed her fingers around the gold coins he had given her? And what was more, he had asked her father to bring her with him the next day! Had that really happened, or was she dreaming?

She strutted proudly as she walked: and why not? She was the woman who had sat next to Napoleon in his seat in the royal marquee, watched by the aristocracy, the mayors of all the towns, the imams of al-Azhar, the most important merchants, the common folk, and everyone, all of them asking, "Who's that girl sitting at Bonaparte's side?" When she stepped into the horse-drawn cart that would take her and her father back to their street that day, the men glared at them with envious resentment, while the women gathered behind the meshrabiyehs watching the girl who had captivated the emperor. All of a sudden, for the first time, Zeinab felt that she had left her childhood behind and become a lovely young woman, capable of charming men and making them admire her. At home, her clogs beat a tattoo on the wooden floor as she repeated a poem someone had composed especially for him:

> The chivalrous Bonaparte, leonine and most capable in the land
> Has conquered kingdoms and his will is done with a wave of his hand.

After the afternoon prayer, she went out with some of her girlfriends. Her mother put the gold coins that Napoleon had given her into a burlap purse which she bound with strong thread and secreted inside her *gallabiya*, and she went shopping. Now she could shop at the stores that only sold European wares, imported and brought in on ships over the Mediterranean from Spain, France, and Greece: wool, carpets, shawls, gold watches, perfumes—the gold coins gave her the right to purchase from such stores, not only browse regretfully as she had used to.

Since Napoleon's campaign, the stores had taken to hanging out their shingles in French, and the narrow alleys were bursting with French soldiers, some of whom enjoyed taking walks on foot, looking around at everything warily, and some of whom hurried by on the backs of mules, which occasionally crashed into each other. It was impossible to deny that conditions in the country had improved under the French compared to the Mamluks: the streets were clean, thanks to the first decree issued by Napoleon, that the streets were to be swept and watered down every day. The folk who used to throw their refuse and the remains of the animals and birds they slaughtered into the street were now careful to throw them away in a remote location reserved for the purpose. The brawls that used to break out every moment throughout the day were completely extinct now, thanks to the powers of the French troops in breaking up fights between ex-convicts, carters, and those who rented beasts of burden. Anyone fighting would be immediately taken off to the police station to receive a stern punishment. Suddenly, the tradesmen kept to posted prices and were careful to provide quality goods. It was a truth that could not be denied: things had changed for the better under the French.

With pride, Zeinab said to her friends, "Look around you! Can you say we're not better off under the French than the Mamluks? It's enough that it doesn't stink and there aren't piles of garbage at every street corner." She waved a hand. "Look, everyone seems more cheerful and their clothes are cleaner."

"Do you think it can go on? People won't keep doing a thing if they've been frightened into it," a friend replied. "It just breeds resentment. Someday, it'll all blow up."

Zeinab laughed mockingly. "Since when have we not been frightened into doing things? At least being afraid has actually gotten us something useful, for once. Before, all we had was ignorance and disease."

"I don't understand you, Zeinab! Are you really on the side of the invaders? Can't you see how unfair and cruel the Frenchmen are to us Egyptians? Haven't you heard of the massacres that happen every day, of them cutting off people's heads and mounting them on pikes on the walls of the Citadel? What about the bodies in sacks that they throw into the river?"

Zeinab ignored her: she had caught sight of a shop displaying velvet and silk imported from Malta and France. Darting inside, she touched the fabrics, wrapping them around her body. "How gorgeous. I'm going to buy it."

When she came home, laden with her purchases, a crowd of people was there: clerics, imams, instructors from *kuttab* Qur'an schools, and blind Qur'an reciters, all standing outside the house of Sheikh al-Bakri to complain. Apparently, they had been fired and their salaries cut off because the Ministry of Religious Endowments had been taken over by the Copts and Levantines appointed by the French. "Now what do you have to say?" asked her friend, gesturing to the throng outside the door. "Now that's injustice if ever I saw it."

Zeinab ignored what was happening, so thrilled was she with her purchases from the market that she had bought with the gold coins Napoleon had pressed into her small hand. Wonder of wonders! She had bought everything she had been longing for and still had money left to spare.

She kept rubbing her palm, remembering how he had touched her hand. She couldn't sleep at night, wondering: had she really been touched by the Emperor of the East? Had the look in his eyes, which had held so many words and so much meaning, truly been for her? Was it possible that he had come to conquer Egypt so that fate might bring the two of them together? Were the distances he had traversed to reach this land and all the cities he had conquered on his way, all the battles he had planned, stepping stones to her fate to meet him, pressing gold coins into her hand, enfolding her with his smile?

She hardly noticed her mother opening the door to her room: she was soaring in the world of her fancies. "What's come over you, Zeinab? It's like you're not even here."

"What happened to me isn't just any old thing. Bonaparte the Commander put gold coins into my hand and smiled at me. He told Father to bring me along when he goes to meet him tomorrow." She sighed. "And then you ask what's come over me?"

"So what?" her mother said. "Don't let your imagination carry you to flights of fancy. Next you'll be telling me you think he fell for you. You're nothing but a child to him. You're the child of the man he trusts."

But she did not let her mother's words quell her joy. "Poor Mother!" she murmured under her breath. "You didn't see the way he looked at me."

Ponderously, her mother waddled to the bed where Zeinab had piled up her purchases, and began to look them over. "Lord, what glaring colors!" she rebuked. "And this fabric's transparent! Have you lost your mind? Zeinab, daughter of Sheikh al-Bakri, wear something like this? Do you *want* tongues to wag?"

"Mother!" Zeinab groaned. "Please, just for once, forget, or pretend to forget, that I'm Sheikh al-Bakri's daughter! I'm Zeinab! I can do what I like and wear what I please!" She straightened. "Besides, people will talk no matter what you do or don't do. Everyone loves to gossip."

"Well, I'll tell your father, and he'll deal with you."

That night, in a spacious bedroom on a brass bed, the portly body of the Sheikh's wife tossed and turned, sleepless. The bed wobbled and squeaked. "Lord," she groaned in disgust, "I'm drowning in a soup of sweat." She heaved herself up and went to open the meshrabiyeh a little, hoping to let in a cool summer breeze for some relief from the stifling air of the room. A little before dawn, she heard the sound of her husband's sandals sliding across the reed mat. She raised her head and watched as he took off his large green turban and hung it on the clothes rack, then got up to help him take off his caftan—the new one that Napoleon had given him.

"You should discipline your daughter. She's too impulsive," she started. "I don't know what's come over her, but suddenly she can't be controlled."

He guffawed. "Let her do what she wants," he reassured her.

"What's that you're saying? How can I let her do what she wants?"

"Have some discernment," he smiled, "don't be thick-headed, there's a good woman. I have something in mind. If it comes to pass. . . ." He stroked his beard, which grew down to his stomach.

"What's that supposed to mean? What are you talking about?"

Maliha, the slave, walked in with a jug of warm salt water, and placed it at his feet. She washed them, then dried them with a towel. "When the time is right, I'll tell you everything."

His words only perplexed her more. She could not fathom what her husband could possibly be thinking.

The next morning, Zeinab woke early. She had only slept a little that night, preoccupied. Maliha prepared a bath for her: she placed the urn of water on the brick oven and, when the steam rose from it, scrubbed Zeinab's body with a rough loo-fah made of sheep's wool, poured water over her head, and massaged her scalp and hair with a bar of soap made from olive oil to make it smooth and silky. Then she rinsed her off with clean water and perfumed her with musk and ambergris, and finally sat braiding cloves into her hair to make it smell sweet. When she was done, she smiled at her and spat at her side three times for luck, spraying granules of salt around and saying, "Lord protect you from the Evil Eye!"

To Zeinab's eyes, there was something odd about Maliha today: she seemed to be sad for some reason. Usually, she never stopped talking and joking, but today she had hardly said a word. "What's wrong, Maliha?" she asked when they had finished.

"My master Sheikh al-Bakri told Rostom to pack. He's going to make a present of him to Commander Bonaparte. He doesn't want to go. But my master the sheikh insists on it." Her tone turned pleading. "Could you speak to him, Miss Zeinab? He won't say no to you."

Does Father really want to give our Rostom to Bonaparte? Zeinab thought to herself. *He has been indispensable to Father since the moment he set foot in the house—he does everything, from going to market and taking care of my brothers and doing the carpentry and plumbing work in the house and even helping with the baking, to gardening and overseeing the vegetable garden, and he guards the house at night as well.* She drummed her fingers against her chin. *Besides, he's my father's most trusted servant and keeps all his secrets.* Could her father sacrifice all of this and present Rostom to Napoleon?

"I'll speak to him," Zeinab finally said. "Now let's see what I'm going to wear."

Zeinab stood at her closet. It was made of beech wood, designed by a carpenter from Malta, and ornately decorated, with brass handles. She wondered what to wear to such an occasion: even if it was just a routine meeting like the ones Napoleon held every day for the important men, the guild masters, and the Azharite imams, it was enough that she was to be a guest in the house of Napoleon, who had insisted that her father bring her with him.

She selected a *gallabiya* with vertical stripes, tight and alluring around the contours of her body. She put on her curl-toed slippers and perfumed herself. The sobs of Rostom rang out loudly as he stood in the courtyard holding his clothing in a sack and saying goodbye to everyone. Zeinab approached her father and whispered in his ear, "Can't you leave him be?"

Angrily, he swept his caftan up over his other shoulder. "No. He's my gift to Bonaparte, who needs him more than I do."

"But I don't know anyone here but you," sobbed Rostom. "I served you with everything I had. You were my family."

"Your star shall rise in the house of Bonaparte, believe me," said her father. "You are a slave trained to be a professional warrior. It's a shame for your talents to be wasted in buying vegetables from the market and watering the garden."

It was clear that Sheikh al-Bakri had made up his mind, and Rostom could see that it was no use arguing. He had not the right to decide his own fate: his destiny had always been in the hands of others, since the long-ago day he had been loaded onto a ship to be taken to Constantinople and sold at the slave market. There, he had been bought by a rich merchant who had gifted him to a friend of his a few months later, and that man in turn had taken him to Egypt and gifted him to Ibrahim Bey, a Mamluk prince. The latter had trained him to fight in his division, teaching him the art of mounted combat, until he rose to be a formidable warrior in the Mamluk army. But fate is fickle: the winds of change arrived in the form of the French Campaign, blowing away everything in their path. The Mamluks ran away and dispersed through the cities of Egypt, and Rostom ended up with Sheikh al-Bakri, who had been friends with his owner, the prince. He had promised the latter to make Rostom his servant and faithful guardian—and Rostom was faithful and loyal in every sense of the words.

Sheikh al-Bakri mounted his horse and Zeinab a mule, while Rostom dragged his feet weakly in their wake—Rostom, who used to run like the wind—his sack of clothes in hand. His tears flowed more copiously with every step he took away from the house, toward an unknown fate with this man who killed and slaughtered without compassion or mercy.

They turned toward Ezbekiya and crossed the bridge leading to Harat al-Ifrinj, the Alley of the Franks. On the way, they saw the Mamluk palaces and mansions that the French had appropriated for themselves, plundering their precious booty. Here the Mamluks had lived; here was the house where Rostom had lived with Ibrahim Bey, one of the most famous Mamluks, the center of attention in every street and marketplace. No sooner did he set foot outside than everyone would start to stare at his opulent clothing, his horse adorned with silk and gold. His spacious mansion had been transformed into a restaurant for the French, a sign on the door saying,

"All French dishes are prepared by a French chef." He peered inside to see the tables and chairs laid out in the garden with peerless elegance—an elegance unknown in Egypt at that time, where people ate with their hands, dipped their fingers in dishes, chewed loudly, and were not ashamed to release the occasional loud belch.

They stopped at the place where Napoleon lived, by the lake Berkat al-Rathle. Guards in military uniform surrounded the palace on all sides, wearing feathered hats, weapons hanging at their sides. They looked incongruous, as though they had been placed in this location by mistake. Sheikh al-Bakri received permission from the guards to enter. They told him to leave the horse and mule outside, which he did, and they entered on foot.

They walked through the gates into a spacious garden filled with flowers whose perfume wafted everywhere. In the center was a mosaic fountain inlaid with Damascene tiles. The instant Zeinab and Rostom stepped into the garden, they trembled, and their heartbeats sped up with fear and trepidation. Neither knew what fate awaited them within the palace walls.

The place was labyrinthine: rooms within rooms, corridors leading onto corridors, entrance halls that were alternately broad and narrow. The floors were smooth marble and the windows were inlaid glass. In the central atrium, soft seats had been placed all around to receive guests, while in one corner was the large conference room where Bonaparte held his meetings.

The palace was bustling with activity, busy as a hive of bees, filled with soldiers coming and going in shiny black boots, footfalls loud where they trod on wooden floors. Her father perched on the edge of the couch, while she stood at his side like a frightened squirrel, Rostom behind them. They were not the only people awaiting an audience with the great man; a great many Azharite imams and religious scholars were lined up in rows, some barely concealing their resentment and hatred behind the mask of a false smile. Their eyes raked over her, one question evidently in their minds: *What brings her here?* She looked at the floor and shuffled behind her father's bulk.

A loud noise burst through the atrium, and Napoleon strode in, flanked by his officers. He greeted everyone in French, whereupon some of those present remained silent and others tripped over their own tongues. Catching himself, Bonaparte made a visible effort to recall the few words of Arabic he had memorized and, in a French accent, said, "*al-Salam alaykum wa rahmat Allah wa barakatu,*" peace be upon you, and the Lord's mercy and His blessing. Zeinab could hardly keep herself from laughing, and she could not suppress a small giggle.

Bonaparte went to her, took her by the chin and raised her face to his. The murmurings of the men grew loud and resentful as if to say, "Have some decency! You have an audience!" Bonaparte's eyes then fell upon Rostom.

"This is the boy I told you about," said Sheikh al-Bakri.

Napoleon nodded without speaking. He spoke softly to one of his guards, then turned and headed for the conference room, the assembled crowd following him. Zeinab was so confused she had no idea what to do, so she followed them with hesitant steps. When she tried to enter the conference room, the guard to whom Napoleon had spoken barred her way and told her to wait outside.

The guard disappeared for a moment down the corridors of the great palace, then reappeared in the company of a Frenchwoman. Her face betrayed nothing of her age. She appeared serious and stern, looking Zeinab up and down from head to toe. Then she let loose a torrent of incomprehensible French, as though something had irked her. Zeinab had no idea why the woman was speaking, but a look at her face was enough to tell that she was displeased. With a haughty gesture, the Frenchwoman motioned to Zeinab to follow her.

Zeinab followed the woman down a set of marble stairs that led to a long corridor, to the right and left of which were closed doors, rooms concealing their secrets. The woman took her into one of these: inside were several sewing machines and long tables with sewing equipment on them: scissors, needles and thread, fabrics of every type and description, and a boxful of the feathers used to decorate the soldiers' hats. If one fell off, Zeinab thought, they would have no trouble finding a replacement.

Zeinab stood before the woman, who took her measurements without saying a word. Zeinab loved to joke and laugh, and she knew that if she had been at her own seamstress' place, she would have filled the room with giggles and good-natured fun. But with this woman, it was different. She finished taking her measurements and commanded her to go. The guard was still waiting for her. All Zeinab could think about was the clothes the woman would make for her. Would she make them like the ones worn by the French women, the long, puffy dresses that made them seem as if they were floating? Could her dream really be this close to coming true? She had only recently been wishing to be rid of this hateful *gallabiya* she was draped in, and wear a dress like theirs!

The French soldier marched on, and she followed him to what fate she knew not. What was Bonaparte preparing her for? The guard led her into a room with bookshelves lining the length and breadth of the walls, laden with Arabic and French books and magazines. The air smelled of books and burnt pig-tallow candles. Several Frenchmen were sitting at a large reading table, half-hidden behind stacks of books. In a corner was a desk with an elderly man sitting at it. He appeared to be a man of great knowledge, dressed in the French style, what was left of his white hair tied back in a ponytail. He appeared both serious and kindly. The guard launched into a long conversation with him, and when he finished speaking, the man looked long and hard at Zeinab. Then he smiled. "Welcome," he greeted her in Arabic.

"Thank you," she replied.

He motioned her to a seat. "What is your name?"

"Zeinab."

"Do you know any French words?"

"No."

"Right. You're here because General Bonaparte has asked me to teach you French, at least a few words, so that you can speak with him."

Her jaw dropped. "So you can speak with him"? She repeated the phrase over and over in her head, asking herself, *Am I going to speak with him?*

The kindly old gentleman seemed to notice that the girl was perturbed, and smiled to calm her down. "Don't be afraid. French is simple and easy. You'll like it. Now, come on, we'll start our first lesson."

Meanwhile, Rostom was still waiting outside the conference room, bundle in hand, just as the guard had told him to. Everyone who came and went stared at him, for his incongruous clothing, the sack in his hand, and the place he was standing in were all conspicuous and piqued their curiosity. Hours later, when the meeting was over and everyone had left, Napoleon sent for a guard to bring Rostom in. He was still standing in place, not having moved an inch.

Rostom stepped into the conference room, finding the great man standing at his desk with Sheikh al-Bakri. Napoleon examined Rostom carefully, then asked, "What's your name?"

"Rostom."

"Where are you from, Rostom?"

"I'm from Georgia. I was kidnapped as a child from my family, and sold and resold several times, until I wound up in Egypt."

"Are you an adept fighter and horseman, Rostom?"

"I am a Mamluk of the class that is trained in the arts of battle. You are aware that ordinary Egyptians are not permitted to bear arms, but I am. My specialty is mounted combat."

Napoleon went to a closet and took out a magnificent sword with a diamond-studded hilt, and two pistols with worked gold handles. "From now on, you shall be my personal slave and my loyal guard."

Rostom nodded without speaking: his trepidation had swallowed up his words. Sheikh al-Bakri rose and patted him on the shoulder. "I hope you won't let me down," he said.

That was their first meeting, Napoleon with his low, soft voice and perpetually furrowed brow, and Rostom with all the questions he kept locked inside as to the mysterious fate that had propelled him through time from place to place, to finally bring him face to face with the most powerful man in the world—to be given a diamond-studded sword the like of which he had never imagined to own in all his life, and what was more, to be his personal guard and protector.

Napoleon left his tent, and Rostom exited to be initiated into his new profession by a guard, while Sheikh al-Bakri sat in the atrium waiting for his daughter, swallowed up somewhere, he did not know where, in this wonderful palace.

More than three hours passed with Zeinab in the company of the elderly gentleman, absorbed in teaching her French. He wrote out the letters of the alphabet and read them to her, asking her to repeat after him; he had her copy out each letter; then he asked her to try and pronounce his name. She was a quick study in copying the letters, although it took her a long time to learn how to hold the quill and dip it into the inkwell, then use it to write. The strange thing was that, although she was usually by no means patient, the hours did not drag on her and she felt no tedium; on the contrary, she felt full of enthusiasm. Her eyes shone with an unusual light, and her smile broadened whenever he said to her, "Bravo!"

Finally, the man folded up the papers and held them out to her, together with the quill and the inkwell, and asked her to memorize them like her own name. "I'll expect you in three days, same time, same place."

She thanked him and walked out of the library, weighed down under her pride. She was on her way to being special, and the knowledge filled her with delight. The guard, who had been waiting outside the library, took her back to the atrium, where her father waited. She looked around, searching for the emperor, but he was nowhere to be found.

On their way out, Sheikh al-Bakri asked her what had taken place while she had been away, and she told him everything that had transpired. He smiled, then said something under his breath that she couldn't make out. "Do you know," he said, "that the man teaching you French was Venture de Paradis, the chief translator for the French Campaign? He is Bonaparte's personal interpreter." He became more expansive as they walked through the garden. "He lived his life between Istanbul and Syria, then moved on to Egypt and Marrakech. He speaks Arabic, Persian, and Turkish in addition to his native language, and he was a French interpreter for a long time at the Turkish Embassy. He is an important man indeed, respected and feared by Napoleon himself." They arrived at their mounts. "Do you know what it means for Napoleon to entrust your teaching of French to a man of such stature?"

Naturally, she knew what it meant for Monsieur Venture de Paradis himself to be teaching her French. She gave a sly smile at knowing just how taken Napoleon was with her.

That evening, the moon was bright and the weather unbearably hot. From time to time, a cool breeze blew. Zeinab's mother asked the slave woman to set the table for dinner in the courtyard, which she did on a big brass tray upon a central table. Everyone gathered around the table, set richly with birds and meats and the duck soup that was Zeinab's favorite. She ate with great appetite, which was unusual for her: but her unaccustomed appetite was not due only to the duck soup. The day she had had was enough to give her an appetite, not only for food, but for life. She chattered away to her family about everything that had taken place in euphoric tones bursting with joy, and they listened, enthralled. The only one who plied her with questions was her mother. "Didn't the woman who took your measurements ask you what you wanted your new dress to look like?"

"I don't remember hearing her voice. Perhaps she's dumb?" Zeinab shrugged. "She was quite different from the French teacher. He never stopped talking. And he smiled at me! And he said 'Bravo' to me several times!"

In their bedroom, her mother sat on the edge of the bed while Sheikh al-Bakri lay on his back in bed. Suspiciously, she asked him, "What does Bonaparte want with our daughter?" She narrowed her eyes. "What is that *invader* preparing her for?"

"Fortune," chuckled al-Bakri, "has smiled upon our daughter."

"Fortune? What fortune? What ill-luck awaits us with that infidel?"

"An invader," he mocked, "*and* an infidel?"

"What else should I call him?"

"I'm tired," he said, "and not up to discussions right now. You'd best go to sleep." And with that, he turned his back on her, and a few moments later was snoring loudly. But his wife's rest was uneasy, plagued with suspicions and doubts, and she could not sleep a wink.

She was not the only one who couldn't sleep that night. In the next room, Zeinab lay awake as well; but unlike her mother, she could not sleep for joy. By candlelight, she pored over her notebook, dipping the quill into the inkwell and copying out the letters. This was the language that would open closed doors to her—the doors of a new world. A world brighter and more spacious, more beautiful and more wonderful, than anything she had heard of, nor yet imagined, not even in her dreams.

*

At nine every morning, a magnificent carriage crunched over the gravel, its horses beating the ground with their hooves, cutting through the narrow alleyway and raising a cloud of dust in its wake that blocked all sight. It was Bonaparte's personal carriage, driven by a special coachman, next to whom sat a French guard in a cap with a feather in it that fluttered in the wind, come to pick up a fifteen-year-old girl, a girl with braids that lay over her shoulders and a shy smile set in innocent, childlike features. From there, it took her to Bonaparte's imperial seat, where she resumed her French lessons with Monsieur de Paradis, the kindly old man who was patient with her to an unimaginable degree. He never begrudged the time it took her to learn to pronounce the sounds and spell the words, patting her gently and kindly on the shoulder, and never tiring of repeating the words over and over again. She could not remember a single time he lost his patience with her.

One day, when her lesson was over, the guard took her, not to the carriage as he did every time, but commanded her to follow him to the room where the seamstresses worked. Could her dreams be coming true? It was all she could think as the seamstress turned her this way and that, adjusting the cut and drape of the dresses over her slim figure, for the design of the gowns seemed to resemble those she had seen on the women at the ball Napoleon had hosted a few weeks ago, the one she had watched from behind the meshrabiyeh, wishing so desperately to be like them, to wear what they wore, and speak their foreign language.

The seamstress folded the dresses and placed them into boxes, then gave them to Zeinab. She looked at her, and for the first time, Zeinab heard her voice. It was dry and hoarse, like the touch of an autumn leaf. "There are accessories to bring out the dresses," she said, and spent some moments demonstrating how to wear corsets and heels. Then she gestured to the traditional Egyptian crescent-shaped gold necklace at Zeinab's throat. With some haughtiness, she went on, "This type of jewelry does not suit them. Also, these braids have to go. Please, don't spoil what I've worked so hard to create." Then she straightened. "The next time you come to the palace, you must wear these clothes." Then she left Zeinab and disappeared into the bowels of the dressmaking workshop.

Zeinab shook her head: would it kill the woman to smile? Still, she staggered out of the room under a pile of boxes, helped with her burdens by the guard who supervised her while within the palace. They arrived at the carriage that was waiting for her outside, and he placed the boxes into it. They set off for home.

The boxes did not contain dresses only, but the other necessities of smart attire, without which the look would be ruined, as the stick-dry woman had said. There were high-heeled shoes, big hats of different shapes and sizes and colors, and most importantly, the wire crinoline that must be worn under the skirts to give them their shape. Zeinab ran and jumped for joy like a little girl, opening each package, putting on the hats each in turn, wrapping each dress around herself and swaying to the left and right, putting on and taking off the gloves—but she stopped at the high-heeled shoes, looking at them with fear and awe. She had no idea how she could walk in them. She avoided even the high clogs in public bathhouses, made of a broad, high platform of wood to keep women from slipping and falling. How would she manage these thin, too-high heels?

Her father could not wipe the sly smile off his face, while her brothers looked on in astonished curiosity. Only her mother, preoccupied and upset, retreated into a corner of the courtyard. Eager to show off her new dress, Zeinab ran to her. "What do you think, Mother? What do you think?"

"Of what?" her mother said dolefully. "Where do you think you can go, dressed like that?"

Zeinab wasn't listening. The sound of her happiness drowned out her mother's sorrow. But the next morning, the answer to her mother's question became apparent.

The streets were bedecked with decorations. The French put up a giant flagpole in the middle of Ezbekiya Lake, hoisting flags and a mock Arc de Triomphe, next to which was a long marquee emblazoned with the words "*La Ilaha Illa Allah, Muhammad Rasul Allah*"—there is no God but Allah and Muhammad is His prophet—the Islamic declaration of faith. In the center of the square was an obelisk with a pyramid-shaped top, about seventy meters high. Emblazoned on one of its sides were the words, "République Française." On the other side was "Ousting the Mamluks."

Three gunshots heralded the start of the celebrations, followed by more pops and bangs. Napoleon Bonaparte himself stood tall among the people to give a speech. His soldiers and officers cheered when he came to the line, "The eyes of the world are upon us." On that day in particular, it was impossible to believe that these people joking and laughing and celebrating with the Egyptian populace were the French soldiers who had killed and been killed, mere days ago, to take Cairo. French tricornes mingled with Arabian turbans, and snatches of French and Arabic conversation rang out and intermingled. Banqueting tables were laid out, bearing a combination of Egyptian and European dishes. After the great banquet, when everyone had eaten, the horse racing commenced. When evening came, everyone's eyes were on the sky, where the French had fired several joyous shots and burned gunpowder to create fireworks, lighting up the heavens in an enthralling spectacle.

Zeinab was invited to the private party that Napoleon was giving at his palace for the occasion. The invitation arrived early in the morning with one of his guards, who knocked twice on the door and waited politely until the slave opened it for him. In refined French, he asked her for Mademoiselle Zeinab al-Bakri. The serving girl gawked. He presented the invitation, smiled and left, leaving her still rooted to the spot, staring after him.

Having only understood 'Zeinab' out of all he had said, the slave realized that the missive was for her. The message was written in graceful handwriting on expensive paper, and signed by Napoleon Bonaparte. The invitation did not include her father, not even mentioning him, although he had gone to offer his congratulations along with a number of Azharite imams and the members of the Diwan, and several high-ranking Copts and Levantines. Earlier, they had put on their cashmere turbans and taken out their best mounts to listen dutifully to the speech of the French bishop, who had stood under the giant flagpole and sermonized and sought to inspire them with courage, talking at them in French.

At sunset, the celebration for the common people drew to a close, and Napoleon and his retinue made ready for the private party, to which Zeinab had been invited. Sheikh al-Bakri was not upset that the invitation did not include him: he had no objections to his daughter going alone to a party to celebrate with the French community. On the contrary, he was filled with pride that out of all the men and women in all of Egypt, she had been invited.

When evening came, Zeinab prepared herself with the help of Seada, the grooming lady who helped women get ready for special occasions and weddings. She sent Maliha out to fetch her, and in an hour she arrived with a wicker basket containing her supplies: henna powder, rough loofahs, pumice stone, kohl, rouge, powder, musk and ambergris, and combs and hairpins. Zeinab took her straight to her room: there was no need to bathe or depilate her, for she had had her slave already do it—the woman had been surprised to be asked to remove the hair on Zeinab's arms and legs, for girls never did that until the Henna Night, the night before their wedding day. Zeinab had made the excuse that her body hair was so thick that the new clothes would reveal it, making her look ugly, whereas she wanted to be at her prettiest and every bit the equal of the foreign women.

It was not only the serving woman who was astonished at Zeinab's request; Seada the grooming expert also found it odd that Zeinab wanted her to pluck her eyebrows. No virgin girl had ever dared make such a request: plucking was reserved solely for married women. Still, she pulled her tweezers out of her basket and started to pluck the girl's brows, chattering incessantly. Zeinab laughed at her way of pronouncing her *z* as an *s*. "The people," Seada said, "are growing resentful at the Western laws that the Franks are imposing." She plucked a few stray hairs from the center. "Every day they issue a decree stranger than the one before it. Isn't it enough for them that we have to sweep the streets every day and splash them with water and light the oil lamps over the gates of our houses? The worst of it is these papers they're having us make out when each new child is born or when someone dies. Even traveling abroad, you have to get a paper for that too, if you can believe it! The newest fad is to take down a list of the people living in every house, and their names and ages to boot. And they've imposed strict penalties against mocking any French soldiers wounded or vanquished in any battle. Oh, and get this—they even ordered us to hang out our washing in the sun and air out our houses well, so as to stop the spread of the plague. . . ."

"Seada, enough of that. This isn't the time for this kind of talk. I'm getting ready to go to dinner in honor of the emperor, and you're talking about laws and taxes and plagues? What do I care about that?"

"True," Seada said bitterly, "what do you care?"

She looked like a princess, a creature neither of the East nor of the West. Her crowning glory, her hair, she had plaited into two braids wrapped around her head and then concealed beneath a large hat decorated with fur and feathers. Everyone in the household came to look at her: her father, her mother,

her brothers of all ages, and all the slaves and servants. They all looked at her and wondered, "Who is she?"

Her father approached her, saying, "*Subhan Allah*, you are so lovely! What a change in you!" Meanwhile, her mother stood observing her, eyes full of sorrow and anxiety, saying nothing. But when Zeinab was just about to go out, she approached her and took her by the hand, and whispered in her ear.

"Safeguard your honor. Don't let anyone touch you or approach you. Don't let anyone go too far when they speak to you. Those people are devils incarnate. Don't forget that Bonaparte, for all he seems gentle, gives the order to have four or five people beheaded every single day, not to mention the ones he has thrown into the Citadel dungeons, never to be heard from again. Are they alive, or did he get rid of them and throw them in the river? Look how many bodies come floating up to the surface in burlap sacks day after day. Don't trust him. Beware of him."

Then she put her hand on Zeinab's head and murmured blessings and recited verses from the Qur'an.

Zeinab listened to her mother's advice and nodded in silent acquiescence. She knew that any further discussions with her mother would lead to a fight, and she wanted nothing to ruin her happiness this evening.

Bonaparte's carriage was due any minute, coming especially to take her to the ball. As usual, the coachman drove at top speed, heedless of the whirlwinds of dust his horses kicked up behind him, rattling to a stop outside the door. He rang the bell of his carriage to let Zeinab know he had arrived. That evening, Zeinab was the center of attention not only for her family, but for everyone in their street, if not their entire neighborhood. All the men and boys thronged the street to see her, and the women and girls clustered behind the meshrabiyeh to watch her enviously, one thing on their lips: "Look at Zeinab, Sheikh al-Bakri's daughter! Look what she's done to herself!"

"How can her father allow her to go out with her face unveiled, wearing see-through clothing?" they whispered.

Zeinab had always worn a long, wide veil that fell to the ground and covered her face; she did not catch anyone's eye, concealed as she was beneath mountains of fabric. But the women of the neighborhood always made much of her beauty, and it was every young man's dream to see the face of Zeinab, Sheikh al-Bakri's daughter. Today, the dream of the men and boys of the neighborhood had come true, and here Zeinab was, her face on display. The women with their matronly busts under their black *gallabiyas* and their veils covering their heads stood whispering, some twisting their lips in disapproval and others beating their breasts in shock and dismay. But who could dare to stand in the way of Sheikh al-Bakri's daughter on her way to a ball given by Bonaparte himself on the French day of celebration?

The carriage arrived. A few meters away, Napoleon's palace was bathed in light, and the sound of music wafted outside. With a nervous tread, Zeinab walked down the path that led into the palace. She remembered her mother's words about those who had been drowned, and suddenly her ears were filled with the screams of the people thrown into the darkened dungeons. Louder and louder, she heard the murmurs of those trying to get out of the sacks before they were thrown in the river, and she saw the heads of the traitors mounted day after day on pikes at the Zuweila Gate to the city. Fear and apprehension coursed through her; she tripped on a marble step and would have fallen, if a strong hand from behind had not caught her. "Thank you," she said, looking back to offer her gratitude to whoever it was. She recognized him. When the French officer had barred her way, this was the man who had stood up to him, rebuked him, and cleared the path for her to pass. Again he had saved her, as though it was her fate to be rescued by him.

He was handsome, that was undeniable. It was hard to tell his age or origins: he seemed to be in his early thirties, a

Frenchman perhaps, or an Italian, or a Greek. "I would have fallen for sure," she smiled, feeling proud at her command of French and the fact that she could communicate in that language. Where would she have been, she thought, if she couldn't speak French? What language would she have used to thank him? How grateful she felt to Monsieur Paradis, her tutor! If it wasn't for him, she would never have managed it.

He gave her a friendly smile, then went on his way. The major-domo met her and looked at her for a moment; then he bowed. "*Bonsoir, Mademoiselle.*"

It was like stepping into another world, a world she had never thought to experience or be a part of. All the men were in tuxedos, and as for the women, it was a positive competition of elegance and beauty. Some had come with the Campaign, and some were part of the larger French community already living in Cairo and Alexandria, which had incidentally been the reason for the campaign on Egypt—if the ruler Murad Bey had not subjected that community to great injustices, their mayor would not have written a letter of complaint to the French Consul, who in turn wrote to Napoleon urging him to send a campaign to keep the Mamluks in line and tempting him to come and invade these bountiful lands.

Turks, Armenians, Levantines, everyone who was anyone, merchants and consuls, Zeinab could see them all here at the celebration. Streamers decorated the walls and hung down from the ceilings, an orchestra played Western music, and servants moved around bearing trays of crystal glasses filled with liquor. For a moment, she felt lost among this great crowd: she knew no one, and no one knew her, and she did not know who she was. She was no longer the simple Egyptian girl with skin the color of Nile silt, and yet she bore no resemblance to the French women, but stopped somewhere in the middle, where it was difficult to take a step forward or backward. In such a position, questions start to come up: *Who am I? What do I want? Who brought me here? Do I really belong here?* Although she finally had the look she dreamed of, and acquired a good deal of French which allowed her to move forward in this new world she had entered, she felt no joy or pride. Something was missing. Perhaps she had lost her own self.

Bonaparte was standing among a group of commanders of his army, in full regalia as he was most of the time, never seeming to take off his uniform. The major-domo led her to him so that she might congratulate him on the anniversary of victory. Reluctantly, she followed the man, who stopped directly in front of Bonaparte. The general saw her and nodded for her to introduce herself. She managed to choke out in low tones, "Zeinab al-Bakri."

Bonaparte's eyes raked over her in a flash, astonishment filling his face. Then he burst into uproarious laughter. "Is it possible? Look at you! You're completely changed!" He laughed again, as the men around him fixed her with curious glances. On his right was Caffarelli, one of the leaders of the Campaign, who was also known as a painter. Napoleon turned to him. "Look at this beauty, Caffarelli! What would you think about painting her?"

Caffarelli laughed, rocking on his wooden leg, but his features did not soften. "It would be an honor for me to paint such loveliness," he said, "but I only paint the victories of Napoleon Bonaparte." He raised his glass to the general, adding, "I am no longer entranced by women's faces. But wait!" He pointed at someone else standing nearby. In a moment, the man Caffarelli had pointed to came over. Her heart filled with gladness to recognize her savior of earlier. He bowed to Napoleon and congratulated him. "This is Alton. He is an accomplished artist. He came with the rest of the Campaign, and his job is to document important matters. There is nothing more important, I believe, than painting such authentic Egyptian features."

Napoleon nodded approval. Caffarelli touched her cheek with his fingertips. "What do you think of this face?

Isn't it worth painting? Don't these features have the right to be documented in a painting that will survive across generations, across time, a constant reminder that such loveliness once existed?"

Alton looked directly into Zeinab's eyes. Her heart beat faster and she felt herself flush. He was scrutinizing her, taking in every detail, as though weighing the man's words. Finally he said quietly, "Definitely this face is worth painting. The moment I set eyes on her, I was certain that she was not French, despite her clothing and her language. Her deeply Oriental features proclaim her true identity." He looked at her directly again and she felt as though his gaze pierced through to her core. More lightly, he said, "I think you would be lovelier in your Oriental clothing."

Napoleon smiled at Alton, downing his glass in one gulp, then commanded the major-domo to take Zeinab to Madame Pauline and her lady friends. He took her to a group of women standing in a corner of the atrium, approaching one of them and whispering in her ear. The woman smiled a welcome at Zeinab, taking her in from head to toe. And with that, she stepped into the closed circle of the aristocracy, and she might as well not have been there. For more than half an hour, she said not a word. She made no attempt to cut into their conversation, for what would she have had to say? The women were all talking about the deplorable state of the country, the even more deplorable state of the Egyptians, the unbearable heat, the mosquitoes and flies and insects everywhere, the dirty streets, the disgusting odors. "If Bonaparte had not issued his edict," one woman said, "I do believe we would all have suffocated from the stench!"

Another woman spoke up in a high, squeaky voice. She wore a puffy dress and a hat adorned with several feathers, each a different color, giving her the air of a parrot. "The Egyptians care for nothing but sleeping, eating, and reproducing," she exclaimed. The women tittered along with her.

A waiter passed with a tray and they plucked glasses of wine and liquor from it. He offered it to Zeinab and she hesitated: should she reach for a glass or not? But if she did not, she would be the laughingstock of these brainless women. Besides, hadn't she dreamed of being like the women at these parties? To dress like them, to dance like them, and even to drink like them? And now that her dream had come true, what was keeping her from reaching out and taking a glass?

She took a sip; it was sharp and bitter. She was forced to swallow it, but realized she wouldn't be able to drink any more, and pretended to be drinking and enjoying it. The women's talk had turned to another topic: Paris and the gossip of those who lived there. She lost interest and stood there, hardly listening to the conversation about people of whom she knew nothing; what did she care about the doings of Mademoiselle So-and-So and the misadventures of Madame Such-and-Such?

Looking around, she caught a glimpse of Napoleon deep in conversation with Muallim Yaacoub, the leader of the Coptic community. So the rumors must be true: Yaacoub was completely on the side of Napoleon, he and the Copts were at his command, and he had offered the services of several young Copts in the service of the Campaign!

She took a few steps away from the women; nobody noticed her departure. She was of no consequence to them. Alton came up to her, took her by the hand, and led her into the courtyard in the rear.

The courtyard was redolent with privet and night-blooming jasmine, the perfume blowing around with the cool summer breeze. They stopped under a large oak three that hid them from prying eyes. "But tell me," he said, "what's your name?"

"Zeinab."

"Zeinab," he repeated. "Zeinab. . . . What does it mean?"

She did not know what her name meant. She shrugged carelessly. "I don't know. What's yours?"

"Alton." He paused, then answered a slew of questions she had never asked. "I'm twenty-eight. I studied painting at art school in Paris. I came with the Campaign to draw and paint everything strange and unusual that my eyes fell upon, and you are the most beautiful, exotic thing I have ever seen." The French she had learned was insufficient to keep up with this gentleman who spoke in a rush, so she tried to pick up a word here and there to understand what he was saying. "But forgive my asking: why are you here?"

She repeated the question to herself. "Why am I here. . . . ?" Then she remembered. "Because Napoleon wants it."

He scoffed, thinking, *What does Napoleon see in this innocent little girl, who knows nothing whatsoever of life? She has none of the skills of any of Napoleon's lovers; besides, he prefers women who are older than him. Or maybe he likes that she's different.*

The major-domo announced that dinner was served. Bonaparte led the way, sitting at the head of the long table that seemed endless. He gave a short speech of welcome to the guests and raised his glass, "To France!"

She sat next to Alton; he was her lodestar in this strange place, and without him she would have remained lost. Having him with her made her feel safe. She marveled at the table setting, the likes of which she had never seen before. At every seat was a plate, knives and forks of pure silver, and a white napkin with embroidered edges.

The waiters began to serve the meal. She saw everyone unrolling their napkins, so she followed suit. After the soup, the waiters removed the plates while others replaced them with another dish; and so it went, as waiter followed waiter, and course followed course. She was overcome with nervousness, as she had never used silverware before, but with a glance at how the people around her held their forks and knives, and since she was intelligent, she managed to pick it up.

As she sat at the long table, she thought of their round table back at home, around which all the family gathered, and how they only used their hands to eat—hands were good enough for everything, after all. Here, there was no conversation while eating, no sound but the clink of fork and knife, one ate with one's mouth closed, and one's teeth performed their function slowly, not like the threshing machines that her family's jaws became as they chewed their food. Her family loved to talk with their mouths full, as though there were no better time for conversation.

The meal ended when the final dessert dish was served. It was an odd kind of sweetmeat, shapeless in form and texture, but it was delicious, so she demolished it to the last spoonful.

Napoleon rose, announcing the conclusion of the banquet, and everyone followed suit. The musicians started playing again, and the glasses started making the rounds once more. Someone came up to Alton and asked for a word with him; he excused himself from her and left, promising not to be long.

She had only been standing alone for a few moments when Napoleon's private secretary came to her and asked her to follow him. She reluctantly followed him, trembling like a leaf in the wind. What fate awaited her? What did this man have in store? Her mother's words rang in her ears: "Don't trust him. Beware of him." Her hand crept up to her neck in terror, but she shook her head sternly, dismissing the idea. Certainly Napoleon would not harm her. Why should he? If he had wanted to hurt her, why did he have her taught French? Perhaps to hear her beg for her life in a language he could understand?

She ascended the marble staircase and walked down a long passageway. It was carpeted with a long, red rug with an Oriental pattern, and on either side of her, the walls were lined with paintings. There were small side tables bearing statues of genuine Limoges porcelain. She walked slowly, hands lifting the hem of her dress. They reached a room at the end of the passage. The man stopped and knocked at the door. A male voice came from inside: "*Entrez!*" The major-domo left her to her fate, but not before he had looked long and searchingly at her with a question in his mind: *What does the general want with this girl?*

She found herself stepping into a strange room, a mix of East and West so complete that it would have been hard to tell where one was on this great Earth. The rug on the floor had an Oriental pattern; the bed was in the French style; the lantern in the ceiling was arabesque; the vases were Limoges with a Romeo and Juliet pattern. Not so strange, after all, for a man who would appoint himself Emperor of the East and West, to bring them together in this tiny corner of the world. Had he not given a speech to the Muslims on the day of the Prophet's birthday, handed out gifts and largesse, and worn a turban and a caftan? Today, he was celebrating the anniversary of the French Republic, raising a glass and drinking wine.

He stood with his back to her, looking out of the window of the palace, legs slightly apart. At last he had set his hat aside: his thinning hair was smooth and chestnut-colored. He left her standing in the sea of her shyness for a few moments, and she said not a word. Then he turned to her. His hair was creeping down over his forehead and partly covering his eyes. There was no trace of the renowned cruelty in his features, nor the strength and courage he was known for. He had the face of a shy and innocent boy. Could appearances truly be this deceiving?

He approached her and took her hat off, tossing it onto the bed. Then he whispered her name into her ear. "Zeinab. . . ."

She had never heard her name said so sweetly before. Could the man saying it in such tones be Napoleon, the great warrior? Slowly, he ran the tips of his fingers up and down her cheek and neck, a pleasant sensation. The scent of musk and ambergris still clung to her from where the slave girl had added it to her bathwater that morning and burned it in incense, and now it hung in the air between them.

He came closer and put his nose to her neck, inhaling her scent in ecstasy. "How wonderful you smell," he murmured, "how lovely you are!"

He took her by the hand and gently led her to sit next to him on the bed. She found herself sitting close to his medals, proudly hanging from his uniform jacket. Conflicting feelings rushed through her: pride and guilt, confidence and unease, panic that stopped her breath at what was about to happen, like a tiny fish in the presence of the vastness of the sea.

The room was lit by candlelight. The overpowering scent of his masculine perfume filled her nostrils, and he was only a few breaths away. He took off her hoop earrings, opened her small hand and placed them into it. Then he began to undo her braids one by one, lock after lock of hair coming free, and with every lock, he plucked out the cloves that Maliha had braided into her hair. He pursued this task with great care and patience, making sure not to hurt her when he separated the tangles in her hair. Silence weighted the room down, making her feel as though time was passing impossibly slowly, as if it had stopped. One question filled her mind: *What was to come after undoing the braids?*

Finally, her hair hung free, cascading like a waterfall down her back. He gently stroked it, then said, "Go now."

Had the greatest and most powerful man in the world truly been undoing her braids with matchless care and patience, like a man preparing his lover for a night of love, taking off her earrings, inhaling the perfume of her body, loosening her hair? How much time had he taken, undoing her braids? Nearly an hour. He had not spoken a word in that time. Then to ask her to leave?

She stepped outside the room, sighing with relief, still flustered and shrouded in fear. Down the long corridor she went, trying to gather up her loose hair and twist it into a bun at the top of her head, jamming the hat down on top of it to hide it. It was no use, though; her hair slipped out, long locks of it straying free. She hurried down the stairs, although she was aware that no one had noticed her disappearance, just as no one had noticed her presence. They were dancing joyously, well into their wine by now.

She had been wrong. One person had noticed her disappearance, and after searching for her everywhere, had convinced himself that she must have had to leave in a hurry without saying goodbye. All of a sudden, as he lifted his glass to his lips, he caught sight of her coming down the stairs, flustered and uneasy. Their eyes met; she saw a question in his eyes and a cynical smile. For the second time, she slipped and would have fallen, if Bonaparte's secretary had not caught her—he had been waiting at the bottom of the stairs until his employer had finished his rites of passion with her. He caught her and propelled her to the carriage that was waiting outside to take her home.

The carriage rattled all the way, scraping against the walls of the ancient houses on both sides of the narrow street. The moon disappeared behind a cloud in the black velvet sky. August was hot and humid, and the darkened streets were swallowed up in mist, but for the light of an oil lamp here and there. Everyone was deep asleep at such a late hour of the night. Only this girl of fifteen was awake, asking herself all the way home: *Was what happened real, or was it a flight of fancy? Did I truly sit close to Napoleon? Did he take off my earrings and undo my braids? Did he kiss my neck and inhale my scent? And the handsome artist, did I truly meet him? Was what happened real?*

A few days after that celebration, the stiff festoons put up for the celebrations were shattered by a gale, leading people to be optimistic that this heralded the end of the rule of the French.

8

Cairo: Autumn 2012

WHEN HE LEFT HER THAT day, he was heavy with sorrow and consumed by a terrible sense of guilt. How could he have remained so ignorant all the time they had been together? How had he not understood that a terrible secret lay behind the sorrow on her face, her sudden silences and preoccupied air?

He tried to fall asleep, but ever since he'd given up drinking and sleeping pills, sleep had been slow in coming. It was always the same: no sooner did he lie down in bed than he was flooded with everything that had happened that day and the days before that, if not even further back in time. Sometimes the memories were pleasant, but most of the time they were unhappy, and if he did manage to fall asleep, a sensation of falling would take hold of him. But that night, his insomnia did not bother him: he was happy to stay awake because it allowed him the opportunity to think about her. It was time to rethink their relationship. He had always blamed her for breaking it off in such a humiliating manner, laboring under the delusion that he had been the perfect lover; but how could he have been, without ever realizing that his beloved held a terrible secret of such magnitude?

Throwing off the bedclothes, he climbed out of bed and went to the window. The weather had changed again, and a light rain was falling. The leaves on the trees shone wetly in the moonlight.

"I've been selfish," he muttered. "Yes, I have. I've been selfish."

He padded to the kitchen and began to make coffee: it was no more use trying to sleep anyway. When she had come into his life, he had been in the iron grip of a new phase, which he had dubbed his 'Purification Phase.' He had decided to reinvent himself as a new man, a different person. If she had known him when he was younger, she would certainly never have left him. He would have given her everything she could possibly need or want.

He had been twenty-four when he had gone abroad to do his postgraduate studies, not out of a love of learning but a desire to escape his surroundings: his society, his friends, his family, his relatives, his country's problems. In short, his whole life. His joy had been indescribable when he got accepted into a Swedish university, one he had applied to some time before in an endless search for architecture scholarships in Europe. The acceptance letter arrived along with a class schedule and a notification that the scholarship would cover half his tuition and provide housing, the rest falling to him. He did not waste time thinking about how he was going to cover the rest of the tuition or come up with living expenses. His father was a simple government clerk who would barely be able to come up with the money for the air ticket.

He had known that the cost living in Europe was high, but he had not realized that it would be that expensive. From the very first day, therefore, he decided to look for work. He had a BA in architecture and was a postgraduate student at the foremost university in Sweden, so no doubt some important job awaited him, or so he thought. His dreams were shattered, however: all his interviews ended in failure, and when he finally lost hope of getting a job commensurate with his abilities, he was obliged to take several jobs in his first year: a supermarket checkout clerk, a salesperson at a store selling athletic shoes, a room-service waiter at a hotel. One day, the hotel posted a job for a waiter at the hotel bar. The pay was excellent, so he applied and was accepted, having already proved himself in room service. Times were tight, so he never spared a thought whether it might be a sin to work in a bar and serve alcohol. Even the unpleasantness of the drunken customers he managed to put up with without a murmur. The drunker they got, the better they tipped.

The day he saw her, his life changed. She was older, dark-skinned with long black hair and a voluptuous figure. Their eyes met and he could tell from the way she flirted that she was taken with him as well. Her nationality was a mystery to him: if he had had to guess, he would have said Italy or Mexico—she was certainly not Swedish. When he approached her to set down a few glasses of vodka at her table, she was talking on her cell phone in Arabic, her accent that of the countries of the Arabian Gulf. At first, he couldn't believe his ears. She kept talking, and loudly too. When he became certain she was Arab, he said, "Welcome," to her in Arabic.

"And to you," she said in the same language. "Are you Arab?"

"Yes," he said, "Egyptian."

She gave a coy laugh. "I guessed as much." She asked his name and what brought him to Sweden; he missed speaking in Arabic, which made him chatty, and in a very short time had told her his entire life story. He talked about his hometown, his family, his career, and the circumstances that brought him there. Finally, he left her and went back to work. When she asked for the check for herself and her friends, he brought it in the little leather folder, and she put in two cards: her credit card and her business card. The former he gave to the cashier; the latter he kept.

He could hardly wait for the end of class the next day. He dialed her number, afraid she might be sleeping—he assumed that the types who spend their nights at the bars slept all day. However, she sounded bright and lively, contrary to his apprehensive expectations. "I'm on the way to an important meeting," she said, "but I'll expect you in the lobby of the Hilton at two o'clock."

On their first date, she told him everything about herself. Her father was Arab and her mother Swedish; she had spent most of her life moving back and forth between the two countries. After university she had opened her own business, a real estate development and construction company that specialized in building resorts and buying and restoring old mansions to convert into hotels while preserving their appearance and architectural character. She made him an offer to join her company. As it happened, he had only a few days left until graduation, after which he would be free to accept.

A few days later, Nirvan, for that was her name, told him she did not want to spend the night alone, and led him to her room in the villa where she lived. He was inexperienced and his shyness and apprehension only made matters worse. She took the lead and laughed when they were done, kissing him on both cheeks: "You're going to need some training, that's for sure!"

That might have been true at first, but in a few weeks, he became an expert in the rules of the game, and excelled, not just in bed, but in his new job. He learned quickly that with enough money, anything is possible: commissions over and under the table—and from the side and round the back as well—paved the way to buying government-owned plots of land. Old historic houses were assessed at a fraction of their real value, and every tender the company took part in, they won.

He was to spend half his life country-hopping from airport to airport all over the world: he met with Wall Street brokers in the morning, and agents in Milan in the evening. The morning after would find him in a new town with new people to broker a new deal. With the slew of titles and positions that introduced him to clients, no one suspected his veracity or cast doubt on his integrity: he was, after all, an expert in architecture and construction, a consultant and assessor with a postgraduate degree from one of the world's foremost universities.

In a short while, thanks to Nirvan and to his own acumen, he went far. The fame and fortune he achieved came at a cost, however. The greatest sacrifice was his own peace of mind. He could not sleep without being plagued by nightmares; he could not eat without indigestion. After a checkup, he was diagnosed with an ulcer, brought on by stress, exhaustion, and constant anxiety. Meanwhile, his relationship with Nirvan only grew stronger, helped along by the fact that there was no possessiveness on either side, except for the moments when their bodies became one, leaving each free to go their own way when they weren't together. She never asked him whom he had been with, and he never asked her whom she had known. Although he had slept with many women much more beautiful and many years younger, the blond cover girls offered to him by his clients by way of a thank you never satisfied him the way she did. There was a certain affection between them that he could not name: it did not deserve the name love, but perhaps admiration or gratitude for the immense opportunity she had offered him. His whole life, he had never dreamed of being half as rich as he had become.

He could not deny that he had been drawn to the jet-set world at first: its parties and soirées, its trips and jaunts, were all like dunes of soft sand pulling him deeper and deeper down. As time passed, he realized that money in and of itself was these people's ultimate goal, and money was all they believed in. Money could buy anything: happiness, ambition, security, love, and marriage. It was a world he had regarded with curious interest while still on the outside, looking in: he remembered wondering what life meant to these people. He had wondered, more mundanely, what paths they traveled, which countries they visited, which doctors they went to, and on and on; now that he had come into this world and become one of them, he knew for a fact that it was empty. Oddly, their lives, like their thinking and even their appearance, were all the same. It was hard to tell their women apart, for they went to the same plastic surgeons to remake them all in the same mold: the same nose, the same perfectly pouty lips, even the same shape to their eyes. They had the same bleached blond hair, fake tans, acrylic nails, and augmented breasts and hips. Their men were not much different, similarly stripped of any individuality: they wore clothing in the latest style, owned the most expensive top-brand watches, smartphones, and other electronics, and sported tattoos over their gym-built, toned bodies while their hair gleamed with product. They all spoke in the same fake, polished tones, their body language languid and mechanical. This was how they chose to present themselves: they saw and heard nothing of the world's sufferings unless it was through their own blinkered view. As for their romantic lives, they were something of an incestuous clique, one within a very large family: this woman was X's girlfriend today, Y's girlfriend tomorrow, and the same with the men, all traveling within the same circles.

Sooner or later, one must tire of such a life, devoid of all feeling. Five-star hotels and restaurants, fortunes in every currency accumulating in numbered accounts, the latest model of luxury automobile, beautiful plastic dolled-up women: one must tire of all this, and of one's own self. At the same time, there is no outlet for one's anger, and no way out of this fake world.

But Sherif, unlike the other members of that crowd, managed to make the decision to shake off its anxiety, anger, and tedium. To leave such a world was like stepping out of a dream to fall headlong into cruel reality. The first step to leaving it was dissolving his business interests with his partners. The financial loss was devastating, but he had made a decision and there was no going back.

A few months before his decision, something had happened that had affected him deeply, and fueled the fires of his unease. He traveled a great deal for the company in order to assess the worth of historical and ancient sites for purchase and refurbishment as hotels. The company had recently put in bids for various properties in Britain, France, and Greece, as well as in Istanbul, Cairo, Damascus, and Baghdad. His current trip, to a place called Konya, was not the first time he had visited Turkey, for he had been there several times and was very fond of it. He loved everything about the country: the climate, the geography, the history, the streets, the architecture, and the friendly people. Whenever he felt he needed a change of scene, it was the first place he would go. Although he was a regular at the Bosporus Hilton, which commanded a breathtaking view of the river it was named after, in Turkey he felt he could escape the pressure of social status and walk through the narrow streets and alleyways, his mind at ease at last.

9

WHEN HIS FLIGHT LANDED IN Konya Airport, Sherif closed his book and got ready to disembark. He took a taxi and gave the driver the name of his hotel. The weather was chilly, but a golden glow of sunlight reflected off the buildings and the trees, giving them a friendly warmth. The city was historic, its buildings and mosques reflecting its prominence as a twelfth- and thirteenth-century capital, despite some modern buildings and Western-style restaurants and cafés; however, its most striking feature was the tall Islamic gravestones with sun symbols and men's headgear carved into the tops, planted all around the city in a circle as though embracing it, casting shadows of grief and melancholy.

His Turkish wasn't up to much, despite his repeated visits: he had not even managed to pick up a few words to help him shop and communicate with taxi drivers. It was difficult, therefore, to ask the driver about the tall turbans carved into the gravestones. He remained silent until they arrived at the hotel, its modern façade incongruous in such an ancient city. There was a line of tourists in front of a large mosque, extending all the way into the middle of the street. The driver helped him carry his bags to reception and Sherif tipped him several extra liras in thanks. "Here's my number if you need a lift anywhere," said the driver, handing him a business card.

Check-in was accomplished quickly, and he asked the receptionist to have a cup of Turkish coffee brought up to his room. The balcony looked directly onto the mosque, offering a grand view. He stood there, momentarily mesmerized by its arresting beauty, until the waiter arrived with the coffee. "What's that mosque called?" he asked.

The waiter smiled proudly with the reflected glory of the magnificent building that his country boasted. "It's the Mosque of Suleiman the Magnificent, Kanunî Sultan Süleyman."

It was not the first time he had seen an opulent mosque in his travels to various Turkish cities, but this was by far the most marvelous and certainly lived up to the sultan's title, 'the Magnificent.' Despite the fine Turkish coffee, he found himself tired and lay down on the bed, closing his eyes.

He was startled from his nap by the ringing of his phone. It was a local number, not an international one: it could only be Borhan Bey, the client from whom his company wanted to purchase a house. He spoke to the gentleman, who wanted to meet in an hour, and agreed although he was in desperate need of sleep. "Oh, well," he said to himself, "it's not as if there's any nightlife in the city. Might as well avoid napping in the afternoon so as to get a good night's rest." Sherif had never contented himself with what meets the eye, always eager to know the story behind historical cities, so he pulled up Konya on his iPad. In a few seconds, several sites came up purporting to offer details about the city he was visiting for a scant three days.

Borhan met him in the lobby of the hotel and introduced himself, shaking his hand and greeting him warmly like an old friend as was the Turkish custom. He was a squat, portly man of just over fifty, with graying hair and a ruddy and fine-featured face. "You must be starving!" he declared. "Let's go to lunch first."

He then led Sherif out to the hotel garage where his BMW waited, and turned on the air conditioning despite the pleasant weather. He stopped in a commercial area outside a restaurant which, Borhan told Sherif, was the oldest in the city, and served the traditional cuisine Konya was famous for, most prominently *etli bamya*, dried okra soup. He would not permit Sherif to order for himself, but told the waiter, "Two *etli bamya*, two bread with meat, two *çiğ köfte,*" which turned out to be lettuce leaves stuffed with spicy raw meatballs. "All traditional Turkish dishes," he smiled cheerfully at Sherif after the waiter had left.

The restaurant was old, high-ceilinged, and furnished in an old-fashioned style; it seemed not to have been renovated since the day it had opened. There were wooden tables covered in white plastic sheeting and rattan chairs; the overhead neon lights glared palely, and a ceiling fan rotated monotonously, circulating the air and the delicious smells of cooking throughout the interior. A window displaying the dishes on offer stretched horizontally across the wall, behind which the fat cook was working. On the walls were displayed several photographs of the restaurant owner with his most famous guests: a framed photo of Kemal Atatürk and one of a whirling dervish performing in his white skirt. Traditional Turkish music filled the restaurant.

Their orders arrived. Borhan dug in with gusto. "Turkish cuisine is the oldest in the world, you know," he boasted between mouthfuls, "and I daresay the finest. We've kept to our traditional recipes."

Sherif nodded politely.

"We Turks love a good meal. You won't find us chasing after Italian restaurants and American-style food the way it is in other parts of the world."

Borhan's appetite for talking was as good as his appetite for food. Sherif just smiled, nodded at the appropriate junctures, and otherwise let his client chatter happily on.

Looking up, he found himself staring again at the photograph of the dervish. He could almost see him whirling—no, it wasn't an illusion. The man was dancing, actually whirling. Sherif blinked his eyes and stared. Borhan, noticing, asked in concern, "Something the matter?"

Suddenly, the dervish stopped whirling. Sherif must have been more tired than he realized, or else it was the man's endless chatter that had him seeing things.

After the meal, Borhan drove Sherif into the old quarter, coming to a halt outside an imposing wooden doorway. Sherif had noticed that although most of the houses in the area were historic, the vast majority of them sported signs emblazoned with the word 'HOTEL.' Konya, he knew, was full of old buildings that had been restored and reopened as hotels. The new generation of tourists preferred places like this to luxury hotels. He felt uncomfortable telling Borhan that his company was one of the foremost to profit from this new tourism trend.

Borhan unlocked the door with a large, rusty wooden key that let out a piercing squeak as it turned in the ancient lock. The house they stepped into was wooden, surrounded by a large, neglected garden. It was as silent as a graveyard inside, with a cold, depressing atmosphere that made Sherif shiver. He buttoned up the top button of his woolen jacket. "This house was built hundreds of years ago," Borhan boomed, shattering the silence, "by one of my ancestors. He built it to live in with his family. He was a teacher and also the imam of a Sufi order; later, he set a part of the house aside for a madrasa, a school for religious instruction, and a *tikiya*, or guest house, for his dervishes and followers. You know that was common for a lot of imams of that time."

He guided Sherif from room to room and corridor to corridor, showing him around the house. It was divided into two: the *haramlek*, or women's quarters, set aside for the imam's family and his womenfolk, with its own staircase and entrance; and the *salamlek*, or men's quarters, part of which was devoted to the guest house and its visitors. "Here we are," the man said, pointing to the rows of rooms: classrooms, meditation rooms, and the one they walked into, the *sama' khana*, a type of auditorium or listening room. It was a spacious chamber layered with Persian carpets that seemed untouched by time and Ottoman couches set all around. Hanging from the ceiling was a chandelier composed entirely of brass candelabras. In one corner was a collection of reed flutes and tambours, clearly exactly as they had been set down by the last hand that had played them. "This is the *sama' khana*, where all the singing and dancing took place."

The smell of incense was rising. Sherif's ears caught the melancholy wail of a reed flute, growing gradually louder and louder. The dervish was there again, whirling and spinning all around the room. His skirt wafted a perfume that struck Sherif in the face. He turned lightly around, his speed breathtaking. Sherif's head spun, but this time it was worse: he flung himself down on one of the couches, straining to stare harder and harder at the whirling specter. In the blink of an eye, their eyes met. The man's eyes were sharp, powerful, piercing. They seemed to bore into Sherif's soul. He trembled. "I need to go," he stammered to Borhan Bey.

As they walked out, Sherif's eyes fell upon an oil painting hanging on the wall, of a number of dervishes in costume and tall felt turbans, whirling all around a man bearing the hallmarks of dignity and grandeur. Sherif froze, staring at it. It was the dervish whom he had seen moments ago, the same one whose image he had seen on the restaurant wall. His eyes were sunken, dark around the edges as though adorned with kohl, and topped with thick, furrowed eyebrows. They were the same eyes he had just looked into. Their gaze pierced his very depths, as though the man in the picture was aiming the arrows of his glances at Sherif and only him. He stared at the picture so long that the man noticed his interest in it. "That's my great-grandfather, the imam of the Sufi order and the owner of this guest house, with some of his followers and dervishes."

"Tell me, Mr. Borhan," Sherif breathed. "Why do you want to sell the house?"

Borhan chuckled. "As you see, because it's locked up, and no one's using it."

"Why didn't you try to make use of it? Turn it into a hotel perhaps, or open it up to tourists, or rent it out?"

"There are a great many of us heirs to the place," Borhan explained, "and each of us wants to do something different with it. That's why we settled on selling it. As you see, it's in poor condition and will cost a lot to renovate."

Sherif was on his way out when Borhan called out, "Wait! There's a basement as well. My grandfather's buried in there with his family and some of his most faithful followers. It's a nice mausoleum down there. . . ."

Sherif stared. "You bury your dead here?"

"Yes. It's tradition. The imam and his followers are buried in the same spot."

Sherif shook his head. "I don't think I need to view any mausoleums. Let's just go."

On the way home, Borhan took to chattering about the value of the property and its unique location, but Sherif was not really with him.

10

SHERIF LAY DOWN IN THE bed, the full moon lighting up his room from behind the glass of the window with a lovely silvery light. He fell asleep for a few hours, waking up to the sound of the dawn call to prayer. The muezzin's voice gave him some measure of peace, with his repetitions of *"al-Salatu khayran min al-nawm,"* prayer is better than sleep. He had given up praying a long time ago, but now the phrase preoccupied him. He felt a sudden need to pray. He went out onto the balcony and saw several men hurrying to the mosque. He dressed and joined them.

In the large courtyard of the mosque was a fountain of white marble with brass taps for those who wanted to perform ablutions. He placed his hand beneath the cold water and slapped his face with it—once, twice, three times, not so much washing his face as slapping himself awake, slapping away the veil over his eyes to see life from a new perspective.

The inside of the mosque was an architectural masterpiece. Giant chandeliers hung from the ceilings; its walls were inlaid with shining marble and adorned with Qur'anic verses in beautiful calligraphy. The faithful arranged themselves in rows, shoulder to shoulder: a dervish's headgear could be seen toward one of the front rows, taller than all present. After prayers, Sherif again glimpsed the man with the tall headgear. It was the same whirling dervish. Yes, it was he, the man from the oil painting on the restaurant wall, and the painting on the wall of the house. But how could he be here? It must be just an uncanny resemblance; the two men were centuries apart. Unable to resist his curiosity, Sherif went up to him. "Excuse me, but have we met?"

He couldn't help noticing that the man had an extraordinarily bright complexion that seemed to be glowing. The light was not just coming from the man's face: it was a glow that haloed him. He inclined his head slightly. "You must have seen me with the eyes of your heart."

Sherif just stared. At the time, he had not known what the man meant, but something stopped his tongue and stilled any further questions. The man's eyes, black as pebbles, penetrated Sherif's defenses. In an instant he felt them going deep into him, into his innermost heart. "Follow your heart's footsteps and release the fetters of the sins that weigh you down. Give your soul room to breathe."

Sherif opened his mouth to rebuke this impertinent stranger, to say to him, "Who are you to say such things to me?" Instead, he found himself saying, "I'm trying. But it's hard. Harder than I thought."

The man smiled. "Nothing is hard." He laid a gentle hand on Sherif's shoulder. "Try, and you *will* succeed."

His recollection of what happened after that was not very clear. He seemed to blank out for a moment; when he looked around him, there was no one. The man was gone. Sherif looked around in hopes of finding him in some corner or other of the mosque, but there was no trace of him. He hurried outside the mosque, looking left and right, still thinking he might find the man; there was only silence and darkness.

Back in his room, he couldn't stop thinking. Was what had happened real, or was it a dream? But how could it be a dream when the man's words still echoed in his ears, when he still could feel the loving touch of his hand on his shoulder, when the scent of his perfume still lingered in his nostrils? Perhaps it was only a dervish who looked like him; but then, why had he suddenly disappeared as though he had never existed?

He dismissed these speculations from his head, focusing instead on the man's words: "Follow the footsteps of your heart and release the fetters of the sins that weigh you down." But this advice only led to more labyrinthine avenues of confusion: how could this man have known that he wanted to leave everything behind and start anew?

He had strange dreams that night, but he could remember nothing of them. He breakfasted in the hotel restaurant, and at exactly ten o'clock, Borhan called, telling him he was outside the hotel to take him on a tour of the city as he had promised the previous day.

That morning, Borhan's greeting was brighter and his demeanor friendlier than it had been the day before. "I hope you slept well?"

"Very well. Except for a few nightmares."

"Oh," the man smiled, "that always happens to me after I take a flight to a different country. Change of place and time zones, and all that."

"Mr. Borhan," Sherif ventured, "would you mind another visit to your grandfather's house? I . . . would like to give it another look."

The man seemed taken aback to hear Sherif's request; Sherif, after all, had told him yesterday that everything was in order, and that he would commence writing his report. Noticing that he seemed disgruntled, Sherif hastened to reassure him. "Don't worry. Everything's still fine. It's just that there are parts of the house that I didn't assess carefully enough, and you know how important it is that my report to the company be complete."

"Well, I'm at your service, Mr. Sherif. Let's be on our way."

He turned the BMW around and they set off. They opened the house to reveal the same perfume: the scent that had filled his nostrils the other day, the dervish's perfume. "What's that smell?" Sherif asked carefully. "Do you use a particular incense or freshener in here?"

"I actually can't smell anything," Borhan sniffed carefully at the air, turning his head this way and that, "but then again my sense of smell isn't that acute. I can smell mold and mildew, but that's all."

This time, it was Sherif who led Borhan to the listening room. He walked straight up to the dervish's portrait, standing directly before it and staring to make sure it was the same man he had seen in the mosque the other day. "What is it about this dervish?" asked Sherif.

"I don't know what you mean," Borhan said, his pleasant demeanor disappearing and his features tensing. "I'm sorry, what do you mean, 'what is it about him?'"

More insistent now that he scented a secret, Sherif repeated firmly, "Who is he? What do you know about him?"

"Why are you asking about this particular dervish? Did someone tell you something about him? I know the people of this city, they never stop gossiping and making up lies and creating superstitions and making up stories!"

Sherif planted his feet more firmly on the ground. "Mr. Borhan, let's be frank. There's no need to beat around the bush. I'm here to write a report to close a big deal, and we're going to be paying a lot of money. I'm asking you to be honest with me about everything to do with that dervish."

Borhan mopped his bald pate and forehead. "Wouldn't you like to look at some other part of the house?"

"No."

"Then let's go," Borhan gestured nervously, "and I'll tell you all about the dervish over coffee."

Sherif reluctantly agreed. He didn't really want to leave this place, filled with the spirit of a man who was no longer there. He wished the dervish would reappear, so that he could see and speak with him again. His presence had made

Sherif feel at peace, and his conversation was a balm to his aching soul.

Borhan glared silently throughout the drive, as though some catastrophe had struck him and rendered him dumb—a stark contrast to his garrulousness of before. Finally, they sat at a sidewalk café and he ordered them two cups of coffee. "Okay," he said. "I'm going to be honest with you: I'll tell you everything." He mopped his brow again. "Let's start at the beginning.

"One of my ancestors built this house to marry and start a family there. Then he joined a Sufi *tariqa*, or order, and became a prominent imam with his own followers and students, so he converted almost all of the house into a school and guest house for the dervishes. He and his family only lived in a small corner of it. As you know, these guesthouses open their doors to one and all, and dervishes from every corner of the globe are welcome to stay there for days, weeks, even months. On a cold December day, this man came knocking at the door of the guest house. He was trembling with cold, with snow in his hair and beard. They made him welcome and gave him a seat by the fireplace, and the cook gave him a bowl of hot soup. That day he didn't speak much, only telling him that he had had a long journey, because he had come from Azerbaijan to Konya especially to study under my great-great-great-grandfather, now that he had become famous all over the world.

"My grandfather accepted him as one of his students, and he quickly became a favorite. He was a man of few words, and did as he was told. One time, as they were gathered in the listening room, playing and dancing, he asked to be allowed to dance in circles as they did. My grandfather refused, as he was not yet ready for the whirling dance."

"But does that dance need any training?" Sherif asked, taking a gulp of his coffee. "It's just turning around and around."

"Mr. Sherif," Borhan said seriously, "the thing is very different from what you imagine. It is an ancient ritual dating back to the start of what we call human knowledge—the knowledge that allows a human being to take the path back to the Lord. It was first known in Persia. The whirling dancer departs his earthly life to spin high up into the Kingdom of God. My grandfather warned him at the time, 'Not yet. Transmutation hurts you if you are not ready. Transmutation touches the heartstrings, and brings on such a flood of emotions that it becomes a temptation. Such a temptation blocks spiritual growth for those who immerse themselves in it merely to fulfill their emotional longing. Because of this, before transmutation, the heart must first abandon its burdens. When a dervish goes forth to the whirling dance, this is his path to the Complete Human.'"

"The Complete Human?" Sherif repeated.

"Yes," Borhan explained, "the Complete Human refers to the wise creature whose ultimate goal is to reach God. To reach Him, he must pass through four portals. The passageway leading to these four portals is the four parts of the dance. The first portal is sharia, religious law, and the second is the *tariqa*, the Sufi order, that is the mysterious inner dimension of the Mevlevi Sufi order. The third portal is *al-ma'rifa*, knowledge, and the fourth is *al-haqiqa al-mutlaqa*, absolute truth, where the skirted dervish shares his wisdom: when he opens his right hand above his head, he is drawing blessings upon himself from God, and when he opens his left toward the floor, he is conferring these blessings upon others. And thereby the dervish is reborn."

Sherif blinked. "I see."

He had not known that the simple-looking whirling had such a weight of ideas and beliefs behind it.

"If you like, I can take you to a Mevlevi retreat, and you can see them for yourself."

"I'd definitely like to do that, but tell me the rest of the story about the dervish."

"There's nothing to tell. This dervish refused to heed my ancestor's advice. Once when they were dancing, he slipped in among them and began to whirl with them. My grandfather punished him by banning him from dancing for six months, even if he were to become ready during that time. But no one saw him again after that night, in the guest house or outside it. They looked for him high and low, but he was gone without a trace. Ever since, there have been rumors that his spirit roams the guest house and the streets, wearing his white skirt and performing the whirling dance."

Sherif stilled, lost in thought. Clearly afraid he would change his mind about the house, or put down in his report 'Dancing dervish in the house,' Borhan started to convince him. "The only reason for all the rumors was the way the dervish disappeared. There's no truth to them, none at all. Please don't believe them." He mopped his brow. "Or write them down in your report."

Sherif let the man prattle on, finally cutting him off. "Where do you think the dervish went?"

Borhan took a breath. "Nobody knows. They do say he was a mysterious one, who never talked to anyone. And everyone knows that dervishes like to travel far and wide, across God's green earth. Look, come on, let me take you to the retreat and show you the ritual."

It was late at night when Sherif came back to his hotel room, after a long evening where Borhan had initiated him into the secrets of the dervishes' hidden world. He had taken Sherif to a Sufi order, where he had watched the dance, and had the different parts of it explained to him by Borhan. The most enthralling to him had been the state of mind into which they entered while performing the whirling dance, the spiritual ecstasy so intense that he fancied he could see them levitating off the floor.

He thought long and hard about the divine love that transported them to this state, as though they were in a completely different world from ours. He wished he could have risen to join them and whirl and spin as they did, to join them in this world of theirs. But was he ready? It was then that he understood the dervish's overpowering urge to dance.

Borhan took him to the graves of the dervishes with their tall hats carved into the top of their headstones, telling him that a dervish's hat was always buried with him. The hat was an important part of the ritual, and the worst punishment that could befall a dervish who had committed some sin was to be forbidden from wearing it. They ended their tour by visiting the graves of the famous dervishes Jalal al-Din al-Rumi and Shams al-Tabrizi. Sherif was consistently astonished by the depth of the man's knowledge about a world of which Sherif knew nothing: to him, before today, a dervish had been only a dancer in a white skirt.

Sherif flung his exhausted body down on the bed, and, unusually for him, fell asleep at once.

He saw himself wearing the costume of the dervishes, complete with tall hat, spinning and whirling. Suddenly, a voice whispered in his ear: "Not yet . . . not yet . . . transmutation hurts you if you are not ready."

He bolted upright, turning his head this way and that in search of the voice. Had it been a dream? He had been asleep, but the voice that woke him . . . that had not been a dream.

The muezzin's voice rang out with the call to dawn prayer: *al-Salatu khayran min al-nawm*, prayer is better than sleep. He leapt out of bed, did his ablutions, and went out to the mosque.

The wind whistled loudly as he made his way across the square, chilly gusts that nearly blew him off his feet. He crossed the road quickly and went into the mosque. He scanned the rows of the faithful, hoping to find the dervish among them, but he was not there.

Sherif did not leave the mosque like the rest of the men who had been praying. He sat in a corner saying fervent prayers, the name of God on his lips, praising Him and asking for His mercy and forgiveness. A ray of light shone down from the sky and found its way into his heart, filling it with light and faith. He didn't know how long he sat there, apart from reality. Through the veil of his tears, he saw the hem of a white garment: looking up, he saw him standing there. "You?" he breathed, overcome with love and gratitude.

The man smiled without answering.

"But are you really the dervish who disappeared long ago? Tell me. Are you real, or am I imagining you? Dead or alive?"

"Dervishes never die. They live on in silence." Sherif was still thinking of these words when the man went on, "Don't stop. Keep going and you'll get there."

When Sherif opened his mouth to speak, the dervish began to whirl. He spun at breakneck speed, his perfume spreading like a breeze, then faded away and vanished, still spinning.

Dawn was breaking when Sherif left the mosque, a weak light trying to push its way up and dislodge the weight of the darkness. Gradually, it grew and grew until it filled the world with brightness, light, and warmth. The light dispelled not only the darkness in the sky, but also the darkness in Sherif's heart and soul. This was the time of day he usually crawled out of the clubs he frequented, but he had never thought to notice the darkness gradually clearing the way for the sun to spread its light anew. The darkness that had settled over his soul had blocked him from seeing anything of beauty.

He didn't feel like going back to the hotel. He went to a café and ordered tea and pastries stuffed with cheese and vegetables. He ate with great appetite, and then took a walk all around town. While the dervish didn't appear again, he remained with Sherif in spirit. He saw him whirling and turning all around him, his wide white skirt touching the whole of creation.

Going into a stationer's that stocked dervish-themed gifts, he found figurines of dervishes in different shapes and sizes, and books on their history. He bought several books on Sufi mysticism and their different orders, the dervishes, their lives, rituals, and guest houses. As he was walking out, he saw an enormous earthenware statue of a dervish, wearing a wide skirt, with one palm raised to the heavens and the other pointed at the floor. He bought it.

Back in his room, he checked his phone to find more than ten missed calls: from the office, from friends, and from his partner asking him for his report. There were also two calls from Borhan. Sherif returned these first. Borhan's voice came tersely through the phone. "Good morning, Mr. Sherif. I called you a couple of times, but you didn't answer. Did you sleep late?"

"Not at all," Sherif said curtly. "I woke early." He let him stew, imagining curiosity eating him alive. Borhan couldn't very well ask him why he hadn't answered his calls, and Sherif imagined that his short responses were making him uneasy.

"Mr. Sherif. Please don't mention that business with the dervish in your report about buying the house. It's just a superstition, I told you."

"Of course," Sherif took pity on him, "of course, I know it's just a superstition. Don't worry about it."

"And about the dervishes buried under the house. . . . We can demolish the mausoleum, and move the remains somewhere else. They've been buried for three hundred years at least, and the remains won't be more than a handful of dust."

Sherif thought about all the years that the dervish had been in this world, the man who had disappeared from the city without a trace. Had he really left Konya? And if he had, why had his ghost remained in the same location, going around the place performing the dance of which he had been deprived, openly defying his imam? Here he had remained, for decades, dancing and dancing. 'Dervishes never die . . . they live on in silence,' he remembered. What had the man meant by that? Had he been hinting that his ghost and his soul were there for

94

eternity? So many questions flashed lightning-fast through his mind, Borhan's voice snapping him out of his reverie. "Mr. Sherif? Mr. Sherif? Are you with me?"

"Yes, yes." Sherif took a breath. "Don't worry about the house. It'll all be fine."

He did not leave his hotel room all day: he began to read a book of biographies of the dervishes in the Mevlevi order founded by Jalal al-Din al-Rumi. It gave details about their rituals, their lives, their clothing, their creed, their dances, their hopes and dreams, the circumstances of their lives, and even of their deaths. From time to time, he ordered coffee from room service to help him concentrate. Humming, he recited the dervish's mantra that the author had quoted: *There was a dervish . . . the dervish opened a shelter for dervishes . . . his wide skirts scattered secrets . . . but no one knows what they are. . . . There was a dervish . . . the dervish opened a shelter for dervishes . . . his dance rises high to the sky . . . his beard touches the ground below him . . . and his lips scatter secrets . . . but no one can hear them.*

The book drew him in and filled him with astonishment. He couldn't put it down until he had read it from cover to cover. He closed the book, still chanting the mantra. He contemplated the image of a dervish on the cover: suddenly the image changed to that of the familiar ghost, smiling and chanting.

He was still frozen with astonishment when he felt a strong hand pulling him up from where he sat. The dervish began to whirl around the room. Sherif found himself dancing with him, one hand splayed above his head and the other pointed at the floor, turning and whirling with the dervish. He felt an incomparable lightness, as though his soul had left his body and floated far away into another world. He was transmuted into nothingness; he was not present on this earth. He remained thus until a tremor through his body brought him back to the mortal plane, pulling him out of the spiritual.

Here he was, he who had sampled this world's every pleasure and experienced the extremes of ecstasy, overcome by an ecstasy that was matchless, a pleasure that was peerless. He decided not to think: however he cudgeled his brains, he would not understand.

Sherif ended up spending twenty full days in the city. During that time, he went to the dervishes' retreat that Borhan had taken him to, and met with their imam, and spoke to him of his desire to join their order. They had a long meeting that day: Sherif laid bare everything about his life and his past, and his desire to liberate himself from it and start anew. However, when he tried to mention the dervish, something stopped the words from coming out.

In his report on the house, he assessed the price accurately, not overpricing or underpricing it. It might have been the first time where he did not fudge his report, or try to convince the seller that his property was worth a lower price. It was his modus operandi to try and find a loophole to bring down the price, and if none existed, he would make one up out of whole cloth. Borhan's property, with its Sufi order, was positively riddled with holes—all he had to do was tell Mr. Borhan that his house was haunted with the ghost of a dervish that wouldn't leave, and he'd be forced to accept any price the company offered. But he didn't.

11

Cairo: Winter 2012

WITH GREAT CARE, SHE PLACED the painting into the trunk of the car, and drove to the Cairo suburb of Maadi. On the way, she thought of what had taken place with Sherif yesterday. The oddest feeling had come over her since he had held her: she could still feel his embrace, feel his strong arms encircling her and the tenderness he had offered. Because of it, she had gone to bed happy that night. Now she felt stronger than before, no longer a feather in the wind.

She parked outside the address on the business card, remembering what Dr. Khalil had said about this man: "He's an expert on painting, a graduate of the Florence Academy of Fine Arts. He's been a voracious learner ever since he graduated, always reading about the newest ways to examine a painting. He worked at the National Institute for Fine Arts here in Egypt, and oversaw the conservation of a lot of paintings in state-owned museums."

The place was a two-story building in a quiet street, surrounded by a wrought-iron fence and tall trees that blocked the view inside. The owner had built it especially for the conservation of privately-owned artwork that would otherwise have been discarded, or at the very least permanently removed from display. She pressed the intercom button. A scratchy, electronically distorted male voice grated, "Who is it?"

"It's Yasmine Ghaleb."

"Come in." The door buzzed. She entered, carrying the painting that had preoccupied her since the moment she had laid eyes on it. The entrance was marble, the stairway flanked with two marble statues of lions. The wooden door stood open, revealing a reception hall beyond it, furnished with leather chairs, and a blond secretary behind the counter who welcomed her with a smile. She asked one of the assistants to take the painting from Yasmine and she and the assistant took the elevator up to the second floor.

The expert welcomed her with a smile and shook her hand warmly. "Good to meet you." He was middle-aged, somehow managing to look both conservative and bohemian at once. He wore a black wool jacket with a partly unbuttoned white shirt underneath, and black dress shoes. His hair was in a ponytail, and he had leather braided bracelets on his wrist. She liked him at once: he did not seem rigid or pedantic, as was typical for those who worked in research and conservation, nor disorganized and chaotic, which seemed to be the rule for artists. "How do you like your coffee?" he asked, which was a prelude to an interesting conversation about painting. "Do you know," he said, "I have found that people's relationships with their artwork has little or no relation to its value. Most of the paintings I've restored are neither signed nor dated, nor even by any artist of note. On the contrary, most were by amateurs, and many were copies of famous masterpieces. But in every instance, there is a relationship between a painting and its owner. It's that which makes people keep the same painting on the same wall for years, and look at it from time to time as if they're seeing it for the first time. When they move, it's the first thing they think of taking with them, and they're careful to re-hang it in a prominent place."

Eventually, the conversation turned to her painting, and Yasmine told him of the information she had managed to acquire in her research into it, with her experience as a professor of art history. He listened attentively and did not seem surprised by her attachment to the painting, clearly used to it from his clients. What did surprise him was when she told him about the locks of human hair in the girl's braids.

"We'll analyze the hair," he said. "If it's human hair, your suspicions will be proved. Then we'll ask what would bring an artist to do that." He drained his coffee, put on his spectacles and got up enthusiastically. "Shall we?"

They went into the lab, putting on white coats and gloves. He placed the painting on the easel and looked at it. "Remarkable. What an artist." He shook his head. "Unfortunately, it's in a deplorable state. It must have been stored improperly. Moisture alone will do that to a painting, and this one has most probably not been hanging on a wall. I'll wager it was stored in a cellar somewhere. Thank goodness the rats didn't get to it." He turned to Yasmine. "But where did you find it?"

"It came to us from storage at the Gezira Museum."

"Storage in the Gezira Museum?" He approached and touched the braids. He looked closely at the girl's face. "Truly beautiful." Then he straightened. "Now for the moment of truth. We'll put it under the machine and we shall see what we shall see."

He took a jar from a shelf and withdrew several drops of some liquid from it. He selected a minuscule corner of the painting and carefully dispensed the drops onto it. The color dissolved instantly, and he immediately withdrew it with a pipette and placed it under the microscope. Then he placed the painting into a large device that took up an entire corner of the room. He pressed the button to activate it and it produced a series of ringing sounds.

Time passed while he was hard at work. It was almost time for her next class. Eventually, he noticed that her eyes were darting from the wall clock to her wristwatch and that she was looking impatient. "The examination will take a while," he said. "I need to run several tests, including one most important one, x-ray photoelectron spectroscopy. That will tell us how the artist mixed his colors and the elements that went into creating them. If you have somewhere to be, you can go, and I'll let you know when the results are ready."

"Okay. " She pulled out a business card and gave it to him. "When you find out anything, please give me a call."

All the way to work, one question was in her mind: what could this man possibly find? Might he find another painting concealed beneath it, like the discovery made recently by art experts restoring Picasso's *The Blue Room*? A palimpsest of a man wearing a tie, sitting in a chair, driving everyone into a frenzy of speculation as to the man's identity?

After class, on her way back home, Sherif called. "Would you like to come to dinner?" he asked. "I'm nearby, at a restaurant in the Marriott."

Although she was exhausted and preoccupied, it was an invitation she couldn't refuse. He had outsmarted her, for he knew her weakness for the Marriott. The ancient palace, long ago converted into a hotel, was where she had first discovered the meaning of art. She used to go there on walks with her father, who told her stories about its history. "It was a great palace built by Khedive Ismail to house the guests he had invited to Egypt for the opening of the Suez Canal," he had said, "especially Empress Eugénie, the woman he was in love with. She stole his heart and mind." He would show her the life-size portrait of Eugénie, and mention that the largest banquet hall still bore her name, having been converted from the wing originally set aside for her. Yasmine grew attached to the place and its history, and let her imagination roam free: whenever she set foot inside the Marriott, she stepped out of the present and everything in it, and lived once again in the glory of bygone days. She could see Empress Eugénie, decked out in her magnificent clothing, glittering gems decorating her delicate neck, taking part with the khedive in the soirées he held in her honor. This fantasy world she had built for herself as a little girl never faded, not even as an adult. Her postgraduate studies had been on the use of art in khedival architecture, and it had been a positive delight to write about this palace, its style, and its art collection in her doctoral thesis.

She passed through the interior of the hotel to reach the central garden around which the rooms were built, strolling through the mosaic-paved pathways to reach the open-air kebab restaurant in the garden. He was waiting for her, all alone but for the company of his tobacco. He wore a tie that matched the greenery around him. The trees in the garden were centuries old, deep-rooted, ancient, sturdy. They seemed to form part of the foundations of the place, the opulence of the hotel matching the trees' awe-inspiring nature.

He saw her coming and greeted her with a smile. With a quick glance, he could tell that she had something on her mind. "What's up?" he asked. "You look like something's happened. Will you tell me what it is?"

"Have you been learning how to read minds?" she said.

"It's not mind reading. You just have to know how to read people is all."

She shrugged, dismissing their exchange. A menu appeared before her, proffered by a Nubian waiter in a traditional embroidered *gallabiya* and cap, a uniform enforced by the management to give the place an old-world atmosphere. She picked up the menu and glanced through it. "Today I went to a lab to get the painting analyzed, and left it there with the experts."

The waiter came back and Sherif ordered two mixed grills. "What do you plan to do with what you find out?"

"That depends what we find out," she sighed.

"Is it going to put an end to your chasing after it?" Sherif chuckled. " As soon as you get what you want out of a thing, you lose interest and run after the next thing that catches your eye. You were definitely a child who got everything she wanted."

"Is that really what you think of me?" she rebuked him, uncomfortable and not a little offended. "Do you really think I'm that shallow?"

"Of course not. Who said anything about being shallow?"

"If what you just said doesn't mean that," she challenged, "then what do you call it?"

He shook his head. "Being *shallow* . . . it means being empty. Not chasing after anything. Your curiosity and excitement, those are things that drive you to achieve what you want, to work for it. That's the surest indication that you have your own goals."

"Oh." She sat back, wondering whether he had been hinting at their relationship, namely that as soon as she had been assured of his love, she had lost interest in him and chased after another man. But it had not been all her fault. Their relationship could have survived if he had known how to make her miss him and want him. He had waited too long between phone calls, between dates; he had been too cagey with his feelings, never expressing himself enough. It was only natural, she thought to herself, for their ardor to cool.

She opened her mouth to tell him as much, but her phone rang. It was the art expert. "I've made an exciting discovery," he told her without preamble.

"Really? I'll be right over." She gathered her things and pushed her chair back. "Sorry, Sherif, I've got to go at once. The expert has something he wants to show me."

He opened his mouth to suggest they have dinner and then go to the art lab together, but he knew how important it was to her and held his peace. He said goodbye with a regretful smile, and watched her retreating form running out of the restaurant.

He thought again of their conversation when she had told him about her mother, and how their family had been scattered far and wide. Despite her attempts to conceal her pain and pretend to forget it, there was a glimmer of hidden sorrow in her eyes from time to time. How many times had she been laughing at the top of her lungs and paused suddenly, her face filling with grief? Didn't she always get flustered and lose her concentration whenever she had to speak of her childhood and family? It was so obvious in hindsight, but hard to guess the full extent of the unhappiness she had endured. At the start of their relationship, she had always changed the subject when he had asked her about her family or wanted to meet them. Although she had carefully kept the secret, it had all tumbled out of her in a mad rush in the moment the dam had finally collapsed, bursting forth like water that had been confined.

The music in the restaurant mingled with the smell of grilling kebabs. The scent which had been so appetizing a while ago now turned his stomach. He paid the bill for his uneaten meal and hurried out.

12

She almost caused several accidents, not because she was driving at speed, but because she was so distracted she could barely see the road, the other cars, or the pedestrians. Dr Khalil was waiting in the lab, eyes all but invisible behind thick-lensed magnifying spectacles. "This was painted in the eighteenth century," he told her by way of greeting. "It was painted by a professional, as we can tell from his technique of mixing his colors. The colors are blended with sea salt and sand, which makes them exceptionally long-lasting and capable of producing subtle variations in shade. It was painted directly without a preliminary sketch, another indication of a professional."

She didn't care about any of that. She was waiting for something more important, staring at his lips as though willing them to move and say something more important. "And the girl? What about the braids?"

"They really are made of human hair," Dr. Khalil told her, "glued down by the painter after laying down the first layer of color. He then covered them up with another layer of color created by mixing clay with gesso and water to achieve the greatest possible stability, and also to conceal the hair itself, which it did, as you can see. The color never faded, and the painting's over two hundred years old," he enthused, "and the hair itself didn't show until you were scraping off the dirt on the painting to restore it."

Her shoulders slumped. "Is that all?"

"Yes. That's all." He smiled triumphantly. "All the information I managed to glean is in this report," he tapped a folder, "right here."

He handed her the report and she leafed through it. On the final page, she found something important he hadn't mentioned. *The back of the painting*, the report read, *bears an inscription in French: Zeinab.* "But," she looked up, "you didn't tell me about the name on the back of the painting."

"Yes, yes," he nodded. "Forgive me. This painting has me all in a dither. It's got a name written on the back in Roman script, 'Zeinab'."

"So her name is Zeinab," Yasmine whispered, staring at the painting. "Zeinab," she repeated, fascinated. "It suits her."

Cairo: October 1798

"Zeinab? What does it mean?"

Out of all the momentous events that had taken place that night, this was the only one that stuck in her memory, the sound of her name on his lips, and his question about the meaning of her name. That man whose affectionate gaze embraced her, the only one in that place who had cared about her at all. She stood admiring herself in the mirror, wondering: *Was he attracted to me as well?*

Her mother burst in, looking harried and anxious. "Tell me every detail! Tell me everything that happened from the minute you left the house till the second you came back in!"

"Now?" Zeinab replied. "Tomorrow. I'm tired right now."

"Right now, this minute!" her mother thundered. "You're going to tell me everything!"

There was nothing for it, in the face of her mother's insistence, but to sit on the edge of the bed and tell her about everything she had seen, heard, said, and done from the moment she set foot in the palace until the end of the ball.

But she couldn't speak when she came to the encounter with Napoleon in his room, and so she said nothing at all. Finally, her mother was satisfied that her daughter's virtue was intact, and left her room.

The next morning, she awoke with the excitement of the party still lingering around her. She liked this life! This French lifestyle, their language, their food, their drink, their music, their dancing, their parties. "Why shouldn't I be one of them?" she asked herself. "After all, I wore their clothes and I speak their language."

At noon that day, thick clouds mercifully blocked the sun's glare and heat, and Zeinab sat in the courtyard in the shade of a lemon tree, enjoying the invigorating summer breeze and reading *Courrier de l'Égypte* as well as she could, trying to pronounce the words out loud and make sense of the articles. It was a newspaper put out especially by the French Campaign in Egypt. Her brothers crowded around her, listening and laughing, mimicking her as she spoke word after word in this odd, alien tongue.

> At the end of Venesi Street, in the home of Citizen Follmard, is a distillery for wines and liquors. Citizens Faure, Naseau & Co. distill all manner of spirits at Berkat al-Feel Square, at reasonable prices.
>
> Tonight the gardens of the Champs-Élysées and Tivoli will come to life in the skies of Cairo. Tonight is the grand opening of Casino & Restaurant Dar Ghivel, an exclusive event for elite society only. Emperor Bonaparte will be the guest of honor. Tomorrow, the restaurant will open its doors to the general public, at 90 *bara*s a ticket.

What would the opening be like? Zeinab wondered. It would no doubt be wonderful. But it was open only to the aristocracy. If only she were one of them, so she could go.

Her elder brother gestured to her, impatient and trying to get her attention. "Are we French now? Acting like they own the place, like Egypt belongs to them!"

She looked up. "What's gotten you so worked up? You liked the Mamluks so much? They were ignorant boors and cruel as well." She tossed her head. "Compare now with then. You can see the difference."

"At the last meeting of Napoleon's council," her brother said, "someone announced that Cairo has a population of three hundred thousand. They said they were going to start to settle a lot of French people in Egypt, bring them here to start farms and be merchants and sell stuff." He folded his arms. "They said it would make Egypt 'the most attractive and the most useful of all their colonies!' That's what they said. Do you know what 'colony' even means?" His eyes met hers, challenging. "It means that the riches of this country won't belong to its people any more. It means the people are just colonized natives with no rights to anything."

"And since when were we not colonized?" Zeinab retorted. "Do you want to convince me that we weren't colonized under the Mamluks? At least *these* colonizers want to change this country for the better!"

He looked at her askance. The light smattering of hair on his upper lip indicated that he was just inching into manhood, but he had a strong personality. "It's no use talking to you. You're just like Father; of course that's what you'd think. You don't even wear the same clothes as us any more, you wear theirs, and you want to be just like them. Aren't you ashamed of yourself?"

"Not at all." She laughed out loud. "I feel proud, not ashamed. What I should have been ashamed of was how I looked before."

He glanced at her with derision and adjusted his turban on his head, preparing to go. "You know what? It's no use talking to you. It's just a waste of time."

A soft knock came at the door, then another, and another after that. The hesitant knocking indicated that whoever was outside was a stranger. Halima went to see who was at the door. Someone spoke very fast in French; she couldn't understand a word they were saying, but one of the things the man said was "Zeinab al-Bakri," so Halima realized he wanted Zeinab. Before she could speak to her, though, the man had placed an envelope in her hand and left.

Halima gave the envelope to Zeinab, who tore it open with hands trembling with excitement. It was an invitation to the grand opening she had read about, at seven that evening, near Ezbekiya Lake. A proud smile lit up her face: her wishes were coming true, one after the other! "What shall I wear?" she thought at once. She had to be elegant, beautiful, as befitted elite society. The invitation card in her hand was proof that she was now a member of high society.

As Zeinab rode through the streets of Cairo on her way, the doors were already locked for the night, the oil lamps put out. Night watchmen were asking people for passwords for their neighborhood gates. Meanwhile, Dar Ghivel was brilliantly lit up to welcome its clientele, its music ringing out far and wide, rousing the neighboring Egyptians from their sleep. The French proprietor of Ghivel's, in his search for a place where everyone might find entertainment, had chosen a house with a spacious garden next to Ezbekiya Lake, which had belonged to a Mamluk prince. In point of fact, this house boasted one of the largest and most verdant gardens in all of Cairo. It was planted with lemon trees, Levantine and Indian jasmine, cypress, willow, and every type of fragrant tree and plant. The driver stopped directly in front of the gate. The trees were hung around with lights, and paper decorations were wrapped around their branches, making them glitter and gleam. The place was filled with men and women she had never seen before; in fact, she had never imagined that men and women so attractive and elegant even lived in Cairo.

As soon as she entered the main hall, she stood still, looking around. Most of the tables were already occupied with groups of friends and French Campaign officials. Suddenly, she noticed a lady waving to her. A closer look revealed that it was Madame Angele, the wife of a trader from Malta who was a friend of her father's, or rather, a man who shared business interests with him. Madame Angele and her husband had visited them many times at home and they had returned the visits at every feast and special occasion. "Madame Angele!" Zeinab greeted her. Angele introduced her to the women at the table with her: ladies from the upper echelons of Egyptian society and the wives and daughters of eminent merchants, consuls, and diplomats living in Egypt. They were looking at her with frank astonishment, unable to believe that she was Sheikh al-Bakri's daughter; then they burst into a gabble of Greek and Italian so that she would not understand. But then one of them said in French, "I don't believe it! Is this the daughter of an Azharite imam? How did her father ever allow her to take off her veil?"

Zeinab rounded on her. In the same language, she shot back, "I don't see anything wrong with taking it off. And my father has nothing to do with it. It's my decision to make."

Everyone at the table was stunned, not just by her clothes, but by the fact that she could not only understand French, but speak it as well. "The owner has taken great pains to arrange this place just like the casinos of Paris," Madame Angele said, trying to change the subject. "Look! He even set aside a sitting room for the literary salon, in addition to the ballroom and the dining hall! Why, it's just as though I were in Paris!"

"Yes," another lady nodded, "especially with the most famous musicians in Paris playing in the band."

At around eight in the evening, Napoleon came in, surrounded by his guards and a group of senior generals. The

French national anthem was played and everyone stood, applauding and cheering. Napoleon greeted everyone and walked around, looking at the place. Fireworks were set off, lighting up the sky. Afterward, Napoleon went to sit at the table reserved for the emperor and his officers, who had quite abandoned their military decorum and were joking and laughing uproariously, bursting into impromptu song and dance.

"Look at the two beauties on either side of Napoleon!" one of the women at their table said. "The one on the right is the wife of General Verdi, she's Italian, that's why she has black hair and dark skin. The blond on his left is Pauline, the wife of a naval officer."

"Lucky man," laughed another woman, "with a blond on one side and a brunette on the other!"

"There are rumors about him and Pauline," said a third. "They even say he sent her husband off on a military mission in a faraway land so that he could clear the path for their affair."

"Don't believe the rumors, my dear," said the first woman. "Since Napoleon arrived, they've been flying fast and thick, they never stop. The most absurd and low rumor was that he's taken up with a girl from Egypt, and a commoner at that! Imagine! The rumormongers are so stupid as to put it about that he could possibly fancy an *Egyptian* girl. It just goes to show you, my dear: people will say anything."

"What?" said her friend. "An Egyptian girl catch Napoleon's eye? And him having an affair with her? What half-wit started that rumor?"

"You mean what half-wit would believe it," the first woman laughed.

Zeinab pondered their words. It was true: what naïve soul would believe such a thing? She looked around, eyes roving over the guests until she spotted him, standing in a corner of the hall. He was dressed smartly, not in uniform this time, but in a formal tuxedo. If only he would see her! But he was engrossed in conversation with another man, and then disappeared from her sight. In a few moments, she spotted him sitting at Napoleon's table.

When dinner was over, she decided to go home. "But it's still early!" Madame Angele remonstrated. "It's only ten-thirty!"

"I think it's time to go home," Zeinab replied. She said her goodbyes and left.

The women watched her go, walking gracefully on her high heels, picking up her skirts on both sides as the French women did, until she was out of sight.

Outside, the air in the garden was cooler, the evening breeze wafting great breaths of night-blooming jasmine. The loud music from inside was softer out here. In the corners stood a number of people who had tired of the noise and strain of the party, while pairs of lovers sheltered beneath the branches.

"Zeinab?"

She knew that voice; she had been expecting it. She looked behind her, and there he was. He hurried to her and took her hand in his. "I saw you leaving. I didn't think I'd find you here."

"Why not? Because the party is exclusive?"

"No, no. I didn't mean that. But I didn't think this kind of event would be to your taste."

"On the contrary, it's fun. But I don't like the people who come here. They're conceited and naïve. All they care about is gossiping and spreading rumors."

"There's the bourgeoisie for you," he shrugged. "It's the same everywhere, Paris just the same as Egypt. I've never been too fond of that milieu. I try to avoid them, with their gossip and scandals."

He looked at her face for a long time, then gestured to the sky. "Look at that star. You shine like a star, too."

She smiled. "I have to go."

"Wait," he said. "When will I see you again?"

"I don't know."

"Tomorrow they're sending up a hot-air balloon," he told her, "and everyone's coming out to see it. It's going to be a little before noon. I'll meet you in the square."

"I'll be there."

He watched her until she was out of sight.

Outside Dar Ghivel, the music wafted through the narrow streets and alleyways, disturbing the rest of the poor neighbors who asked in perplexity what on earth was going on in there.

Cairo: November 1798

The French had announced the bizarre experiment a few days ago: a balloon that flew via hot air. Rumors flew thick and fast among the Egyptians that the French were going to release a giant airborne ship that could travel from one place to another. Starting early in the morning, everyone took to the streets to watch the unprecedented event. The women were muttering prayers and invocations. The men lifted their hands up to the sky, praying to the Lord to let this day pass without disaster. Only the children were darting around in delight, cheering excitedly.

At noon, the square was completely full. All eyes were on the sky, awaiting the passage of this strange object, this ship that the French had said could travel from one country to another, and from one place to another, at lightning speed.

That day, she picked out a gown of fine mousseline, made for her by the French seamstress. It was simple and elegant. She covered her head with a light silk shawl, lined her eyes with kohl, and painted her lips in a soft pink shade. Her friends came by to pick her up, but Halima told them she was too ill to come and couldn't get out of bed. She waited until they had gone, and went out, accompanied by Halima.

The square was bursting with people. She would never find him in the middle of this crowd. She looked toward the podium, hoping he might be near there; but there was just Napoleon, surrounded by his generals and by imams of whom all she could see was their great turbans, each one different, like great domes above their heads. She knew them by sight: Sheikh Sharkawi, who had a thick white beard and wore a round green turban; Sheikh Mahdi with his white turban; her father, Sheikh al-Bakri, most prominent in his big black turban; only Sheikh Fayumi had not opted for an imposing turban, and wrapped his head instead in a simple cashmere scarf.

The balloon surged into the air, rising to a height of 250 feet. Everyone's necks craned to watch it. Cries and applause rang out: it was deafening. Suddenly, a gentle hand tapped her shoulder. She turned and found him there, with his hazel eyes and sparse mustache covering thin lips, a lock of his silky hair falling into his forehead. Joy, anxiousness, and awe overcame her all at once. "Alton!" she blurted.

He smiled, and life was sweet and joyous once more. No one noticed when he took her by the hand and led her away from the crowd, still cheering for the balloon.

"Where are we going?" she asked him.

He kept walking without answering. With difficulty, they worked their way out of the press of bodies, everyone standing mesmerized at what was happening in the sky, no one noticing that Sheikh al-Bakri's daughter was leaving the square with a foreign man.

They walked down twisting alleyways and narrow lanes, street after street and alley after alley, until they reached the garden of willow and myrtle in Ezbekiya Square. In the center was a large, splashing fountain of Damascene tiles, while all around were blossoming trees bearing flowers of every conceivable shape and description, their perfume wafting over the two of them. There were meandering gravel paths punctuated by benches to sit on, and on a bench hidden beneath the branches of a mighty oak, they sat.

"I have never seen such a beautiful place," he confessed. "I come here daily to be alone under this tree. It helps me collect my thoughts while taking fresh air. It refreshes me and helps me go on."

"True," she sighed, "it seems the most beautiful place in Egypt. That's why I call it," she continued in Arabic, "*Hadiqat al-sifsaf wa-l-aas li-man arad al-hazz wa-l-i'tinas.*"

He did not understand her Arabic phrase, so she tried to use all the French at her disposal to translate for him. Finally understanding it as "the garden of willows and flowers for companionship and peaceful hours," he took off his hat and placed it next to him. She picked it up and put it on, smiling like a child at play. "How do I look?"

He gazed into her eyes. "Beautiful."

"Why did you come to Cairo," Zeinab asked him, "when you're not a soldier or an officer?"

"I came by military decree as part of the Arts and Sciences Committee," he explained. "It has 151 members, all the best French scientists and artists. At first I was enthusiastic about coming here: any artist's dream was to visit the Orient. The reason for coming here, they told us, was to discover the Orient." He sighed. "None of us knew we were on our way to a military campaign. Even the soldiers themselves didn't know. The Campaign was a closely guarded secret, even from the ones who were to be doing the fighting." She nodded, listening intently. "If you could have seen the machines we brought over on the ships—printing presses, magnifying glasses, containers for liquids, special solutions, paper and inks—you would not have suspected for a minute that these ships were on their way to a military campaign, but rather to discover a new world." He sighed. "The day we set sail from the port of Toulon, then and only then, did we learn we were on our way to a military campaign. When we cast off, we saw them: all manner and shape of war machines. It was then that I took my leave of all my dreams to paint the Orient: for how could

I depict the facets and landmarks of a country, with its people terrified and terrorized, and hating us? What's more, when we arrived, I was shocked to see the reality. I had not thought it was that bad. Unfortunately, the only thing the Mamluks cared about was getting rich, and they plundered your country and left it in a deplorable condition: streets unpaved, refuse everywhere, endemic diseases running rampant, poverty and hunger, and the populace stripped of all agency and power."

He rose from his seat and began pacing in a tight circle, then looked at her. "You, for instance. Tell me what you do in life. A girl your age: how does she occupy her time and what is she preparing for her future?"

"Nothing important," she said helplessly, "nothing worth mentioning, anyway. Girls in our country are made only for marriage and doing what our husbands say. Ever since we're born, mothers prepare daughters to be wives and mothers. We're taught how to cook and keep house, then we wait at home to get married. As you can see, we're not allowed to leave the house unless it's with a guardian— a eunuch or a female slave or a parent—and that's only to go shopping or to the public baths. It's the only outing for women here. Life, for us, is a long list of 'don'ts.' Don't show your face, don't do this, don't do that—it never ends." She fell silent for a while; her expression changed. Unhappily, she went on, "And because I broke these rules, because I went out with my face uncovered wearing the clothes of the Franks, and because the emperor's carriage was waiting for me outside the door to my house, looks of derision follow me wherever I go, and I know that every tongue is wagging about me. If it were not for my father's high position and his closeness to Napoleon, I know their anger would have found vent in my direction. But they don't dare." She sighed. "I hear them talking about me. When I approach, they trip over their words and go quiet in a hurry."

She spoke in a low, choked voice, as though she could see some fate awaiting her. "Do you know that the women they think are impure are stoned and thrown into jail? They wake up to find their doorsteps smeared with tar and red wax, and insults and curses scrawled on their walls. As for prostitutes, they put them on a mule with scabies, and parade them around the streets, and everyone comes out to look at them and throw stones and garbage at them."

"But I thought," he interjected, "that this profession was permitted and licensed, and even taxed? Why so much disgust against prostitutes then, when they bring money into the state's coffers?"

"Yes, they're allowed to practice," Zeinab said, "but only in specific quarters and designated places. A woman who practices it outside these places is immediately punished. And in any case, those women are outcasts from society."

He was silent, anger and sorrow warring in his face. "But tell me, what happened in Bonaparte's room?"

She blushed and started to play with one of her braids, tying it into a knot. "Nothing."

A gust of wind sprang up, scattering dead leaves everywhere. He looked her straight in the eye, full of suspicion and disbelief. In low tones, she went on. "He told me to come in and sit next to him on the bed. Then he undid my braids one by one. When he was done, he spread out my hair over my back, patted me on the shoulder, and told me that I was much prettier that way."

"And then?"

"Nothing. He told me to go."

He smiled wryly. "He is indeed an extraordinary man."

"Why?"

"Because as far as I know, he is passionately in love with Josephine."

"Who is Josephine?"

"His wife, to whom he is forever writing love letters, even while he's making campaign plans. He's forever scribbling with pen on paper, telling her how much he loves her."

"Really?"

Alton's voice dropped as he put his hat back on his head. "Beware of him, Zeinab. You'd better not accept his invitation another time."

His eyes embraced her. *Why is he asking this of me?* she asked herself. *Is he jealous? Could he have fallen in love with me?* He had found a place in her affections since the first time she had seen him: it was a strange sensation in her budding heart, a feeling she had never had before toward any man.

She bolted to her feet, jolting out of her dream. "I'm late. I must go," she said in a rush, wrapping her silken scarf over her face in preparation to leave.

"Wait." He lifted the scarf. "When will I see you again?"

"I truly don't know."

"Not tomorrow, then, but the day after, we'll meet here at the same time."

The mighty oak shaded them with its low-hanging branches, reaching almost to the ground, shielding them from prying eyes, guarding their secret—the secret each of them was concealing from the other. He drew nearer and with little more than a breath, dropped a kiss on her cheek, which blushed shyly. He let her veil fall once more, and his eyes followed her as she ran quickly away.

He did not leave that spot. He sat on the wooden bench, wondering what was this girl's secret, to capture the heart of everyone who laid eyes on her. What was so attractive about her? Was it the innocence and spontaneity that radiated from her? Her thick brows, shading wide, dark eyes, filled with wonderment like a little girl just discovering the world around her? Or her voice, like a babbling brook? Perhaps it was all of these.

All the way home, he walked with one question in mind: *What does Napoleon want with her?* Had the great man tired of experienced and expert beauties, and was now hankering after an innocent flower, scarcely more than a bud and not yet in bloom? He was known to have a penchant for women older than himself; had it morphed into a complex that he wished to dispel? And her braids . . . what on earth had possessed the man to undo her hair? Was he proceeding, step by step, preparing her for his ultimate goal? And the girl's father? How could he be positively propelling her into such a fate, knowing that his religion, not to mention his society's customs and traditions, looked upon it as a sin? Could he be truly abandoning her to her fate in his lust for power and position?

He walked all the way home, filled with questions and finding no satisfactory answer, and so he began to paint.

13

Cairo: Winter 2012

SHE LEFT THE LAB WITH a handful of information. The mysterious girl had given Yasmine her name as a calling card. "Zeinab, Zeinab, who are you?" she murmured, as she went down the stairs. She had made up her mind: every ounce of the art historian she was, every particle of her energy, every piece of information she possessed, and every research tool in her arsenal would be devoted to finding out the identity of the unknown Zeinab.

Back home, she sat at her laptop, a giant art history reference book open on the table next to her. 'The key to art history research,' it had been drilled into her, 'is the date it was painted.' This would open every door to her, and without it she would find out nothing. According to the report, the portrait was painted in the late eighteenth or early nineteenth century—the date of the French Campaign in Egypt. This was the first spark of light to illuminate the dark tunnel, so far, of her research.

The information she had to go on was that the artist was a professional and not an amateur, and his technique of mixing color confirmed it. She entered several search queries on blending colors with sand and sea salt and waited for the results. Finding several specialized sites, she finally ascertained that this method of painting was only used by a limited number of French painters in the mid-eighteenth century. She rearranged her query and repeated her search: the painter she was searching for must have been in Egypt during the French Campaign. A professional painter, who might have been part of the Campaign itself.

This was as much information as she could come up with, after searching and cross-referencing several search engines. She woke up exhausted the next day. Her only consolation was that with the information on the French Campaign, she had caught the first thread of the answer.

This piece of information so intrigued her that she went to her former art history professor, the mentor under whom she had studied. She knocked on the door to his office. His dry, distinctive voice invited her to enter.

He welcomed her with his usual smile. Since she had been a student, he had taken note of her love of art history and her enthusiasm for research: she was one of the few who had come to the department out of a genuine passion for the subject, as opposed to the many who only joined it because it was the only option available to them due to poor grades. He ordered them two coffees and she told him everything she had found so far. "Why don't you look in the location where the painting was sitting all this time?" he suggested. "Provenance, and the storage of a work of art, can be an important tool in our field."

"All I know," Yasmine said, "is that it was in storage at the Gezira Museum."

His thick brows furrowed in puzzlement. "The Gezira Museum? It was only built recently. This was one of its acquisitions? I doubt it. Where did it come from originally? That is, where did the museum get it?"

How stupid could she be? If she had gone to the Gezira Museum in the first place, she could have saved a great deal of effort. She drained her coffee all at once, then put down her cup and took her leave. "I'm going straight there. I need to get there before it closes at two."

"Good luck," he smiled. If she had come to him with a story like this in years gone by, he might have accompanied her to the Gezira Museum and helped her look for the history of the mysterious painting. Where, he wondered, had all his enthusiasm gone? He remembered his own youth when, as a postgraduate student in Italy, he had been fascinated by the works of da Vinci and Michelangelo, and researched day and night, from museum to conservation lab and back.

The museum was not too far from her own house, on the grounds of the Opera House on Gezira Island, which also held her neighborhood of Zamalek. The museum was rectangular in shape, the doors to all the different rooms opening onto the spacious central hall. There was a room at the side with screens and electronic remote control equipment. "Is the director in?" she asked the receptionist. After a phone call, he asked her to follow him to the top floor, where the administrative section was. He paused and knocked at a door with a brass plaque bearing the words MUSEUM DIRECTOR.

The director, a friendly faced man in his fifties, greeted her politely at first, then warmed to her and greeted her effusively when she introduced herself with her title. "I do conservation and restoration," she explained. "Currently I'm working on some paintings that came from storage in your museum, and I'm doing research into the history of a particular piece I'm conserving right now. I was hoping you could give me some information about it."

His eyes shone with curiosity. "Which piece?"

She opened up her iPad and showed it to him. "This one."

Several expressions flitted across the man's face: deep thought and finally perplexity. "But this painting. . . ." he looked at it again carefully, "isn't part of our collection."

"Really?"

"Hold on," he told her, "and we can make certain."

He picked up the phone and asked the collections manager to come to his office. The man appeared almost at once:

he had sensed from his boss' tone that it was important. He burst in, looking as though he expected a catastrophe or something of that sort: "Has something happened? "

The director showed him the painting and he looked at it, slowly catching his breath and mopping his sweaty brow. The tension in his expression dissipated and he relaxed. "Yes, yes!" he cried. "You're right. This painting isn't one of the museum's acquisitions. It was transferred here as part of the Egyptian Scientific Institute's collection after the fire."

"The Scientific Institute?" Yasmine repeated in astonishment.

The director dismissed the collections manager, thanking him, but apparently overcome with curiosity, the manager refused to leave. "But is there something wrong?" he asked. "Has the painting been stolen?"

"No," the director said firmly, clearly irritated by his intrusive questions. "Nothing's happened. Thank you once again. Go back to what you were doing."

Miffed, the manager stalked out, while the director kept looking at Yasmine. "When the Institute caught fire on Friday, December 16, 2011, we received several of its acquisitions that had been burned or otherwise damaged. This painting was one of them."

"I wasn't aware that there were paintings in the Institute," Yasmine said slowly. "I thought there were only books, manuscripts, and rare documents there." She looked up at the director. "Even when the painting came to us, there was no indication or anything saying that it was part of the Institute's collection."

The director launched into a lecture: "Napoleon founded the Egyptian Scientific Institute, originally called the *Institut d'Égypte*, in 1798, so that the scientists and artists he had brought with him to Egypt could have a base from which to work and make their discoveries, culminating in the *Description de l'Égypte* as its crowning glory, a comprehensive study of Egypt of the time, along with numerous other books and documents. As for paintings in the Institute, I do not have enough information to confirm or deny that. You can ask the secretary-general of the Institute: he's the only one who can help you with that inquiry."

She thanked him politely and left, filled with renewed hope: although nothing was definite, the information she had gleaned so far was an indication that she was on the right track. She had already ascertained that the portrait had been painted at the time of the French Campaign in Egypt, and that the painter must have been one of the artists who came to Egypt with the Campaign; its presence at the Egyptian Scientific Institute confirmed it. The odd thing was why the painting had remained in the Institute's building all this time; why had it not been moved to a museum to be displayed? Why had the artist abandoned his painting so easily, leaving it behind in Egypt when the Campaign left, an artist who had used such a unique technique?

The questions rattled around in her head; she was jolted out of her reverie by the ringing of her phone. She was delighted to see Sherif's picture on the screen—the photograph he had sent her on his last trip to Prague. The temperature had been below freezing there, so he looked at the camera from beneath the hood of a thick parka, a scarf wrapped around his neck, snow carpeting the ground around him. She loved that picture: he looked like some sort of snow god, so she saved it with his phone number, and enjoyed the way he flashed on her screen with a winning smile each time he called, and his gaze that seemed, effortlessly, to see straight through her. "Still alive?" she said cheerfully into the receiver.

"I only came back to life when you answered," he said. "I live only to hear your voice."

The faintest tremor went through her. How strange! He had never said anything romantic to her, not since the day they parted; he had always been careful to be strictly friendly, despite his loving glances. Why was his voice touching her this way once more?

"Where did you go?" he asked.

She shook herself. "I'm right here."

"Still chasing after that girl?"

"You mean Zeinab?"

"Who's Zeinab?"

"The girl in the painting."

He burst out laughing. "Did she tell you her name?"

"Yes."

"What happened? Did she come to you in a dream and tell it to you?"

"Didn't I tell you," Yasmine said calmly, "that she came to me because she wanted someone to find out her secret? I'm a detective now. I follow her footprints everywhere."

"I think this calls for a coffee and a catch-up."

"It's half-past three now . . . how does five o'clock sound?"

"Okay. The usual place."

14

THE PAINTING HAD KEPT HER too busy to primp or pretty up. She pulled her hair up into a ponytail and shrugged on whatever she could grab out of her closet. She felt she ought to look good for some reason, so she passed by the beauty salon and asked her hairdresser to give her a new style. "How about putting it up?" he suggested.

"I want it wavy," she said. Then she placed herself in the hands of the manicurist, also getting a pedicure, and got her makeup done too. She left looking completely different from when she came in. She felt attractive, beautiful. Spritzing on some perfume, she went to see him.

As usual, he had chosen a corner table outdoors, with nothing between him and the Nile but the thick rope that encircled the place like a guardrail. He was breathing out smoke in slow, lazy breaths. He smiled to see her coming, like a fresh breeze. She told him everything she had been doing in the past few days. "I think you're about halfway there," he said seriously. "The hardest part is done. The painter's got to be one of the French Campaign artists. Might be that he fell in love with her, or maybe the girl, the way she was dressed and the way she looked, was part of his job. The Institute's mission was to document everything about this country."

"Yes," she said, "that's what I hope to find out. I got an appointment with the secretary-general of the Institute to tell me everything he knows."

He put out his cigarette and asked her: "Is it okay if we change the subject? Let's talk about something else."

"Of course," she smiled. "Go on. I'm all ears."

He laughed aloud. "What? Are you expecting me to give a speech? These past few days we've only been talking about the painting and the girl in the painting."

"What do you expect us to talk about?" she countered. "The weather maybe? Or the state of the nation?"

"The state of us," he said earnestly.

"Us?" she repeated. He said nothing, and she found herself deep in thought. She turned to the river as though it held the answers. His hand crept forward to touch her fingertips. She smiled and their gazes intertwined. His every glance said *I love you, I love you, I love you*. Their eyes remained locked until the ringing of his phone broke the spell. He glanced at the screen and stabbed the button to silence the device, but the persistent caller started to ring again, on and on and on, so finally he took the call.

A feminine voice poured out of the receiver. "Sorry," he cut her off firmly, "I'm busy right now." But the powerful voice, full of vim and vigor, chattered on without pause. Yasmine couldn't make out what the caller was saying, but it put a smile on his face. "Don't worry," he said, "I will." Then he ended the call.

She didn't ask who it was, and he didn't tell her. It would have been stupid of her to imagine that women would leave a man this good-looking alone. What did the woman look like, Yasmine wondered? She sounded so alive. She must be in her twenties, probably in tight jeans and tottering on high heels. "Where did you go?" he asked.

"I'm here. I was just wondering what she looked like. The girl who was talking to you."

"Can't you give your imagination a rest, just for a minute? Why don't you ask me? I'll tell you."

"Didn't I tell you that it's my imagination that keeps me alive?"

"Okay, I'll bite," he smiled, leaning forward and resting his chin on one hand. "What did she look like?"

"Tall," said Yasmine. "Slim. Long, smooth white neck. Long, wavy black hair like a gypsy's. Her eyes are outlined in black kohl. She wears skinny jeans and platform heels. Maybe a tattoo on her neck, and a nose piercing, and lots of bracelets on her wrists."

His eyes widened. "I can't believe it," he stammered. "It's like you've met her. How . . . how did you manage to describe her so accurately?"

"It's not a magic trick," she said. "Instinct combined with experience fuels the imagination." She took a sip of her nearly empty glass of juice and leaned back. "I didn't know you liked that kind of girl." When he didn't answer, she added, "Or is she the soul mate for your dark side? When you leave everything behind and cruise on your Harley?" She laughed, pushing her hair back. "Leather jacket and sneakers, helmet and bike . . . all you need is a girl like that riding behind you with her arms around your waist." Although her mocking tone irritated him, he was delighted to hear the jealousy in her voice that she couldn't manage to hide.

A sudden sadness had come over her when she thought of something going on between him and that girl. *What does he see in her?* she thought. Here she was, a university professor over thirty, always careful to look conservative, her only concerns taking care of her old grandmother, doing research, and restoring old paintings. She imagined the girl sitting behind Sherif on his motorcycle, slim arms around his waist, wild hair fluttering in the backdraft and whipping around his face. The girl laughed, filling the world with fun. Her young head had nothing in it but the latest fashions, house music, trips, nightlife, phone permanently glued to her hand, tapping on it with her long, brightly painted nails in long chats with her millennial friends, and of course with him. Maybe in the morning he texted her: *u awake?* followed by a sleeping emoji.

coffee with me? he would text, with a coffee emoji. Did he maybe write *love u* with an emoji of a heart with an arrow through it? Could his heart beat for another woman, she wondered? Could he love someone else?

She had been gazing out onto the river: but now she fixed her eyes on him. She wanted to scream at him, *Could you?* He was smiling, typing something on his phone. She had been right! Here he was, sitting with her at the same table, and chatting with another woman. "I need to go," she muttered, gathering her things and stuffing them into her handbag.

He didn't argue, but asked for the check. He could tell that there was something the matter. This was not her habit; she always looked at her watch, then with a startled 'Would you look at the time!' said that she had lost track of time and must be going. This was different; something was up. Could it really be that she was jealous?

"You can stay if you want," she said.

"No, I'll go—Oh, I just remembered. Here's your invitation." He was just about to put his hand in his pocket to take something out, but the waiter interrupted him with the check and he was distracted with paying it.

In that short moment, her mind whirled with questions. Invitation? What invitation? Could it be that he was getting married and this was an invitation to his wedding? He held it out to her, but she pulled her hand back.

"Whatever is the matter with you, Yasmine? Just take it! It's an invitation to the Mevlevi dervishes' performance!"

She heaved a sigh of relief, unable to hide it, and managed to collect herself with difficulty. "But," she forced out, "I'm not a fan of that kind of dancing."

"It's not a dance. I told you before. It's a type of prayer. A spiritual ritual."

"Are you still into all that?"

"You could say it's a matter of faith."

She gazed at the image on the ticket: a man wearing a white skirt, a tall hat on his head, whirling. His skirt flared out with the movement, while his eyes were fixed on infinity. She tried to pronounce the name of the troupe, finding some difficulty doing so, and he corrected her pronunciation. "It's one of the best-known Mevlevi troupes in Turkey."

She looked from the invitation to him, unimpressed. "Isn't that the same as the *tannura* dance that we have here in Egypt? You know, the one with the big skirts in many colors, and they spin and spin while people cheer and applaud? It makes my head spin."

"That's actually a method adapted from the Mevlevi dance, and it's a pity, they've cheapened it." Sherif shook his head. "They made it into an entertainment to be performed at parties and for drunken nightclub patrons. It's got nothing to do with the real Mevlevi dance, and when you see these dervishes perform, you'll discover it for yourself."

"All right," she said, "I'll come."

"I'll pick you up at eight tomorrow."

He walked her to her car and gave her a wave as she drove away. Sometimes, she thought, he was a strange person whom she could not understand: he was a follower of a Sufi order but wore the latest fashions, rode a Harley and smoked, and listened to music, both instrumental and vocal, which some Islamic sects considered a sin.

15

"ARE YOU STILL INTO ALL that?"

Her question preoccupied him. It was not an interest as much as it was faith. He had been like a ship adrift at sea, and they had been a lighthouse shining to lead him onto the right path. Yes, the idea of salvation had been in his mind, but he had been drowning in the mire, unable to pull himself out; and even if he had managed it, he could hardly have managed to get all the mud off himself. Until he met them and discovered that this world was temporary and ephemeral: the eternal world, on the other hand, was right there, behind a delicate veil, a veil that did not need to be lifted to reveal what lay beyond it. All we must do, he had realized, is purify our souls, and then we shall see everything clearly. He would tell himself: *I was bewildered; my mind was confused, and so was my soul. That man was my guide, that man who appeared to me from the other world. I needed someone to reach out their hand to me: and in our world, where everyone is chasing after their own interests, no one cares or takes an interest in others. On the contrary, they reached out their hands to me to drag me further into the mire of the world they occupied, while those on the outside envied me my wealth and position. No one thought to ask themselves what I had given up to get where I was; and even if they knew that it was my very peace of mind that I had given up, would they have cared? Would they have taken pity on me? Who cares about peace of mind when compensated with fat bank accounts? Screw peace of mind, they would say, and screw conscience as well and its incessant nagging.*

He had come back from Konya a different person. It was not only his mind that had changed, but his face, his eyes, his voice. He told no one of what had happened, of the ray of light that had penetrated his heart and soul. It had catapulted him into a war, not only with his baser nature, but with everyone around him, for all roads led to a single path. Because he knew that the wars where the fiercest fighting raged were with oneself against one's own desires, where if one won, one won everything, he was quick to cut off all ties with his former life. He quit his job, moved out of his house, abandoned the circles he had traveled in, and changed his phone number. He began to establish a new life and a new world for himself.

His trip to Konya had not been just a vacation or an experience after which he could go back to the way he was before; it had been the gateway to a new, purer world. The fireplace of faith needed to be stoked, from time to time, with the logs of purification: he sat meditating for hours at a time, alone with only God for company. His rituals of worship were conducted in a corner of his house in a seaside town, with windows all overlooking the sea and the open sky. The more of himself he liberated, the lighter and freer and happier he felt. Sufi tenets preach primarily the liberation from the self's desires, not repressing those desires, for repression burdens the self, and the heavier the burden on the self, the body correspondingly suffers and with it the soul, which is no way to put an end to the conflict. In the end, evil will release the fetters that tie you down.

He had grown up in a moderate family, not overly religious. He had only prayed on Fridays, and that because his father made him go to mosque with him. He only fasted in Ramadan because it was impolite to be eating in public in the holy month. He had grown up hearing people saying the same old thing: "Pray or you'll go to Hell"; "God's punishment is terrible"; "Hellfire is waiting for you"; "You will bring God's wrath down on your head." These are the words that imams, families, siblings, and friends use to exhort others to obey God's commandments; but these words did not bring him closer to God but quite the opposite. He had found himself unable to worship the Lord out of fear of punishment, but he found it quite easy to worship, speak to, and approach Him out of love. That was why, when that man had whispered in his ear, "Love God and He will love you; come closer to Him and He will come closer to you; He is the best of lovers and the closest of friends," he had thought hard on these words and worked hard to make them come true, based on the central tenets of Sufism: obedience to God and worship of Him out of divine love, not out of fear of Him and His vengeance. Love opens all doors: it inspires worshipers to purify themselves and liberate themselves from sins and transgressions, and so it was that he found his path in love.

It was true that he had not gone deep into the Sufi orders, nor had he officially joined any order as such, but he was always reading about and researching Sufism. He was especially drawn to the Mevlevi order founded by the poet Jalal al-Din al-Rumi, better known only as the Rumi. He had written his best work in worship of the Divine Presence, where he had called upon his students and followers to listen to the melodies of a melancholy flute and dance to its tune.

When Sherif left Yasmine and went home, he found himself pulling on the wide white skirt he had bought in Konya, and putting on the tall felt hat of the dervishes. Then, to the tune of the reed flute, he spun through the kingdom of God, calling and praising the Lord, eyes fixed on the distant horizon.

16

A COLLEAGUE OF YASMINE'S WHO was also a member of the Scientific Institute had secured her an appointment with the secretary-general of the Institute, the contents of which had been devoured by fire on a black, dismal day during the 2011 revolution: all the documents that the invader had been careful to pen; all the information and the discoveries they had collected so assiduously; the treasures they had found and deposited with such care in a safe place; the information that a great number of the most skilled and competent scientists and artists had worked on. How could the people whose homeland it was so casually set fire to it, as if all these priceless treasures were not theirs?

She was on her way to meet the director at Beit al-Sinnari, a historic house preserved as part of Cairo's heritage, in the district of Sayyida Zeinab, in a cul-de-sac at the end of a narrow alley named after Gaspard Monge, one of the artists who had worked for the French Campaign. This was the temporary headquarters of the Scientific Institute, and the temporary home for the Institute's collection, what had survived the fire without damage, until the Institute was rebuilt and the fire-damaged books and manuscripts restored.

She parked on the street close to the sidewalk, as the lane was too narrow to allow her car to go any further. She found the house without having to ask anyone where it was. It stood there tall and proud, a fortress against the ravages of time. It had a large footprint: the central courtyard around which the rooms were built boasted a great fountain. The house itself was composed of several buildings comprising several wings: Yasmine felt very small standing in the courtyard beneath the towering walls.

"Welcome, welcome," the director greeted her. She told him of the reason for her visit briefly and without embellishment, keeping the greatest secret jealously to herself. He adjusted his glasses and said somberly, "Unfortunately, what befell the Institute is a disaster in the truest sense of the word. We are making every effort to restore these things and keep the losses to a minimum. This is a disaster equaled only by the destruction of the Alexandria Library in the Ptolemaic Era."

"It's certainly a great loss," Yasmine commiserated, nodding.

"Egypt will never be able to make up for what has been lost with the burning of the Institute. We had over two hundred thousand documents in its library, manuscripts, ancient books, and rare maps. Only twenty-five thousand survived. These documents were the memory of Egypt since 1798, including an original copy of the *Description of Egypt*, which burned along with other treasures. Other losses include most of the documents that were over two hundred years old, rare printed books from Europe of which only a few copies exist in the entire world, the books written by foreign explorers and travelers, and copies of scientific periodicals since 1920."

"I knew that manuscripts were lost," Yasmine said, "but what about the books?"

"We had forty thousand books in the Institute's library. The most important of them was an atlas of ancient Indian art. There was an atlas of Upper and Lower Egypt drawn in 1952, and a German atlas of Egypt and Ethiopia dating back to 1842. There was *Le Sou Atlas*, which was once part of the collection of Prince Muhammad Ali Tawfiq, former crown prince of Egypt. That's one of the reasons why international museum and library experts had valued the library of the Egyptian Scientific Institute higher than the Library of Congress."

"What's more," Yasmine cut in, "the chaos in the country at the time of the fire was the same as what happened over two hundred years ago. I see it as one of those crises of culture and civilization when everything falls apart." She mused, "It wasn't just a crisis in Egypt, but in the East as a whole. Just like what happened then."

"When Napoleon came to Egypt," he said, "he formed a council of consultants composed of Egyptian scientists, aristocrats, and high-ranking imams. A similar type of council was formed after the January 2011 Revolution, and it was during this council's rule that the Institute burned down. It's a historical correspondence between rejection of change and welcoming it, suspicion and apathy, which resembles the Egyptian attitude toward the French Campaign and Bonaparte's presence in Egypt." Clearly engrossed in his subject, he said, "Abdel-Rahman al-Jabarti, the ancient historian, wrote a detailed note in his diary describing it, which was published in *Aja'ib al-athar f-il-tarajim w-al-akhbar*, or *The Marvelous Compositions of Biographies and Events*, describing the Battle of Imbaba, which took place on the seventh of the Islamic month of Safar in AH 1213, between the French Army and the Egyptian Army, which was led by the Mamluk princes. Foreigners sometimes call it the Battle of the Pyramids."

He continued, "The fighting went on for three-quarters of an hour. Then came defeat. The Egyptian subjects rioted and protested, going off in the direction of the town. They poured into the town in waves, all in deep fear and trepidation, expecting to be killed. The sounds of weeping and wailing rent the air, and prayers to God to spare them the horrors of this terrible day. The women were screaming at the top of their lungs from the houses. On the Tuesday, the tenth of that same month, that is to say, only three days later, the French crossed over to the shores of Egypt, and walked through the marketplaces with no weapons and no aggression; on the contrary, they laughed and joked with the people, and bought their essentials at the highest prices. When the common people saw this, they warmed to them, and came to trust them. They brought sweets out to them, and various types of pastries, eggs, chickens, and sundry foodstuffs.

"That's what Egyptians are like," he said. Then he smiled. "Yes, they have the kindest hearts in the world. They can welcome even an invader and only later revolt against them. But let's get back to the subject at hand. To tell the truth, in my tenure at the Institute, I saw no trace of any paintings: the artwork of the artists of the French Campaign are hanging in museums all around the world. What's more, the Institute has moved to various locations over the years: was the painting transferred with its collection, then, from place to place?"

He got up and went to a bookshelf. "Look what al-Jabarti says about this," he said, taking down *The Marvelous Compositions of Biographies and Events*. He opened it and began to read aloud: "And they demolished several princes' houses, and took their ruins and the marble used therein for their own buildings. They devoted a certain alleyway, Nasiriya Alley, to scientists, astronomers, men of knowledge, mathematicians and their like such as architects, men who understood form, ornamentation, patterns and blueprints, painters and scribes, accountants and builders. The new street and all its houses were placed at their disposal, such as the house of Qasem Bey, the Prince of Hajj known as Abu Youssef, and the houses of Hassan al-Kashef the Circassian, both old and new, and they opened the house of Ibrahim Katkhudha al-Sinnari to a group of the painters who depicted everything, including one who depicted the imams, each standing alone, in a circle, and other important men, and the paintings were hung."

"By 'depiction,' she clarified, "he means 'painting'?"
"Yes."

"And this painting he mentions, of the imams of al-Azhar who joined the Majlis Istishari, the council of consultants to Napoleon, is a collection of portraits of Sheikh Suleiman al-Fayumi, Sheikh al-Bakri, Sheikh Sharqawi, the one at the Musée des Archives Nationales in Paris? I've seen it there."

He sat down in a chair and went on speaking. "This is how the location of the Egyptian Scientific Institute was chosen. It was founded by Napoleon in Egypt to rival the French Scientific Institute in its collection of elite scientists and thinkers to produce information and research and publications that would assist Napoleon in running the colony. As al-Jabarti tells us, he chose the Sayyida Zeinab area, where a number of luxurious, abandoned Mamluk palaces were located. The most important ones belonged to Hassan al-Kashef Bey, Qasem Abu Youssef Bey, Ali Youssef, and Ibrahim Katkhudha al-Sinnari, which is the one we're in now."

Her eyes shone and she looked around the house with renewed interest. "Really? This house?"

"That's right. After the place was made ready, on 20 August 1798, Bonaparte commanded a number of men to live here: Gaspard Monge, a mathematician and a pioneer of perspective in painting, Geoffroy Saint-Hilaire, and Caffarelli du Falga, who specialized in painting Napoleon's campaigns and conquests—he accompanied him whenever he went to wage war or conquer a country to paint and document them at Napoleon's command."

"I've seen Caffarelli's work," Yasmine nodded. "My favorite was his painting of Napoleon in Jaffa."

The man stuffed a pipe with fragrant tobacco and lit it. "I don't usually smoke at work," he said, "but talking on this subject requires a pipe." He took a puff and went on. "Napoleon gave orders to found the Egypt Scientific Institute and select its members. It was divided into four sections: Mathematics, Physics (meaning natural history and medicine), Political Economy, and Arts and Letters. It is noted on the gravestone of Pierre Jacotin, cartographer and surveyor, that he was a member of the Egyptian Scientific Institute during the time of the French Campaign."

"That only goes to show how important this work was, and how important the Institute was."

"Yes, definitely. The Institute may have been built by the French, but the primary beneficiaries of it have always been Egypt and the Egyptians. Even some of the prominent imams of al-Azhar and eminent citizens paid visits to the Institute and used its extensive library, which the French welcomed." He sighed. "The old seat of the Institute remained abandoned until the British consul in Egypt managed to reestablish the Egyptian Scientific Institute to play the scientific role so integral to the Institute's function. Another British professor, named Henry Abbott, together with the French Orientalist Prisse d'Avennes, founded the Egyptian Literary Association to perform the same cultural role that the Egyptian Scientific Institute had. And on May 6, 1856, Khedive Muhammad Said Pasha declared the Institute officially reestablished in Alexandria." He puffed out a long plume of pipe smoke and went on. "In 1880, expert archaeologists restored Beit al-Sinnari, the original seat of the Institute, and it came back to this building, resuming its cultural activities."

She drank in his every word, wide-eyed. "It came full circle. This house having been the seat of the Scientific Institute at its inception, when the Campaign came here, and again when the Institute was moved from Alexandria to Cairo, and then again when the collection came back here after the fire!"

"That's true."

She allowed him to speak until he had finished his historical monologue: finally, she pulled out her iPad and showed him the painting. He scrutinized it carefully. "I've never seen this painting before," he said. "I don't think it's part of our collection." He added, still looking, "But what makes you so sure that it's one of ours?"

"The painting came to our lab from the Gezira Museum," said Yasmine, "one of the damaged paintings that were brought there after the fire at the Scientific Institute. The odd thing is that the painting is damaged, yes, but definitely not at all by fire. It was improperly stored in an enclosed, humid place for a long time."

"I assure you," he told her, "this painting is not part of our collection. In any case, we would not have let such a distinguished piece of art deteriorate to the state it appears to be in. Although, since you say the damage is due to improper storage, it might have been in the Institute's storage rooms. You might drop by and have a word with the storage supervisor."

She took her leave and thanked him warmly for his hospitality. He had been most forthcoming with his information and had not minded her asking questions; on the contrary, he seemed to need no prompting to open up the treasure troves, storehouses, and caverns of the Institute's memory to place everything in it on display.

The storage supervisor was in a room a little way from the office; unlike his boss, he greeted her with a curt nod. When she showed him the painting, he said in a tone that left no room for dissent, "No, this painting wasn't in our storage. There were no paintings in there."

Cairo: November 1798

He waited until she was out of sight, the girl whose innocence and childish smile had touched his heart. Then he went on his way, down streets and byways, contemplating the features of the people he had come to paint. All the Egyptians had something in common, he noticed, however different they looked: it was the pure smile that lit up their faces.

The Jewish quarter; the Armenian quarter; churches forbidden to ring their bells, synagogues with squared-off courtyards, churches with high domes, wooden buildings, the fish market, the caravansaries for rice trading, linen trading, and oil trading, the tailors' street, the Sudanese alley, the Mosque of Abul-Ela, and the mule stop, a spacious square where men and boys stood with beasts of burden, each occupied with washing and bathing his mount, feeding them, and decorating their saddles with velvet covers, then hanging bells around their necks. The mules preened with a sense of importance, and stood tall and proud.

He stood there for a long time, contemplating this strange world, pondering the special relationship between these carters and their beasts. It was something deeper, he thought, than just a livelihood for them. He asked a carter to take him to his house.

"Where?" the man asked.

"Beit al-Sinnari."

The man helped him up onto the mule's velvet-saddled back. With a thick hand, he slapped the animal's back to urge it into a gallop. "Beit al-Sinnari, the one Napoleon took over with all the men who do odd things inside?" he asked.

Alton chuckled and shook his head. "Odd things?" he repeated.

"Yes, they say that a lot of men live there and do odd things, like summon demons, God help us, to share Napoleon's conquests and his new lands." The man, feeling more comfortable with no interruption, went on. "They say he summoned a demon and made him drive the ship that flies in the air. He let them down, and it fell down on everyone's heads, and, but for the grace of God, would have killed many."

"Hmm." Alton smiled, not feeling it worth the effort to undertake changing the man's mind and disabusing him of these notions, for how could a man who thought like that absorb his explanations?

"I've taken a lot of relatives and acquaintances to Beit al-Sinnari. They were a generous household, they always tipped well. What an odd world this is! I wonder where they are now? Ah well, here we are."

Alton disembarked and handed the man a quarter-*bara*. The man's face broke into a broad smile to see the coin, after which he whipped up his mount and trotted away. Alton pushed open the oval wooden door with a friendly greeting to the gardeners inside who took care of the courtyard. He walked in, through the broad corridor floored with *mazut*, solid bitumen, and entered a large room where Gaspard Monge and another scientist were engrossed in an experiment. "Good evening," he said.

"Good evening," said Alton. The sight of the other Frenchmen calmed him, and he suddenly felt at ease enough to speak of his doubts. "With every day that passes," Alton said, exasperated, "I find myself less and less certain of what on earth Napoleon wants from us." He flung himself down into a chair, shaking his head, thinking of an innocent girl's smile. "Why did he bring us here? What was so incomprehensible about this land, so outside the order of creation, that he needed us to explain it to him and set it down in books and reference volumes?"

Gaspard Monge set down his instruments and straightened. "*Au contraire*. This country is full of treasures as yet undiscovered. There are a great many resources as yet untapped. It's up to us to find them."

"Treasures?" Alton sighed. "Resources? That's all very well, my good fellow, but what exactly is required of me? What am I supposed to do?"

Monge fixed him with a proud look. "We are preparing a book on the description of Egypt. That is the volume in which we plan to describe everything in Egypt in words and pictures." He added, "I don't believe you have not yet found something that inspires you to draw! Ever since you got here, the only thing you have completed is that painting of the celebration of the flooding of the Nile."

The words seemed to rattle around in Alton's head. "Inspires me to draw?" he said aloud, while thinking, *What*

145

makes him think I haven't already found my muse, and that the only thing I've thought about since I set eyes on her is to paint her?

He left Monge and went to the studio where the artists and sculptors did their work. He took out a fresh piece of paper and spread it out, preparing to paint her: but something made his brush veer away, changing his mind at the last minute. He felt a sudden reluctance to paint her in public, in that room where anyone could see. He wanted to be alone with her. No one should look upon his brush as it painted the intimate details of her. No one should see him painting with his heart instead of his hand.

He would paint her for himself, and himself alone. He would not allow her to become a part of their *research*. She was not some sort of animal to be caged within the four corners of a painting. He would not allow her to become the laughing-stock of the elite Parisian women who went to museums and stood before paintings—her painting—not bothering to hold back their titters as they made fun of the veil around her head or the striped silken *gallabiya* she wore. They would care nothing for her striking features, nor for the charm and innocence she radiated: he knew such women well, all the women of the bourgeois set, the *nouveaux riches* of the Revolution.

Alton originally came from an aristocratic family, and had always hated the snobbery and artifice of that class. Still, want and a need to earn a living, coupled with the hard times his family had fallen upon after the Revolution, had kept him in contact with a class he hated. His father had been a courtier in the court of Louis XVI; the Revolution had not only imprisoned him, but confiscated all his family's property, leaving them penniless and out in the cold. His mother had lived for a while on charitable gifts from wealthy members of the family who had fortunately escaped the clutches of the Revolution; however, as time passed, these gifts slowed to a trickle and eventually dried up completely. Alton, a handsome and eligible dandy who had many Parisian beauties chasing after him, of the type who went for walks in the Jardins de Luxembourg at five every afternoon accompanied by their maids and little white poodles, was obliged to leave his life of luxury behind to earn his living. His only skill was painting: he went out to Montmartre with his canvas and his brushes, and set up his paints, canvases, and easel on a street corner. Fortunately, he was talented, so the faces and scenes in his paintings made people stop and stare, asking him to paint them, or requesting particular scenes that had tickled their fancy. He sold well, and thanks to his gift, he became quite well known within a short time.

He managed to save a bit of money and rented a garret on the rooftop of an old apartment building that he converted into a studio while keeping his old location on the street corner. He became well-known in Parisian high society and aristocratic families requested him by name to paint their family portraits on special occasions and at their extravagant parties. Circumstance forced him not to be choosy; he needed to be able to live within his current more modest lifestyle, but one thing he never abandoned was his smart attire. Now he was 'the handsome artist,' 'the lively young man,' and so on, and thus still retained the ability to attract young lovelies and women of the world alike. Still, he only had passing flings with them; he would visit this one and accept the invitation of that one with gentlemanly charm, no more, for they always struck him as shallow and vacuous. What was truly strange, even to himself, was that he had left all these beauties behind, traveled all this distance, to meet this ordinary girl and fall in love with her, as though fate had arranged this journey to this land at this particular time only for this purpose, to bring him face to face with her.

He had never planned to visit the Orient. The organizers of the Campaign had not meant to include his name on the roster of its artists. It had all been sheer chance. On a bitingly cold day in February, as the snow was falling outside and the juniper logs were crackling as usual in the fireplace, he heard—as he was placing the finishing touches on a painting before handing it in for a few francs—a horse-drawn carriage pull up outside his house. The brass knocker sounded insistently against his door. When he opened it, he found Monsieur Lombard himself outside. He was one of the most famous artists in France and a professor at the School of Fine Arts. "Come in, come in," he had said, stunned, and Lombard had stepped inside. He was a fiftyish man with a beard that looked as though it had not been trimmed in years, and a pipe that never left his hand even when he wasn't smoking it. He could not begin to guess the reason behind this odd visit at such a late hour. Another man was with Lombard, stern-faced and with the air of a military man. He welcomed them both and set out two chairs. "It's an honor to have you here in my humble studio," he said.

Gruffly and with a supercilious air, Lombard responded as he looked all around the studio as though inspecting it. He blew out smoke from his pipe. "It is humble indeed," he said, "but your work is quite the reverse." He raised his eyebrows. "You have a fine hand, and your talent is unparalleled. That is why we are here."

The other man took up the thread. "Your name is on a military list to take part in an exploratory campaign where we shall be in need of several professional artists to draw and paint everything strange and unusual on our journey, and document what is important on our voyage."

Tongue-tied by surprise, he was obliged to shake himself in order to find something to say. "What campaign?" he asked. "To where? How?"

"You are not permitted to ask questions," the military man said. "This is an imperial command, and you must obey without question. This is not a matter of choice to which you may say yea or nay."

"But what is the purpose of the expedition?"

"That is classified information." He went on to tell Alton that he was not to tell anyone about his upcoming voyage, which was a state secret.

"But what about my family? I'm the only breadwinner."

"You don't need to worry on that score. They will receive a sum of money at the start of every month."

Lombard looked around him at the paintings on the walls and propped up against them on the floor. "This is a golden opportunity, my boy," he said while taking his leave at the door. "The artist who should have gone in your stead has fallen ill, and your name was recommended to replace him. You can take your own equipment with you, the things you can't work without. We will send you a telegram to tell you of the travel date and other details."

Alton stood rooted to the spot on his doorstep after they left, snow blowing in. Finally, half-frozen, he closed it, still thinking of the man's words, "This is a golden opportunity." Was it truly golden? It was a military command that he could not refuse. Sailing into the unknown! That was an exciting prospect that any artist would envy—if he was setting sail of his own free will, to a destination of his own choosing, to draw what his eye desired, not commanded by a military officer. But soon enough he convinced himself to set his misgivings aside. The command had been issued, after all, and he could do little else but obey.

A few days later, he received a telegram telling him that the date to set sail would be at dawn that next Monday from Toulon Square. On the telegram was scrawled, "PLEASE ENSURE SECRECY."

Secrecy? That alone piqued his curiosity. A scientific expedition . . . why would they require secrecy? In any case, he would obey orders; he had no wish to court disaster by disobeying. He made his arrangements and took his leave of his family and friends, telling them that he was going on a brief journey through various cities and towns in France. Only his mother did he tell about his secret: she said good-bye with bitter tears. He promised her that he would write to her. He had resolved not only to write letters to her, but to set down every detail that transpired on his journey from the moment his ship set sail until he set foot on his home soil once more. Perhaps these notes he would write might be important enough to publish later, in book form: many artists and men of letters had written travelogues and published them upon their return.

On 19 May, 1798, at the port of Toulon, two great ships were preparing to cast off. One of them was laden with modern war machines, ammunition, and supplies; the other with laboratory equipment, scientific apparatus, and printing presses. The officers stood in rows to the fore. Behind them were the scientists, and I was among their number. The soldiers stood shoulder to shoulder in the last row: long lines and eyes filled with wonderment, and confused chattering, for no one knew what this man was planning. The crew was moving around busily in preparation to cast off and set sail.

The sun had not yet risen when Napoleon appeared, the usual smile on his face that never left it, even in the bleakest times. He made a short speech, his breath condensing in puffs of vapor in the freezing air as he spoke. For a moment, I fancied that he was a dragon blowing his smoke into our faces and that he was about to attack. But he wished us a pleasant journey and disappeared into the ship.

The address he made to us was a very short one, a few mysterious words of which we understood nothing. He was careful not to betray anything of his plans to us. In under an hour, the foghorns sounded, indicating the ships were setting sail. Where to? To the Orient! This was all the information we were able to obtain.

I was in the company of great scientists on that ship. Because I never kept up with science or modern discoveries, I did not know any of them. Monsieur Monge arranged a meeting to introduce us all to one another, and asked us to all come up on deck after lunch. Only then did I stand there, speechless, as he called out their names. There was a historian, an archaeologist, an astronomer, a physician, and a geographer—and myself! Whatever had brought me there? What brought me into the company of these eminent men?

I met a great many scientists, craftsmen, and workmen, these last powerless and helpless; they had been perforce torn from their homes and the company of their families, forced to leave everything behind—their sweethearts, their wives, their children, their jobs—and go off into the unknown. They could not show disgruntlement or refuse. I made friends with Leon Pointard, a fortyish man whose profession was betrayed by the ink stains on his fingers: he was responsible for the printing presses and the machines that that department comprised. He took me down into the bowels of the ship, and took it upon himself to show me the machines and how they worked: strangely enough, there was one with Arabic lettering. Pointard told me that the Commander-General had told them to bring it along so that they could print circulars and newspapers in Arabic for the people of those lands.

After several weeks' sailing in the wide open sea, one foggy day we sighted land, looking like an extension of the sea. I had not yet known that it was a changeable country, swinging between extremes from one day to the next: one day glittering, the next dark; one day light, the next gloom; extending to right and left, wide as her river and old as her pyramids.

Cairo: November 30, 1798

Since Zeinab had returned home after meeting him in the park, his face had not left her. She was filled with him, her soul clinging to him. His face, his scent, his voice. Was she in love with him? She must be, for what else but love could be making her only live for the hope of seeing him? What else but love could be making her think of him and only him, day and night?

But what could come of this love? In the eyes of all, he was a Frenchman, here with the Campaign to invade her country. He was one of the infidel invaders, as the Egyptians called him. Even though he was only in the country to paint and not to fight, who would understand that?

But what did she care? The tremor that took her when she laid eyes on him was enough. She had been so close to Napoleon that there had been only a few breaths between him and her; he had touched her cheek and stroked her hair; yet he had stirred nothing within her but a feeling of panic and unease. With Alton, everything was different: she had but to lay eyes on him to dance inside with joy. The whole world meant nothing compared to what she felt for him. What had the world given her but cruelty, rebukes, and envy? A mother who cared for nothing but cooking, sweeping, and polishing, and blind obedience to her husband; a selfish father who could give anything away to make his own dreams come true; friends who were only jealous of her; family and relations who only came to visit when they needed something or to borrow money; neighbors who could hardly wait to see some disaster befall them so as to gloat their fill. Alton was the gift that fate had given her: he had come to free her from the clutches of the world she lived in, and she would let him come to her rescue and sweep her away from this life she lived.

Her mother came into the room; she didn't even notice, lost as she was in another world. "Hey!" her mother prodded her in the arm. "Aren't you done dreaming yet? Wake up!" She put her hands on her hips. "Isn't it enough what you've done to us? You've made us the butt of everyone's gossip!"

With wide, bold eyes, Zeinab looked up at her mother. "No, I won't wake up," she said firmly. "Will you not even let me dream?"

"A word of advice," her mother said. "When you dream, dream a dream your own size. That way you won't break your neck when you wake up from your dream in seventh heaven!"

"Let it happen," Zeinab snapped back. "It's enough to have dreamed."

"Get up and help me clean the house and make dinner."

"I'm not cleaning or cooking. The house is full of servants and slaves who can help."

"Now I see!" her mother cried. "That's what comes of your father spoiling you!" She stormed out, muttering curses under her breath.

Zeinab knew perfectly well what her mother was talking about: she thought Zeinab was in love with Napoleon. She was right to be fearful and apprehensive: grown men trembled just to hear the great man's name. No one could presume to know what was going on in his head. If only she could tell her mother that her dream had nothing to do with Bonaparte. If only she could tell her about Alton and her feelings for him. But could her mother even understand what love meant?

Fatima, wife to Sheikh al-Bakri, was deeply worried about her daughter's well-being. What worried her even more was the fact that she knew nothing about what anyone was thinking—not her husband, not her daughter, not Bonaparte. From behind the meshrabiyeh, she could see dark clouds gathering in the sky and hurrying toward her fate, thunderous storm clouds. She had been unable to sleep for thinking and worrying, turning right and left, looking at her husband to find him lying on his back, his fat paunch vibrating to the rhythm of his loud snoring and making her want to prod him, wake him up, and yell, "What's happened to you? Are you that much of a slave to power and position? Would you sacrifice your own family to them, your religion, anything and everything, just to get what you want?" Suddenly, as if he heard the screams she was choking back, he opened one eye and looked at her. He slurred drowsily, "Go to sleep, woman."

Perhaps before, in another time, she would have gone to sleep, feeling she had no choice since he commanded her to do so; but now was the time to reject his commands, now that they had lost their power. He had fallen in her estimation ever since he had agreed to present his daughter as a gift to

Napoleon in exchange for high rank and status. How had he allowed himself to do such a thing? How could he look people in the face, and him a high-ranking Azharite sheikh? She herself could no longer look anyone in the eye. She passed through the streets with her head down, looking at the ground as though she was looking for something she had dropped, while the wagging tongues of those whom she passed by lashed at her back like whips.

She waited until the sun rose, sending its smooth silken threads out to spread light and warmth, then quickly pulled on her burka and slipped out of the house unnoticed. She walked through the streets, head down, taking unaccustomed paths that made her journey longer, so as to avoid meeting other women who she knew would shower her with coarse insults. Through the alleys she went until she arrived at the mule market and cart stop; from there she hired a cart and asked the carter to take her to Harat al-Yahud, the Jewish Quarter, in the district of Moski.

The carter stopped at the gate to the Jewish quarter, telling her that the cart would not fit inside: "The camels, you see, are loading up a bride's trousseau, and we won't be able to get past through that narrow path."

She threw him a quarter-*bara* and went on foot through the alley, stumbling hesitantly and dragging her feet. She saw a woman frying *zalabya* pastry balls, sprinkling them with sugar and placing them in paper cones for sale. She bought one, then walked to the end of the alley. Taking hold of a rusty wooden door knocker, she knocked on an old, cracked wooden door with a Star of David carved into it. She knocked again and again; she waited, and then, when no one answered, decided to turn back the way she had come. Just then, she heard a creaky voice coming from behind the door: "Patience! Patience! Patience is a virtue!"

"I've been as patient as Job," she muttered. "These pastries are stone cold."

The door screeched and creaked open: the old woman behind it invited her in. Fatima followed the woman into the courtyard of the house, to where a table was placed. The woman was leaning on a wooden stick, wearing a threadbare black *gallabiya* full of holes and patches. Her shock of wild hair was the blinding white of snow. She was just as Fatima remembered seeing her the last time. Nothing about her had changed a jot; even her house was the same, with the same stench, the pitted and scarred table still there where Fatima had sat with her own mother many years ago. The fortune-teller busied herself with making coffee, roasting the beans first in a small pan, then grinding them with mastic and cardamom, filling the place with their fragrance. Fatima gave her the cone of pastry. "Leave them, thanks," said the woman, "and we'll have it with our coffee. How do you take your coffee?"

In days gone by, Fatima would have refused coffee; drinking coffee was a sin, or so they said. But now she would not say no to a cup. "Medium sugar, please."

She poured their coffee into two brass cups. "How are you, Fatima?"

Fatima was amazed. Was it possible that the woman still remembered her from when she was a little girl? "Do you still remember me," she asked, "after all this time?"

"Yes," said the fortune-teller, "I recognized you by your scent."

"My scent?"

"Everyone who has set foot inside this house I recognize by smell," said the woman calmly.

"I don't remember putting on any perfume today . . . ?"

The woman laughed aloud, displaying her dark cavern of a mouth, toothless but for a lone canine. "You don't need to wear perfume for me to recognize you. I recognize you by your body's smell: every person has a scent unique to themselves alone, that resembles them. I remember your smell very well, as it's one of the few I've smelled like it in my life: a goodly smell,

155

like virgin soil. True, it is mixed with another scent this time, but the scent of untouched earth is still there." She sniffed the air. "Wait . . ." She kept on sniffing like a bloodhound in search of some thief. "It's the smell of fear. No—not just fear—it's a mix of fear and panic and grief. What is the matter, woman?"

Fatima sighed helplessly. "It's the Franks. My life is turned upside down. No sooner did they come than it seemed they were only there to invade my own home." She sighed. "That brute Bonaparte must have cast a spell on my husband and daughter. They've changed! They're not the same people at all." She took a swallow of her coffee. "My husband—the good, devout man of God—has changed, as if he had never known the Lord God or his Prophet. My pure, innocent daughter! She's changed and is acting like the belly dancers and prostitutes. How could this have happened in the space of a day and a night, unless he enchanted them?"

"The evils of one's self are more wicked than enchantments," the woman said, "and your daughter and your husband have wickedness in their own selves."

"But how? This is my husband whom I have known all my life, and my daughter, raised by my own hands, and I know them better than I know myself!"

"The wickedness within the self is more powerful than anything, and harder than any enchantment. Spells can be broken and vanquished; the ills of the self grow from deep within, and only go away when the soul leaves the body."

"No!" Fatima shook her head. "No. I don't think so. One doesn't change completely in a day and a night! What's happening with them is surely some spell."

There was an old silver pan filled with water on the table, in front of the old fortune-teller. There was something odd about the water: even motionless, it was filled with concentric ripples like those raised by a stone thrown into a still pond. No sooner did the ripples dissipate than they came back at once. "Let us see. Did you bring something of theirs?"

Before coming, Fatima had remembered the fortune-teller asking her mother, long ago when they had first visited, to bring something belonging to the person to examine. She had therefore brought something. From the recesses of her *abaya*, she took out a burlap purse bound with strong thread. From this she pulled out two handkerchiefs, one silk, which was Zeinab's, and the other of white cotton, belonging to her husband. The woman took the two handkerchiefs and began to recite incantations in a strange language. Her voice dropped and grew rough, and her features changed. The more she spoke her incantations, the more the water in the dish roiled and bubbled, as though boiling over a flame.

The woman calmed and laid the handkerchiefs aside: the water ceased its bubbling. "O Auntie, set my mind at rest," Fatima entreated, "what has happened?"

"As I told you," the woman said calmly, "it is no witchcraft nor spell, but the wickedness of the self." Then she fell silent for a moment. In a voice softer than usual, a kinder expression on her face, she said, "God help you, God help you."

Fatima trembled in fear: what had the woman foreseen to change her thus, making her so sad for Fatima, she who was normally so hard-hearted? She could not keep the pleading out of her tone, "Set my mind at rest."

"There is nothing you can do," said the fortune-teller. "Go to the temple of Maimonides at the end of the alley, and call for the mercy of the Lord. Bless yourself with the water of the well there, and take some of it with you, and bathe your daughter and husband in it." And without warning, she left her, rising with speed surprising for one of her age and walking away, still leaning on her stick. "Close the door behind you."

"Auntie! Auntie! Please wait!" Fatima stood too. "Isn't there anything you can do for us?"

The woman shook her head as she walked away.

Fatima left more troubled than she had come, dragging her feet and moving with difficulty. What fate had the fortune-teller seen and refused to tell her?

Outside the house, a group of children were drawing hopscotch squares on the ground with a piece of chalk and playing. She approached them and asked, "Where is the temple of Maimonides?"

"That's it," said a little boy, pointing to a building at the end of the lane. Although she did not know who this Maimonides was, the fortune-teller had told her to go to his temple and be blessed with the waters of his well, so she did. Like a drowning woman, she clutched at any straw.

With halting steps, she entered the spacious temple. Three separate buildings stood before her: one for men's prayers, one for women's, and a third room for blessings and healing. A cold wind sprang up from she knew not where, almost blowing her over. She stood there, hesitant and fearful, not knowing where to go. A student, seeing her, approached, asking her, "What do you need?"

"I wish to be blessed and take water with me to bathe my sick husband," she said.

He pointed to the far end of the courtyard, where she could just see a well. "From this well you can take water," he said, "and go to the healing chamber, where you can anoint yourself with drops of oil for a blessing."

She thanked him and did as he had said. She asked a man whose job it was to help the sick people who came from far-off cities and towns for some oil. "You can spend the night in this room," he said, "so that Maimonides can come and help you recover." She quickly invented the excuse of a baby at home. "Where is your pain," he asked, "that I may anoint it with oil?" She pointed to her heart. It was, in truth, the location of all her pain and trouble. The man dipped a scrap of fabric into a jar full of oil, and handed it to her, asking her to anoint the place where it hurt.

She returned home with a bottle of water from the well and the piece of fabric dipped in the oil, thinking all the way home: what had the woman foreseen? What disasters awaited her? But then, was there any disaster worse than the one already taking place?

Upon the low, round table, the slave girl set out the dishes for dinner: the earthenware pot of baked vegetables with meat, the rice, and a plate filled with green stalks of arugula and bright red radishes. Every hand reached out to eat with good appetite as usual. Fatima was lost in thought. "What's wrong, woman?" her husband asked, noticing. "Someone die or what? What's gotten you into such a dark mood?"

Then he laughed mockingly, and Zeinab laughed along with him. "Mother is always unhappy these days." The gold necklace at her throat gleamed in a ray of sunlight that filtered in through the openings in the meshrabiyeh. Fatima glanced from one to the other, wondering what Fate had in store for them. What would happen, she wondered, if she told them of the fortune-teller's prophecy? Would it make them turn back and abandon what they wanted? But she held her peace, knowing that whatever she said, it would be no use. Besides, if her husband learned she had been to the fortune-teller, it would bring the full force of his wrath down upon her, for he did not permit her to leave the house unless it was for an important matter. What would he do if he found out she had gone out without his knowledge to go to a Jewish fortune-teller to look into the future? Would he, a cleric, accept such a thing? She smiled mockingly to herself as she tried to get up, with difficulty.

The sheikh waited until his wife had left the room and whispered to Zeinab, "Get ready to visit Napoleon tonight. He is waiting impatiently for you. He is utterly captivated by you."

A rush of contradictory feelings surged through Zeinab. Before, she would have jumped for joy to know that Napoleon had asked to see her and was expecting her. Now, though, everything had changed. She did not want to accept his invitation, but she couldn't refuse. Who would dare? "Do you think Napoleon would be in love with me, when he has so many beauties around him?" she asked her father. "Didn't you hear the rumor about him and Madame Pauline? They say he sent her husband off on a military campaign in the desert so that he could be alone with her."

"The heart is one thing," her father said, "and the desires of the flesh are another. You have captured his heart."

She didn't care about capturing his heart: there was only one person whose heart and mind she wanted, only one and no other.

17

YASMINE PUT DOWN HER COFFEE on the desk and sat at her laptop to resume her research. She had now grasped hold of the thread: the portrait had been painted at the time of the French Campaign in Egypt, and she was confident that the artist had been with the Campaign. All she needed to do was uncover his name, and the mystery would unravel.

She searched the names of the artists in Napoleon's French Campaign in Egypt, and read back over the details of the Campaign:

> Napoleon sailed for the East in 1798 with a fleet of twenty-six warships, with thirty thousand soldiers on board, arriving twelve days later in the region of Agami, off Alexandria. The troops disembarked and continued on foot. The Campaign was accompanied by up to 150 scientists and two thousand people including artists, sculptors, carpenters, designers, craftsmen and artisans, and workmen.

How could she find her artist among all these men? She knew that the most famous among them were Vivant Denon, Antoine Jean-Gros, Théodore Géricault, and Eugène Delacroix. She had seen their paintings in various museums around the world. She was familiar with their styles, and none of them even remotely resembled this painter: she would have recognized him immediately if that had been the case. With long experience, one acquired the ability to identify a painter by merely looking at their work; she was rarely wrong, and her intuition was rarely proved inaccurate. An artist's brushstrokes were like fingerprints to her, like a writer's distinctive style, or a poet's. The way one can identify a singer among a hundred voices, she was able to recognize the style of an artist that set them apart from the rest.

Three hours flew by as she was absorbed in her research. Most of the artists that Napoleon had brought with him on his campaign had already been friends of his or at least known to him, and he had been in the habit of bringing them with him on all his previous campaigns. Most of the paintings were depictions of battles or portraits meant to glorify Napoleon and underscore his greatness, particularly those of Denon and Caffarelli.

At last she found a clue: on a site showing paintings of life in Egypt at that time, paintings that documented habits, customs, and fashions of the era, she found a painting titled *The Mule Market in Cairo*. She peered closely at it. There was a strong resemblance between the style of this painting—the brushstrokes, the way the light fell, the color composition, the sense of it—and the painting of Zeinab. She was able to zoom into a close-up of the work, which helped her see that the artist had paid attention to the most minute details and depicted clear emotions on the faces of the different carters at the market. It was clear that they were exhausted, although they were smiling. She found another painting by the same artist on that site, titled *A Street in Cairo*. The painting was full of a great many details: the old houses, the meshrabiyehs that covered the secret world of the women, the giant camels laden with heavy burdens that walked through the narrow alleyways, the two men engrossed in what appeared to be a long discussion, the woman selling oranges in the middle of the road, but most importantly, the work was suffused with a particular feeling:

the warmth and bustle of life which made the viewer feel that they were part of the scene, if not actually a partner in creating this depiction of it.

The paintings were listed under the name of the artist: Alton Germain. She clicked on the artist's name to see what the site had to say about him: to her surprise, the site only listed his name, date of birth, and date of death, but no other information. Art sites usually provided a fairly exhaustive biography of every artist: their birth, their study, their life, their works, and their death, but this site only had the barest of facts: name, birth, and death, as though the life he had lived had meant nothing to anyone—or had, perhaps, remained a secret.

She tried to find him on other sites, but came up empty. She went back to the paintings by him. The site refused to let her download them, insisting she register with a foreign bank card. She picked up the phone to call Sherif, who was always buying all manner of things online and had often complained to her that online sites often didn't ship to Egypt yet, which, he claimed, would save him time and effort.

"Yasmine," came his sleepy voice. "Everything okay? What's the matter?"

"Don't worry," she said, "everything's all right. I need your help with something." Without waiting for an answer, she went on enthusiastically. "There's an art site that's asking me to become a member so I can see the paintings on it. It won't accept my card, I think it needs a foreign—"

He cut her off curtly. "Are you kidding me? You're calling me at three in the morning to ask me about an art site membership?"

She blinked. She had been so engrossed in her search that she had not even noticed it was three o'clock in the morning. Mortified, more so at his brusque tone, she stammered, "Three . . . I'm so sorry! I didn't notice, I lost track of time."

"I know you're crazy about these things, but this is ridiculous!"

"I'm sorry. I'm sorry."

Sherif had changed. He had never been so short with her. She remembered waking him up from sleep many times before, and he had made a joke of it, saying that not only was she on his mind during his waking hours, but she even interrupted his sleep. His love had always rolled out the red carpet for her, guaranteeing her VIP treatment; she seethed with jealousy to think that this new girl had pulled the rug out from under her.

The Mediterranean: May 1798

I found myself on a boat battling the swells of the sea, heading I knew not where. Too much talk, speculation, and guesswork became tedious after a while. The gist of almost all of them was that the campaign was headed to take over Sardinia or take control of Malta, to ensure control of the Mediterranean, while a stubborn minority insisted that we were on the way to Egypt. We were worried and tense. Finally, Napoleon came out and stood at the prow of the ship, his generals around him. He gave a speech that dispelled a great deal of our worries:

May 10, 1798
From Headquarters at Toulon
You were a wing of the army that fought Great Britain. You have fought in the mountains and valleys; you have faced siege; there is nothing before you but a naval battle.

It was a long speech, the goal of which was to raise the soldiers' morale once more, and in that goal it largely succeeded: no sooner was it read out than everything changed. The soldiers whose faces had been awash with trepidation and disappointment quickly changed to euphoric excitement, and snatches of patriotic songs could be heard interspersed with their shouts of enthusiasm. The sails were unfurled in search of a favorable wind to start moving. At dawn on May 30, the ship set sail, and the circuitous route we sailed confounded all the sailors' guesses: first we sailed close to shore and they said "It is Genoa," and then we moved away and they said, "No, we are en route to Sardinia," but we did not stop at either. We were sailing according to the winds, with Neptune as our guardian. Finally, we approached Malta, which we saw as a long-awaited promised land, the land of legends and stories. We took advantage of the darkness of night to allow a few divisions to disembark to start, and when the Maltese saw our maneuvers, they rained down a volley of fire upon us, while our soldiers amassed easy victories. After 24 hours of fighting, the Maltese surrendered unconditionally, and in a scant few hours, we were the masters of an island that enjoyed a fantastic position in the sea. The beautiful, proud island was transformed in a short while into an island in mourning. The city closed its doors in our faces, and wherever we walked, we were met with gazes of hatred and resentment. The streets were filled with grief and sorrow. The women wore black; the children wailed; the men walked through the streets with their heads bowed.

I could not help but feel it odd that the soldiers were so happily celebrating their victory and clinking their glasses in toasts to victory. Why were they celebrating? We had not fought a real battle, neither proving our heroism nor winning in a test of strategy. It was a quiet city, its closed doors concealing the dreams of its peaceful, kind people, and here we were, killing their innocent dreams, and raising the flag of victory over the corpse of the dream.

Napoleon had set the hearts and minds of his solders aflame with his speech where he promised them that they would own the earth: their hearts were filled with envy and greed to take over what they had no right to take. After we had taken Malta, the ships made ready to sail away again, and Napoleon came out to give us a second speech.

You shall make a conquest that shall have the greatest possible impact on trade and civilization in the world. It shall be the greatest strike against England before we vanquish that country with a back-breaking blow: the Mamluks, who prefer to trade only with the British, and whose tyranny has laid waste to the poor inhabitants of the land of the Nile, shall become history as soon as we arrive.

It was then that we became certain that we were on our way to Egypt, and the soldiers began to hope this would be their destination, dreaming of its women, their imaginations fired by The Thousand and One Nights and Letters from Egypt and sundry tales from history. They thought that every Egyptian woman resembled their queen, Cleopatra.

I was imagining, with great excitement, this land that I had so far only heard about: would my feet really tread this ancient, eternal land, the cradle of science and art? Would I see the pyramids? The obelisks? The ruins of ancient temples? Would I walk on the rubble of the cities that had witnessed the civilizations of the pharaohs, the Greeks, and the Romans?

It was drizzling lightly when its minarets and temples appeared on the horizon. The ships dropped anchor and there was a great hullabaloo. The soldiers, scientists, and workmen disembarked, crowding the port, and began to unload the equipment. At the start, a number of Egyptian Mamluk divisions, working for the beys—the aristocrats—attacked us, on the backs of horses faster than the wind. They were richly clothed, armed with guns and pistols, plus gem-encrusted swords. Their features were beautiful but cruel, their eyes like burning coals, sparks flying from their eyes. The mounted fighters fired upon us first, and here the real battle between us and them started. We were greater than them in strength and numbers, and we had better knowledge of the arts of war. They were quickly vanquished, and Alexandria fell with them. But, it must be said, they fought with courage and strength to their last breath.

We set up camp, some within the city and some without. We based our center of operations in the homes of some of the great Mamluk princes of the city. Thus, in an afternoon and a night, the people of this charming and peaceful city found themselves in the midst of war. The smell of the sea changed, for now it stank of gunpowder; clouds of black smoke obscured the clear blue sky, and the fresh sea breeze now bore the stench of the bodies of the dead Mamluks. Napoleon had ten of them beheaded and their heads mounted at the entrance of the city to be an example to the others. The white seagulls that circled above were replaced by severed heads.

Before we had come, the British had put it about that the French invaders were vicious infidels who would destroy the country. Napoleon,

however, was intelligent enough to give the lie to their rumors, and com-
manded that we must show them respect, the lowliest as well as the
highest-born, that we must revere their women and their religion, and
preserve the sanctity of their personal belongings. This made them trust
us, which was exactly what Napoleon wanted. He gave his third speech
addressed to the Egyptian people. He was careful to calm and reassure
them, and the people of Alexandria all came out to listen, thronging the
squares and public gathering places.

From Bonaparte to the Egyptian People
For a long time, the Mamluks who rule Egypt have
taken pains to humiliate the French community here
and oppress their merchants. The hour of retribution
is at hand; for a long time, this riffraff—for Mamluks
were originally a slave class, as you know—bought
from the Caucasus Mountains and Georgia have
been going further and further in their oppression,
imposing a rule of tyranny over the best corner of the
Earth. But the Lord in His infinite wisdom hath fated
the end of their rule.

People of Egypt! They will tell you that I am
here to destroy your religion. Do not believe them.
Say to them that I have, rather, come to give you
back your rights, and punish those who would wrest
them from you. I revere your God, His Prophet
Muhammad, and the Holy Qur'an more than the
Mamluks ever did. Say to them that all people are
equal before God, and that wisdom, knowledge,
and virtue are the real mark that distinguishes one
man from another. Where is that wisdom, knowledge, and virtue in the Mamluks, that they have laid
claim to every element of a life of luxury? Every
good slave, thoroughbred horse, or beautiful estate
has been usurped by the Mamluks, who have laid
claim to all that is good in the land.

This speech fell like an enchantment upon the ears of its hearers, and Napoleon with his cunning managed to win the people of Alexandria over to his side. After the speech was done, the looks of hate and resentment were replaced with friendly and familiar smiles, and some even cheered for Napoleon. The Bedouin, who had been fighting us fiercely the day before, today sent us baskets of bread and gifts for the general.

I was certain that my presence in this land, with a campaign to take it by force, was in error. Thus, I left everyone to their dreams and illusions, and went out to explore this city that had been built by Alexander of Macedonia, this towering city, as towering as the heroes who once set foot upon its soil. I found its people to be strong, muscular, and tall of stature. They were of a complexion between olive-tinted and swarthy. They were almost uncovered but for some rags clothing their nakedness, with turbans upon their heads. They wore no socks nor shoes upon their feet, but walked barefoot and wild-haired. This was the poorest class of the people, working as farmers or day laborers hired by the Mamluks. The rich, on the other hand, wore loose pantaloons of silk, Moroccan slippers on their feet, large turbans gracing their heads. The men and boys of this class shaved their heads, only leaving a small tuft of hair at the top, explaining it away by saying that the Prophet Muhammad would come on the Judgment Day to pull them by this lock of hair up to Paradise. Sometimes I would see little girls and boys walking around completely naked, unable to find clothing to cover them. The houses, similarly, were no less destitute than those who inhabited them: they were mere huts of reeds, while the food they ate was one of two things—three at most—and after meals they hurried to drink coffee and smoke water pipes. Unfortunately, in this city embraced by the sea, whose soil had been trodden by the most powerful men, and where the greatest civilizations had sprung up, this city whose library had comprised the most important books and manuscripts and which I had hoped would yield happy hours to us—we could only find poverty and suffering.

The soldiers' dreams were scattered to the four winds. They began to mutter that the Maltese women, ugly as they had been, were goddesses compared to the Egyptian women. Still, for all that, I saw something else in these women, something unique. Perhaps it was the sorrow buried deep inside that showed in their eyes and made them more captivating.

In my walks along the winding paths, I found a café on a corner, only a few meters from the sea. It was a simple place, simple and unassuming like the city itself. I asked the waiter, who was glaring at me with ill-concealed dislike, for a cup of coffee. He shouted at me in a tongue I did not understand, but it was clear that he did not wish to serve me my coffee: he waved a hand at the sea, telling me to go and jump in the sea.

His treatment of me did not surprise me: it was only natural, for we were the invaders who had stormed their city and upset their lifestyle, and he couldn't have known or understood that it was no fault of mine, or that I had no weapon and was neither a fighter nor an invader. All I had come with was my palette and my brushes, no more. I was here by imperial command and I was nothing but a slave to my orders.

I was preparing to go when a voice came to me, as though it was pushing through the thick winds. "Wait, don't go!" It was the voice of an older man sitting close by me. He left his seat and came to sit at my table, then gestured to me to sit down and glared at the waiter. "Go and make us two cups of coffee," I understood him to say.

The man appeared to be wealthy, although his clothing was not like that of the other rich men. He wore a caftan of Indian cashmere, Muscovite slippers, and a white turban, which, along with his long white beard, gave him a reassuring air. He gave me a long look. "You seem different from them. Are you a warrior?"

"No. I am a painter. I'm here with the scientific expedition."

"Scientific expedition?"

"Yes. Napoleon brought a number of scientists and artists with him, for he plans to discover this country's hidden treasures, and he believes that he will lift this land up out of ignorance and poverty."

The man reached out a hand to shake mine and introduced himself. "I'm Antonio, a philosopher. I'm sorry to have to tell you that it's enough to get in the boat coming to invade Egypt to earn her people's hatred."

"I knew nothing of the military campaign. Napoleon concealed it from everyone. But even if I had known, I could not have disobeyed his orders—I would have been forced to come in any case."

The waiter brought two cups of coffee on a brass tray and slammed them down on the table, looking askance at me. I took a sip. It was sharp and bitter. I was as yet unused to the flavor of Arabian coffee, and almost spat it out, but managed to choke it down. Antonio chuckled. "You'll get used to it." He nodded. "Careful. It's addictive, and you may never want to stop."

I took another sip. This time, though, it tasted less bitter.

"But," he asked, "aren't you afraid of being murdered? You are walking through the city alone and unarmed." He went on, "Don't be too impressed by the reaction to Napoleon's speech: many people did not believe it, and only saw in it the words of an infidel invader with his army."

"I don't fear death," I said, "for it will come sooner or later. The idea of hiding and never venturing into this great city, a city I have heard so much about, would be foolish. I'm a painter, and I draw my inspiration from nature, from cities, from life."

"And has Alexandria inspired you?"

"Its natural beauty is breathtaking. But the people who live here are so unfortunate. The injustice they suffer, and the discrepancy between the lifestyles of the Mamluks and the sons and daughters of this great country, who live in poverty and hunger, all of this has shocked me, I cannot but confess."

"This city was a beacon of science and culture in bygone days," said Antonio. "It was enough for a man to say, 'I was educated in Alexandria.'"

I nodded, then ventured to ask him, "But your name and face are not Arab."

"I am originally from Rome," said Antonio. "An ancestor of mine moved here to study philosophy, astronomy, and mathematics under a famous scientist, and my family has lived here since then." He took a sip of coffee. "One of my ancestors was a librarian at the ancient Library of Alexandria, and his sons took up the profession after him, and so on, until it burned down."

The man kept talking without pause, then suddenly, as though he remembered something, he said, "Come, let me take you to my house."

I trusted his intent implicitly: his appearance and conversation evoked nothing suspicious; therefore, I accepted his invitation. He got on his mule and rented one for me; I followed him through paths, alleyways, and narrow passages. We went past markets rich in fruit and vegetables, and others filled with the smell of fish. We went by the houses of rich men whose windows were adorned with golden handles, and the reed huts of the poor. There were strange faces and diverse nationalities: Armenians, Maltese, Levantines, Italians, and Moroccans. There were women who went out with their faces bare and wafted the scent of perfume, others wrapped in fabric from head to toe, monks in black habits, and old men with white beards. It was a city teeming with life: every inch of it was an inspiration for some brilliant painting. All the way, the man never stopped talking. He was like a tourist guide or some dragoman, waving his hand toward this scene or another, although most of his words were carried away by the wind.

At last he turned his mule toward a quarter where the alleyways were locked up with great wooden gates: it was the Coptic quarter, with a large brass cross hanging on its gate. The inhabitants of this quarter were forced to live with a great many restrictions and prohibitions imposed by the Mamluks: no entry or exit without permission, no wearing certain clothing and certain colors, no riding mules in front of mosques, and so on.

The alleyway branched out into several narrow paths, paved with gravel. From behind the closed doors came the sounds and scents of their inhabitants. Antonio stopped outside a two-story house with a bleached wooden door. He cleared his throat loudly and clapped his hands twice, then invited me in.

Antonio's elderly wife came out to shake my hand. She smelled strongly of onions and spices. She smiled, chattering a great deal in Arabic. Her husband translated for me: she was telling him that dinner would be ready soon. He then took me up a wooden staircase whose creaking informed me that it was on its way to collapsing, and I crept up it with a good measure of trepidation. Upstairs, shelves of walnut—filled with books, magazines, and old papyri— lined the wide corridor. In a corner stood a chest of drawers with whatever secrets it held locked inside. The man gestured proudly at his library: "Here are the treasures of knowledge," he said. "Books on philosophy, medicine, mathematics, astronomy, astrology, magic, and chemistry. They are my inheritance from my ancestors. The city was invaded many times, and every time it was, the library was the first thing to be sacked by the invaders, and every conqueror's

first evil thought is to burn it to the ground. This library is every invad-
er's greatest enemy, because it comprises treasure troves of knowledge and
learning: it is the evidence of a wealth of civilization, and that is why he
wishes to destroy such minds, doing away with their civilization. That is
why invaders burn down libraries." He smiled proudly. "My ancestors
who worked in the Library of Alexandria transferred books secretly, by
night, helped by the people of the neighborhood, to protect them from the
hands of the conquerors. Because there are hundreds of thousands of
books, though, it was hard to transfer them all, but after the fire, the books
that survived were moved here."

I must admit to great shock. "What ignorant mind could burn such
priceless treasures?" I found myself asking. I approached the shelves and
began to look through them, book after book and volume after volume.
They were all in different languages and penned by different hands. There
were volumes of physics and chemistry, comprising complicated equations
and long formulae; volumes of astronomy filled with diagrams of the
sky, the stars, and heavenly bodies; books on the arts of architecture and
construction, mosaics, volumes of graceful Arabic calligraphy, and even a
manuscript painted and trimmed in pure gold lettering and another edged
and embroidered with smooth silk. I could scarcely find voice for aston-
ishment. "These really are treasures," I managed to say, "of knowledge
and the sciences."

By the light of flickering candles in a tarnished old silver candela-
brum, I took my time perusing one of the volumes. Antonio had clearly
read it so many times that he knew it by heart. It was a book entitled
Lives of the Most Excellent Painters, Sculptors, and Architects, *written by the world's most famous art historian, Giorgio Vasari.*

Eventually, dinner was served. When we had finished the delicious
meal that Antonio's wife had prepared, I made my excuses, for I had to
leave before dark. Antonio disappeared for a moment, then came back with
the priceless book and held it out to me. "A gift from me to you," he said.
"A beautiful book on the history of art." He smiled. "I think it will be
useful to you in your work."

I was speechless. It was the most precious gift I could ever have
wished for, and to have it given to me so freely! Because all the thanks in

the world would never express my gratitude for the man's favor in giving me such a book, I thought later of painting his portrait and having it sent to him. I bade him and his wife goodbye, the latter's face reddening in pleased embarrassment when I praised her cooking. "It is the most delicious meal I have ever had in my life," I said quite truthfully. I placed the book carefully in my coat, and the carter took me back whence I had come.

I went with a scientific expedition to the Citadel of Qaitbay. It is an ancient fortress that looks medieval in nature. The more I walked around there, the more I felt the magnificence of history. I could almost hear the hooves of the horses that had galloped over its gravel. There was also Pompey's Pillar, which reminded me of the pillar in the Place Vendôme in France. In the south was a towering obelisk, beside which lay another neglected on the ground. I sat upon it so as to feel humbled and small. One of the archaeologists told us that this had been the location of Cleopatra's palace—the woman who had captivated Marc Antony, the most powerful man in the world, and made him sacrifice his empire for her. Had he truly been that naïve? Or had she truly been that powerful? Or was it love, which works miracles?

One look around us was enough to affirm that we would never bring back to this people all of its bygone glories, or make all of its dreams come true.

Alexandria: July 1798

We were ordered to start moving again. The army separated into three directions: west, straight on to Damanhur, and the third along the coastline to Rosetta. I walked with one of the three divisions under the heat of the burning sun. We suffered terribly from heat, thirst, and lack of supplies. Many died. We lost one soldier after another. Finally, we arrived at Rosetta, and drank all the cold drinks we could lay our hands on, buying poor and overpriced wine from the Jewish distillers there. We rested and stored enough supplies to last us a while, then resumed our journey. And so it went, from place to place and battle to battle. We were not facing a single enemy, but three all at once: the Mamluks, the Bedouin, and the heat, the last of which was the cruelest.

We were forced to march over burning sands under the broiling sun, in addition to the privations of lack of food and water. Many soldiers despaired and fell ill, unable to bear it; suicide took several forms, and appeared to spread like a contagion. Many shot themselves. I saw with my own eyes two brothers taking hold of one another and casting themselves into the Nile. Everyone wished their suffering to end. Death, to them, was more merciful than fulfilling the orders of a mad general. One night, exhausted by heat and relentless fatigue, we threw ourselves down upon our packs, but no sooner had we fallen into sleep than we heard the familiar call, "To arms! To arms!" It was a massacre, a battle between us and the Mamluks. It ended quickly in our favor. Then we went on to Wardan, a region filled with watermelon patches, to which I owe my life along with the Nile, indeed, my life and that of the soldiers. This beautiful, moist, and delicious fruit quenched our thirst and made up for the weakness and frailty that had afflicted us. We not only ate our fill of it, but threw it at each other like cannonballs, laughing hysterically, for we had been close to death or insanity, and if not for this fruit, so like a ball, we would have perished for certain and been only bodies dead upon the road.

I sat upon a high rock, carving a piece of wood with a knife in the shape of an exhausted soldier. The news spread that the general had arrived to inspect the troops. I glimpsed him from afar, walking among the ranks of the exhausted soldiers overcome with despair. He could see it as well, and realized that he would not be able to accomplish his goal with things as they were. He walked among their ranks, speaking to them and conversing with each in turn, encouraging them with phrases such as, "Just a few more days and you shall find much of everything in the capital of Egypt! White bread, tender meats, and fine wines!" Napoleon's words worked like magic on the poor soldiers: no sooner had he spoken than they were filled with renewed life. I cannot overstate his confidence, and the ease with which he infused it into those around him. His boundless enthusiasm was infectious and impossible to escape, especially in these hard times: we were like drowning men clutching at any life raft.

18

Through the windowpane, she watched the rain, listening to the weather report on the radio. "Autumn has arrived," the newscaster proclaimed, "with scattered rainfall and chilly winds throughout the country."

She dressed and picked up her bag, bulging with papers. She said good morning to her grandmother, who was sitting in the hall wrapped in a woolen shawl, lips trembling as Fatima fed her yogurt. Watching the scene, she thought miserably of what makes a person what they are, and the stages of life. From a child being fed by its mother to a mother feeding her children to an old person being fed by their children, it was a continual cycle in which everyone played the same parts. The pathways of our life diverge and separate into passageways, but in the end we meet on the same road.

The ringing of her phone brought her out of her melancholic reverie, so like the autumnal weather today. His smile on her screen made her life cheerful once again. Of course she knew why he was calling so early in the morning: he was usually grumpy in the mornings and usually preferred to avoid talking to anyone right after waking up. He most probably wanted to apologize. She slyly let the phone ring and did not answer.

The window of her office on the ground floor overlooked the college garden. She had always hated offices with locked doors and windows, hermetically sealed away from everything that went on outside. For that reason, she was always careful to open the window and look out onto the world: the congregations and movements of the students, their liveliness and laughter, all of this inspired her and renewed her zest for life.

A knock on her window jolted her out of the grading she was engrossed in. She looked up and saw him waving to her from behind the glass. He traced out her name in the dust on the part of the window untouched by the rain and then, under it, "Miss You." Then he disappeared. She was filled with joy, and it made her confused. She fumbled for her hand mirror in her bag and glanced into it to make sure she looked all right. She put on some lipstick and perfume, and not a moment too soon, for in seconds he was standing there, handsome in a linen jacket the color of the sea and a white shirt with a button open, over which some of his chest hair pushed, like grass climbing the fences of his walled garden. She glimpsed that he was hiding a bouquet of lilies, which she loved, behind his back. "Thank you," she said with a smile when he gave them to her, found a vase, and started to arrange them. "Shall I order you some coffee?"

"It's two-thirty, which means it's lunchtime, not time for coffee. Let's eat."

"But . . ."

"But what? Let's not waste time. I only have two hours before I need to go to a meeting that will go on for several hours."

He took her by the hand and they walked side by side out of the college under the students' curious stares. They took his black luxury car and, with a fleeting glance at the man next to her, smartly dressed and elegant, she said, "I can't believe that the man sitting next to me is the same man who wears a skirt and headdress and spins around and around."

"That's when I shed my skin," he quirked a smile, "like a reptile. I take off these clothes and with them everything they represent, everything they are connected to. The Pierre Cardin and Rolex and Mercedes-Benz you see are only for appearance's sake, a social thing. I am only really me when I take off all this and find myself in that simple skirt: nothing is wider or more welcoming."

"But all these brands and this bling are the opposite of the simplicity you were talking about."

"Unfortunately," he said, "in this town, people judge you by appearances, and calculate your worth by these 'things.' If I had this position in Europe, I could have biked to work. Besides, simple doesn't mean tasteless. Or do you want me to live like a wandering dervish?" he chuckled. "In any case, it's not about what we wear, but what's in here." He placed a hand over his heart.

She was completely convinced. At her favorite restaurant on the Nile, the waiter gave them a corner table for two, with a white lace-edged tablecloth, a lit candle, and a bud vase with a single red rose. Moments passed in companionable silence, each of them looking at the view around them. The mood music was dreamy. Both of them felt at peace and a sense of calm stole over them in the cool breeze springing up from the river. More quietly, he apologized for what had happened the night before.

"I should be the one apologizing," she said. "I lost track of time completely. I had no clue that it was any time even close to three o'clock."

"What's the name of the site?" he said, unfolding his iPad. In a few minutes, he had opened her an account, allowing her to see the paintings behind the paywall. "But why this artist in particular?" he asked. "What's so special about him? Do you really think he's the one who painted that portrait?"

"I couldn't swear to it," she said, "but I definitely suspect it. My gut tells me it's him."

"How so?"

"Every artist has their own style," she explained, "like a fingerprint. Like your voice, or mine. You can recognize a person singing from the sound of their voice, and it's the same with painting, or sculpture. You can recognize an artist by their brushstrokes and style."

"It needs a lot of experience."

"Experience, and instinct, too," she explained. "You get it from years working in the field. This artist's style is the same as the one who painted the portrait. I get the same feelings and emotions from his work. The most important thing is what I call the artist's spirit, something that comes out of them and fills the painting. It's what makes each artwork different." She went on, "Some artists have the ability to put themselves into their work, and that makes it always feel like it's full of some sort of life."

Their waiter arrived with a smile. They had been so engrossed in conversation that they had not even thought to look at the menu. He quickly ordered a veal piccata with vegetables and she ordered an escalope: there was hardly any need to look at the menu, it had all the usual things.

"That man came to Egypt with Napoleon's campaign," she said, "and the dates of the paintings of his I found fit this theory."

"Is there any information on his visit to Egypt?"

"I'm trying to get more information on the paintings I found," she told him, "a painting of the mule market in Cairo, but I haven't found anything yet. Still," she mused, "the painting itself is enough. It was of two French soldiers getting on a pair of mules. They wore the French Campaign's uniform." She reached for his iPad. "I just remembered something."

The waiter arrived with their orders and put them on the table, but she didn't notice. The delicious aroma of the food went ignored. He tapped the edge of his fork against his plate. "Could you possibly see your way to leaving your research long enough to eat something?" he smiled.

"Of course." She smiled back and set the device aside.

"Do you know," he said, "I only have a good appetite when we're together?"

"Me too."

His phone rang and he put it on speaker. A mellifluous feminine voice came through. "Hi, how are you doing?"

"I'm good, and you?"

"I'm good as long as you're good."

He smiled. "Where are you now?"

"On my way to the office. I thought I'd come early so we could have a coffee and talk."

"I'm sorry, I'm having lunch out."

"I'll expect you then. Bye."

She watched him speak, trying to read in his face any feelings that would betray the nature of his relationship with this girl, but he put on a smooth smile that revealed nothing. He was clearly expecting her to ask him who the woman was, but she didn't. He answered the question she was thinking, but didn't ask. "Nirmine is a student in her final year of architecture school. She's doing her graduation project and needed some help. A relative of hers, a good friend of mine, asked me to help her."

"She seems very invested in her . . . project."

"Yes."

"Sometimes," she said, "I get students who are . . . enthusiastic about me, but it's just a crush. That's why I always advise them, and try to be kind to them."

He understood what she was getting at and said with a sly smile, "Usually we don't like a woman to be older or more experienced than a man, but it's different when it's the man who's older."

She averted her eyes, not wanting him to see that she was jealous, so she pretended to be engrossed in her food. They remained silent all the way back. He was thinking: did she have any right to be jealous, she who had once come to tell him straight out that there was another man? She was wondering: could he really be starting to fall for this girl? And if he did care for her, then why was he with her, Yasmine, now?

They arrived at her car. "See you later. Take care of yourself," he said with a smile. He watched her go in the rearview mirror. Her body was full and curvy, her buttocks high and round. Her intelligence and success only made her more attractive, a beauty in every sense of the word. She was the last person in the world he wanted to hurt, even peripherally. He loved her to his dying breath, and she remained within him. He would not deny that the young Nirmine piqued his interest, but it had nothing to do with love: his attraction to her was based on her enthusiasm for the work and her passion for life. Only Yasmine owned his heart, leaving no space, however small, for anyone else to take her place.

From the first day he had seen her, his feelings for her had not changed. When she had come to him that day, swaying confidently as she walked with the air of one who knows her own worth, tall and graceful, captivating in every sense, enveloped in a warm, mysterious perfume, he had been confused and flustered, which in itself had been exciting, alluring. He rarely felt that way toward any woman. A woman like this, natural in every sense of the word, was different from every other woman he had known in his previous life. She was frank and truthful, with no trace of pretension, her allure lying in her childlike simplicity. When they talked, she tilted her head back to toss a persistent lock of hair back that had a habit of falling into her face. He remembered wishing back then that he could reach out and push it away himself. It was a shock to him that he fell for her in this way.

Cairo: July 1798

Finally, we came to Cairo and the soldiers saw the great city on the banks of the Nile. They rushed to the water, desperate with thirst. We had known that the enemy held the keys to the Nile, and was lying in wait for us on either side: but thirst, heat, and exhaustion made us mad. No sooner did the enemy glimpse the soldiers drinking, bathing, swimming, and splashing themselves with water, than they beat the drums of war.

They beat the drums seven times: the city itself seemed to vibrate and our hearts trembled along with it in fear.

Suddenly, the Egyptian people all seemed to have turned into soldiers defending their land, all unskilled in the arts of war as they were. The pashas had saddled their steeds and rode in on them; the tradesmen bore arms; the gardeners, bakers, painters, carpenters, tanners, grocers, builders, teachers, salesmen all, all, came out to fight. We found ourselves face to face with a mass of humanity of every stripe and color, their cries filling the place. The sunlight reflecting off the Mamluks' weaponry and clothing blinded us. Everyone attacked us, calling out "Allahu akbar!" which means "Glory to God!"

A mounted division galloped toward us, and their leader, Murad Bey, attacked us, followed by his men. But our eagle-eyed artillery division was already upon them, and they fell with the first salvo. Many of them ran away, while others fell wounded. After a long and fierce battle that went on for hours and where many were killed and those who were not remained at death's door, General Bonaparte asked them to surrender and told them that they would be treated as prisoners of war: in other words, their lives would be spared and they would be treated with dignity. But they refused, and kept fighting.

I was close to the battle, with no choice but to watch helplessly. I was horrified by the sheer loss of life in what seemed like the blink of an eye. The battle finally over, it left behind decapitated heads, severed arms and legs, and a stench of gunpowder that stopped the noses of thousands, a cloud of black smoke belching up toward the sky and obscuring the eye of the sun.

The ground was littered with bodies, and a foul stench pervaded the place. The faint moans of the wounded filled the air, and owls hooted mournfully. Wherever you turned your eyes, you could see a horse tottering without a rider or a piece of wood burning. I was asked to draw the battle: I was certain that no matter how I tried, I would never be able to capture its thunderous roar or depict the scale of the destruction.

The battle had raged close to the Pyramids of Giza, next to which we stood like dwarves, asking ourselves, 'Will we be able to vanquish the descendants of the geniuses who built these towering monuments?' Our battle was not, in point of fact, with the descendants of the pharaohs, but with the alien invaders, the Mamluks. Still, the entire Egyptian populace, of every sect and division, came out to assist them. Everyone fought bravely to the best of their abilities, all untrained for war as they were. We crossed the Nile and arrived at the opposite bank after more hours of battle with the enemy, who was concentrated on the other side to defend Cairo. After some resistance, we entered Cairo, taking it and doing away with the rule of the Mamluks. When we came in, Napoleon, as was his habit, gave a speech to reassure the people of Egypt: but was the scene we had just left in our wake any cause for reassurance? Who could have possibly trusted him or believed him?

He stood upon a high hill, which made him appear small, and tried to combine harshness and leniency in his tones. "Let everyone who fears be calm. Let everyone who has left their homes return there. I have only come to free you from the line of the Mamluks. Hold your prayers as usual. Fear not for your homes, moneys, and women. Fear not for your religion," he said, "for which I have the greatest affection and respect."

Several people from the town gathered around him, and their voices rose in yells of both support and rejection. Those who had benefited from the Mamluks and their running of the country would have stood to gain from their continued rule, so they cried out in dissent, whereas those who hated the Mamluks cried out in welcome of Napoleon and his soldiers; there was a third class, one that had no power and held no sway, and all they wanted was to live in peace, to eat, drink, and sleep in safety. Despite the humiliations they endured under the rule of the Mamluks, they had been more merciful, or so they thought, than the cruel invader Napoleon. This third class constituted the vast majority of the populace.

The foreign community welcomed us: to them, we were saviors from the abuses of the ignorant Mamluk soldiers. At last, they could expect to be treated with humanity, after living under a list of prohibitions and regulations that seemed endless. Many of these joined the army, and some offered their services to the Campaign. To bear the title "a man of the Campaign," one had to perform many services, not least among which were spying and bringing news to Napoleon in exchange for full protection.

We despaired when we entered Cairo. Contrary to our expectations, the streets were narrow, the roadways unpaved, and lighting at night non-existent. Refuse and waste piled up in every corner, and most of the houses were mere dismal huts. When they collapsed, their inhabitants did not trouble themselves to rebuild them, merely building new ones in another location, and leaving the ruins of the old one to lie where they had fallen.

Wherever I walked, you could see the miseries of poverty and the opulence of wealth. It was enough to walk through the places the Mamluks had built for themselves by the Ezbekiya Lake, the opulent palatial mansions, and actual palaces with their walled gardens loud with the screeching of peacocks and the gobbling of turkeys. It was enough for a Mamluk to walk next to a common man in the street to see the injustice in the country by means of a speedy comparison between the two.

I have never been a supporter of this campaign. I believe that the army of a country had no business entering the land of another country without good and just reason, or else it was merely opportunism of the basest kind. But the discrepancy between the Mamluks and the common people in every possible thing made me angry. The beys of the Mamluks were living a life of luxury, building palaces from the sweat and toil and moneys of the Egyptian people: they saddled their horses with gold and jewels, they wore silk shot through with gold and adorned with diamonds, they brandished the most modern weapons imported from London, and flashed around their Damascene shields encrusted with precious gems. Anyone could see the injustice under which the poor citizens were groaning from a single glance into the private gardens of the Mamluks, extending as far as the eye could see, filled with every bounty the earth had to offer, while the people could not find their daily bread.

Entertainment was limited to boating on the Nile, sitting in cafés to smoke water pipes and chat, and the soldiers' and officers' only pleasure was riding the mules that ran like the wind. It was a common matter, then, to see the officers and their solders galloping at top speed through the narrow streets, amid the stares and questioning glances of the passersby. But the worst of it, the worst blow to the soldiers' hopes and expectations, were the women of Egypt, of whom they had painted wondrous mental pictures of beauty and coquetry—hopes that were dashed when they encountered reality. The women in this country are of two types: respectable harem women and wives, whom no eye may see: they pass by you in a flash, concealed under layers of clothing in mule- or horse-drawn carts. The second type are prostitutes and belly dancers who can be seen in their revealing clothing in alleys and cafés all over. They have lost whatever lissome litheness they may have once had, and have a vulgar and common manner; they harass and pester you so badly that it is best to stay away from them.

During my wanderings, I discovered a small island between Cairo and Giza, called Roda. It is the island where the Nilometer rests. It is covered with many varieties of trees and plants of varying forms and colors, the perfume of which wafts over you from hundreds of meters away. To me, this island was the loveliest thing in all the city: I went there from time to time to take the air in its gardens, inhale the scent of flowers, and enjoy the refreshing breezes of the Nile, watching the boats that came and went bearing people from one shore to the other: tradesmen, older gentlemen, and laborers. The most beautiful of these boats were painted in gold, and these were private crafts whose owners engaged in a friendly rivalry as to who could build the most luxurious and eye-catching boat, and even encrusted them with gems and all manner of stones.

Cairo: July 1798

After we had been in Egypt for a short time, everything began to take on a French character. Restaurants and cafés sprang up serving French food and drink; the Jews and Greeks who manufactured wine and had sold alcoholic drinks in secret now hung out shingles in French and Arabic announcing that they served alcohol. The streets of Cairo acquired a distinctly Parisian aspect: not only because of the new cleanliness and order which Napoleon had been careful to impose since his arrival, but due to the names of the stores that were now written in French. The goods in the stores were now imported from Spain, France, and Italy, and it was now a simple matter to find a store selling French hats and perfumes.

My presence in this country was different from that of the other men of the Campaign, who cared only for fulfilling the general's commands, whatever they were. They fought and battled with great gusto, despite their differing beliefs, mobilized by a single idea: everything they were doing, they were certain, was a national duty. As for me, I was certain that Napoleon was in Egypt out of greed, wishing to build a French empire in the East, making him the Emperor of the East and West. Egypt had been chosen by him for its strategic location and its many natural resources, and more importantly, the weakness of its ruling class. Since he could not rule over a mere substratum of ignorant riffraff, he had brought with him scientists, architects, engineers, experts, doctors, and artists of every stripe, to beautify this new empire and make it worthy of his name and status when he finally appointed himself proud emperor of all he surveyed. To achieve this end, he cared nothing for the wives he had widowed, the children he had orphaned, or the households that were now in mourning.

While the men of the Scientific Campaign were pursuing their research and discovery day and night, I went out to explore the world living around me. I wanted to see behind these smiling faces, accepting the fate that befell them and theirs. Day and night, their bathhouses were filled with men and women, their cafés were filled with patrons, their Nile was filled with flowing water. I walked through the narrow alleyways, from place to place and path to path, drawing faces, customs, manners. Little girls playing primitive games; little boys wrapping turbans that looked too large for their emaciated bodies around their heads in imitation of their elders; I walked through the markets glutted with goods, where the tradesmen laid out their wares to dazzle the eyes of the customers and lure them to stop to test the quality of a fabric or the strength of a carpet. The tradesmen's voices rose up in organized song, at the sound of which a customer could not but stop and buy.

The more I walked, the more the various aromas assaulted my nose, smells that filled the streets: the scents of spices, fresh fruit, delicious sweetmeats, grilled meats, and fried fish. Tables were spread out outside the doors of restaurants with cane chairs set at them and bolsters stuffed with straw; and the cooks, in embellished costumes and mighty turbans, their great paunches extending what seemed like meters before them, offering the delicious dishes prepared by their own hands. "We have the most delicious food you ever tasted!" they boast. Whenever the smell tempted me, I would go into a restaurant and sit there to watch the street bustle all around me. Once, opposite a restaurant, I found a café with a group of men sitting and smoking water pipes and playing cards. Another time, I saw a camel burdened with a heavy load, who almost ran over a small boy hanging onto the hem of his mother's gallabiya: the woman screamed at the camel driver and a fight ensued, whereupon people gathered around them and separated them, each eventually going their way and smiles once again winning the day.

This is life in Cairo: it has a magical side that enchants me and makes me want to leave everything behind and go out to draw and paint. What is war and conquest to me? This man who has appointed himself a god wishes me to paint them and him, in battle on his horse. I cannot. I can only paint and draw that which tempts me, and I have never felt life batter at my defenses and push me bodily toward my easel as I do in this life here today, among the Egyptians, this strange people who, in spite of everything, find small ways to celebrate and to smile.

My stay in this country has forced me to live as its people do. I follow their customs and manners and respect them so that I can live in peace among them and get to know them better, in hopes that they may accept me. But I have set limits to this: I do not chase after their world like General Jacques-François Menou, who changed his religion and married a woman of Egypt, had himself circumcised and put on a gallabiya and turban. Did Menou convert to Islam out of conviction? Or was it his love for Zubayda that made him do so?

Without warning, the image of Zeinab came to my mind, and her smile, radiant like the sun, was there, pushing away the darkness of my life and spreading light in its stead. Her smile grew broader, dimpling deeper and deeper. My heart beat faster with my love for her. It started with light beats, then grew stronger and stronger still, until it crashed through the doors of my heart, and she burst in and is now seated on the throne. Yes, I am in love with this girl; I will do anything to be close to her.

A noise roused me from my reverie. A group of people had gathered in a street around a conjurer doing tricks in a café. Their applause and cheering revealed the most common two types of people that one is likely to see in the streets and alleyways of Cairo: the water carrier and the carter.

Each of these has his own market, and a trading center with its own systems and rules. They are both extremely important for the Egyptians: water only comes with water carriers, who carry bags of deerskin upon their backs, and brass cups in their hands, their faces leathery from the sun and tanned to an attractive dark shade. Similarly, the only means of transportation are mules and donkeys.

I must confess that these scenes gave me the energy that brought me back to life: I go back to my studio filled with renewed passion to depict everything I have seen within the four corners of a painting. I painted a street scene, the mule market, and here I am, almost done with the painting of the water carrier. I painted him groaning under the weight of the bag upon his back, and in spite of the clear fatigue on his face that has been baked by the sun like a round of pita bread, he was smiling at the woman to whom he was giving his water.

19

Yasmine watched an episode of her grandmother's favorite Turkish soap opera with her that evening, to keep her company. The events of the soap were like a black-and-white movie whose story she had seen repeated scores of times and knew by heart, but she feigned surprise and amusement while the old woman laughed wholeheartedly or cried bitterly from scene to scene.

Eventually, her grandmother went to bed, and Yasmine made herself a cup of coffee to banish the sleepiness that weighed down her eyelids. Then she went online.

She was surprised that she had never made the acquaintance of Alton's work before, despite his skillful brush and varied subjects. "How did he get past me?" she murmured to herself. She had studied eighteenth-century painting and its most prominent artists and schools of painting. Why had his works never caught the eye of critics and historians? All his works were in private collections, it appeared, not exhibited in public; although his work was every bit the equal of the great masters she had encountered, this was the fate of paintings and artists: either to shine, or to live forever in obscurity.

Her eye was caught by a painting entitled *Battle of the Pyramids*. It was a scene of fighting between French and Egyptian forces in the desert beneath the Great Pyramid. No information about the work was available: again, only the name and the date.

She was examining a painting entitled *The Man of Life*, a portrait of a water carrier in the streets of Cairo, before water had been piped into homes and cities. The man seemed to bear the weight of countless years upon his back, and he wore a short *gallabiya*, breeches, and leather boots up to his knees. A woman was holding out a pot to him into which he was pouring water, and it was clear that they knew each other from their air of easy familiarity. They seemed deep in friendly conversation: his eyebrows were knitted together and his eyes widened in surprise, as though she had let him in on some secret. She scrutinized these details of the painting and felt she was part of the scene, standing between the pair and listening to their conversation, almost able to hear the man's gruff voice and smell the woman's perfume. She looked more closely at the woman: she was wearing a white *habara* veil and her face was covered with a silken scarf; only her wide black eyes showed. She looked deeper and deeper into those eyes: she knew them. "Oh!" she suddenly found herself crying out. "It's her! It's her! It's Zeinab!" Surely, this was the most powerful clue yet that this was the artist of her painting.

She wrapped up her research for the night, falling asleep overjoyed with this new lead.

The next morning she went straight to the office of Dr. Khalil, who welcomed her with a broad smile, as was his habit. "Good morning!" he said warmly. "I sense something important behind this visit."

"Yes," she smiled, "there is." She told him about the art site and the painting she had found online the day before, and the resemblance between Zeinab in the water carrier painting and the other one, and handed over her iPad to show him.

Khalil took his time examining and comparing the two paintings. "Yes," he said at long last, "there is a strong resemblance, particularly around the eyes. But we can't say for certain that it's the same girl. The veil covers part of her eyes, and you can barely make out one of the irises."

"The irises are the eyes."

"Wait," he said. He connected the iPad to his printer and printed out the painting of Zeinab. With a pencil, he sketched out a veil covering the girl's face. When he was done, he returned to the other painting, comparing his copy with the penciled-in veil with the painting on the screen. He looked from one to the other, expressions of surprise and perplexity chasing one another across his face. "Yes," he admitted finally, "there is a strong resemblance. Still, I couldn't say for certain that it is the same person."

Although the picture of Zeinab in her newly acquired veil did resemble the woman in the painting, Dr. Khalil had not positively confirmed it. Still, that did not sway her from her task: she knew what Khalil was like, a meticulous art historian who would not say anything for certain unless he had proof positive in his hand. When something was *almost* certain, he would never lean one way or the other, which was just how he was in his profession. "Thank you," she said sincerely. "I've got to get to class."

She was distracted, and her students noticed. They exchanged glances and smiles, especially when she misspoke and said an artist's name wrong, then caught herself with an apology, only to make the same mistake once more. *Heavens, what's wrong with me?* she thought to herself. *I've got to get my head in order.* On the way home, a horn blaring from the car behind her prodded her to notice that the light had turned green and the cars had started to move, while she was still lost in thought.

Cairo: December 1798

"Who are you?"

"I am Zeinab."

"Yes? And who's Zeinab?"

The woman spoke with a haughty air, looking at the girl with derision. "I am Zeinab," the girl replied, "the daughter of Sheikh Khalil al-Bakri."

The woman snorted. "And is this any way for the daughter of a sheikh to dress?"

Zeinab had no idea how she was supposed to respond. She had no experience with the slyness and cunning that some women possess. She merely lowered her head without a word.

"But tell me," the woman said, "why are you here?"

"The general sent for me."

"The general? Which general?"

"Bonaparte."

The woman pointed at her as though she was an insect. "You? Bonaparte sent for you to come here?" Then she burst into gales of laughter.

Nearby, Rostom was standing and watching what was going on between them. He approached them. "The general invited her," he snapped at the woman, "and is awaiting her in his private suite."

Zeinab noticed that Rostom was greatly changed from the way he had looked when he used to work for them. He was more elegantly attired, positively glowing in an embroidered jacket adorned with gold and diamonds, his gem-encrusted Damascene sword hanging at his waist, a dagger in his jacket pocket. Clearly, he was now a man of some standing in this palace, for the woman fell silent at once and obeyed his command without a word. Rostom's words, which had silenced her, bore the hidden meaning: 'Don't interfere in matters which are none of your business.' Her face darkened and filled with disgruntlement and jealousy, twisting her attractive features.

Rostom took Zeinab by the hand and took her up to Bonaparte's suite. He whispered to her, "Take care. He loves to pinch ears until they redden." Spontaneously, she found her hands rising to her ears, but she thought, *If it's only ear pinching he wants, that's safe enough.*

This time was different from the previous one. She was clearly unhappy and preoccupied; after all, she was in love now, and her heart beat for another man. She had realized now that the heart meant more than all the gold medals that glittered on Bonaparte's military tunic, more than the feather on his tricorne. She stood at the door of the room, transfixed, thinking. What if he touched her, or kissed her, or asked her to share his bed? What could she do in that case? So many thoughts burned through her young head. Could she push him away? Run? Cry? Scream? What could she do, powerless as she was? Perhaps he would let her go if she told him that his touching her was a sin in her religion, punishable by stoning to death.

He was sitting in his chair, his legs extended in front of him, propped on the chair opposite. Rostom approached him and bent to whisper into his ear. Bonaparte nodded and commanded him to leave. Alone with her, he looked thoughtfully at her for a while. His eyes appeared filled with thought, and his visage was dark. In a tone filled with guilt and blame he asked her, "Are you telling anyone of what goes on between us?"

She shook her head violently. He could barely make out her "No."

"Do you believe it yourself?" he asked. "What goes on between us?" He went on staring at her. "Have you ever asked yourself why you are here, for instance?"

"No."

He rose languidly, walking toward the bed and sitting on the edge. He motioned to her to come over. With halting steps she came and sat next to him. When she looked down, he took her by the chin and lifted her head, forcing her to look at him. "I like the way you smell," he said. "It is a smell that owes nothing to perfumes; it is the smell of nature." He thought deeply, then went on in a near-whisper, as though talking to himself, "The soil after rain. Fresh-cut grass. Seaweed on the shore at night." Drawing closer to her, he added, "I hope that time never changes it. Time never lets anything alone."

His voice changed, his face overcome with some sadness, a veil falling over his eyes all of a sudden. He bolted up, and began pacing to and fro across the room. "Would you believe me if I told you," he said, "that my schoolmates made fun of me? Some of them even called me 'Old Saggy-Stockings.' Others called me 'Corsican,' because I originally come from that island. They mocked me because my French had an Italian accent. It showed as soon as I opened my mouth." He paced back again. "That was why I abandoned everyone, all friends, always alone, with only books for company. When I entered military school at eleven years old, I was the only student who spent all his free time in the library, reading books on history and battles. I saw myself in every hero." He came to a stop at the window. Standing silhouetted in it with his back to her, hands clasped behind his back, he continued his monologue. "Do you know the real reason I came here?" he asked. "It's Alexander the Great. He made himself an empire and established his awe-inspiring rule in this part of the world. This is a land that makes heroes of men, and makes heroes immortal. The mighty pharaohs are looking down upon us now, to see what we shall make of their land. They cheered when we arrived to rid their descendants of poverty and backwardness, and the reign of the Mamluks." His voice softened. "Do you know? I wept when the Sphinx's nose was broken off. We came here to build a civilization, not to destroy it." His next words were barely audible. "But was there not some moral to the breaking of his nose? It might be a good omen, indicating that this land and its people, with its blessings and its beauty and its ugliness, too, would be putty in our hands, and that I was to become the Emperor of East and West."

He clenched his fist hard. His voice changed and became harder. She trembled in fear of him. It was the first time she had seen him like this. Half-turning, he noticed the fear on her face, and approached her, sitting next to her. With the back of his hand, he lightly touched her cheek. "Fear not," he whispered. "You are a descendant of Cleopatra. Shall a woman descended from Cleopatra know fear, when her ancestor made the greatest and most powerful men slaves to her love, her beauty, and her flirtations? With her brilliance, she made the greatest man in history offer her his reign on a silver platter." He smiled. "Cleopatra vanquished Antony with the power of her beauty and charm, which is a power before which the greatest of military schemes and the most modern war machines all fall useless." His voice seemed to fill with passion as he said, "Can you do to me what your ancestor did to Antony? She made him fall in love with her. Do you know that she used to dance for him?"

He took her hand and drew her up slowly. "Come. Dance for me as Cleopatra danced for Antony."

Zeinab, who had no idea who Cleopatra or Antony were, nor any clue what this man was talking about, slowly took off her shawl and wrapped it around her waist as the belly dancers did. Then she swayed to the tunes of a melody she conjured from memory in her own head. She raised her arms aloft, then brought them down; she took a step forward, and another back, then swayed her slender hips and thin body; then she spun, and spun, and spun.

"Stop!"

He approached her. He undid her braids and spread out her black hair over her shoulders and back. It was like a shawl all around her. Then he undid the ties of her dress. It slipped off her onto the floor, leaving her in only her shift. "Don't tie up your hair," he said. "I like it like this, down your back. Go on," he said, taking his seat back on the chair, putting his feet up on the table in front of him. His eyes narrowed as he stared at her.

She pointed her toes a little and shook her shoulders and hips as she swayed. She turned in circles and her hair swirled around with her, images and faces chasing each other in her imagination. The look of sorrow and reproach in her mother's eyes; the worry in Alton's eyes; the pride in her father's eyes; the prying eyes of the neighbors, their fingers all pointing at her, and their mutterings tearing her virtue apart. "Look at the debauched daughter of Sheikh al-Bakri, look what she does!"

Time passed and she began to tire, beads of sweat gleaming on her golden skin. She did not stop. She whirled and whirled, the faces in her imagination whirling along with her. The whispers grew louder and louder in her ears. Unable to stand them any more, she raised her hands to her ears with a cry, then flung herself down on the bed.

When she awoke, she was alone in the room, darkened but for the dim glow of a single candle. It was a while before she could remember where she was. She hurriedly yanked on her dress, fixed her hair, and put her shawl back around her shoulders. When she made to go out, she found Rostom outside, guarding her. He examined her with narrowed eyes, like a fox, seemingly seeking out traces of Bonaparte on her body. But all he saw was a frightened, confused, flustered little girl. "The general left," he said. "He gave orders that we were not to wake you or disturb your sleep."

She tried to remember details of what had happened. She remembered being exhausted and flinging herself down on the bed. Clearly, once the show was over, Napoleon had left the room to see to his own affairs, letting her sleep undisturbed.

In the entrance hall, several men were sitting with the woman who had opened the door, who was now looking at her with envy and disdain. The men ignored her, engrossed in their own conversation, except for one whose expression betrayed astonishment and curiosity.

She burst out of the palace, running through the garden. Alton—for it had been he—caught up with her, reaching out to catch her by the shoulder, whispering, "Zeinab! Zeinab!"

Rostom stood at the gateway to the garden watching what happened. Although she tried to smile, he only saw unshed tears and grief in her eyes. "Meet me at five o'clock in the same place, in the garden," he said. She merely nodded; she had no voice to answer him. Questions crowded insistently in her mind: why did she feel such a strong distaste for Napoleon now, when a few days ago she had been in transports of joy because he had chosen her above everyone? Why did she feel so shamed and disgraced? No, it was not only because of Alton and her feelings toward him; she was now aware that she was committing a crime against herself, her religion, and her society. The last of these would never forgive her.

She asked the carter to take her to Harat al-Qassaseen, the Dressmaker's Alley. There, she knocked on the door of Auntie Tafida, who made her clothes. The woman welcomed her warmly, although her eyes held the question, *What brings you here?* Tafida cleared a space for her to sit down among the piles of fabric and thread, and insisted on serving her lunch—which was strange, because Tafida was known for being tight-fisted. "No, thank you," Zeinab excused herself, "I'm really not hungry. Have you finished the dress you're making for me yet?"

The woman slyly eyed the French gown Zeinab was wearing, crafted in taffeta and organza. "And will you really wear that *gallabiya* made of cotton," she said, "after these gowns? I know you're a fine lady now who only wears the clothing of the Franks! I hear you speak their language and act like them."

Why should Zeinab even try to defend herself? It was the truth. She wore their clothing, but did she really act like them? She let the woman chatter on as she pleased, and when she finished, she asked her for a glass of water. The woman waddled off, and quickly and with some sleight of hand, Zeinab stole the scissors the woman used for cutting fabric and concealed them beneath her clothing.

The woman arrived with a brass cup. She waited until Zeinab had slaked her thirst and then asked, "Do you think you could ask the general to give my son Hassan a job? I heard that the men who become soldiers earn a good salary and that's besides the generous gifts."

Zeinab left, now knowing the source of this woman's uncharacteristic generosity, and also knowing that there was not a single household in the land of Egypt that did not know of her dalliance with the general. It was enough that it was known by this gossip of a seamstress who knew everyone and went into everyone's household.

It was still early for her meeting with Alton. She didn't want to go home; she didn't need her mother's interrogation. The strange thing was that her mother blamed her, knowing full well that it was General Bonaparte who had taken a shine to Zeinab, and it was by his imperial command that she went, something no one could refuse. To say no to the general was to be imprisoned in a dark dungeon or even killed.

Zeinab sat underneath the trailing branches of the willow that hid her from prying eyes. She unbound her hair and began to cut it off, weeping quietly. Lock after lock of hair fell off, until it barely covered her neck. She collected her shorn locks and bundled them up into her shawl. She embraced the shawl, curled up into herself around it, and wept.

She didn't see him arrive; he found her lying on the bench. With a start, shamefacedly straightening up, she stammered, "How long have you been here?"

"Zeinab! What have you done to your hair?"

He approached her and pulled her into an embrace, patting her back comfortingly. "Calm yourself, my dear. Why all this?"

"I got rid of it so Bonaparte wouldn't touch it again. I hate when he touches me. I hate the way people look at me, and their gossiping about me." She choked. "He told me to wear my hair loose always because he prefers it so. So I got rid of it. Maybe he won't want to see me again."

With deep suspicion, Alton asked, "Did he . . . do anything to you?"

"No. On the contrary. Today he was a different person. He told me about his unhappy childhood, then asked me to dance for him. He left me all alone. But I'm afraid he will want more from me, and I won't be able to say no."

He patted her small shoulder. "That man doesn't like to be opposed. With what you've done, he will only grow more attached to you."

They fell silent for a while.

"What do you plan to do?" she asked. "Will you stay in Egypt or go home to your own country?"

Her question surprised him. "I . . . haven't decided," he said. "But I can't live in a country whose people hate me with such a passion." He sighed. "To them, I am nothing but a French invader, here to kill innocents. They will never believe anything else of me, even if I tell them that my being here is all a mistake."

"It wasn't a mistake," Zeinab whispered. "It was fate that sent you here, to me."

He enfolded her hand in both of his. It calmed her and filled her with a sense of peace.

"But who was that woman you were sitting with in the hallway?"

"It was Madame Pauline Fauré. She is beautiful, but arrogant." Sensing that she was jealous, Alton added, "But you are the loveliest woman in the world in the eyes of my heart."

20

Madame Pauline Fauré, Yasmine read, had been an attractive Italian woman, the wife of Lt. Fauré, with blue eyes and blond hair, who had disguised herself in her husband's military attire so as to come with him to Egypt: there were no women allowed on Napoleon's campaign ships, except for a few seamstresses and cooks. This was depicted in a painting entitled "The Scientists of the Expedition" of a number of men, Napoleon in the center of their little group, and a woman among them. Was the artist in this painting, she wondered? She had found no trace of this artist, not even a self-portrait. She searched the names of the Campaign artists who had visited Egypt, but the long list of names held no Alton Germain among them. She found this unsettling: was he really one of the Campaign artists? His paintings documenting the French Campaign, its battles, and the Egyptian street did not constitute incontrovertible evidence that he had come to Egypt with the Campaign; there were many Orientalists and indeed artists who had created paintings of the Orient without ever having visited there. But then again, the painting of Zeinab and the date it had been created strongly suggested the artist's presence in Egypt at that time.

Before shutting down, she scanned her email: the only thing of note was an invitation to a conference held by the Association for Art History in France. *I'll have to email them back and tell them I'm too busy,* she thought.

As she was driving to work, a sudden impulse took hold of her. She turned in the opposite direction, heading for the headquarters of the French Campaign, Beit al-Sinnari, the place where Alton had lived when he was in Egypt. The secretary-general of the Institute had told her in her last visit that the painting had not been among the items damaged in the fire; indeed, it had not even been in the Institute, and the storehouse keeper had told her the same thing. The documents she had perused the day before had told her that the painting had come to the Conservation Department with the paintings damaged in the fire at the Institute, even though the damage to the painting had not been caused by the fire, but by improper storage. All the information led to a new theory: the painting had never left Beit al-Sinnari. It had been painted there and then hidden in a place where no one could find it. When the collection had been moved to the Institute's new location, it had remained in its hiding place, and when the Institute had caught fire, the collection had found its way back to Beit al-Sinnari, and somehow, at that point, the painting had been found, making everyone think that it was part of the Institute's collection. They had then sent it to be conserved.

"Welcome back," said the security guard who had first met her at Beit al-Sinnari a few days ago.

"I'd like to meet the curator of Beit al-Sinnari's collection," she said.

The man led her to a long corridor ending in an office. After several knocks on the door, a weak voice quavered from behind the solid wood, "Come in!"

Although the sun was shining brilliantly outdoors, the place was dark and damp. "Good morning," the man cheerily greeted her. His face was so lined and wrinkled that she could not properly tell his age. He was sitting at a desk surrounded by a huge collection of large, ancient volumes, and peered at her from behind thick spectacles. "Welcome, I'm sure. Are you from a newspaper?"

"No, I'm not. I'm conserving a portrait that was damaged in the fire at the Scientific Institute, and was moved here with the Institute's collection, then was sent to my university's conservation department—that's where I come in—but what was strange about it was that the director of the Institute said it wasn't part of their collection, and in fact no one seems to have ever seen it before." She went on, "So, I suspect that this work may never have left this location, not since it was occupied by the scientists of the French Campaign."

"Well," he said, "this house was, indeed, their base of operations. I've been in charge here for a long time, and I know pretty much everything about it. Which painting are you talking about?"

"It's a painting of a girl in a striped *gallabiya*, with her hair in two braids." His eyes narrowed and he appeared lost in thought. "Wait," she said, "I'll show it to you." She held out her iPad so that he could see it clearly.

He peered at it for a time, then shook his head. "No. I don't remember seeing it."

"Perhaps," she suggested, "it was in storage and just wasn't noticed."

He shrugged. "It's very possible. There's something strange about this house. The spirits of everyone who has lived here before inhabit it."

"How so?"

The man reached under the wooden desk at which he sat, taking out a tray with coffee-making paraphernalia on it: a small butane stove, a jar of coffee, and another of sugar. He began to prepare coffee slowly and carefully, as though everything in the outside world had ceased to matter as long as he was making coffee. "I'll make us coffee," he said, "and we can talk." Without asking her how she took her coffee, he spooned it in and stirred it slowly and patiently with a long gilt-handled spoon. It was only seconds before the delicious aroma of coffee spread through the room, clearly firing up his memory and preparing him to tell his tale.

"This house," he explained, "was built by Ibrahim Katkhudha, whom they called Ibrahim al-Sinnari, in a reference to his home town of Sinnar in the region of Dunqula in Sudan. He was a Berber who left his city and came to Cairo after first living in Mansura. He had worked as a night watchman in that city, and learned how to read and write. He read a great many books of magic and astrology, until he became quite the authority and acquired a bit of fame. He went to Upper Egypt after that, and worked with Mustafa Bey al-Kabir. By then, he had learned Turkish and was famous and rich as well. After that, he came to Cairo and built this house. They say it was one of the most attractive houses of the era. To tell the truth, it is still worthy of that reputation today. They say that he went to Alexandria to attend an important meeting held by an Ottoman prince called Hussein Pasha and a group of the most important Mamluks, on the seventeenth of the Islamic month of Jamadi al-Akhar, in 1801, and they were all murdered."

"So what you're saying," she said, "is that he was murdered in 1801, after the French Campaign left Egypt." She rubbed her chin. "How did it come about that the Campaign took his house as a base of operations?"

"It is said," he replied, "that he was thrown out of his house by order of the French, who took it over; there are rumors that he escaped to Upper Egypt with the other Mamluks." He took a deep draft of his coffee. "What do you expect of a historic house whose owner used to be an astrologer and a fortune teller, and carried out his experiments here?" He smiled. "I promise you, when I'm in here I find myself living in another world, a different one—the world of the Unseen. I often see Ibrahim al-Sinnari, who owned the house, a man with black skin and broad shoulders, in his white *gallabiya* and his turban upon his head, with a long string of ninety-nine prayer beads, wearing yellow slippers curled up at the toes, walking slowly around the house, looking left and right as though he's checking up on the place and making sure it's all right, or looking for something. Sometimes he ignores me, and other times he smiles at me and keeps right on going." He shook his head. "I also see the members of the French Campaign walking around, in their foreign suits and chattering in French. One of them has one leg and walks with a crutch. There's a blue-eyed, blond woman with them, her hair down her back, wearing clothing so diaphanous that it makes me feel ashamed—I have to look down and say 'Cover yourself, woman!' and all she does is give me a coy laugh and then she goes on her way."

By now, Yasmine was all but staring, in open-mouthed surprise, which he noticed.

"That's not all. Often I will hear noises: music and singing, giggles and laughter, and champagne corks popping and the clinking of glasses. I go out to see what's going on, but I can't see anything, and the sounds stop as if they'd never been there—but when I go back to my desk, it starts up again." He shook his head. "It's not only the spirits of the French folk that haunt this place: there are Mamluks and Ethiopian slaves, servants, and guards of the house. I see everyone in their different clothes, and I hear them chattering in different languages."

"Ah," she nodded sagely, thinking to herself that this man was definitely losing his marbles. He was certainly old enough. But then, what about Caffarelli and Pauline, whom he had described with great accuracy? "What of the spirit of this girl in the painting?" she found herself asking. "Haven't you seen her pass by as well?"

The man seemed to sense the hint of disbelief in her tone. "You're making fun of me, aren't you," he said calmly. It was not a question. "I swear to you that this house is inhabited by the spirits and shades of everyone who once lived here, as if there's something about it that makes them reluctant to leave it."

"Can I visit the storage room?" she blurted out.

"Yes," he nodded, "of course."

He opened a drawer and took out a round keychain with a disc hanging from it, crammed with brass keys. "I can't believe it," Yasmine couldn't help saying. "This is your security system? In this day and age?"

"And why not?" he replied calmly, rising and starting to head out of the room. His back was bowed and he shuffled slowly on his way, feeling his way with each step so as not to slip.

Yasmine followed. "There are newer ways of keeping things safe: self-closing doors with programmed keys and passcodes or fingerprint locks." He chuckled to himself, walking a few steps ahead of her. At the end of the corridor was a door to the left; it opened onto a passageway that ended in a spiral staircase. She followed him down to another old wooden door, which creaked in a series of staccato bursts when he pushed it open.

The storage room took up the entire cellar of the house, equal in area to the size of the structure above it. She noticed immediately that it felt cold, damp, and musty, with no ventilation or sunlight: this could be the source of the damage that had befallen the painting, especially if it had been stored in here all this time. The smell of the canvas that the portrait had been painted on was saturated with the smell of this place, already familiar to Yasmine.

"No ventilation at all down here?" she asked.

"This is the cellar or the shelter," he said, "designed to be used in times of danger. The scientists of the Campaign used it to safeguard their secrets and important discoveries, especially after the Revolt of Cairo in 1798, when the people stormed the homes of the French and attacked them and burned them to the ground, destroying what was inside."

Yasmine nodded thoughtfully. "What about the damaged pieces in the Institute's collection? Were they put in here as well?"

"Yes, they were kept here temporarily under great secrecy, but now they've been sent away to the labs to be conserved."

Everything the man said indicated that the artist had used this shelter to hide his painting away to keep it safe from theft or damage. Yasmine paced slowly around, taking the place in, now looking at it as a researcher, now as a detective, which was, after all, what she had become since she had found the painting. Several closets and cubby holes, she noticed, lined the walls, perhaps built to store papers and tools. The warping and creases in the canvas in her possession indicated that it had been folded up. The artist must have shoved it into one of these, perhaps hiding it under a table or similar, and it had only come to light when the storage shelter was combed meticulously to move the damaged works to a restoration center. "Everything indicates," she whispered to herself with a new certainty, "the painting never left this room since he painted it."

She left, happy in her new discovery; she was convinced now that the artist who had painted the portrait was indeed part of the French Campaign and that he had lived and worked here. And if he was one of the Campaign artists, the other works she had tracked down would have been painted while he was stationed in Egypt.

She arrived home filled with energy from her discoveries. "Hello, Grandma!" she sang out.

Her grandmother did not return her enthusiastic greeting.

"What's wrong, Grandma?" Her grandmother often took to childishly pouting when something upset her. Yasmine was aware of why she was upset. "Look, I'm sorry. I'm just very busy with something these days. There are . . . problems I need to solve. But don't worry, I'm nearly done with them and I'll be free to spend time with you again."

"I don't want you to be free to spend time with me. You hardly talk to me. I sit alone all the time with nothing but the walls for company."

"How can you say that, Grandma? What happened to all your relatives, your family, your friends you talk to for hours?"

The woman looked away. "They're busy too."

She knew she wasn't spending enough time with her grandmother, the old woman who was as dependent on her as a small child. What would she do about her, she wondered, if she married?

Married? She rolled the word around in her head. Why had she not been preoccupied with marriage like every other girl she knew? She had never felt the ticking clock or nagging thought of marriage, although she was past thirty. Had she devoted herself to her studies and research without noticing her life slipping past? She knew that her mother's suicide had made her despise the social construct known as marriage: it was a cheating husband that had driven her to kill herself. This was at least part of the reason why she had commitment issues with Sherif, running away the minute she got close. She had never daydreamed of her wedding day, or thought what her wedding gown might look like; she had never looked at bedroom sets or children's rooms in stores and thought of them one day being hers. And when she went to a wedding, she had never jostled with the other girls to catch the bride's bouquet.

She unclipped her hair, put on her pajamas, and flung herself, exhausted, onto the bed. She suddenly thought of the man she had met today and what he had said about ghosts and spirits in Beit al-Sinnari. She smiled, then fell into a deep sleep.

Cairo: November 1798

On my way home, I carefully carried the bag she left in my care before leaving the garden with entreaties to take good care of it. I am now certain of her feelings for me: she sacrificed her crowning glory so that it might not be touched by another man. This young girl possesses enviable courage. She did it without fear of Bonaparte, the man feared by the strongest men. I shall never abandon Zeinab.

Gaspard Monge, the head of the artists, spied me straight upon my entrance through the door. He instructed me to draw the house in which we live. It is to be documented in the great volume being completed by the scientists of the Expedition, to be entitled The Description of Egypt.

The house is designed in a style which displays these people's uniqueness in their Islamic architecture. Despite the ubiquitous ignorance and poverty, there are clear glimmerings of their keen intelligence and artistic sensibility, although this intelligence, sadly, lies fallow, without proper direction.

I sat down to draw the plot, some 1150 square meters in size, with 810 of those occupied by buildings, in addition to a garden some 345 square meters in area. This is the house where I roam freely, seeing splendor to rival the palaces of Paris, but with a unique Oriental aura. It is composed of a ground floor and two upper stories; it may be divided into five main parts. First, there is the entrance; then there is the part devoted to movement and communications; there is a service area; there is an area devoted to the reception of guests; and finally, a women's quarters. The house has one façade, which is the north side, looking onto the north. There are three courtyards in the house: one for the entrance, one private for the womenfolk, and an internal courtyard annexed to the service areas.

What inspires sorrow is that this house was forcibly rid of its inhabitants that they might be replaced by the Sciences and Arts Committee. Although this permitted me the luxury of inhabiting this splendid place, I cannot but grieve for them. It is certain that whoever constructed a place of such beauty to live in would be stricken to be expelled from it and for others to be brought in to take their place. This is more true for the fact that we have changed some features of the house: we have taken over the women's quarters as our painting studio, and the storehouse for foodstuffs and clothing has become the place where we store our equipment. This is not the only structure that we have documented in The Description of Egypt: *we have documented a goodly number of buildings, including Beit Hassan al-Kashef and Beit al-Alfi, Bonaparte's headquarters. Of all these, though, Beit al-Sinnari is by far the loveliest.*

Day after day, meetings and celebrations are held at the seat of Bonaparte's reign for the leaders and scientists of his campaign, but I make my excuses and refrain from attending. I take more pleasure in going out and walking around this place, looking at faces and learning about the different trades. These smiling, content faces that make haste to assist you, I say, for I frequently take a wrong turn on my return journey due to the narrowness of the alleyways and passages and the fact that they looked all similar, but no sooner do I ask for directions than I have a volunteer to convey me to my destination, despite the fact that my language and my features indicate that I am a Frenchman, and they hate with a passion all that is French. Still, this never impedes them from assisting me, and this odd nature of people has enamored me of them. I admired their determination to defend their homeland, for all Bonaparte's efforts to ingratiate himself. He knows full well in what high esteem they hold their faith, and his speeches glorify their religion, its prophet, and its rituals. Even Zeinab, an innocent girl, was not taken in by him; she was not enamored of his uniform, his medals, or his illustrious name, a name that shines like a sword in the sunlight. His feigned tenderness and softness with her did not fool her, nor did his patience in undoing her braids one by one. She cut them off and sought to free herself of him.

21

SHE PASSED BY A BAKERY famous for its French pastries to buy her grandmother's favorite chocolate cake. She had decided that they would spend the evening together to make up for the days she had neglected her in favor of the painting. The strange thing was that there was no one but her to keep her grandmother company: her other grandchildren were all over the globe, and only called her on the telephone on feast days and special occasions. Other than that, there was no one: everyone she had known in her life was no longer in the land of the living, friends, family, and neighbors all. It is a painful thing to have to live on without everyone with whom we have grown up and lived our lives while we await our own death, like a person packed for a journey that will start soon, very soon, although we do not know when exactly.

She put the cake on the table and made two cups of tea, her grandmother sitting and smiling like a happy little girl. Her hands shook so much when she took the plate of cake from Yasmine that she asked, "Haven't you been taking your nerve medicine?"

"I have," she said, "but what can medicines do for these old nerves? My nerves are shot and no amount of medicine can fix them."

She watched her grandmother fight the tremors in her hand to cut up the cake with her fork, not trying to help her, as she knew that would make her feel patronized and feeble. "I used to make a chocolate cake every Thursday," her grandmother reminisced, "and invite our family, friends, and neighbors over. My home was always full of guests. I liked them and they loved being there with me. Funny, they stopped visiting me and calling. The telephone hardly ever rings."

Yasmine let her be: why tell her? Tell her that they were all dead, and she was the only one left.

Her grandmother kept reminiscing. "On my high school graduation—it was a girls' school, and it had the best class of girls in Cairo—we learned embroidery and crochet and sewing and dressmaking and home decoration and flower arrangement and cooking and all the arts to prepare a girl to be a homemaker of the best and smartest class." She took a bite of her cake. "On my high school graduation," she resumed, "I made a white lace gown, and embroidered it with flowers, with little pearls in the center." She smiled. "Everyone was wild about it. The teachers adored it, and the girls went crazy over it. I was the top of my class, and the girls offered me huge sums for it. But I refused. I kept it just as it was. I never even dreamed of wearing it!"

"But why not?" Yasmine asked, caught up in the tale.

"I don't know," her grandmother shrugged. "I was afraid of it getting dirty or torn, I think. I wanted to keep it pristine, untouched by anyone's hand and without anyone wearing it."

Yasmine leaned forward. "What use is it, then?" she asked. "What use is a piece of art if nobody can see it or have a chance to admire it?"

"I don't know. It was like a precious jewel. I wanted to protect it from everything, even from people looking at it." Her grandmother's eyes shone. "Let me give it to you for your wedding dress."

"Me?" Yasmine said, stunned. "Me wear it?"

"Yes. It's just your size."

"Do you know how long it's been in the closet?" Yasmine cried out. "The fabric must have rotted away by now. It'll be all yellow . . . not to mention it'll be out of style."

"No, no!" her grandmother shook her head hard as if denying some accusation. "It's as fresh and new as the day I made it. I put it in plastic to stop it fading. As I was flipping through the channels on the TV yesterday, there was a fashion show by a famous French designer, and one of the models was wearing a dress just like it."

Seeing nothing for it, Yasmine said meekly, "Yes, Grandma."

"But when are you and he announcing your wedding?"

She made a vague positive response to please her grandmother and save herself the trouble of a fruitless and pointless conversation. "Soon."

Later, she thought about her grandmother's words, and of the man who she assumed was her granddaughter's future husband. She thought about how he had changed since that new girl had come into his life. He had not called her in a while. He gave her less attention. With the intuition that every woman possesses, she could feel that something was the matter. But she could not blame him, in any case.

She went into her room to resume her research on the other man who had come into her life all of a sudden. She found a new painting by him entitled "The Revolt of Cairo." The painting depicted two sides locked in fierce combat: the French in their military costume, their horses so lifelike you could practically hear their loud neighing, and the common people of Egypt who had come out to confront Napoleon and his army. Looking at the painting, you could see the power evoked by the military uniforms, representing training and knowledge of the arts of battle, in the face of men filled with honor and dignity standing unarmed in defense of their land with all the courage, valor, and chivalry they possessed—quite unlike the other, more famous historical painting of the same subject, which depicted Egyptians as a weak, powerless rabble crushed beneath the hooves of the French fighters' horses.

All the paintings of the Campaign had depicted Napoleon as almost a god, perched high atop his horse while everyone clustered like slaves around and beneath him. But this work showed a battle of equals, the Egyptian confronting the Frenchman, the artist seemingly wishing to depict a truth that many ignored.

Day by day, the picture had grown clearer: it was all based on assumptions, true, with nothing certain as yet, but all the threads of her investigation were leading her somewhere. The one stumbling block to her theory was the absence of Alton Germain's name from the list of the French Campaign artists.

She woke the next morning with one thought in her mind: she must go to France to attend the conference. This would help her with her search for this man, in the place he was from. The emails she had sent to the website asking for more information and whether he was an artist of the Campaign had gone unanswered. She rang up the airline and booked her ticket.

At noon, Sherif called. "How's Zeinab?"

"She's fine."

"Anything new?"

"You care about her more than me. You didn't even ask about me, just about her," she joked.

"Haven't you noticed recently that she's all you care about?"

"Yes. And haven't you noticed recently that all you care about is that girl whose name I don't remember?"

She had been expecting him to respond that he only cared about her, and to ask what girl she was talking about. Instead, there was a moment of silence on the other end, after which he changed the subject. "So, have you found anything?"

"I've found a lot, but nothing for sure. I'm going to go to Paris to see for myself."

"Paris?" She could hear him blowing out smoke. "You didn't say anything about leaving the country."

"I only decided a few hours ago," she explained. "I was invited to the annual conference of the Association for Art History, and I wasn't going, but now I think it's a good chance to do more research there."

"I hope to see you before you go. If you have time, that is."

"Of course, we'll meet before I go."

His voice held a gentle reproof, the source of which she could not guess.

Cairo: October 1798

We were graced with calm in the country for some time. Those of lesser intelligence imagined that the Egyptians had accepted matters as they were. I knew that it was the calm before the storm.

I woke this morning to the sound of pot lids clanging against one another. It was a terrible racket, growing louder and louder until it drowned out all other sound, deafening. I did not know what this could mean: why were they doing this? When I saw the masses of humanity in the street, it dawned upon me that this had been the signal to congregate. Men—old men, young men, boys, and even children of every stripe and manner— poured out into the squares and gathered on every street corner and in every passage and alleyway and in the mosques and churches and synagogues. They spilled out into the streets, rage on their faces, bearing all manner of impromptu arms such as sticks, staffs, knives, and daggers. Some went directly to the houses of French people to exact their vengeance. When General Dupuy, the commander of Cairo, heard the news, he took a contingent of men out to fight, and went straight to the home of the Turkish judge, Ibrahim Adham Effendi. The Egyptians were gathered outside the house of the judge, complaining loudly of the injustice they suffered, and calling for justice for Sheikh Muhammad Karim, whom Bonaparte had ordered to be executed by firing squad in Alexandria. Moments after General Dupuy arrived, his head was cleaved from his body.

It was as if the cry of demons had reverberated throughout every corner of this calm city. In every place, at the same time, there was robbery,

215

looting, and murder of Frenchmen. At the moment when Dupuy was murdered, the army bakers were being slaughtered at the hands of the people of Bulaq, and General Caffarelli's house was robbed and looted, and his architectural equipment and personal equipment destroyed. An attempt was made on his life, but he escaped death by a providential miracle. Not only that, but they scattered the heads and other body parts of the dead in the streets and alleyways. It was an extremely painful and repulsive sight.

The people of Cairo had neglected to take over the rooftops; the French positioned themselves there, aiming their weapons and cannons onto the heads of the populace. French fire erupted from the Citadel into the city; it was aimed at al-Azhar Mosque, the coal market, the Ghuri market, and the Carpenters' Alley. The neighborhood of Bulaq was completely destroyed. The French continued their barrage on al-Azhar. Not only that, but they galloped into the heart of the mosque on horseback, and burned and ruined its religious books and valuable manuscripts and documents. Flames leapt up from within al-Azhar, and the horses urinated and defecated inside that holy place. This incident in particular incited redoubled hatred for all Frenchmen within the hearts of the Egyptians: al-Azhar was not only a mosque or a square to them, but a symbol of Islam, of faith and piety. Al-Azhar is also a university to which students come from every land throughout the world, known as 'Qiblat al-Nour' and 'Qubbat al-Iman,' the Mecca of Light and the Dome of Faith.

Our soldiers destroyed everything in their wake. Both sides had run amok, unfettered, and the vanquished Egyptians had fought bravely: Egypt's poor, its peasants, its itinerant salesmen, and its craftsmen, those who knew nothing of fighting and battle and whose only weapon had been their love for their country. The loud reverberations of their hate for us rang out to equal the neighing of the leaders' horses whose hooves pounded the streets, their turbans upon their heads their only shields against swords and lances.

By nightfall, all was calm. All at once, the streets and alleyways were void of the throngs that had crowded them earlier, although they were filled with dismembered corpses. Dogs came out and howled, and noxious odors pervaded the atmosphere. The cries of night owls and ravens echoed through the air.

The next morning, the fighting raged anew, but considerably less fiercely than the previous day. A delegation of imams, led by Sheikh al-Bakri, went to Bonaparte, asking him to call off his soldiers, in return for which they would call upon the people of Cairo to return to their homes. Bonaparte imposed a condition for this cessation, namely a list of names of the men who had organized this revolt. In the face of Bonaparte's unbending insistence, they provided him with a list of the imams who had organized and incited the revolt, whereupon he ceded to their request and commanded the immediate cessation of fighting. Concurrently, the imams went out asking the people to give up and return home. Then, Bonaparte issued the order to have the imams who had incited the revolt executed, their heads mounted on the wall of the Citadel, and their bodies thrown over its walls. The execution was carried out, which only fueled the people's hatred for us. They had only to see one of us in the street for their anger to be unleashed, cursing at us and pelting us with dirt and refuse. The situation had become untenable; any return to the relative calm of before was now unthinkable.

The members of the Campaign were saddened at the death of one of their senior architects in the Cairo Revolt. Testifout had been a kind and keenly intelligent man, and his name had been foremost on the list of assassinations because he had been planning a new layout for Cairo, which meant the demolition of old houses and mausoleums, and the first thing he had done away with were the gates to the neighborhoods that were locked at night and without which Egyptians did not feel secure. These gates had meant security and privacy to them, and that man had come and demolished them, so they had not only killed him but mutilated his corpse, beheading him and mounting his head on one of the gates he had ordered to be destroyed. On the same list were the names of the surgeons who dissected human corpses; this was a violation of the sanctity of the body under Islam, which states that a body must be buried intact. But what I found truly incomprehensible, and was a great blow to me, was the murder of Dupré, an artist whose only concern since we arrived here has been to draw the architecture of the houses, streets, and mosques of this fair city.

One thing I admired and found odd in equal measure was that our neighbors and the inhabitants of the neighborhoods occupied by the *scientists of the Campaign, around the palace of Hassan al-Kashef Bey or Beit al-Sinnari, and other far-flung quarters, protected us from being murdered. A number of men had gathered and formed a protective barrier all around the house and prevented it from being looted. This is the Egyptian people: a people to perplex and astonish. Why had they done this? Did they know the value of what we were accomplishing in their country, what works we would leave to history, although they knew not what we were executing or what work we were doing?*

I was grateful for the attitudes of the water carrier and the man who sold the licorice drink. They had not forgotten that I had once painted their portraits, and that my only weapons were my brush and palette, so they stayed close to my house with several of their friends to protect me. It was a wonderful way to return the favor: this is a people that does not forget, and can distinguish between those who seek to harm them and those who seek to do them good.

Cairo: October 1798

It had been a strange day from the start. The sun did not rise as usual, obscured by a great dark cloud. Rain began to fall. Was it truly rain, or the tears of the sky lamenting what was to happen on this day?

Ravens had been cawing on the walls of houses, at the gates of alleyways, and on the tops of palm trees, a cry of ill omen, since early on. Zeinab woke to the sound of brass saucepan lids clanging together. Everyone in the house ran to gather in the central courtyard. "Heavens!" Zeinab cried, hands clapped to her ears. "What's that sound?"

Her mother rushed out, muttering garbled prayers under her breath, the verse of the Qur'an that says, *Allah is the best guardian, and He is the most merciful of the merciful.*

Sheikh al-Bakri was not immune to the fear that swept the household: he hurried out with his head bare of the great turban he usually wore, forgetting even to put on his caftan over his house clothes. "They've done it! They've carried out their plot!" he cried, wringing his hands.

"What plot?" Zeinab's mother asked.

"Yesterday," he said, "some of the imams from the council addressed the matter of exorbitant taxes, the breaking down of the alley gates, the ransacking of houses, and the confiscation of horses, cows, bulls, and weapons, and demanded that Napoleon cease and desist, but he refused. Several of them plotted a revolt!" He shook his head. "It's the head of the serpent, Sheikh Abdel-Wahab al-Shabrawi! And al-Jawsaqi, the head of Ta'ifat al-Imyan, the order of blind imams!"

"That makes you mad, does it?" she sneered at him. "Don't they have the right to plan a revolt? Or are you the one who's blind to the injustice of the French?"

"You don't think we've a chance of winning against them, do you?" he moaned. "We'll get nothing out of it but that we'll anger the general, and killing and ruin as well!"

Sheikh al-Bakri tried to keep his son Ahmad from going out and taking part in the revolt; but Ahmad, with the impetuous courage of youth, refused. For the first time ever, his eyes held disdain and resentment toward his father. "Shame on you to keep me from it! And shame on you for not taking part!"

Sheikh al-Bakri vacillated between bouts of rage and spells of silence. His wife kept on muttering Qur'an verses under her breath. Zeinab felt a strange combination of fear and worry for Alton on the one hand, and pride and a sense of challenge that they were standing up to the French, on the other. She wondered what would happen to Alton if the revolt succeeded. Would he be killed? Would they throw him into prison, there to be tortured to death?

Sheikh al-Bakri closed the doors to the house and bolted the courtyard gates, then hid in his bedroom, refusing to eat or drink. The sounds that came to his ears from outside told him and his family the story of what was happening. After a time, the weeping and wailing of women came to their ears, and the cries of battle rang out, echoing throughout the city. The next day, the sound of cannon fire was deafening, and smoke belched into the sky from the fires everywhere. Houses were demolished, their walls falling in upon the heads of those living there, and thousands died under the rubble. Everyone within the house was weeping and crying in terror.

There was a knock at the door. At the first it was a regular knock, gradually increasing in force and speed, indicating that some disaster had struck. Fatima's heart trembled in fear for her son. Had something happened to him? She ran to the door to open it, praying to God that she was wrong. "God have mercy!" she cried, working the bolt and flinging the door open.

At the door was a great delegation of Azhar students and imams, asking to see Sheikh al-Bakri. Sheikh al-Bakri, who had sequestered himself in his room for a day and a night, thinking of the black fate that awaited him if the revolt succeeded, enjoyed a renewed surge in confidence. He put on his turban, donned his fur caftan, and stood puffed up like a peacock listening to the entreaties and pleas of the delegation, who knew all too well how close he was to the general. They begged him to go to Bonaparte and ask him to cease bombarding the city.

"Of course," he told them, head raised with his usual arrogance, "I could easily convince Bonaparte to cease firing, but it is no easy matter to get him to forgive those who plotted the revolt. I expect a severe punishment to fall upon their heads."

The man's response to the entreaties of the delegation betrayed the pride and arrogance that ran in his blood. This was confirmed to Zeinab, who was watching the entire scene from behind the wooden barrier.

Napoleon agreed to cease firing, on condition that they give him the names of those who had plotted the revolt. The delegation fell silent, suddenly struck dumb. Napoleon threatened to resume firing. Sheikh al-Bakri looked at the delegation, and in a threatening, menacing tone, said, "Perhaps we must sacrifice a few men for the sake of the lives of the people . . . or else there will be no end to the fighting." He went on, "With one look at what is happening outside, at the severed heads rolling in the streets, the burned bodies, and the people expiring beneath the rubble of demolished homes, we know the fate that we are heading toward."

The men murmured loudly among themselves, consulting with one another. Sheikh al-Bakri added in order to convince them, "Be assured that with every moment that passes, more of our children and wives are dying."

At last, they agreed to give the names of the men. One of the imams took on this distasteful duty, grating the names out through a tight throat. He spoke a great many names, foremost among which were Sheikh Abdel-Wahab al-Shabrawi and al-Jawsaqi. Napoleon was pacing back and forth, and as was his habit when preoccupied, had one hand folded behind his back and stamped his feet loudly, while his secretary took down the names and made out an arrest warrant.

The men left Napoleon's seat weighed down with guilt and shame. None of them could say a word. Silence reigned over them. A few days later, the heads of the imams were mounted on the Citadel walls.

Cairo: October 1798

I was in my studio painting The First Cairo Revolt. *The scenes I had witnessed bent my brush to their will; I could draw nothing but this. It was injustice incarnate. I did not obey the commands of our power-mad general by immortalizing him in a painting exalting his courage and strength. I cannot but depict the bravery of this people who came out in defense of their land, bearing whatever makeshift weapons they could lay their hands on—stones, kitchen tools—and took to the streets to resist with these primitive implements in the face of cannons and artillery.*

Monge watched me as I painted. When the painting was done, he expressed displeasure. He did not approve of the manner in which I had depicted the Egyptians' valor in facing down their enemy. I gave his comments all the attention they merited, that is to say, none at all. In art, it is your brush that leads you, and I heeded mine. It is the brush that paints, and not the artist.

After the First Cairo Revolt, something changed about the Egyptians' attitude toward the Campaign and its leader. This great hatred was a thing that permeated every heart and mind, expelled with the very air they exhaled, until the atmosphere was laden with it. None had forgotten the scene when al-Azhar had been violated, when they had galloped in on their horses and blasted it with cannons, burning and defiling copies of the Qur'an. None had forgotten the sight of the corpses that had filled the streets and the screams of men, young and old, and even of women, being arrested from their homes in dead of night, their bloated corpses bobbing up on the opposite bank of the Nile days later. None had forgotten the heads of the imams mounted next to one another, their mouths stuffed with straw, on the Citadel wall, a choice meal for the worms and ravens.

The populace grieved. Those who had previously been generous with us merely cast us a look of derision. The tradesmen and the bakers, the butchers and the water carriers, would no longer have dealings with us. In the face of this great hatred that surely heralded dire consequences and would doubtless put paid to Bonaparte's plans to win over the people, the emperor must do something.

The way into Egyptians' hearts, in his view, was through their religion: but the Azhar incident had destroyed everything he had worked toward. Therefore, when he held a meeting with the leaders and senior scientists of the Campaign, we found him crying out, pounding the table with his fist, "What if an invader stormed the sanctuary of Notre Dame Cathedral, for instance, and wrought such havoc? Would our own people have taken it lying down? Indeed not! What occurred was a mistake and a grave one at that." This time it was even worse, for what well laid plan could he possibly have made to make these resentful masses forget what had happened?

But he was a genius when it came to strategy, and was not without a plan for long.

It was a little past midnight when one of Napoleon's men knocked at the door of Sheikh al-Bakri, who was deep in slumber. Not giving him the time to adjust his clothing or properly settle his turban upon his head, the messenger took him off straightaway. Al-Bakri wondered what on earth was going on, stroking his long beard and asking himself what he could want with him at this hour of the night. Would his fate be the same as that of the imams who had been executed? He shook his head vigorously, rejecting the idea. He had, after all, done nothing: on the contrary, he was Napoleon's faithful man in Cairo. But no one could know the general's intentions, or what he had in mind. He tried to coax the servant who had come to get him into conversation, hoping to glean something, but he received no answer.

Sheikh al-Bakri went into the meeting room, rumpled and his turban askew, with a heart that trembled in terror. But his fears were allayed when Napoleon greeted him with a broad smile, "Sheikh al-Bakri!"

The door closed on the pair of them: they did not come out until three hours later, when Sheikh al-Bakri and Napoleon had finished penning a convincing speech to erase all that had taken place from the memories of the Egyptian people. Lines were written, erased, written and erased again, to be replaced with other, more convincing phrases. Finally, Bonaparte was satisfied with the speech and went out to give it to the populace at large.

The Lord God has commanded me to be merciful and forgiving to the populace, and so I have been. I am disappointed by your revolt, which has deprived me for two months of my customary meeting with your Diwan. But today I return to you, clerics, descendants of the prophets, religious scholars, and imams of mosques. I would have you declare that he who sets himself against me in enmity will have no safe place to escape to in this world nor the next. Is there a person who can deny that it is fate that guides all my campaigns? I could judge each person for the slightest emotion they hold within their hearts, for I know everything that is in your hearts, even that which you have told no one.

It was a rousing, religiously inspired speech, where he informed them that he was fated to lead them, and that they must follow. He thus appealed to the fatalistic nature of the Egyptian populace, who fell under the spell of his speech thanks to that very fatalism. It was so convincing that there were rumors that the general would soon convert to Islam and trade in his tricorne for a turban and have himself circumcised. As for Napoleon's generals and the scientists of the Campaign, they were provoked by that speech, all asking as one man, "What does Napoleon hope to achieve by speaking so?" He became the butt of jokes for some, and the target of disapproval and astonishment for others. A third, smaller, contingent believed that this was the best way to guarantee the safety of the Campaign and achieve its ends.

That was not all. Napoleon paced back and forth in his office in his military boots, thinking of different ways to win back the trust of the Egyptian people. To this end, he enlisted the help of a number of trusted Egyptians and Frenchmen. Day after day, circulars were printed in Arabic and French, and pasted up in the largest squares. Some of these justified what the Campaign had done to Egyptians during the revolt, while others attempted to convince the people of Napoleon's good intentions and that he had only set foot in their land to save them from the Mamluks. Although these gambits did succeed in convincing some, they never managed to completely erase the resentment in the hearts of others toward the French Campaign and its men.

Cairo: November 1798

Zeinab's mother gasped. Her daughter's hair had been so long she could sit on it, and now it barely covered her neck!

"Good Lord! What have you done to yourself?" she gasped. "How could you? It was your best feature!"

She flung herself into her mother's embrace and sobbed bitterly, brokenly. Gently, her mother moved her away and looked her in the eye. "What did he do?" she asked. "Did he do anything to you? Did he hurt you?"

"No, Mother, it's okay. He didn't do anything. All he did was undo my braids, slowly, patiently. That's why I got rid of my hair. It's so he won't ask to see me again."

"What a strange man he is!" Fatima shook her head. Ever since the fortune-teller had told Fatima of the ill-luck that was in store for them, she had been preoccupied and unhappy, repeating, "God protect us from him, his followers, his soldiers, and all his men" over and over. Although she believed her daughter was truthful when she said that nothing had transpired between her and Napoleon, Fatima could tell that there was something else on her daughter's mind, something she could not explain. There was a lost look in her eyes: she appeared defeated, broken. Zeinab had always been proud of herself, vain even, strutting around as though the world and everything in it belonged to her. She had not been fond of this arrogance in her daughter, but to see her crushed grieved her.

"Come on," she said, "let's go to the baths. The change will do you good." She called the slave girl and asked her to prepare the reed basket in which they put their bathing paraphernalia. "Make some henna so I can dye my hair. It's all full of white hairs. And put the sheep's-wool loofah in there and the ambergris perfume, and the pastries I baked this morning."

The slave girl put the basket on her head; Fatima put on her abaya and Zeinab covered her face; she and her mother got on two mules while the slave girl walked behind them. The bathhouse was in a narrow alleyway a few streets away. Zeinab knocked on the brass door knocker mounted on the heavy wooden door. The owner of the bathhouse opened the door, but she was lackluster in her welcome, unusually for her, for she was always garrulous and never stopped asking for the news of family and friends. "Morning," she said curtly, and handed each of them a towel without looking at them.

A large marble basin occupied the center of the place: several women were bathing in it, others sitting at the edge, chattering and smoking water pipes and eating sweets. As soon as she came in, Zeinab put on a pair of the high clogs provided by the bathhouse: they were wood and ensured that she would not slip. In one of the side chambers they undressed, and Zeinab sat before an Ethiopian grooming woman with a glass bead dangling from her nose. She was used to coming to this lady in particular to scrub and wash her. "Wait," said the woman, and came back with a bar of soap. In a whisper, so that no one would hear, she said, "This soap is made of olive oil. It comes especially from merchants from the city of Nablus in Palestine. The owner only uses it for her friends who come here. Let me wash your hair with it; it's worth it."

But the moment she saw Zeinab's hair, she cried out, "Good heavens! What have you done to your hair?"

Zeinab sadly lifted a hand to her hair, only to find that it wasn't there. She remembered when the woman used to tease her, 'It'll take me a whole day to wash and style it!' Her mother jumped in to her rescue. "She got sick and it was falling out. The spice expert who deals with such things advised us to cut it off."

"It must have been the Evil Eye," the woman volunteered, scrubbing Zeinab's body with the rough woolen loofah. "What a shame. It was her best feature."

Zeinab sat alone in a corner of the room while the grooming woman worked on her mother. It was impossible to see for the steam that came in through openings in the stone walls, but there was a face that kept appearing before her: Alton, with his hazel eyes, and the lock of hair that kept falling into his face, and his pencil mustache. Suddenly, it was as though his strong arms were wrapped around her and holding her close. The grooming woman finished scrubbing her mother with the loofah, then began to apply henna to her hair. Now, all that remained was for them to take a dip in the central basin.

Zeinab unwrapped the towel and flung herself into the tub, whereupon every other woman in the water reacted as though the Devil himself had jumped into it. They hurried out, looking back with glances of derision and scorn. A fat woman cried as she heaved herself up out of the bath, "Get out, girls! This water's been polluted."

"We need *pure* water to bathe in!" another cried.

In the face of the flood of insults heaped upon them by the women, Zeinab and Fatima could not even raise their eyes to them: they dressed in haste and hurried away. All the way home, Fatima could not stop crying, the words ringing in her ears, "This water's been polluted"; "We need *pure* water to bathe in!" Both of them knew perfectly well what those words meant: the story of Zeinab and Napoleon was known to everyone in Egypt. Truly life is changeable. Before the French came to the country, the women had received Zeinab's mother with warm greetings and kisses on both cheeks, vying with one another to offer her sweets they had made: she was the wife of Sheikh Khalil al-Bakri, and that in itself was enough to confer an aura of aristocracy and respectability upon her.

At last they were home. Fatima collapsed on the wooden couch, while Zeinab undid her veil. "It's like I committed some act of debauchery," Zeinab shook her head.

"You did," her mother responded. "It's enough that you took off your face veil and wore the revealing clothes of the Franks. If your father wasn't a favorite of Napoleon's, they would have beaten us up and kicked us out. But it's not your fault, it's your father's."

Zeinab shuddered. She knew the fate of a girl from a good family who was considered sullied or debauched: she was paraded through the town, riding backward on a scabied mule with bells around its neck, while the doorway to her house was stained with tar and red wax. She brought shame not only on her family but on her neighbors and friends and anyone who knew her. If she were not killed, she would probably never show her face again in the same neighborhood.

That night, Fatima raised her voice to her husband for the first time. "Our daughter's reputation is ruined," she said, "and so is her future. Who will marry her now that her affair with Napoleon is common knowledge in the whole town?"

"Lower your voice, woman. You'll always be like that, understanding nothing. Your daughter will marry Bonaparte. He is in love with her. She will be the empress of all the Orient."

"Marry Bonaparte?" Fatima beat her breast in shock. "You would marry your daughter to a killer, not to mention that he's a Christian?"

"Bonaparte will convert to Islam soon, be sure of it, like General Menou. He's a French general who converted and became known as Abdullah Menou, and married Zubayda, a girl from Egypt."

Cairo: December 1798

Other than General Menou, I had no dealings with the Army, neither generals nor soldiers: we were two things apart. The scientific campaign had its own motives and ends: namely, the advancement of science, and we were here to build and establish things, while the military campaign had only resulted, so far, in ruin and destruction.

I have been friends with Menou, now General Menou, since childhood: we grew up in the same quarter. Although he has converted to Islam and married a Muslim woman, it has not affected his standing in the army; quite the reverse. He is one of its highest-ranking generals and an indispensable cornerstone of Bonaparte's forces. One day I met him in a small tavern run by a Greek fellow. He was in the company of several other generals and enlisted men, all enjoying themselves. Everyone was drinking wine, but he was having chilled water. There was some discomfort in the group due to Menou's conversion to Islam, his having changed his name, and his evident infatuation with Egypt. He had been trying to lead his comrades by example and reason, not by harshness or cruelty. "How can we be true Frenchmen," he was saying, "yet be dealing with these people in a manner devoid of all civilization?" He explained, "A great many liberties are taken by some of our soldiers at the expense of the Egyptians. We must act with nobility, respect the elderly, and respect women." He took a sip of his water. "Tell me, what glory can you get from injuring a man who trembles at the mere sight of you? This is our role as leaders. We must always repeat this to our men."

Some of the generals around him were clearly disgruntled by his words: they approved neither of his vision nor of his means of enacting it. They believed that the Egyptian people were a horde of barbarians who must be quelled with harshness and force, and had no qualms about saying so, entering into a heated debate that almost came to blows but for Menou's restraint.

Over time, I became even closer to Menou, who was a more intimate friend to me than the other artists. Remarkably, this military man possessed a more compassionate heart and a more open mind than even them. One day he invited me to dine at an Oriental restaurant. I confessed to him that I was enamored of an Egyptian girl.

"But do you truly love her," he interrogated me, "or are you merely enraptured by her Eastern beauty? Will you grow used to her, nay, tired of her, with time, and know that it was not love at all?"

I took his questions to heart. I could feel my features changing as I mulled it over. He comforted me, seeing that he had upset me: "If your love for her is genuine, then let nothing stand in your way."

I laughed loudly. His face darkened and he flushed, thinking I was making fun of him. "Do you know," I quickly said, "what might stand in my way? Merely a little matter called Napoleon Bonaparte."

"Bonaparte? What has he to do with your amour?" He shook his head. "I don't think he would see fit to intervene in such matters. When I told him I was going to convert and marry an Egyptian woman, he did not object, but congratulated me." He nodded. "In fact, to him it was a trump card, something to help him win over the people and gain more of their trust."

I felt the words fall from my lips, bitterly, "He is my rival."

He repeated the words slowly, then said, "I had not known that Bonaparte loved a girl from this country."

"It is Zeinab," I said, "the daughter of Sheikh al-Bakri. He saw her at some event or other, and she caught his fancy."

"Ah." He stroked his chin. "But what of her? Does she love him?"

"She is a girl of sixteen. She is the living embodiment of every kind of innocence. It never went beyond some pride at being chosen over all the other girls of Egypt."

"Beware," said Menou. "Napoleon is unyielding when it comes to land or women. If he has taken the girl to his bed, she is his."

"No! She has never shared his bed. And that," I continued, "is what I find so strange. Although he is clearly attracted to her and has chosen her out of all the women and girls of Egypt, he has not touched her."

"He is a professional huntsman," said Menou. "To fall upon his prey all at once spoils the pleasure of the hunt. Thus he lays his traps, step by careful step."

The man's words inspired fear and worry in me. Was this man truly grooming Zeinab to be his bedmate? Teaching her the arts of seduction step by step? He had undone her braids one day, unlaced her dress the next. What did he intend to take off the next time? What did he intend to do to her? I burned to think of it: only then was I certain that I loved this girl with a mad passion.

The licorice-drink seller encountered me on the way home. I asked him to pour me a cup to quench the flames burning in my breast. Frequently, this man with his clothing and his tools had given me cause to stop and gaze at him, especially the magical way in which he poured the beverage in a curving stream from a spout in the brass urn upon his back into cups of metal, calling out, "Life and health is licorice!" As soon as I went into the studio, I began to paint him. I painted him just as he was: his interesting garb, the brass urn on his shoulder, and his bare feet. I was deeply engrossed in painting the portrait when I found several Campaign men all around me, insisting that I accompany them to a house of ill repute. I refused, whereupon they began to mock me for being a saint, or else, they hinted, there must be something wrong with my manhood, and in an instant, made me the butt of their jokes. I was so incensed by their jibes that I agreed to go with them, and with no little curiosity to see a new side of this world, something that might later be a subject for a painting.

Rostom, Bonaparte's personal slave, was waiting for us in a smart carriage drawn by two horses. Bonaparte had given him the task of seeing to the needs of the scientists and artists of the Campaign, thanks to his vast knowledge of the secrets and hidden aspects of the city. He knew the best places to take the scientists, oftentimes telling us of historical sites worthy of our visits. Today, though, was different. As he said, we needed some entertainment and diversion, especially after the events that had recently transpired.

Rostom was garbed in colorful clothing, wearing a cap on his head that was tied in an eye-catching manner. His shining sword lay dormant in its scabbard, his features betraying that he was from a far-off land. He did not resemble the Egyptians. Although he wished to appear stern, as befitted Bonaparte's personal slave, there was a certain kindliness that shone from his childlike eyes.

No sooner were we settled in our seats than he tapped the side of the carriage and we were off. It rattled all along the way, scraping against the sides of the older houses in the narrow alleyways we drove through. Street after street and narrow path after narrow path, we left behind quarter after quarter, now filled with poorer houses, now opulent mansions. It was a refreshing winter night, with a wash of pleasantly chilly air. There was no sound but the cry of a night bird or the meowing of a hungry cat, and the barking of stray dogs in the distance. From time to time, cooking smells would waft over us, mixed with the smells of people, and sometimes fragrant flowers.

At last, the carriage stopped outside a tight passage into which it could not fit. We alighted and followed Rostom, who held a lantern aloft to guide us, although it gave off barely enough light to see where we were putting our feet. We arrived at the end of the alley. Outside a small house directly on the riverbank, Rostom stopped and knocked repeatedly at the door. I was overcome with a sudden distaste for stepping into that darkened *house, but it was too late. A strong arm whose owner had glimpsed my hesitancy to come in took hold of me and forcibly propelled me inside.*

Behind the door was a lovely woman in a tulle gown, almost completely transparent, wearing a great deal of makeup and powder. She took us inside. The lighting was dim and came from brass candelabras scattered around. The floor was scattered with cushions of red velvet, a large tray in the center laden with all manner of fruits and sweetmeats. There were also water pipes standing around here and there. The place was clearly familiar to Rostom, who flung himself down between two lovelies, both paragons of beauty, who began to play upon musical instruments. We started to hum along with them as they raised their voices in song. One of them stood and began to sway to the music, soon joined by another, and another. They were well-formed, their features charming, and most importantly, they were perfumed with musk and ambergris. What a difference between these and the prostitutes of the common road and the café! It was clear that they had been carefully selected to provide their services to a better class of gentleman.

The serving girl went around with a large tray bearing pastries topped with sugar, and others stuffed with nuts. Jugs of a spicy liquor called arak were placed before us. The music continued, and the girls took turns dancing. One of the girls wore a face veil, teasingly transparent like the morning mist. She would not take her eyes off me. She was not the loveliest among them, but there was something different about her, unlike the others. She had an angelic gaze, filled with innocence—an innocence far removed from this place and these women, as though she found herself there by mistake. When I began to return her glances, I felt as though I were in a different place—wider, more luminous. When we looked away from each other, it was like waking up from a sweet dream to the shock of bitter reality. But did this girl truly possess such charm, or was it the cheap liquor that had me imagining things?

One member of our group, now thoroughly drunk, went upstairs with the girl who had been sitting next to him. Minutes later, another couple went upstairs. I looked around for Rostom, but did not find him; he, too, had disappeared. Only I was left. I leaned back on the cushion and gave the girl a flirtatious glance. She lifted the veil off her face: she shone like the moon at its fullest. She poured me a glass and drew near to me; she took my shoes off and massaged my feet. Then she came around behind me and began massaging my shoulders. She undid her hair and it fell like a waterfall to cover her face. She drew nearer and kissed me. Kiss followed kiss until I surrendered to her completely. Her kisses were unusual: sweet, yet spicy.

Upstairs, her bedclothes were rose-colored. The burning candles filled the air with the scent of the clove oil they were made of. It was the scent of Zeinab. The smell possessed me, consumed me. I found her standing before me, in the flesh. I pulled her to me and drank my fill of her lips. I lifted her dress and the fabric rustled: the jingle of her finery reverberated in my ears. Her earrings; her anklets; her bracelets. We kissed deeply again, a kiss that was only extinguished when our bodies moved together.

22

SHE SPENT A LONG TIME looking at the painting of the lico-rice-drink seller that she had printed out from the site. The man practically burst from the page, as though he was stand-ing before her in one of the narrow alleyways of the city. There were a few itinerant salesmen sitting around here and there, while the man smiled broadly at his female customer. A closer look at her face and Yasmine was sure it was her. Although all that was visible was the side of her face, it was her, reaching out a graceful hand to take a brass cup from the vendor. It was her hand, her long, slim fingers. "It's her in all his paintings," she whispered. But what was the secret that meant that she appeared, as the main figure in all his work, again and again and again? She was an ordinary girl, not all that different from any other girl. Had there been something between them? And where had he met her? Had he met her by chance in the street and taken a liking to the way she looked, and drawn her? Per-haps he had asked her to model for him, and she had said yes. But how would her family have let their daughter model for an artist, and sit before him for hours while he painted her—those families that would not even let their daughters go out with their faces unveiled?

Her head was awhirl with questions, and she was suddenly nervous and confused. Perhaps a walk by the Nile would help her get her thoughts in order. She put on her running shoes, put her hair up and her headphones in, then went out.

With her favorite songs playing, she walked through the streets until she reached Abul-Feda Street. She crossed over to the side directly overlooking the Nile. A chilly breeze wafted in her face, refreshing her. There wasn't much traffic in the streets at that hour. She walked the length of the street, and toward the end, she found Sherif's car. It was parked outside a restaurant called Sequoia—his favorite place. She decided to go in and surprise him.

The restaurant was quite empty, unusually for that hour. She looked over at the table where they usually sat. Sure enough, there he was. She went straight over to him, without noticing that there was a woman sitting opposite him, obscured by a hulking man sitting in the seat between her and Yasmine. She didn't see her until she was right in front of their table. Opening her mouth, she blurted, "Hello."

His mouth fell open and he exclaimed, "Hello! What a surprise!"

"I was taking a walk," she said, "and I saw your car. I thought you'd be here."

He introduced them. "Dr. Yasmine, Nirmine." The girl shook Yasmine's hand with a faint smile. "You must sit down. . . ."

"Oh, no, I couldn't," she said, "I was just taking a quick walk. I have work I need to get back to."

"Sit," he said commandingly. "Ten minutes won't make a difference."

The girl remained absolutely expressionless except for her lukewarm smile. With a quick glance at her, Yasmine ascertained that she was attractive, but not beautiful: olive-skinned with a mane of loose, dark curly hair, she wore jeans and a white shirt, a woolen jacket and brightly colored scarf. It was clear that she was deliberately ignoring Yasmine: she kept her eyes glued to her phone, pretending to be absorbed in it.

"Are you all ready to go?" he asked her. "To France?"

"Yes," she said.

The three of them sat at love's wintry table, giving off waves of jealousy and insecurity that heated the chill air, watching one another with tentative glances. But no one can tell what goes on inside another person. The girl's perfume was overpowering, insistently pushing itself into the spaces between them. Some perfumes are premeditated; some perfumes pass by fleetingly with the breeze; yet others are barely there, a scent one tries in vain to catch. Yasmine's name, which means jasmine, was enough to bring its scent with her: had her name infused her with a passion for everything natural and things from the earth? The scent of petrichor, the aroma of tea, orange blossoms, seaweed. . . .

In a casual tone, the girl asked her, "Where are you going?"

"Paris."

With more enthusiasm, she responded, "Paris! Oh, you're lucky. I love Paris. Are you shopping or sightseeing?"

"Neither. I'm going to an art conference."

The girl looked astonished. "But Chanel's summer collection is coming out next week! You must go to the show, you'll regret it if you don't."

Yasmine gave a half smile while Sherif took up the thread of the conversation. "Dr. Yasmine is a professor of art history. She spends her time going to conferences, researching historic paintings. She's not interested in things like that."

"Says who?" Yasmine responded. "I always find time to have fun, just like you do." She pushed her chair back. "I really do need to go. It's been good catching up."

"What's your hurry? Stay a while."

She waved goodbye and left without answering. She strode purposefully to the exit, then once she was through the door, she broke into a run.

She ran, her rage propelling her forward. The meeting had not lasted longer than thirty minutes, but it had her incensed. If they had had a normal relationship, she would have had the right to upbraid him, to reproach him, to yell at him. But she could do none of it, and the very fact of it filled her with resentment and unhappiness. Now she knew for a fact that there was no room in her heart, her mind, her soul for anyone but him, for anything but her love of him. From the girl's curious glances, filled with jealousy, Yasmine could tell that she was in a relationship with Sherif, and not just an intern in his office as he had said. An attractive girl in her early twenties, clearly infatuated with him, devoting all her time and attention to him. What would he see in Yasmine, preoccupied with the ghosts of the dead, caring only for her research?

As usual on the nights before she was traveling somewhere, she couldn't sleep. It was even harder to get any rest because she had an early morning flight; she ended up not sleeping at all. It was not only travel jitters, though: the jealousy tearing her apart was what made it impossible to get any rest.

She gave her grandmother a big hug goodbye, and gave the nurse her instructions. She was employed by an office that provided elder care. Yasmine taped a list of her grandmother's forbidden foods to the refrigerator so it would be always in the woman's sight.

She wrapped the painting carefully up, then placed it into her hand luggage. A few days ago, she had made a request of the head of the conservation department to take the painting with her to Paris to continue her conservation work there, claiming that the damage required more experience and state-of-the-art equipment than was available in Egypt. He had agreed at once, and given her a permit to take it out of the country. She left, dragging her carry-on behind her, a wool coat over her arm. The weather forecast had told her that there would be snow waiting for her in Paris.

In the taxi on the way to the airport, her phone rang. It was Sherif, telling her that he was on his way to drive her to the airport. "No need. I'm already on my way."

"I'll meet you at the airport, then," he insisted.

His phone call dissipated some of the clouds that had gathered around the walls of her heart since she had seen him sitting with the girl. But the question that preoccupied her, for which she could find no answer, was: Why was he doing this? Was this love, or just friendship? Or did he have some sort of misplaced sense of responsibility for Yasmine? He had often told her he felt like he needed to take care of her.

He was waiting for her at the departures terminal, smartly dressed as usual. A broad smile broke over his face when he caught sight of her. He suggested they have a coffee at the airport Starbucks. "Why did you come?" she asked as soon as they were seated. "Don't you have to be at work?"

She was trying to get him to relinquish his closely guarded reserve and hear him say that he would cancel any plans for her, or that he was here because he was going to miss her. But he disappointed her as usual. Instead he asked her, "Where are you staying in Paris?"

"The Paris View Hotel."

"How long are you staying?"

"I'm not sure yet. It all depends on how much information I can find."

"All for this man you're thinking about day and night?"

She laughed. "Yes, well. At least that man was here 250 years ago and isn't around any more."

He took her meaning, but ignored it. He looked at his watch. "You need to go now. It's getting close to boarding." He patted her on the back. "Take care of yourself." He saw her to security and left.

She looked behind her once she was through security. He was still standing behind the barrier. She waved at him and went on her way.

23

Paris: Winter 2012

THE CAPTAIN ANNOUNCED THAT THE flight was about to land at Charles de Gaulle International Airport. "The temperature in Paris is -3 degrees Celsius," the announcement went on, confirming what awaited her there.

When she stepped out of the airport, chill winds almost blew her off her feet. She did up her coat tightly and took a taxi from the rank, giving the driver the address of the old hotel. She had chosen it because it was convenient for getting to the Eiffel Tower, the Champs-Élysées, and the Louvre, and was in the center of the places she loved best in the city. The receptionist at the hotel welcomed her. She told him her name and he found her booking on the computer, nodding, "Yes, here's your reservation." She signed a few papers and he handed her the room key card and wished her a pleasant stay.

Although she was tired and in desperate need of a hot bath and a nap, she could not wait. She took the painting out of the bag and went immediately to the Académie des Beaux-Arts to meet Professor Charles Stefan.

The taxi dropped her at the gate of the Académie, one of the oldest in the world, founded by Louis XIII in 1648 out of a love for art. Most of France's best-known artists and the most famous painters and sculptors in the world had passed through its doors, and it had also been where Yasmine had studied for her doctoral degree.

The minute she set foot in the place, the same sensation stole over her that she had felt the first time she had walked into the place long ago: the history and grandeur of the building made you feel taller, prouder, as if you yourself had become part of it.

She went straight to the office of Charles Stefan, who had been her supervisor. He had praised her enthusiasm and hardworking nature and always encouraged her and been generous with his assistance. She had sent him an email a few days ago telling him that she was visiting Paris for the conference, and would be dropping by for his help on an important matter.

"Yasmine!" he welcomed her warmly. "How have you been? How are things in Egypt? How's work?"

"That's exactly what I was hoping you could help me with," she said, getting straight to the point.

She launched into a detailed history of everything that had happened since she had found the painting, right up to the moment of her sitting there in his office. He heard her out, listening carefully and paying close attention. "But a work of such stature as you describe," he said, "how could it have remained neglected for so long without anyone noticing it? And to be allowed to fall into such decay?" He leaned forward. "How could an artist of such significance, with such talent and skill—and one of the Campaign artists if your suspicions are correct—go without a single mention in the books, volumes, and histories of art? It doesn't make sense."

"That's another thing," she said. "The names of the artists of the Campaign are all listed in a document that I have seen and examined myself. His name isn't among them." She tilted her head. "Perhaps he signed a different name on his paintings? That makes about as much sense as anything."

"Where are the other paintings you think are his?"

He opened his laptop and she showed him the pictures. "This is the site of the French Association for Art History.

We can pay them a visit and meet whoever posted the artist's paintings on the site in person."

She had infected him with her enthusiasm. Immediately, he put on his coat and they went out together. She couldn't help a sly smile: her expectations had proved correct. Her professor was passionate about his subject and enthusiastic about getting to the bottom of a mystery, which was why he had been the first person whose help she had thought of enlisting in Paris. She sent up a small prayer of thanks that the years had not dimmed the fire of his zeal. "We can go on foot, it's walking distance," he said. "It's only ten minutes. It would take longer to drive there because we'd have to take main roads, which will be clogged with rush-hour traffic at this hour. We'd arrive after closing time."

She did not argue, although she was not exactly keen on walking any distance in this weather: the wind was chilly and the rain was pelting down. He sheltered her under his big black umbrella: although he was over sixty, he walked with vigor, and she had a hard time keeping up.

He led her through a series of narrow, crooked streets, finally coming to a stop outside a small building surrounded with a wrought-iron fence and thick bushes. "Here we are."

The iron gate creaked as they pushed it aside, the sound serving as a de facto doorbell that summoned the security guard. They asked him for the director, and were informed that the man was in his office. They ascended the marble steps leading into the building. The steps gave way to a large entrance hall with a reception desk. "The director's office is at the end of the corridor on the first floor," the receptionist told them.

The director welcomed the professor warmly, but looked doubtfully at Yasmine. He was in his mid-sixties, with thick white hair and sharp features. "Mademoiselle Yasmine is a professor of art history," Stefan introduced her. "I was her doctoral supervisor, many years ago now. She was always one of my best students, so hardworking. I advised her when she left never to stop researching, and she has clearly heeded my instructions. She is here today doing detective work."

The office was warm, returning the feeling to her limbs. She took off her coat. The man smiled and invited her to explain further, as if to ask, 'What business is this of mine?'

"After the Egyptian Scientific Institute burned down," she began, "the works damaged in the fire were brought to us to oversee their conservation. One of these was a portrait that dates back to the French Campaign in Egypt. An internet search led me to your site, where there are several paintings by an artist named Alton Germain. He is most probably the artist who painted the portrait. The issue is, though, that his name is not listed among the Campaign artists. There's no information listed about him either."

In a robotic voice that made Yasmine feel uncomfortable, the man said, "Mademoiselle, in 1798 orders were issued to the Minister of the Interior to form a committee of the most talented architects, scientists, and artists, and sources indicate that the Campaign went to Egypt with over 160 scientists, artists and inventors. The official websites definitely do not list them all." He went on, "The more famous names, such as the chemist Pilote, the mathematician Gaspard Monge and Claude Louis, Nicola, Jacques-Pierre, Simone Gerard, an architect who designed palaces and highways, Vivien Denon, a soldier and an artist, Jean-Marie Joseph and François Michel, the inventors and pilots of the hot-air balloon, who went to Sinai on a scientific expedition to develop the system of transporting the ancient obelisks that would later be moved to Paris, and we cannot forget Jean-François Champollion, the scientist who unlocked the symbols of the Rosetta Stone. Those were the most famous, and therefore the ones mentioned in the history books for their towering achievements. But what is certain is that there are many others whom the books do not mention."

The man was overcome by a violent fit of coughing. "Excuse me." He went over to the floor-to-ceiling bookcase against one wall, pulling out a great volume. He opened it and flipped through the pages. "Look here," he said, "it says, for example, that the head of the artists was Rigo, and the head of the design department was Denon Cacita Pierre, and the head of the sculptors was Fouquet Gusticas. The sources mention the heads of the various departments, but they do not list everyone who was working there."

With difficulty, Yasmine managed to get a word in. "I'll show you his paintings."

She pulled out her iPad and opened the paintings she had saved, handing it to him so that he could see them. He took off his reading glasses and put on another pair of spectacles, slowly looking them over. After a few moments of examining them, he said confidently, "These paintings are from the pages of *The Description of Egypt*."

"But I've read it carefully. They're not in there."

He handed back her device, responding unwillingly, "*The Description of Egypt* is a vast collection of the research that was conducted in Egypt during the French Army's expedition. It is in twenty-three volumes. After the expedition arrived in Egypt, the Minister of the Interior gave orders that eight of its members were to take on the task of collecting and publishing the research. The first edition was published in 1809, the original imperial edition. Between 1809 and 1830, new editions were issued in different forms. Eighty artists and four hundred coordinators and revisers were appointed to supervise the monumental task of reissuing these new editions. Over the years, a number of paintings and entries were deleted from the original edition. Some of these were reprinted; others were excluded by imperial command."

"Imperial command?" Yasmine repeated.

"Yes. Some artists and scientists were kept out of the volume and their names expunged." He nodded. "They were completely forgotten. It was not only the scientific expedition that received this treatment; there are also several military leaders who are never mentioned. The reason may be that they voiced opinions that were unpopular or challenged the beliefs of the army, or ran counter to Napoleon's policies, or opposed his campaign in Egypt and the Levant."

"And you believe that this artist may be one of those who were expunged?"

"Definitely," he nodded. "Try to look at his paintings again—not with the eye of an artist, but with the eye of a layperson—and you shall see something in common in all of his work." He surged up from his chair. "Come on."

He led them to the exhibition hall. On one wall was a giant screen. He took a moment to connect her device to the screen, projecting a brilliantly clear and detailed image of the paintings. He clicked through to the first. "Let's look at the paintings," he said. "This one . . . and this one. . . ." He only left them on the screen for a few moments, using the remote to zoom in on certain parts of the scenes, punctuated with his cries: "Look. Look at this . . . look at that . . . and this part here. Do you see that?"

After several minutes of this, Stefan broke the silence. "It's very clear," he said thoughtfully, "that that artist did not employ his art in the service of the emperor." He explained, "I mean that he did not show Napoleon's conquests in a favorable light, nor depict the man himself as a god, as he preferred to appear." He looked at the director for confirmation. "This would be, then, the explanation for his works and his name being expunged from *The Description of Egypt*?"

"Yes," the director confirmed. "That is abundantly clear." He clicked back to the first painting, one of the Battle of the Pyramids. "Look how he has depicted this battle. The Egyptians here are battling the French face to face, and clearly fighting them with great strength and vigor." He pointed to Napoleon on his horse. "Here, while Napoleon is sitting on his horse, he is being faced down by an Arab man without any of the trappings of glory, yet he has dignity, strength, and courage, still fighting with only the sword in his hand. Meanwhile, if we look at the face of Bonaparte, we can glimpse fear and awe in his expression." He unplugged the device. "There's another painting by the same artist that confirms what I'm saying. It's not on the website, but I'll show it to you. Just a moment." Crossing over to the room's bookshelf, he took out a CD and put it into the computer connected to the projection device. Rushing through dozens of paintings, he stopped at one.

It was a depiction of the return of Napoleon's army from their conquest of the Levant. "Look here." He gestured. "This painting doesn't show Napoleon fighting another army: the enemy was nature. Nature proved to be Napoleon's most destructive, most powerful enemy." He went on, "The endless expanse of desert; the burning sun; thirst; the plague that decimated his soldiers; this painting shows the suffering and pain endured by the soldiers in that ill-considered campaign. Napoleon's greed and his thirst for power and control drove him to force his soldiers to their death, nothing more."

"The faces of the soldiers," said Professor Stefan, "are full of misery. They're suffering, you can see it. They can barely walk, and it's true, there are so many bodies around them—soldiers dead from fatigue, not wounded in any battle."

"After these paintings appeared in the first edition of *The Description of Egypt*, they were immediately expunged from all future editions, as they displeased Napoleon. To him, he possessed the greatest army in the world, and his warriors were supermen immune to fatigue, illness, and death. He gave orders to Monsieur Denon, who oversaw the publication and later became director of the Louvre, that these paintings be removed from all future editions."

"But who is Alton Germain?" Yasmine burst out, giving voice to her most burning question.

"The fact is," said the director, "the books make no mention of him, not even in passing; but his name is mentioned once in the circular that used to be published in Cairo and distributed in France, and that covered the news of the soldiers and the Campaign and its various achievements. One of his paintings was published in it, and the news item said that it depicted the Egyptians' celebration of the Feast of the Flooding of the Nile, and mentioned the name of the artist, Alton Germain."

"But you say that his works were in the first edition of *The Description of Egypt*!" Yasmine protested. "There must be some information about him there!"

"The first edition of the *Description* is lost to history. It disappeared after it sold out. There were very few copies to start with, and most of them were handed out as gifts to military leaders and important personages in French society. It was so important, and the pictures it contained so beautiful, that a few artists copied works from it, thus producing new artwork."

They followed him back to his office. Yasmine's shoulders slumped, her hopes extinguished: the artist had disappeared, taking all traces of his presence with him, as if he had never existed at all, despite the significance of the wonderful paintings he had produced. His paintings should have taken pride of place in the foremost museums of the world. But with a word from a resentful emperor, they had all vanished.

The man felt bad for her: she had come all this way for assistance in her research, but her hopes of finding out more about the artist had come to nothing. Trying to dispel the despair that was clear on her face, he said, "In any case, the conference of the Association for Art History tomorrow has invited several members of the Association for Military History. I'll introduce you to a military historian whose specialty is this period in history. He has a lot of information on the French Campaign in Egypt, both military and artistic." He smiled. "I'm sure he'll be able to give you some information about that artist. Be careful, though," he cautioned, "some of this is classified, even all these years later. Military historians are like deep wells full of secrets. So my advice to you, so you can get all the information you need out of him, is to try not to make him suspicious. I suggest you tell him that you are researching the artists of the French Campaign in general—I know it seems odd, but don't ask him specifically about Alton Germain at first. Bring the conversation around to it later."

She thanked the director, and later thanked Professor Stefan, refusing his offer of lunch in favor of a shower and a nap. They said their goodbyes and he went back to the Académie des Beaux-Arts.

Outside, the rain had let up, but there were still strong gusts of wind. She opted to walk, needing to feel surrounded by people, walking in their hurried footsteps taking them here and there. Her phone rang. It was him. "Welcome to Paris."

She could hardly hear him for the wind, and all he could hear was blustery gusts into her speaker. "I can't hear you out here," she said. "I'll get to the hotel and call you back."

Cairo: March 1799

Bonaparte's presence in Egypt has led his hopes to grow more grandiose day after day; he has gone to Suez to study a planned canal to link the Red Sea to the Mediterranean: with such a canal, France will have control of the greatest trade passage in the world. Glittering delusions have captured the fancy of our leader, trickling down to his leaders, his companions, his scientists, and his soldiers. They have started work on several agricultural and industrial projects, and conducted careful studies for a modern method of running the country and fortifying it to allow him to remain there indefinitely. They are all laboring under the delusion that they are now masters of the shores of the Nile. But fate is not always favorable: the agents of Great Britain are conspiring with the Mamluks and the Bedouin against us. Rumors are afoot that the Ottoman Empire is making ready to expel the French from Egypt, and Gazzar Pasha of the Levant is making ready to confront our forces, assembling a mighty army to face them.

We have received instructions to head to al-Arish and thence to Syria to do battle with Gazzar Pasha. We set forth in haste with our equipment and supplies, which were soon exhausted. I was one of the few artists chosen to accompany the campaign. Instead of a weapon, I carried my brushes and palette to depict the army and paint its victories. But what was I to paint? The soldiers were exhausted from marching in the merciless burning heat of the desert sun; their food was eaten and their water almost all drunk. We waited impatiently for night to fall, that we might fling down our exhausted bodies upon the sand and watch the moon lighting up the beautiful cloudless sky above us. It seems so close that I could reach out and touch it. We needed no fire for light: the moon was enough. We merely lit a few sticks to keep the wolves at bay.

When I looked around me at the sleeping bodies scattered around the desert sands, I found that many of them were not sleeping at all, but lost in deep thought, preoccupied by a single question: are we ever going home? Some occupied themselves by playing cards, or sitting in circles and making bawdy jokes, or passing around a glass of wine, given to them by some officer, with barely a sip in it.

I met Lautrec there. He came to watch me drawing the exhausted soldiers lying on the sand. With a weak, reedy voice, he said, "I can draw, too."

I espied a young man about twenty years of age, with soft features and a sparse mustache. "Good," I said. "You must nurture this talent."

"Unfortunately," he said, "I have not the time. The woman my father married after my mother died sent me to military school. I was not yet eleven years of age, and my nature was as far from that of a soldier as it is possible for you to imagine. But I was too young to object. During the holidays, I felt like an unwanted guest at home. But for Jeannette, I would have found any pretext to spend the holidays at school."

"And who is Jeannette?"

With a dry twig, he drew a heart in the sand and wrote her name in it. "Jeannette," he sighed, full of tenderness and longing. "She lives next door. I fell in love with her when we were children. We grew and so did our love. She said goodbye with tears in her eyes. She cut off a lock of her blond hair and gave it to me." He put a hand in his jacket pocket and took out a small tin box. From this, he took the lock of hair and handed it to me. "Look. It is like silken thread."

The lock of hair took me far away, to Zeinab's thick black hair. My heart trembled. I remembered how she had grieved for her hair that day. I wished I could burst into Bonaparte's tent and scream at him, "What do you want with Zeinab?" and punch and strike him, and tell him how little she liked him, that she cut off her crowning glory so that his dirty hands stained with the blood of innocents would never touch it again!

The young man noticed that my mien had changed. "I beg your pardon if I have caused you pain," he said.

"No, not at all," I said, handing him back the lock of hair. "Go on."

"When she asked me that day where I was going, I could find no answer," he said, "for I did not know. But I sent her a message with a friend on the frigate that left for France a few days ago."

"What did you write to her?"

The question surprised him as it did me, for what would a young man in the very jaws of death write to his beloved? Would he promise her to return and entreat her to wait for him as I had done with Zeinab, a few days before my departure?

"I only wrote one thing," he said, "'I love you.'"

It was enough. those three little words that held the meaning of all words ever spoken.

Day after day, my friendship with Lautrec flourished. He was a gentle and kind fellow. We penetrated deeper into the desert around al-Arish, suffering always from the burning sun, the lack of food, and the scarcity of water. To these was added a new and greater peril, that of the sand dunes. These lethal traps were composed of soft sand that swallowed up the unwary man who set one foot in it. After a long and arduous journey, we saw fields, trees, lotus blossoms, and the blue waters of Gaza and Jaffa on the horizon, embracing lush groves of olive trees that stretched as far as the eye could see. Confronted with this beauty, we forgot all the privations we had endured: we ran to the waters and leapt in, in an instant turning into children splashing one another, laughing and calling out, building castles in the sand that we knew full well we would never inhabit and which would soon collapse.

The goal of the campaign in the Levant was to take Acre, an essential position for the defense of Egypt. In the beginning, there were many victories, which boded well; but failures followed on their heels, one after another. Acre was larger and better fortified than we expected; the British battleships were anchored in her bay, and managed to capture the flotilla of gunboats, which held the artillery and had been sent from Egypt. This was the first step in our descent toward abject failure.

We resumed fighting, and Bonaparte managed to take Jaffa. A brief battle ensued in which Bonaparte, his soldiers, and his officers committed crimes that went beyond the boundaries of decency and honor in wartime, indeed that went against every principle of the fledgling French Republic. He and his soldiers became rabid beasts, committing atrocities, massacring, sacking the city and looting, leaving it littered with bloody shields, spears clotted with human flesh, dismembered horses, and in the night, shrieks to chill the blood, and the moans and groans of the victims' last breaths.

This man's baseness and wickedness became clear to me when three thousand Ottoman soldiers, including four hundred led by Omar Makram, declared their surrender to the French and threw down their arms, asking Bonaparte to be treated as prisoners of war. Initially, he acceded to their request, and received their arms, which they gave to him willingly: then he commanded them to stand in one long line on the seashore for inspection, to ensure, or so he said, that they were free from the plague. They stood in single file, shoulder to shoulder, facing the sea, their eyes skyward in supplication. The wind blew cold; the clouds were thick and the waves high. The gulls circled overhead, crying out and beating the air with their wings. Bonaparte gestured to his soldiers, who stood behind the prisoners of war, weapons trained on their backs, to pull the trigger. A sudden hail of bullets ensued, the men's heads dropped to their chests, and they fell down dead. Some of the bodies were swept out by the tide, while others made a good meal for the birds.

Bonaparte had violated every agreement and protocol of war by murdering soldiers who had surrendered. He justified his deed with an excuse almost worse than the offense, namely that he had done away with them because he did not have the resources to feed or guard them. It was a rank untruth; he had done it to take his revenge upon the Ottoman sultan for daring to fight him and allying himself with the British against him. The evidence for this was that he had spared the Egyptian soldiers and their leader Omar Makram, and instead had them returned to Egypt on board a special ship. He did this not, it was certain, out of love for Egypt, but out of fear that her people might turn against him once more.

We stumbled upon the corpses of innocents, which piled up in every street and alley of that fair city, and all the length of her seashore. Days later, the stench of rotting flesh, disease, and death filled the air. Plague spread through every corner of that luckless city. The people barricaded themselves behind the doors of their homes, and ceased to venture outside, thinking thus to avoid the reach of the pestilence; but the disease was borne on the air, the water, and the sand. The corpses were washed with vinegar and lime, then transported on ox-drawn carts, these carts whose bells and squeaking wheels never stopped sounding as they clattered over the stones of the street, both day and night. The bodies piled up; they were buried with no washing and no shrouds in graveyards that grew too small to contain them, with no gravestone to proclaim their name, as though they had come in error into the world.

The fair city that we had entered, its sweet perfume reaching us several kilometers before our entry, was now a ghost town marred by the stench and smoke of corpses rotting and being burnt, in accordance with the general's edict. The sky grew black with swarms of flies and carri- on-eating birds that flew over our heads: we had, after all, provided them with the tasty meals of these dead.

What did Bonaparte leave behind in every city he visited but grieving mothers, orphaned children, maimed men, and destruction and ruin? The cities whose doors had stood open with joy and pleasure now locked their gates to keep in their sorrow, the sounds of crying and wailing creeping out from behind them. Mon Dieu! What devastation was this? What manner of man was he?

24

SHE ARRIVED AT THE HOTEL and turned through the revolving door, just as she had been going in circles since she had set eyes on that painting. The receptionist greeted her with a broad smile. In the glass elevator that gave her a view of the entire hotel, *La vie en rose* was playing. Was life truly as rose-colored as the great chanteuse made it out to be, she wondered? And if it was, why had her mother so hated it that she had bought a one-way ticket to the next life? Could she have been persuaded to change her mind if she had heard Edith Piaf sing, with all the passion and power in her voice, ringing out to proclaim that life was beautiful? Could Edith have convinced a woman with depression that whatever happened, life was still worth living, and that something might be waiting for her that could turn her life around—something that might be closer than she thought? She might have stumbled across that something on a street corner someday, or perhaps received it in the mail, or on the wind, borne on the wings of fate, in the rain or on the breeze.

Her mother had been a beautiful woman, energetic and full of joy. She used to start her day at six o'clock, opening the windows of her life and her house to the light, watering her plants and feeding her cats. From the kitchen, the smell of her coffee would waft out; she always made a joyous little ritual of drinking it, listening to Fairuz, her favorite singer. Afterward, she would start making breakfast: she baked little pastries stuffed with cheese and vegetables and made omelets. She would always wave Yasmine and her sister Shaza goodbye until the school bus was out of sight. But in the long hours between when they left the house and came home from school . . . what had her mother done then?

She unclipped her earrings with a jerk and placed them on the dressing table. Yasmine looked at herself in the mirror. She moved closer and looked at her reflection as though seeing herself for the first time. "How many times," she thought to herself, "will I go over and over these memories?" Yes, it had been years, and time had changed her: the years she had lived showed on her skin. There were fine lines around her eyes and on her forehead. She scrubbed at her face with a wipe to get her makeup off, rubbing as if she also sought to erase the traces of time.

As she brushed her teeth before bed, she noticed under the harsh light of the bathroom mirror that several white strands had crept into her hair. She knew that these signs of age could be concealed: her hair could be dyed and her wrinkles would disappear completely with a shot of Botox. But this was not the issue; it was that time flashed by like lightning.

She brushed harder and harder at her teeth, wondering: how had her mother occupied her time?

She would have cleaned up the breakfast dishes, of course; gone to market to buy groceries for dinner and pick up the things everyone in the house needed. Yasmine couldn't remember a time when the house had not been full of anything one could possibly have an appetite for, and she had never needed a pen or notebook and not found one in her desk drawer. Her clothes were neatly hung up in her closet with care; often, she had found new dresses, socks, and hair ribbons in there. With all this, her mother had taken care with her appearance, always attractively and smartly dressed. She had had a few friends whom she made a habit of meeting at the sporting club every Thursday: they talked about diets, their children's schools, cooking, and fashion. She had lived an organized and lady-like life—it had just not been suited to the time she lived in, for she had been more like a perfect 1930s housewife, her husband and children the center of her life, everything revolving around them. Her grandmother had often reproached her mother for not going out to work, ". . . and you a graduate of the American University in Cairo!" She had tried to urge her to find a job to prove herself, be independent, and have her own world outside the home, even if she did not necessarily need the money.

Yasmine splashed water on her face, thinking furiously. If this woman had abandoned her outdated ideas and found a job, if she had had her own sense of self, perhaps then her husband's betrayal would not have driven her to take her own life. Her life would have been filled with other people and relationships; but was a social support network enough to hold a fragile psyche together? She did not think so. Depression attacks a person whose psychology cannot fight back, and creeps in slowly, painting everything in life with the same drab color.

There was a knock at the door: it was room service bearing coffee with milk. She stood at the window, looking out at the Eiffel Tower, snow piled up on its top, as flurries whirled around it in the wind. *Just like these cold memories,* she thought, *that won't get out of my head.*

The specter of her mother appeared before her, making herself a cup of coffee in the kitchen of their home, wearing her white silk robe, her blond hair spilling over her back. Yasmine was standing on tiptoe, trying and failing to reach the glass of water on the kitchen table. Her mother laughed and picked her up, handing her the glass of water with a kiss. She panicked: what if she dropped it? She folded her tiny fingers fiercely around it, and found herself just as fiercely gripping the mug of coffee in her hands as though it might slip away. Time seemed to soften and flow. Where was she now? Which

257

of them was she? The little girl who couldn't reach the table, or the grown woman alone in a room in Paris overlooking the Eiffel Tower? And why had that woman left her and gone away, when Yasmine still needed her?

She rested her head on her mother's shoulder and fell asleep. Her mother laid her gently on the bed. Her mother's specter was teasing her: a tall, slim figure she could feel walking around the room so as not to wake her little girl, then turning off the light and closing the door behind her as she left.

Trying to shake off the past, Yasmine got up off the bed and went to the window, but the memories came thick and fast. She remembered that long-ago winter with the biting cold of its days and nights and perpetually cloudy sky. When her mother had found out that her husband had betrayed her with her best friend, she had started out angry, threatening, screaming. Her father had left the house and gone to stay at a hotel. Then some close friends had intervened and convinced her to take him back, explaining it away as a momentary weakness that most men suffered from. When he came back, she would not share his bed and slept in another room. Day after day, she became a different woman: beaten, weak, and passive. She kept house as usual, but she performed her tasks mechanically, with no joy, and it seemed to take all her energy to do things. She no longer bestowed a smile here, a word there: even the things that used to bother or irritate her, such as walking on the rugs without taking off your shoes, or leaving wet towels on the bed, or leaving dirty glasses on the tables, no longer evoked any reaction. When her housework was done, she would retire to a chaise longue in a remote corner of the hall until the next day. She was absent, as though in another world.

As time passed, she no longer took any care with her appearance: she stopped bathing and doing her hair, and never even changed clothes. Yasmine was sad and bitter because she didn't know what to do to help her. She tried everything to get a rise out of her: she undid her braids so that her mother would have to rebraid her hair, she asked her to let her help with the housework, or invited her to sit and watch one of her favorite movies together, or told her she needed new clothes and wanted them to go shopping. Her mother would always refuse. A sense of real danger came over Yasmine, and she had talked to her grandmother about how far gone her mother was and how she was acting. The next day, when she came home from school, she found them together, and for the first time in weeks, she could hear her mother's voice in the house. She was screaming hysterically at her grandmother: "Me? See a psychiatrist? Do I look crazy to you? What would I need a psychiatrist for? Leave me alone! I hate you, I hate you all!"

She had wanted to run to her and hug her, and tell her how much she loved her. In a matter of weeks, her mother shriveled up like a dried fruit: her face grew pale and her form fragile and brittle. She ended her life, as the coroner told them, at 9:00 a.m., a little after they had all left the house. She must have planned it the night before. Yasmine remembered exactly how she had been that morning: she had been different from previous days. She had woken early, washed up, fixed her hair, and put on a pretty dress. She had baked pastries and made coffee and turned the radio on to Fairuz. Yasmine had been so delighted to find her that way, and a feeling had come over her that perhaps her mother would go back to being her old self, that she had found a way out of her problems and her sufferings, and that they would finally have a happy home again. She said goodbye to Yasmine and Shaza that day with a big hug, and stood at the window once again to wave them goodbye until the bus was out of sight.

On the way home that day, Yasmine had been eager to see her mother, as if she was back from a long journey: the woman who had lived in their house had not been her mother, but a stranger. When she had placed the key in the lock and turned it, silence had filled the house. It was a strange silence, tinged with sorrow, fear, and suspicion, as though it concealed a shattering blow.

She went straight to the kitchen. Everything was clean and in order, but she wasn't there. "Mom? Mom?" she had called. She walked through every room in the house, looking for her. She thought that perhaps her mother had gone to the hairdresser, or shopping, or perhaps to visit her grandmother. She waited another hour and then called her grandmother to ask, "Is Mom there?"

"No, she hasn't been here today," her grandmother answered, "and I called the house this morning and no one answered."

If her mother had been in her regular state of mind, her absence would not have been so concerning: Yasmine sometimes came home to find the house empty. For a moment, she thought that perhaps her mother had packed up and left the house entirely. She rushed to the bedroom and flung open the closet, but found everything in its place. She picked up the phone again and asked her father where her mother was, and he had no idea.

Her grandmother arrived in haste and bombarded her with questions. "Did something happen? Did that man fight with her? Where could she have gone?"

The phone never stopped ringing; neither did the doorbell. Her grandmother had called everyone they knew, family and friends alike, asking after her. She paced in circles in the room, questions circling around her as she did so. "Please, don't worry so much!" Yasmine had begged her. "It's okay! This morning she was feeling much better: she was smiling again, she listened to Fairuz, and she hugged me and Shaza when we left for school. She hasn't done that in forever!"

The words stopped in her throat. Had her mother been saying goodbye because she was getting ready to leave for the last time? Fear chilled her and her heart clenched. She retreated to a far corner, suddenly sensing that something had happened—a disaster so momentous it was inexpressible.

She watched them scurrying around and pacing the hallway, rushing to the phone whenever it rang, running to the door whenever the doorbell chimed, hoping it was her. Only Yasmine knew that she was never coming back. Her eyes never left the wall clock: its hands rotated monotonously, hour after hour, and the air grew heavy with a weight that pressed on the soul, making it groan, only affirming Yasmine's intuition when her father announced that he was going out to search the hospitals and the police stations for her.

He went into the bedroom to get dressed, then let out a yell that shook the house to its foundations. He had tried to open the door of their en-suite bathroom to wash up, but found the door blocked with something heavy. It was a body, lying on the bathroom floor, the soul long gone and flitting like a butterfly far away. How had no one looked in there before?

Shaza and her grandmother rushed to the scene: Yasmine never stirred. Her feet were rooted to the spot and she felt the room spin. She lost consciousness. It had been a mercy: she never had to see her beloved mother's body lying in a pool of her own blood on the bathroom floor.

Her mother had chosen a sharp blade to slash her wrists. Later, the question would not leave her: where had her mother gotten the blade? Her father had not used that type of razor for a long time, having switched to an electric shaver years ago. Had she gone out and bought it specially? Yasmine couldn't imagine it: someone going out to buy a tool to end their life.

She found herself speaking aloud, alone in the cold room: "Were you hiding in that corner all those weeks and months to plan it? What a damned painful end! Why couldn't you have chosen something kinder to yourself and to us?" Her voice rang out in the empty room. "Why did you pick that morning to make yourself up, to put on perfume, to wear a nice dress? Did you like the idea of leaving us that much?"

Tears were rolling down her face. "Why didn't you think of us? Of your two little girls who needed you?" She was screaming now. "You never stopped to think it would be a nightmare that would haunt us for the rest of our lives!"

Her mother had slit her wrists in her parents' bathroom on a grey day in February, and the curtain had fallen on the final scene of their marriage. Afterward, their father—whom everyone had blamed for what happened—had left the country, and the girls had gone to be raised by their grandmother. The apartment had been closed up, its grief locked inside it for years, until her grandmother had decided to rent it out, furnished—with all its furniture, bedclothes, photographs and paintings on the walls, and all the memories of the family who had once lived there.

Everyone avoided talking about what had happened, and many neighbors, friends. and family members could or would not realize that the woman who had ended her life in this fashion had not been "a sinner," as they called her. She had been ill, and her illness had been what had led her to end her life in this manner. In her normal state of mind, she would never have done it: she loved life, and her family, and her husband. The source of her unhappiness was that she had loved too much; if she had loved less, she would not have met such a fate.

Painful memories flooded forth like a waterfall in that hotel room in Paris, as though the gales blustering outside had only stirred them up. "Smile! You are in Paris!" a tourist sign had proclaimed. "Smile," Yasmine said to herself in the mirror, "you're in Paris." She pasted a smile on her face. She had to get herself out of this pit of painful memories. She dialed the numbers of a few friends she had made during her student days in Paris, and made dinner plans.

The next morning, she chose a classic, elegant outfit, to match the event she was to attend, and had breakfast at the hotel. She lost count of the cups of coffee she drank to wake herself up, then hurried off to catch the opening session of the conference. The radio announcer at *Good Morning Paris* rattled off the weather report: sunny with some clouds and rain in the afternoon. The taxi took her to the Paris Hilton, where the conference was being held.

The conference hall was thronged with people: association members, artists, journalists, and a large contingent of the general public. She caught sight of Professor Stefan sitting in the audience and sat next to him.

The conference started with an introductory speech by the head of the association, and for two hours, the conference speakers presented their papers. In the break, everyone went to the dining room for coffee, tea, and cakes. She found herself sitting at a round table with Professor Stefan and the director of the association who had received them in his office the previous day, and several other men. Suddenly, the director shot to his feet and made a beeline for two men standing in a corner. He interrupted their conversation, addressing himself to one of them, a tall, athletic-looking man with carefully coiffed hair. After a minute, the director gestured to her to come over. "Mademoiselle Yasmine Ghaleb," he introduced her, "a professor and researcher of art history from Egypt. Monsieur René Andrea, head of the Military History Archives."

The man eyed her as they shook hands. "She is making preparations to begin an exhaustive research project into Napoleon's campaign in the East—military, artistic, and scientific."

Andrea's military rigidity unbent, and he smiled, suddenly appearing attractive. "I would be honored to assist you," he said, "you are more than welcome at any time. You can come by my office today after the conference if it is convenient: I will be there until five."

"Where is 'there'?"

"The Musée de l'Armée." He gave her his business card.

"Thank you," she smiled and nodded, making her way back to her table, rejoined a few moments later by the director of the Association for Art History.

"You will find all the information you need with Monsieur Andrea," he told her. "His field is Bonaparte's military history. He knows every detail of Napoleon's campaigns and wars. With a little judicious questioning and a little discretion, I'm sure you will be able to find the information you're looking for."

His words rang in her ears as she made her way to Andrea's office after the conference. The taxi rattled through the streets and the trees flashed past the window, one after the other, "With a little discretion," he had said, "you will be able to find the information."

The taxi let her off a few meters from the Musée de l'Armée, which was surrounded by a high wall. Cars were not permitted inside, so she had to walk. In any case, it was two o'clock in the afternoon, and the weather was warmer at this time of day. As she walked through the grounds, she wondered what he had meant by "with a little discretion."

The museum was guarded by an impressive security presence. She informed the guards at the door that she had an appointment with the head of the museum. She passed through a great many electronic doors until she finally made her way inside. The building was quiet. There were several exhibition halls displaying the various weaponry used by the military and the uniforms worn by soldiers and officers through the ages. There were even special display cases for boots, helmets, and ammunition. On her other side, there were paintings glorifying the wars undertaken by the French Empire throughout its history.

The silence was broken by the click of her heels on the wooden floors. She stopped at a case bearing a gold necklace with a diamond embedded in it. Underneath it was a plaque: "The Grand Master Medal: The Medal of Honor of Napoleon I." She took a tour around the entrance, which displayed many military pieces: cannons, pistols, helmets, arrows, and all the instruments of killing that had been used in wars. There was a great cannon in the center of the hall, with a plaque beneath it indicating that it had been used in Napoleon's campaign in Egypt. *I wonder how many Egyptian lives were lost to you?* she thought. *How many mothers lost their sons, how many children you orphaned?*

Having seen enough, she hurried up the stairs to the first floor, where Andrea was waiting for her.

The room was as elegant as its occupant. He welcomed her warmly and invited her to take a seat. He had the window open, and the room felt freezing. Noticing that she had wrapped herself more tightly in her coat, he got up and closed the window. "Right. Fill me in."

For a moment she lost her concentration, unsure where to start. He noticed and left his desk, heading for the coffeemaker on a side table. He busied himself with making them two cups of espresso, and handed her one. Watching him, she could see that he seemed younger and less formal than his position would seem to indicate. They sipped their coffee and made small talk of the weather, Paris, and his last visit to Cairo. She felt comfortable with him, and forgot her first impression of him and Professor Stefan's words of warning. She began to talk, telling him of everything that had transpired since she had found the painting, and her long journey in search of the artist, that had brought her to his office. He listened with what seemed to be rapt attention. "Rest assured," he said, "I'll do all I can to help you. I like you."

She did not quite understand what "I like you" could possibly mean. Did he mean he liked her as a woman, or that he was interested in her research?

"What's the name of the artist?" he asked.

"Alton Germain," she said.

His eyes narrowed and grew unfocused, and he seemed lost in thought. Then he got up and entered the name into his computer, checking their archive. Seconds later, he said, "Yes. That artist was on the boat that took the artists and scientists to Egypt. It set sail from the port of Toulon on July 29, 1798."

She felt her eyes shine and felt light with relief. With this confident declaration, she felt certain that this was the painter of the portrait. After a pause, the man said, eyes still on his computer, "Alton Germain was an artist of great skill and compassionate temperament. He never sought any positions of power: he was only on the ship by sheer chance, as his name was not originally on the list of Campaign artists. At the last moment, an artist fell ill, and a replacement was needed: Alton Germain was chosen. He was an opponent of Napoleon's policies: his paintings did not properly glorify Napoleon, instead depicting the customs and manners of the common people. The few paintings he was compelled to paint depicted Napoleon and his soldiers as cruel and evil invaders, while the Egyptians he portrayed as equal in stature to the French. The greatest disaster was the painting he created of Napoleon's campaign in the Levant, when he painted the soldiers suffering in the desert, enfeebled and miserable, awaiting death.

"His paintings were in the original first edition of *The Description of Egypt*," he continued, "and when Napoleon saw them, he ordered that every painting by that artist be expunged from the book and that it be reprinted."

"That's why he removed every trace of him," Yasmine nodded, bursting with excitement, "and he may have imprisoned or killed him!"

"He did erase him without a trace," said Andrea, "but he didn't imprison or kill him." He looked at his watch, indicating an end to their interview.

"Well," she said, picking up her handbag from the desk, "I have to go now."

"I'll expect you tomorrow at two o'clock," said Andrea,

"and we can finish our conversation. You can bring the painting you think is his: we can take a color sample and run some tests on it to see if the colors match his other work. That way we'll be certain."

She nodded, shook his hand, and left.

The weather bureau had been absolutely correct: it was raining and a chilly wind was blowing. Luckily, she had remembered to bring an umbrella. She liked walking in the rain: it made her feel washed clean. Still, it was hard to walk in the rain in three-inch heels. She took a taxi instead. It was a good thing she had, as the heavens had opened up and the taxi driver could barely see for what seemed like buckets of water falling from the sky. The windshield wipers barely managed to wipe the rain away, sweeping back and forth in a dull rhythm.

She mentally replayed the conversation she had just had, pausing at, "The greatest disaster was the painting he created of Napoleon's campaign in the Levant."

Between Haifa and Acre: March 1798

Disease was rampant: it spread through the soldiers like wildfire. First there were the buboes that sprouted on men's faces, under their arms, and on their thighs; then they would grow and blacken, followed by vomiting and fever. We used an abandoned monastery between Haifa and Acre to set up a field hospital, and moved the afflicted soldiers there. Their numbers increased day by day. I volunteered, along with a number of doctors and nurses, to work in the hospital: this was no time to be painting pictures to glorify the emperor, with ruin and devastation around us everywhere we looked.

The beds filled up with plague-ridden soldiers; the new arrivals we were obliged to place on the floor so that one could scarcely walk through the hospital. All of them were suffering from fevers, buboes covering their bodies, their cries filling the halls. I assisted with all the strength I could muster. I did not fear this black plague nor run from it, as many of the Campaign scientists who were with us did— they excused themselves from assisting—or as the officers and soldiers did, diverting their path to take them away from the hospital. I know that death and life are fated and not within our purvey to control: the junior officer who refused to enter to comfort his soldiers with some word that might bring them peace on their way to the afterlife, we heard was killed that same day in battle. Death awaits us wherever we are: so why fear? All I did was take the necessary precautions: I did not take off my gloves or mask, I disinfected myself, and washed my hands well with vinegar and lime.

One evening there was a loud clamor: we ran to see what was the matter. A large group of afflicted soldiers had been brought there from Acre, their comrades bearing them upon stretchers. Among their number was Lautrec, lying upon a stretcher. His face was ruddy and covered with boils, which marred his beautiful features. He had wasted away to nothing, a mere skeleton of a man. Because I had the unwelcome skill of knowing which of the afflicted was closest to death, I knew that there were mere hours between him and death. I was greatly pained at the knowledge and could not restrain myself from weeping. It was as though all the tears I had held back since leaving from the port of Toulon had found a suitable excuse to fall now, without stopping.

I approached Lautrec. He tried valiantly to smile. Despite it all, that beautiful smile was unchanged. I removed his clothing and disinfected his body, then bandaged his buboes that had grown huge and burst, oozing pus and blood. I wept in silence throughout. I remembered the night he had told me the story of his life, and that he had always been an unwelcome guest in his own home. Had he come here, I thought, to die?

As he was in his death throes, he gestured weakly to his jacket. I handed it to him. He pulled a letter out of an inside pocket and held it out to me. In tones scarcely audible, he whispered, "Please . . . give it to her."

He was holding the lock of her hair to his heart. He held it there until his heart stopped beating.

I covered his face with the sheet and grieved for him.

In this manner, the beds emptied, then filled once more. Death after death brought it home to me how much ruin this rash man had brought down upon the young men of his country to fulfill his grandiose dreams, by forcing them into a war whose consequences he had not considered.

News came to us of the resounding defeat our soldiers had suffered at Acre, bringing disappointment to everyone. One morning, there was chaos in the hospital: there was news that Bonaparte was going to pay the hospital a visit on his way to Cairo. It was a good thing, for perhaps it might be good for the troops' morale. At eleven o'clock in the morning, he strode into the hospital surrounded by his senior officers, having practically bathed in disinfectant and covered his face so thoroughly that only his eyes were visible. He hurried through the rows of beds, then rushed outside, with no word of comfort, consolation, or encouragement. I looked into the eyes of the afflicted men, seeing grief and disenchantment there: he had led them to their death, and then he had all but ignored them.

That day my colleagues and I—doctors and volunteers—gathered at a table, and I saw deep shame in the eyes of those who had seen Bonaparte as a great hero, and justified all his deeds hitherto. In a choked voice, Monsieur Shalimar, who had been one of them, said "He has the face of defeat. It is nature that defeated him. His greatest enemies were the desert and the plague."

"That is not to say," someone added, "that he did not throw us into the jaws of the lion without an adequate plan for this project. He only cares for his own interests, for acquiring the title of 'Emperor of East and West.' For the sake of this, he is prepared to sacrifice anything and everything."

"He rejected the British offer to take his plague-ridden soldiers of Acre on a special ship that would have taken them to France to be treated," said a doctor, "for his pride would not permit him to owe a single word of thanks to an Englishman." He exhaled heavily. "He would rather let his soldiers sicken and die than accept their offer."

"As if that were not enough," said a volunteer, "out of sheer baseness, he commanded that those with incurable cases of the plague be poisoned, to relieve the burden upon the army."

The next day, before he left for Egypt, Bonaparte gave a speech. "You have crossed the desert that divides Africa from Asia," he said, "as fast as any army could. You have vanquished the army that would have come to invade Egypt, taken its commander prisoner, and destroyed their machines of war. There is nothing for us but to face reality and keep what remains of the army, and return to Egypt."

The joyous cries of the soldiers rang out, glad to hear the news of our return. Caravans set forth one after the other. The officers gave orders to start on our way. I and those responsible for the oversight of the field hospital refused to leave the sick and dying behind. In flagrant disobedience of orders, we stayed behind. We resolved to divide ourselves into two groups: one to transport the men who were recovering, and one to stay with the dead and dying until they had expired.

We moved the recovering men on stretchers. The soldiers carried them on the return journey, which I privately entitled "The Journey through Hell" for all the hardships and privations we endured. It was as though everything conspired against us: the return was tragedy incarnate. We were all of us exhausted and weak, barely able to carry our own selves, let alone stretchers laden with plague-ridden soldiers, leaving aside the risk of contagion. Each pair of men bore a stretcher, one to the fore and the other to the rear, and thus we dragged our feet through the heavy and burning desert sand step after painful step, beneath the scorching sun. We had not sufficient water and were obliged to ration what we did have.

Hundreds of thirsting soldiers, wounded men, and plague sufferers lay motionless in the desert. Many shot themselves to be rid of their unrelenting torment. Exhaustion sapped the strength of those who had volunteered to carry their comrades, and they were unable to continue. Some tipped the sick men off the stretchers, then threw the stretchers themselves aside, and staggered on their way half-mad with weeping and shouting, and I could not blame them: they were scarce able to move under their own weight. The cries of the wounded men we left behind split the burning desert, echoing through the boundless cruel silence, crying, "Do not abandon us! Please take us with you! Save us! We would not die here alone!" But circumstance overpowered us all.

I thought amid all this suffering that it might be punishment for some sin we had committed: perhaps some bereft mother, widowed wife, or orphaned child had cursed us after the French army had killed their sons, husbands, or fathers; perhaps all the defeat and death we endured was divine retribution. I dragged myself on, drained and enfeebled, and we dragged our defeat along with us. The idea took shape in my head of painting this scene, a moment of inspiration in my darkest hour. Death's raucous presence and merciless tyranny loomed over us all.

In the night, beneath the moon I could almost touch—my only com-
pany in my loneliness in the night—I would take out my brushes and
palette and paint the men's suffering faces and dying bodies. I painted sand
dunes paved with corpses and carrion-eating birds. I painted ravening
wolves, while overhead the owls and ravens filled the desert night with
their cries. I painted shame and the betrayal of those who had allowed this
thing to befall us. The painting cried aloud with all this pain: I would not
obey the orders of a mad general and paint him as he wished. I would not
paint the false victories of which he made empty boasts. True victory is
over an enemy capable of fighting back, not an unarmed victim.

I was afflicted with fever: I burned. It was then I knew that the dis-
ease had struck me as well. My body had borne the contagion through my
time in the field hospital, and now the symptoms had begun to make them-
selves known to me. A high fever; enfeeblement as my body failed me; and
other sensations that I longed to dismiss as sunstroke or mere exhaustion.
But when the first boil appeared on my face, I knew: it was the plague.

Day after day, my condition worsened, until I was but a breath from
dying. Still, I refused to surrender to my illness. I took up my brush, now
heavy in my hand, and fought my illness by painting.

The physician examined me and said that my case was serious. He
said nothing, merely giving me a pitying look that told me I was well on my
way. I prayed to Heaven that I might not expire here in this pitiless desert,
to be devoured by wolves. At least let me have a grave and a headstone of
marble proclaiming, "Here lies Alton Germain," even if no one sees it.

When we reached the outskirts of the city, I was quarantined along
with all the other men afflicted with the plague. I lay on a humble bed,
surrounded by a great number of sick men. I was in the last stages of
the disease, delirium and hallucinations and phases of unconsciousness,
repeated over and over again. In my moments of consciousness, there was
one name on my lips: Zeinab.

I delivered the painting I had completed depicting Bonaparte's cam-
paign in the Levant to one of the doctors, with instructions to deliver it to
my artist colleagues in the Campaign. I remembered the soldier Lautrec,
and the letter he had pressed into my hand to deliver to his sweetheart,
laughing at the irony of fate: here I was, facing the same end, and I dipped

my quill in ink to write to her. I did not know what language to write in, I who knew no Arabic, so I wrote down one phrase, meaning everything: I love you.

If I had not finished her portrait, scant days before going out on the expedition to the Levant, I would have grieved. It was the only painting that I had painted, not with my tools, but with my heart. I secreted it in one of the house's hidden passageways, used only for storage. It was nailed to the underside of a wooden table, hidden from prying eyes and grasping hands. This portrait I painted for myself alone, so that I might see it on my wall wherever I went. I had concealed locks of her hair under a layer of black paint: no one who saw it could tell it was there. I had done it to allow her braids to rest softly on her shoulders, as she always wished.

25

At last, exhausted, she got to the hotel, dropping into a brief nap. She awoke to the ringing of her phone.

"How are you?"

"Doing okay. You?"

"Tell me, did you find out anything?"

"Yes! Lots of things. Tomorrow I have an important meeting where I'm going to find out more."

There was a beat of silence. "I miss you."

He always blurted it out in the middle of a conversation, like one of those pat phrases we say without really meaning them, but this time he sounded sincere.

"We just saw each other only a couple of days ago," she said, effectively shutting him up.

She clearly wanted to hear a response from him, something to the effect of "I always miss you, even when we're together." He resolved to disappoint her as she had disappointed him, saying, "You're right at that. It hasn't been long at all. Anyway, take care of yourself."

He hung up in a hurry, leaving her hanging on, alone in her hotel.

Yasmine called her grandmother to make sure she was okay, and then she found herself standing at the window, looking out: the Eiffel Tower, covered with snow; close-set apartment blocks with window boxes on the balconies; narrow, crooked streets washed with rainwater. She had always loved this city. Everything in it urged you to live, to love, to create art. For a moment she imagined the man she was searching for in the corridors of history: the man who had painted with passion and honesty. Which of these alleyways would he have emerged from? Which of these streets would he have walked down? Didn't streets recall the footsteps of those who had walked down them long ago? If only she could make the streets speak, and tell her where he had come and gone. She imagined him as a slight young man, a lock of hair falling into his face, walking down the streets of Paris, ages ago. He went out with his palette and brushes to capture life on his canvas. The paintings that she had seen of his were proof that this artist was inspired by real life, by the footsteps of passersby in the streets around her. Her sense of being in the same space where this man had once been made her feel close to him, filling her with peace and contentment. His ghost was here, in the corners of the city, all around her, trying to provide her with clues to who and where he was. He urged her to go outside, to walk in the fresh air and down the very streets he had traversed so long ago.

The hotel phone rang, startling her. Who would be calling her here?

"Hello?"

A heavy silence weighted down the other end of the line. She was about to hang up when a voice scraped down the line, as though from the depths of the past: "Hello, Yasmine. How are you?"

She was intimately familiar with this voice and its distinctive tones, but she could not be sure it was him. "Who is this?" she asked.

There was silence on the other end of the line. What should he say in response? Reproach her for not recognizing his voice at once? And what right did he have? "I can't blame you for not recognizing my voice. It's been a while," the voice replied.

It was a shock. Her legs could not hold her and she dropped down to sit on the bed. "How did you know I was here?"

"Is that all you have to say, after all these years?"

His voice was enough to stir up every memory of the past, dredging up her most painful memory from the mists of her recollection. She had always tried not to remember him.

"I moved to France years ago. Yesterday morning I read that the Association for Art History was holding a conference, and your name was on the list of people attending."

"How did you know I was staying here?"

"I called the conference organizers to ask about you, and they gave me the name of the hotel where the attendees were staying."

"Well, you found me. What do you want?"

"To see you. I promise not to take up too much of your time. I just want to see you and talk to you. I've missed you so much."

"I'm sorry," she said, "I don't have the time."

"Please, Yasmine. It's been a long time. You're old enough to understand now. Just give me a chance to speak with you, and then make your decision."

She didn't know what to say. She felt a strong resistance to meeting him; still, some shred of nostalgia told her to say yes.

"Please."

Hearing the entreaty, the pleading in his voice, she gave in. "Okay. Tomorrow at eight at Café du Monde."

His delight was clear and his voice was transformed now he had what he wanted. "Thank you! I'll be there early."

She ended the call and lay down on the bed. Picking up the receiver had lifted the lid on every memory she had tried to keep suppressed.

She had always had a special relationship with her father. She had adored him and he had always spoiled her. She remembered how her little hand used to disappear completely inside his big one as they walked from place to place. He took her to museums and libraries and, during school holidays, planned trips for them to historical sites. He was deeply cultured and widely read, and she was not too young for him to supply her with culture and knowledge. She was a little girl with long braids and big questions, always greedy for information: thanks to his large library, she had become a bookworm at a very young age. She never tired of being with him and listening to his conversation and anecdotes. To her, he was as deep as the sea: she imagined that however much she took, the source would never dry up. He was never just a father to her: he was the lighthouse that lit up her life. To her, he had been a god who could do no wrong, a man above suspicion, above sin. Then suddenly, without warning, it had all been scattered to the winds. Her idol crumbled like the sandcastles they had built by the seaside, washed away by the waves without a trace. She had been doubly betrayed by him, doubly bereft.

She needed to close the door of memory and get ready to go to dinner with her old colleagues. She found them already waiting for her at a café on the Champs-Élysées, at the same table where they used to sit when she had been a student in this city. At this café, built some three hundred years ago, everything retained its original form: even the customers seemed to be part of it. Only the electronic devices in the hands of the patrons betrayed the old-world charm.

Her friends greeted her with warm hugs, arriving one after the other. Their table filled up and long conversations started. They spoke of who had come and gone, who had gone into academia and who had pursued art as a hobby; the one thing everyone had in common was a passion for the history of art, for its tales and myths. They plunged into long discussions about the latest discoveries in the field. She knew that if she told them about the painting, they would be full of curiosity and seek to help her in any way they could: they might even take her on an expedition to find the home of the artist. But something made her clutch the secret jealously to her heart, for herself alone.

Cairo: June 1799

That morning, the sun was veiled in mist. Thick clouds soon obscured it completely. The rooftops of Cairo, now within sight, looked like a row of teeth. Whether the houses were of stone or wood, the meshrabiyehs were locked and the doors barred, the dogs hungry and the cats dead, the stench of rotting flesh filling everyone's nostrils.

Death loomed over Cairo like a fog that would not dissipate. It permeated every nook and cranny, carried on the wind and mingling with our breath. No one left their houses. The voices of itinerant vendors crying their wares no longer rang out through the streets. The water carriers no longer came knocking every morning, and footsteps were no longer heard in the streets and alleyways. Everyone stayed where they were. Heavy curtains covered the windows of every house and thick fabric blocked the gaps under the doors. People stayed at home praying. The women had removed their finery, the men let their beards grow, and everyone abandoned luxuries and frivolities in the face of the waiting specter of death.

They said that the wind brings the disease, or the water, or perhaps it was a contagion from the food, or from prostitutes, or from the French, who never washed properly. The carts bearing corpses passed by day and night. The squeaking of the wheels over the stones of the city was enough to strike fear into one's heart, and the carter himself was a fearsome sight. Wrapped in a caftan of rough sackcloth, he had his head covered with a cap and a black mask over his face; the only things showing were his cruel black eyes. His passage was an ill omen. If he went into some street of a morning to take a corpse or two, he would come back at night to take more than ten or twenty.

That morning, Zeinab went outside, ignoring the warnings. She wrapped herself up well and washed in vinegar and lime, then passed from street to street until she arrived at the house where Alton was staying. It had been barricaded with bolts and chains since the campaign had left for the Levant. Conflicting feelings filled her with worry and trepidation, and the silence that pressed down upon every part of the city made her even more afraid. Where was the friendly noise of the people? She nearly returned home, but at the last minute it occurred to her to drive her mule to Beit al-Alfi, the seat of Napoleon.

"Who do you want?" asked the guard.

"I wish to see Bonaparte."

"He's not yet back from his campaign in the Levant," the guard told her.

"Then I wish to see Madame Pauline."

The guard, who was used to seeing her coming and going, asked her to follow him. He left her waiting in the hall for a few moments, then gestured her over to a room at the end of the hall. "She's waiting for you."

Impeccably dressed and coiffed, Pauline sat at a round table surrounded by several of her friends, Frenchwomen and Egyptian wives of the aristocracy. There were glasses on the table, and a tray piled high with all kinds of fruit. The woman looked at her curiously, examining her from head to toe. The few times she had seen Zeinab, the latter had been dressed up in French finery, but today she had abandoned her smart attire, wrapped in a faded black burka and the signs of sorrow and exhaustion clear on her face, like one burdened with the weight of the world. "There you are!" said Pauline. "So this is how you really are. How could you set foot in this place looking like that? What if the general saw you looking like a beggar? You'd turn his stomach! He'd never touch you again."

The women tittered and some laughed outright at Pauline's mockery, but Zeinab remained still as a statue. The woman's words didn't hurt her and she did not care about her mockery. "I'm here to ask after a painter, Alton," she said.

The woman's jaw dropped. "Alton? What do you want with him? How long have you known him?"

She was taken aback by the woman's questions coming in quick succession, and stammered, "He was doing a painting of me. I wanted to see it."

Pauline let out a peal of laughter. "Alton, paint you?" she said, pointing at her with a manicured fingertip. "An artist who paints noblewomen and countesses and the cream of Parisian society, paint you? Who do you think you are?" She snorted. "If Napoleon has taken you to his bed, it was a dalliance to him, no more. A bit of fun. But you need to know that you mean nothing to anyone."

Zeinab gave no answer. She turned and left, her footsteps heavier than before.

"Zeinab!" Rostom, who had seen what happened, chased after her. He caught up with her in the garden. "Wait!"

She paused. "Yes, Rostom."

"You were asking about Alton, weren't you?"

Her eyes shone with hope and she nodded.

"I heard that he's being held in hospital in quarantine."

"Hospital? What? Why? Was he wounded in the war?"

"No," Rostom sighed, "it's nothing to do with the war. Plague broke out among the soldiers and more than half the army died. He was infected."

Time stopped. A veil seemed to fall over her sight. "Can you take me to him?" she whispered. "Or just tell me where he is. I want to see him."

"You could get infected," warned Rostom.

"I don't care," she begged. "Please. Tell me where he is."

Rostom nodded. "I will. Come with me."

She traveled there through a veil of her tears, which flowed incessantly. The carriage passed through narrow streets, and she looked out onto the deserted alleys and squares. Even the tree branches were bowed with grief. They rode quite a distance, through many streets and various neighborhoods, until it seemed unending. Finally, they stopped at the outskirts of the city. The guards hurried toward Napoleon's grand carriage, imagining that some high-ranking visitor was in it, perhaps a friend of Bonaparte's there to visit someone he knew. "Wait in the carriage a minute," said Rostom, "while I obtain permission for you to enter."

He spoke to the guards for a long time: Zeinab watched them from behind the curtain of the carriage. From the tones of their voices, she could tell that they were unwilling to let her in.

A great crowd was gathered outside the quarantine hospital: mothers awaiting the return of their sons, friends waiting for friends, traders waiting for their suppliers coming from abroad with goods, and envoys and translators waiting for their fellow countrymen. The wind bore snatches of conversation in every language. Everyone who had come across the sea or across the desert to the town was held in the quarantine hospital for examination. Only those not infected with the plague could pass. The sick were made to go back whence they had come, or stay in the hospital until they were cured and could pass. Since recovery from the plague was unlikely, the only place most of them passed on to was the grave.

The guard scrutinized her from head to toe, as if to ask, "Who is this girl, come in Bonaparte's personal carriage to visit a Frenchman at death's door?"

He asked her, "Do you not fear contagion?"

She shook her head. He led her inside and another man, a nurse, handed her a mask. She put it on, although it would not keep out the unbearable stench. A soldier motioned her over to a ward. "That's the ward where the Campaign men are."

The hallway was full to bursting with dying men, their groans filling the air. With difficulty, she managed to step among the men lying on the floor until she got to the ward that the guard had pointed out. She stood there, a curtain between them. Her hand trembled as she pushed it aside.

Cairo: June 1799

Suddenly, between sleep and waking, I saw her. Was she a dream, or was she real? I knew not. I saw her draw closer. She was wearing a mask, but that would not keep me from recognizing her. Her footsteps, graceful as a gazelle's, were enough for me to know her.

I did not wish her to see me in such a state. I knew precisely how horrifying the sight of men with this affliction was, especially in the final stages of the disease. She sat close to me and whispered, "What has befallen you?" She was weeping

"Zeinab," I managed to croak. "Why are you here? You'll contract the disease."

"Please don't leave me," she entreated. "Please don't go. There is no life for me without you."

"Your life lies ahead of you, my love," I whispered.

"What good is it without you?"

I wanted to see her, to look my fill of her, to print her image on my eyes and keep it within always; but I did not want to ask her to remove her mask, fearing for her life. As though she had heard my unspoken thoughts, she lifted it off her face.

I drank in the sight of her with the certainty of one who knows he is about to leave this world, knowing it would be the last time I laid eyes upon her. Her eyes filled with tears. If only I could have extended my hand and wiped away her tears. I wished my illness were not con-tagious, that I might press her close in my embrace and take my final leave of her. I had come here in the stead of another; I had come to know what love was, the love that would not have touched my heart without seeing her; I had come here to give up the ghost on this soil, as though this narrow corner of the world was where I was fated to experience life's two greatest truths: love and death.

I took my final message out from under the pillow and held it out to her. I looked my fill of her and closed my eyes to the sight of her.

Paris: Spring 2012

At last the sun came out that day after a week of clouds, filling her with an uplifting sense of hope. But then she thought of that evening's date, and her heart twisted, her serenity shattered.

After the conference was over, she went straight to the Musée de l'Armée. Andrea welcomed her with a polite smile, but his once-over of her was more intent this time. "What is the secret of Egyptian women?" he smiled.

She didn't understand. "What secret?"

"The secret of your charm. Egyptian women possess an attraction that captivates even the world's strongest men. Look at Antony and Cleopatra. He gave up his kingdom and his throne for her. And the common girl who captured the heart of Napoleon Bonaparte himself."

"Military men," Yasmine shot back, "often have an over-abundance of sentimentality to balance out their warlike tendencies. Bonaparte is proof of that, writing love letters to his Josephine as he was planning his military campaigns." Then she blinked. "What Egyptian girl who captured Napoleon's heart?"

He smiled slyly, then motioned to the painting she was carrying. "Show me the painting."

She laid it out on the table. He looked at it for a long time, then picked up the phone on his desk and asked someone to come to his office. He handed him the painting, asking the man to take both the painting of Zeinab and another painting, located in Exhibition Hall No. 4—he scrawled some instructions on a scrap of paper detailing the latter painting—to the art viewing room for testing to see if the same artist had painted them both. The employee left to carry out his orders.

Andrea moved to sit in the seat facing Yasmine's. "May I smoke?"

Her eyes flickered to the No Smoking sign, and she made a feeble gesture toward it. "But you've put up a sign. . . ."

"I must confess," said Andrea, "when it comes to smoking and women, it is hard to stay on the straight and narrow."

"Who," she asked again, "is the girl Napoleon loved?"

Andrea nodded slowly. "Napoleon had an affair with an Egyptian girl. We don't know if it was love or just a passing fancy, or how far it went—if it was truly an affair or just over-blown by rumors. There are no definite answers, but what is certain is that he took a fancy to a girl whose father was an Azharite imam."

"Even though," Yasmine interrupted, "Napoleon was deeply in love with Josephine in that period?"

"Napoleon met Josephine at a party and fell in love with her," Andrea conceded, "and she found in him what she was looking for: power, influence, and authority; and he was sure to provide her with the social position and protection she craved. That was why she broke it off with all other men and accepted his proposal of marriage. They had such happiness together that Napoleon is said to have declared, "*Vivre en Joséphine, c'est vivre au Paradis.*" He spoke slowly, clearly enjoying his subject. He opened a desk drawer and took out a box of chocolates, placing it on a small table between them. He plucked out a chocolate from the box, unwrapped it slowly, and bit into it with languid pleasure. Yasmine watched, hoping he would stop eating and resume speaking. "A short while after their marriage, he settled upon a campaign in the East. Josephine wanted to come to Egypt with him, to be a queen of the Orient; she was unconvinced of Napoleon's excuse that she was too spoiled and delicate to endure the hardships of the journey. When she saw his ship and the preparations they had made for the campaign before departure, she saw that Napoleon's bedroom was luxurious and well-appointed. It even had a bed with special wheels to prevent him getting seasick. She laughed and said, "What hardships? Look at this place!" But for the first time, Napoleon did not weaken to her pleas and insistence; he stood firm, as he knew how dangerous the campaign would be."

He held out the box. "Chocolate?"

"I. . . ."

"You'll like it. It has candied chestnuts inside."

Yasmine took one and Andrea went on. "Napoleon had a small library on his ship. His best friend, Louis Antoine Fauvelet de Bourrienne, used to read to him all the time, mostly on the history of the Islamic world. One day, Napoleon conducted a surprise inspection of his troops, and found them reading novels and poetry. He rebuked them, saying, "This is reading for chambermaids! Men should only read history." In the evenings, he would spend time with his generals and speak to them without shame of his love for Josephine." Andrea chuckled. "Imagine that! A few days after they had set sail, he missed her so much that he sent a frigate to have her brought to him, but funnily enough, she had left Paris for Plombières-les-Bains, to bathe in a lake said to cure childlessness. Unfortunately, the old boarding house where she had rented a room collapsed, and she was seriously injured with several broken bones. Before this accident, Napoleon had been overcome with unease because a locket had broken that he used to keep her picture in. He supposedly cried out, feeling it was an ill omen, 'Either something has befallen her, or she is being unfaithful!' It turns out it was both."

Andrea leaned forward. "One day in July 1798, Bonaparte was marching in the desert with General Jean-Andoche Junot, who told him that his wife was being unfaithful to him with a man called Hippolyte Charles. He went into hysterics, screaming and yelling, and then fell into a deep depression. He refused to see anyone. He stopped talking to the others and joining in their soirées. He had loved her madly and had been faithful to her, and thought only of her during their separation. He sat down to write long letters to her, telling her how much he loved her and missed her, while she was in the arms of another man. And since he believed in an eye for an eye, he decided to be unfaithful to her as well, so as to forget her and entertain himself and perhaps escape his depression."

"Just like that?"

"Yes," shrugged Andrea, "and he became preoccupied with the idea and determined to carry it out. But how? In a country like Egypt, women were not permitted to mingle with men—except for prostitutes and belly dancers in the streets and cafés, and that kind of cheap woman would never appeal to Bonaparte. When he resolved to be unfaithful to Josephine, he was determined to choose a woman who would be her equal—if not in beauty and elegance, then at least a woman of good family, not some tawdry lady of the night. He looked for a woman all over Egypt, and came up with quite a few girls, the daughters of merchants from Malta and Greece, or of ambassadors and consuls—men who would not object to their daughter being Napoleon's mistress, and on the contrary welcomed it. It was an unrepeatable opportunity in their eyes: all their dreams would come true through their daughter's lover!" He shrugged. "But none of those girls truly pleased him: they were too fat, too thin, too boring, too plain, or too smelly."

Yasmine sat transfixed. "What a strange man."

"One time," Andrea said, "an Azharite imam brought his daughter with him to the annual celebration of the flooding of the Nile. She caught Napoleon's eye. She was lovely, dark-skinned and slender. Some people say there was something about her that looked a bit like Josephine. Napoleon found an excuse to get close to her and inhale her scent, and he liked her perfume. He decided that this was the one. The father was fine with it, and he gave the affair his blessing, knowing it would be good for him—the man had dreams too, you understand, and it was Napoleon who would make them come true. Bonaparte got attached to her, and they called her 'the general's Egyptian girl.' He asked to see her from time to time, but no one knows what went on between them."

"But I read," Yasmine interjected, "that he was having an affair with one of the officers' wives at the time?"

"There were three hundred women on the ship," Andrea said, "at least, the ones officially allowed on the boat to cook, clean, sew, and nurse the sick. Apart from these, there were strict orders that no woman be allowed on board. Still," he half-smiled, "several of the officers' wives and girlfriends disguised themselves as soldiers and officers and got on the boat. The wife of General Fauré was one of them—a beautiful woman named Pauline, blond-haired and blue-eyed, irresistible in her husband's military uniform. Napoleon saw her at a soirée and was surprised to see one of his generals' wives in Egypt. He decided to discipline her and her husband, but she flirted with him and pleaded with him to forgive them, and he forgave her because he was attracted to her. He never let anything stand in his way when he wanted something, no matter what it cost: he sent her husband off to battle to get him out of the way. During a party hosted by General Dupuy, the governor of Cairo, some coffee spilled on her dress and she went upstairs to change. Napoleon offered to accompany her and they disappeared for quite some time. After that, she moved to a house close to his in the neighborhood of Ezbekiya, and he had her brought to see him from time to time. He didn't even try to be secretive about it, as though he wanted Josephine to find out. Pauline's husband divorced her and Napoleon made her a promise of marriage."

"Did he marry her?"

"Of course not," replied Andrea. "He even left the country without telling her or anyone, in secret, and left General Kléber to rule in his stead. Bonaparte and Kléber had been sworn enemies: now everyone to whom Napoleon had been close was on the list of persona non grata. Pauline was at the head of that list. When she learned that Napoleon was gone, she went to Kléber and asked him for permission to return to France. He agreed immediately, not to please her but to embarrass Napoleon, since Kléber knew she was not a woman who forgave easily. When she arrived in France, she tried to see Napoleon, but he avoided her and wouldn't see her. He gave her a hefty sum and a house outside of Paris to be rid of her pestering." He smiled. "Later, she married a man from the East who had been a commander in the Ottoman army, and spent her life painting and writing novels. As she grew older, she became eccentric, wearing men's clothes and smoking a pipe. She died in 1869 at ninety, fifty years after Napoleon's death. But she never forgot their affair, and talked about it until the day she died."

"That's not unusual," Yasmine mused. "Love is like that."

"Well, even if she loved him, her feelings weren't returned," said Andrea. "When he left, he took a slave called Rostom with him instead of her."

"Rostom?"

"Yes. Come. I want to show you a painting of him in one of the exhibition halls."

Soon, Yasmine stood transfixed before the painting of a handsome middle-aged man, attired in the French style with an Arab turban upon his head. "He was originally from Georgia," said Andrea, "and he was bought from Constantinople by a Mamluk prince and ended up in Cairo. He was freed and made part of the Mamluk cavalry. After the French Campaign forced the Mamluks to flee, he went to work for Imam al-Bakri in Cairo. Al-Bakri made a gift of him to Napoleon. He served the general for fifteen years, traveling with him all over the world. He was his secret-keeper, personal guardian, and secretary. He always wore that Oriental turban and walked at the head of every procession. He even wore it to Napoleon's coronation. Look, there he is in this painting of the coronation. Napoleon always liked to be seen in his company because his presence reminded everyone of his conquest of Egypt. The Parisians took a liking to him and would go out just to catch a glimpse of him at the emperor's twice-daily parade in the morning and at sunset. Napoleon would sit in his closed carriage drawn by several horses and surrounded by eight mounted guards glaring at everyone in sight, dressed in embroidered uniforms and sporting Damascene swords decorated with jewels. Rostom would lead the procession on a proud Arabian horse, displaying the muscles in his arms and back, a great white turban of glossy silk around his head. When the procession went by, people would yell, 'Rostom! Rostom!' and forget to call out for Napoleon."

A secretary came in, telling Andrea he was needed. He left, gesturing to the paintings. "I'll leave you with these for a moment."

Cairo: August 1799

Grief and mourning lay over Sheikh al-Bakri's house like a shroud. Zeinab had fallen ill and was lying in bed, too weak to stand. She had stopped eating and speaking, and no one knew why. Fatima knew that the fortune-teller's prophecy was coming true: here was her daughter at death's door. All the prescriptions and cures of the physicians and the spice merchants had failed, and the prayers and talismans of the holy men had come to naught.

When Zeinab had come home after her meeting with Alton, tears flowed silently from her eyes. Her mother asked, "What happened?" She had not been able to tell her that she was head over heels in love with a man—a Frenchman who painted the people in the streets like those her mother called "maniacs," and that he had loved her in return, perhaps the only one who had truly loved her in this life, so much that her name had been on his lips as he lay dying.

She could not stop thinking of him since their last moment together, as if her memory would only hold his image as he lay dying. A few days later, Rostom told her, "It's over. He's dead." The words had struck her like a thunderbolt: she hadn't known that words could have the power to do this, to turn to flames that destroyed her hopes like wildfire; to strike like a bullet at the heart, to maim like an errant arrow. She had never let go of his letter, the one that only said *I love you*, and her grief only increased.

Before he secretly left for France, Napoleon sent for her. Had he missed her, or did he only want to say goodbye? In any case, they sent word that she was ill and could not leave her bed; but he was unconvinced, and sent Rostom to bring her to him, even if she were ill, sitting in his room waiting for her. There was a knock at the door and he smiled, thinking it was her: but his brow knitted to see that it was Pauline. He nodded. "You seem to be waiting for someone," she said.

He looked away without answering.

"All right. But let me tell you something. The girl you're waiting for came here a few days ago. What a pity, it wasn't you she asked after. She came looking for another man."

His eyes narrowed. "Who?"

"The painter, Alton," she sneered. "Poor girl, her voice was shaking so with love when she said his name!"

His eyes blazed. "Alton? But how? How could he dare?" Jealousy swept him, but not jealousy over her; it was over his own self. A girl whom he had invited into his room was his private property, and no one else had any right to look at her. He burst out of his room, yelling at his private secretary like a madman, "Go and bring me the painter Alton at once!"

His secretary informed him that he had died a few days ago in quarantine after contracting the plague. The man had barely finished speaking when Rostom hurried in. "I found Zeinab very ill. I would have carried her and brought her here, but they said it might be the plague, so I didn't bring her. I feared she might infect you."

"The plague?" whispered Napoleon. He burst into frenzied pacing as was his habit when deeply disturbed, his heels clicking on the floor. He would not get his revenge on the couple; Alton had been snatched away by death, and she was well on her way to it.

A few days later, Napoleon returned to France in secret, only informing his most trusted generals. He set off by boat at dawn one day, without anyone knowing that the man who had come filled with hopes and dreams of becoming king of the Orient was on board, slinking away after these dreams had foundered on the shores of reality. He had lost his battles, his soldiers were dead, and there was no longer any reason to stay.

After Napoleon's departure, rumors flew that Zeinab had fallen ill because her lover had abandoned her and left without her. Neither she, nor her mother and father, nor any other member of her family, was able to escape the whispers and winks of the neighbors. Napoleon had discarded their daughter and taken Rostom, his faithful servant, with him instead.

26

SHE WALKED THROUGH THE EXHIBITION halls until she came to a glass case that contained two skulls, one marked "Suleiman al-Halabi, criminal," and the other "Kléber, hero." She smiled wryly. Had Suleiman al-Halabi, who assassinated Kléber, really been a criminal? He had rid the Egyptians of a dark and dismal fate, and as a result been executed in the most horrific way: the *khazouq*, impalement with a metal spear. She was seized with the sudden urge to break the glass and swap the placards, so that each would be in its proper place.

The sound of his footsteps behind her brought her out of her thoughts. "I got a phone call about the painting," he said. "The tests are being run. The results will be out in two days at most."

"That's good news," she said, "but I have to go now. Thank you for your time."

He bent over her hand to kiss it. "You are welcome at any time."

She was starving, so she went to a nearby restaurant and sat at a table for one, watching the people go by. She saw a pair of lovers kissing, undeterred by the noise and the passersby. There was no reason the sight should make her think of him. Her thoughts came and went. Where was he now, she wondered? Was he with her? What were they doing?

But why should she give in to her thoughts? Why shouldn't she dial his number and put an end to her musings? She had missed his voice and the sight of his face. She decided to Skype him so that she could see him; but there was no reply. She called his phone, but it was off. She was overcome with conflicting emotions: jealousy, worry, unhappiness. But she did not want these feelings to ruin her pleasure at being in her favorite city.

She paid the check and went for a walk along the Seine, to experience everything she loved about Paris: to breathe its air, to embrace its history, to inhale the perfume of its elegance. The Turkish author Orhan Pamuk tells us that every city has its voice, and the voice of Paris is the whine of the Metro. To her, the voice of Paris was the echo of history.

The more time passed, bringing her closer to her meeting with her father, the more nervous she felt. She could just not go, and change her hotel for another. But she did want to see him. She was eager to see how he looked after all these years, and where life had taken him since he had packed his things and left, never to return. He had not abandoned them; in fact, he had been adamant about taking the girls with him. It was Yasmine and Shaza who had refused to go and live with him. They preferred to stay with their grandmother, who had stood up to him like a lion, refusing to allow him to take them away. He had not been in a position to insist on his right to raise them, and so he had quietly left.

She arrived at the Café du Monde exactly on time, and looked at the tables, wondering if she could see him. She would surely recognize him, no matter how much he had changed. He was her father.

He was not waiting for her. She sat, eyes moving between the revolving door of the café and the wall clock. She ordered a café au lait and browsed on her phone to calm her nerves.

The hands on the clock read 8:15 when the revolving door finally regurgitated him. She saw him looking around, searching for her. Would he recognize her after all this time? She had changed completely now; she had been just a little girl with her hair in braids when he had left, and today she was a woman.

It only took him a few seconds to recognize her. He headed for her table, his steps weak. His hair was shot through with white: his face was sagging and his eyelids drooped. He wore a brown woolen coat and black oxfords, still elegantly dressed after all these years. The closer he came to her table, the faster her heart beat until she thought it would burst right out of her chest. He stood there looking at her for a few moments, his face morphing into a succession of expressions—astonishment, bewilderment, joy, anxiety—like a man who has been looking for something and at last has found it.

She found herself rising from her seat to embrace him. His eyes filled with tears and he stroked her hair, whispering her name over and over sorrowfully.

They sat there for a long time. They spoke for a long time about the affairs of her life and his. She noticed that his hand was trembling so hard that he ended up spilling his coffee down his jacket. "Have you seen a doctor about that?" she asked.

"Yes, several. They said my nerves have a severe inflammation brought on by stress and worry and, uh, unhappiness." He tried for a smile. "Oh, it's much better now. I couldn't walk properly or drive or write. I couldn't work for some time; I kept changing jobs and moving from place to place. It's why I settled here."

"Did you ever think of coming home to Egypt?"

His face filled with sorrow and pain. "Often," he admitted. "But at the last minute I always changed my mind. I can't set foot in that country again. Everywhere there are memories. Even the way the air smells stirs up memories I'm not strong enough to resist. You can see I'm not built for endurance any more." Then he asked her about her own affairs and her sister's, how they had been living, and she told him everything.

They fell into a silence that seemed to last a long time. Each of them seemed to disconnect and lose themselves in

their own thoughts; the place had quieted down and the hub-
bub around them had subsided. Weakly, he quavered, "I don't
want to go into details. But I want you to know that I never
loved another woman." He added, "I believe you're mature
enough to know that passing fancies have nothing to do with
love. Your mother wasn't just my wife. She had my heart."

Your passing fancy, she wanted to scream at him, *made a
woman kill herself.* But what good would it do?

They shook hands goodbye. Each of them opened their
umbrella and took shelter underneath it, then went their separate ways.

27

AFTER TODAY, SHE DEFINITELY NEEDED a rest. She had been tired to start with, and her meeting with her father had pushed her from fatigue into exhaustion.

The hotel lobby was crowded with tour groups, both arriving and departing. She slipped her card into the door and when it swung open, the room smelled strongly of a wonderful perfume. She went straight into the bathroom for a hot shower—just what she needed before she went to sleep. She reached for the robe and found that there were two of them, one pink and the other white. What if he were here with her, sharing this comfortable room? The soft light, the paintings on the walls, the comfy armchairs, the gauzy curtain over the window fluttering to reveal the Eiffel Tower lit by night—everything about it was romantic.

After her shower, she flung herself down on the bed and started flipping through the TV channels. She found her favorite song by Dalida, "Nostalgia," playing, so she turned up the volume and sang along. Suddenly, there was a soft knock at the door. She turned down the sound. *Oh, no*, she thought, *I must have disturbed someone with the noise.* She raised her voice without getting out of bed. "Who is it?"

No one answered. She got out of bed and stood by the door. "I said, who is it?"

There was still no answer. She opened the door a crack. Through the narrow opening, she saw a bouquet of flowers. She flung the door open to find him standing there.

Her heart nearly stopped to see him. He looked even more handsome in a winter coat and black sneakers, a purple scarf around his neck. Was it really him standing there or was she imagining it? Could her incessant thoughts of him since her arrival in Paris have summoned him here? When we want some things and wish for them sincerely, they can come true—and here he was before her in the flesh, with his subtly handsome features and slim build. She cast every caution to the wind, took leave of what remained of her senses, and threw herself into his arms.

He held her tightly and kissed her hair and face, his lips seeking out hers. She wished she could stop time and keep this moment forever. It was the most wonderful surprise. At last they drew apart, and he smiled at her as he shrugged his way out of his coat and scarf. He sat on the chair by the window. The curtain rippled, revealing more of the view. He looked at her. Her hair was still wet, her face innocent and fresh without makeup, like a flower when it first blossoms. She perched on the arm of his chair. He pulled her hand to him and buried it between both of his own, then pulled her into his lap. She leaned her head against his chest. He was so close that she could hear the beating of his heart.

"So," he said. "What have you found out?"

"Not," she matched his playful tone, "until you tell me what you're doing here."

"I needed a break. It's been a hard few months at work."

"But why Paris in this miserable weather?"

His smile was his only answer. She wanted him to throw caution to the winds and tell her straight out, "I had to come, I missed you, I've thought only of your face since you left, you're the only one I think of, you're the only one in my heart." He didn't say a thing, but there were other ways to express these words.

Their bodies melted together in the soft glow of the lamp-light. They sank down together, eyes closed, fingers interlacing, letting go only to clasp again desperately. Their lips met, parted, met again. Whispered words, endearments, moans. The world erupted into bliss. There was nothing more to say: in this moment, a single word would have been too much.

Afterward, he stood, adjusting his clothing and putting his coat back on. He said, voice still rough, "I'll wait for you in the hotel lobby. Get dressed and we'll go to dinner."

"Now? I'm tired, I was just going to go to bed."

"It's only ten o'clock, and we're in Paris."

"Why not eat here?" she suggested. "Look out. History and beauty around us everywhere." She pushed the curtain aside to show him the view: the Eiffel Tower, the Seine, and the winding roads. "Isn't it enough?"

"Of course it is," he said, "or it would be if I were staying indefinitely. Darling, I'm only here for two days. I'll wait for you downstairs." He left the room.

She went through a tumult of emotions after he left: joy, bemusement, shock. Then she remembered that he was wait-ing for her and that she had to get ready. What to wear? She had never wanted to look beautiful and sexy more than she did at that moment. She reached for a dress she had brought with her to attend the closing ceremony of the conference. It was long and black and completely open at the back, reveal-ing her pale skin. Should she wear her hair up or down? She tried piling it up onto her head and pinning it in place with a rhinestone pin: that looked good. She pulled on glossy tights and a pair of high heels, and made herself up like a woman going on a date with her lover. She put on her black coat, and a perfume that she loved.

He smiled and his eyes sparkled admiringly when she came down. He put an arm around her and led her into a limousine provided by the hotel that was waiting for them. She sat close to him, engulfed in his energy and surrounded by his scent of perfume and tobacco. She laid her weary head on his shoulder. The rain was falling down in sheets, and her heart was beating out of her chest. She wanted the ride to last forever, or time to stop; but every dream ends with waking.

Ten o'clock in Paris means that only the main thoroughfares are still busy. The other streets were filled with silence and calm. In a dark, deserted street, the driver stopped outside a bookstore. She looked around: perhaps there was a café or restaurant she hadn't noticed? But there was nothing. He took her hand and opened the door, leading her bemused into the bookstore. "Sherif, what's this? It's a bookstore."

"Yes. You like bookstores, don't you?"

"I do, but what bookstore is open at this hour? What's going on?" She added, "I'm not dressed for a bookstore! Who wears a cocktail dress to a. . . . ?" She looked around. "You said we were having dinner out. . . . Are they serving dinner in bookstores now?"

He stood there, calm and cool, which only made her more agitated. She looked around again, casting about for any clue. Her eyes fell on the cover of a book. It was a new novel by her favorite French author, Patrick Modiano. In spite of herself, she picked it up and distractedly leafed through it.

He smiled. "Now," he said, "are you still mad at me for bringing you here?"

He took the book and replaced it on the shelf. "Let's go." Taking her by the hand, he led her down a long corridor ending in another passageway. Along one wall were bookshelves.

"Wait!" she said. "I wanted to buy that book."

Ignoring her, he stopped in front of a shelf, pulled a book toward him, then replaced it. The bookshelves immediately parted; he took her by the hand, they stepped through, and it closed quietly behind them once more.

She walked behind him in a state of shock, only coming back to herself when he invited her to sit down. Purple, green, and orange spotlights flashed; house music pounded so loudly she could barely hear him. Waiters came and went with drinks; the dance floor was packed with couples pressed together, some kissing, in a world of their own. The strangest thing was that such a staid and sedate bookshop could conceal such a noisy and vibrant world. "How?" she managed to yell over the music.

"This is one of the top ten hidden bars in the world!" he yelled back.

"Why hidden?"

"It helps keep it mysterious and attract customers," he explained, moving closer to make himself heard. "It's a throwback to Prohibition in the US, but of course nowadays they don't have to fear law enforcement."

"We could have gone somewhere quieter," she yelled. "I never knew you liked cloak-and-dagger stuff!"

"I figured it would be exciting for a change," he said. "Instead of a door, you pick up a book, or dial a secret number in a phone booth. The first time I went to a secret bar was in Hong Kong. A friend took me to a bar hidden in a store that sold used umbrellas. You had to open an umbrella to activate the secret door."

"Does this place have a name?"

"Lulu Whitesmith, after an African-American lady who ran a brothel."

She looked around her, frankly impressed. "When did you plan all this?"

"I didn't plan anything. Fate plans everything." She was aware that he was an absolute fatalist, and that this was the source of the equanimity with which he took blows and setbacks. "Have you heard about the butterfly effect?"

"Butterfly effect?" she repeated, shaking her head. "No, I haven't."

"It's the theory that if a butterfly flaps its wings in one place, it can result in hurricanes and volcanic eruptions on the other side of the globe."

She gave him a slightly mocking smile. "Really?"

"It's a metaphor for chaos theory. Edward Lorenz made it famous. It basically says that every big event that happens in our lives resulted from some very small thing that happened to us a long time ago."

"I still don't get it."

He lit a cigarette. "A simple example. I got very high grades when I graduated from school, enough to qualify me for a top college. My dad wouldn't allow me to let the opportunity go to waste, or that was what he said, and he made me study architecture. I graduated and started working. We have a bunch of consultants in baroque art and architecture that we always use, like Dr. Khalil. One time he couldn't do the job and recommended you and that was how we met—you remember he introduced us at that conference?"

She gave him a sly smile. "Of course I do."

"Look at the way things lead to other things. If I hadn't gotten top grades, I wouldn't have gone to the Faculty of Engineering. I would never have been in this field, so I would never have met Dr. Khalil, and if he'd been available, he wouldn't have recommended you to us." She was still mulling over what he had said when he added, "And I wouldn't have fallen in love with you and not known how to fall back out of love."

She was flustered; she was reassured; she was overjoyed. He had confessed his love again. What could she say to him? What was the appropriate thing to say to make up for all the pain and defeat she had put him through? Perhaps, "I love you too, I never stopped loving you." Would that be enough?

He smiled; they chatted a while; they laughed; they were filled with joy. The evening passed like a dream, and he said good night at her door with a hug. Embracing him was like having everything in the world she wanted in her arms, filling her with warmth and tenderness, and what was more, the security she had never had.

*

When he turned on his phone the next morning, he found a text from her. *Gone to the conference, will call as soon as I'm done.*

He was disappointed; he would have loved to have shared the Paris morning with her. He sat in the hotel lobby, drinking his coffee and reading the newspaper. Then he decided to take a walk.

At noon, Yasmine's phone rang. "I'm ready to show you the lab results."

"They're out already?"

"Yes. I just got the report and there are amazing surprises."

She raced out of the conference hall and hailed a taxi. On her way there, she called Sherif. "I'm on my way to the Musée de l'Armée. I have an appointment with the director of the Military Archives. He's had the painting analyzed and I'm going to get the results."

"Shall I come with you?" he asked.

"The man's an eccentric. He wouldn't allow you to be there. To him, every conversation is a military secret and classified. If I hadn't been introduced to him by a close friend of his, he wouldn't even have agreed to help me."

Andrea received her with a polite smile. He handed her the report to read. She skimmed down to the conclusion:

The colors in the painting of the Oriental girl match the colors used in the paintings of Alton Germain, and the canvas it is painted on is the same type and characteristics as that used in the artist's other known works. As in this painting, the artist was not in the habit of signing his work, only initialing it.

Based on all of the above, this constitutes a positive confirmation that the painting is the work of Alton Germain.

She felt her shoulders relax and her face melt into a smile. "It *is* him," she breathed.

"Yes," the man responded, "just as you expected. Your hunch was right. I'd bet the girl he painted was his sweetheart. He painted her and hid her away from everyone's eyes, not to hang in a museum, but only on the walls of his heart."

Her eyes sparkled. "Yes, I think so too. Not only because her face found its way into more than one of his paintings, but because there was something in this portrait that that made me feel he was in love with his subject. It was in his brush-strokes, in the way he painted her." She paused. "But it was strange, a French artist falling for an ordinary Egyptian girl. What attracted him to her?"

Andrea gave a sly smile. Getting up from behind his desk, he came around to sit opposite her as he had done before. "The simple, innocent girl you're referring to is the same girl who was the lover of Napoleon Bonaparte."

"Bonaparte's. . . ?" she stammered, her eyes betraying her shock.

"Yes. It's the same girl. Zeinab, daughter of Sheikh al-Bakri, the Azharite imam, the one I told you about earlier." Watching her staring, he went on, "When Napoleon learned that the girl fell in love with the artist, he was furious. How could the artist have dared to presume to love a woman who belonged to Napoleon? That was one thing. The other thing was, when he saw his works and found that Germain had painted him as a heartless, merciless thug or a cowardly weak-ling, that was the final straw. He had his paintings expunged from the *Description of Egypt*, and banned them from being hung in museums."

The words fell upon her ears like a thunderbolt. An Egyptian girl, of no particular importance, with two rivals fighting over her, one of them the most powerful man in the world and the other a painter? One with an overabundance of military power and a mind preoccupied with strategy and military maneuvers, and another filled with the sensitivity of a true artist—what could ever bring them together to want the same woman, no, just a girl with her braids and striped *gallabiya*?

Andrea handed her the painting and the report and they shook hands. She thanked him profusely for his assistance. Before she left, he stopped her and went to his bookshelf. He pulled out a book and handed it to her. "I recommend you read it. I think you'll learn a lot. It has answers to a lot of your questions about Napoleon's relationship to the girl."

All the way home to the hotel, she was preoccupied with one question: who was Zeinab al-Bakri that she had captivated not one, but two men of such stature?

28

Cairo: June 1800

KLÉBER'S DEATH AT THE HANDS of Suleiman al-Halabi rein-vigorated the Egyptian Resistance. The assassination of the supreme French commander gave them hope that they could do even more, that the myth of the invincible French invader was on its way to oblivion. At the same time, the French con-tingent was weakened and demoralized by the death of their leader. A grand military funeral was held for him. His coffin was draped with the French flag, and a military march played as a carriage drew it slowly through the streets, followed by rows of officers, soldiers, and the men of the Scientific Cam-paign. The populace turned out in the streets to view the funeral of the French commander on his way to his final rest-ing place, with triumph in their gloating eyes. At the same time that Kléber was being buried to the tune of a military march, his assassin, Suleiman al-Halabi, was impaled on a spear, having been sentenced to this horrible death. His body was strung up in the city's largest square to be seen by every-one who came and went, and people crowded beneath the body, cheering for him and throwing flowers.

General Menou was appointed in Kléber's stead. He was less brutal than those who had gone before him, polit-ically minded and more liberal. In any case, the Campaign was breathing its last. Agreements and treaties were signed between both parties, culminating in the Campaign leaving

Egyptian soil. Life returned to Egypt, to its inhabitants, streets and thoroughfares, to its skies, its earth, its Nile. The invader was gathering up the remnants of itself to leave, after two years pressing down on them and cutting off their air. Since he had come into the country, every door had locked its misery in behind it, the streets had darkened, and bodies and severed heads and human remains floated to the surface of the Nile. In the night, in the darkened dungeons of the Citadel, the screams and groans of innocents rang out, imprisoned without charge and forgotten in its depths. It was time for a new day to dawn; it was time for the houses of Egypt to open their doors and windows to the sun. At last, there were no circulars posted on the doors and walls bearing rigid and strict laws and long lists of prohibitions. The printing presses no longer printed French newspapers, their front pages emblazoned with images of people killed and hanged for contravening military decrees. Most importantly, the French soldiers no longer sauntered through the streets in their dismal uniforms.

The Egyptians celebrated and exchanged congratulations. Trays bearing juices, beverages, rice pudding, and delicacies of all kinds were passed around. Women let out ululations, taking off their black clothing and donning bright colors. The wealthy slaughtered camels and sheep, handing out gifts of meat and holding banquets. Others took to avenging themselves and exacting punishment against those who had supported the Campaign and stood by the French: the merchants who had had dealings with them, the judges who ruled in their favor, the Azharite imams who had failed to condemn them, the rich landowners who had had business dealings with them, the women who had offered themselves to the men of the Campaign—even the café boys were not safe from those who wanted to settle scores.

And Zeinab was Napoleon's lover. What would they do to her, an Egyptian girl who made free with her honor and accepted the position of mistress to General Bonaparte? It was she who had gone around proudly in the streets with her face unveiled, as if to say, "I am Napoleon's mistress: who would dare reproach me?"

No one cared to find out the truth of her relationship with him, whether or not he had ever touched her. The mere fact that Napoleon's carriage had stopped outside the home of Sheikh al-Bakri to take Zeinab to his debauched parties was damning evidence of her crimes. Zeinab was not an ordinary Egyptian girl—she was the daughter of Naqib al-Ashraf (the Head of the Prophet's Descendants) and a high-ranking imam of al-Azhar—and so her crime was multiplied, its punishment redoubled.

29

He was waiting for her in the hotel lobby. His eyes held the expression she recognized when he was upset with her, but his face softened when he found her as thrilled as a little girl who has been given a new dress on her birthday. It was all he needed. She took off her gloves and coat and unwrapped her scarf from around her neck, everything she had discovered bursting out of her. "My hunch was right! It's the same artist! I found him! And I found out an amazing secret. The girl in the painting, the one he was in love with, she's the same Zeinab al-Bakri who was Napoleon's lover!" Seeing a passing waiter, she ordered a coffee. "Imagine, an ordinary girl from Egypt, with two such important men fighting over her."

"Well, she was descended from Cleopatra," he said.

She gave him a shy smile. Finally, she could relax. It was as if she had been running without pause since she had set eyes on the painting, desperate to uncover its secret.

He gazed at her admiringly, as though seeing her for the first time. "I'm really impressed by your perseverance. Anyone else wouldn't have looked so hard into that painting, and I know it wasn't easy: you kept running into brick walls."

"What can I say?" she shrugged. "I love my work."

"Now that you've found out, what are you going to do with the information?"

"I don't know yet."

His eyebrows went up in astonishment. "So there's a chance we could have lunch?"

She laughed. "That's for sure."

They went out and she pulled her coat tightly around her, as they walked together under his umbrella. He put his arm around her, and she felt warmth spread through her. The scene reminded her of Caillebotte's *Paris Street; Rainy Day*. The painting depicted a man and a woman walking together, sheltering from the rain under a large black umbrella, in the same place where they walked.

He hailed a taxi and directed the cabbie to a restaurant not far from the Luxembourg Gardens. As they drove past the wrought-iron fence, she sighed. "Every time I go by the Luxembourg Gardens, I feel so unhappy. Khedive Ismail had the Ezbekiya Gardens built as an exact copy of them and now hardly any of them remained, paved over and turned into streets and a parking lot. Is the fault in the government, or in us?"

"It's the whole system," he said.

Sitting at a table on the glass-fronted second floor, they had a wonderful view out to the whole of the garden. The waiter laid the menus on the table and left them alone together. Sherif reached into the pocket of his coat and pulled out a cardboard box with the Celine logo on it. He handed it to her.

She smiled cautiously as she took it from him. "What's this?"

"I read that the wizards who make perfumes invented a way to imitate the scent of the earth after rain. I know you love the way it smells. It's a limited edition, made out of rare ingredients."

Her eyes shone with joy. She took it out of the box and spritzed her wrist. She inhaled deeply. "It's wonderful."

"I don't want to shock you," he said, "but did you know that this smell is caused by a type of bacteria that lives in the soil, and becomes more active after rain?"

"Nature is strange," she breathed. "It's a miracle of creation. Bacteria living in the soil and producing the most wonderful scent?"

"Yes. You feel the whole world is full of that smell after rain. But to get it into a perfume, that took time and effort and science, just for a few bottles." He chuckled.

"I love it," she said. "Thank you."

"Let's talk seriously," he said. "This game of cat and mouse we've been playing has me beat. . . ."

The waiter arrived with their orders and she pretended to be absorbed in her food, a sudden shyness flooding her.

"Hasn't it been long enough?" he prodded her. "Say something. For once in your life, just one time, say something."

"What can I say?" she said. "Do you think I'm not sorry for letting you down before? How can you ever trust me again?" Her eyes flickered to the table. "I never had the courage to tell you I loved you, but I never stopped thinking about you. But would you have believed me? Whenever I open my mouth to tell you, something stops me and I can't say it." She looked off to the side. "I'll never forget the day I told you there was someone else. I can't believe I did that to you."

"Do you think if I'd believed you were really in love with him, even for a second, I'd be here with you now?" he said. "I know we were in a slump just then. Maybe I wasn't the Romeo you dreamed of, the lover who brings flowers and sends poetry and love letters. When I met you I was just coming into a new stage in my life, or you could say I was trying to erase everything I used to be and start fresh by acting differently. That was why I stayed away from anything I saw as frivolous. If I had met you in the world I used to live in, I would have been the lover you dreamed of. I would have made you happy." He sighed. "I didn't get it then. A woman always needs to be surprised."

He was looking straight into her eyes. His words were arrows straight to her heart. "The day you said there was someone else, yes, I was unhappy, but I knew I was only going to miss you, not lose you. I trusted that one day you'd come back. You can't twist someone's arm to make them feel a certain way; you have to let people do what they need to do."

There was no need for an answer. All she wanted to do in that moment was hold him.

They finished their lunch and went for a walk. Through the streets they went until they reached the river. "Now, in front of the Seine, in this place where every inch calls you to love, will you marry me?"

She smiled. "Of course I will."

"What do you say to getting married right here in Paris?"

"Here?"

"Yes, here."

"How? What about our families? Our friends? My grandma?" She shook her head. "My grandmother has been so impatient to hear the news. It would break her heart that we got married abroad and didn't have a wedding. And we need to get so many things ready: furniture, the dress, there'll be so much to do!"

"Okay," he said. "As you've gotten to the bottom of that painting now, there'll be nothing to keep you from your preparations for the wedding."

"Yes! I'll be able to shop in the couple of days I have left. When does your flight leave?"

"At eleven tomorrow morning."

Cairo: August 1801

The house of Sheikh al-Bakri was shrouded in fear and sorrow. The mother was already in mourning over a fate foretold; Zeinab had lain there since Alton's passing, neither dead nor alive. Sheikh al-Bakri was an outcast who did not dare leave his house; everyone had abandoned him after there was nothing to be gained from knowing him now he had lost his position. Napoleon had left secretly for France,

Kléber had been killed, and Menou had signed the deal for the French presence to leave the country. Sheikh al-Bakri had no more standing, and the flatterers who sought their own interests no longer saw him as a revered imam, but as a base man who sold his religion and his honor. His son had been dismissed from his job, his employer cursing him and his father, the same man who had used to send his greetings to their family. His eldest daughter came back to live in her father's house after her husband, the son of Sheikh Omar Makram, had divorced her because of her sister's and father's bad reputations.

Al-Bakri did not know that there were men preparing to take vengeance against him and holding meetings to decide his fate. A representative of the Ottoman Empire met with the Wali of Egypt, Muhammad Khosrow Pasha, and several imams, and were holding a trial for him on numerous charges, foremost among which were allowing his daughter, a girl no older than sixteen, to go out with her face unveiled. On a day when the sky was lowery and filled with thick black clouds that obscured the sun, a little before sundown, galloping hooves stopped directly outside the door to the house of Sheikh al-Bakri. Several men of different ages dismounted. With angry footsteps, they strode to the door and knocked. Fatima felt a tremor run through her. The slave girl went to open the door, but Fatima stopped her. "No. Don't open it."

The household, except for Zeinab, gathered in the inner courtyard, exchanging doubtful and fearful glances. The knocking on the door grew harder, escalating into hands slamming against the door and the sounds of kicking feet. No one went to open it. They were all staring at their father. It was his habit to open the door himself when he was at home: he would adjust his turban and drape the hem of his caftan over his shoulder. Then he would clear his throat and rasp out loudly, "Patience, patience!" But now he stood tongue-tied, huddling in a corner like a frightened mouse. He knew who they were and for what purpose they had come.

The visitors broke down the door with a group of men from the neighborhood. Al-Bakri thought of escape, but it was too late. With faltering steps he went to meet his visitors. A scowling man demanded, "Where is your daughter Zeinab?"

"Why?" he quavered. "What do you want with Zeinab?"

"The judge has called on you both."

"What does the judge want with Zeinab?" Fatima screamed. "No! Zeinab isn't going anywhere!"

The men tromped up the wooden stairs, almost smashing it under their boots as it creaked dangerously. They crashed into the room without knocking. As soon as Zeinab saw them, she realized what was happening. A man pulled her off her bed and another flung her abaya at her, grunting brutishly, "Cover yourself."

She could barely walk, surrendering completely to whatever befell her. She went down the stairs, surrounded by several men. Her mother held her tight and screamed at them, "Let my daughter go! Take me instead!" She tried to pull her out of their grip, and one of them slapped her hard. Zeinab stumbled to the ground and clutched at the hem of her mother's clothing. One of the men reached out a big hand and grabbed a fistful of her hair, dragging her bodily away from her mother. He threw her into the cart, where her father already sat, his fingers repeatedly adjusting his turban on his head. The people of the neighborhood gathered around the cart. Beating drums and sounding horns, they sang traditional songs of public humiliation, "Pull the turban out of shape! Under it you'll find an ape!"

The horse-drawn cart pushed its way with difficulty through the milling crowd. Through the meshrabiyehs, women and girls watched the procession and poured out bowls of dirty water onto them, while children chased barefoot after the cart, pelting its occupants with pebbles and stones.

Zeinab remembered Napoleon's carriage that used to wait outside the door, where she used to ride in all her finery, while the same eyes that were watching from behind the meshrabi-yehs longed for the honor of riding in that carriage. Why had none of these men come out back then and asked her to go back home, or made her? Or taken her to their houses and protected her from going to Napoleon? Why now, now that Napoleon was gone and the Campaign had ended, did they find their voices, speaking of honor and decency, raining foul curses upon her and her father? In times gone by, they bent to kiss his hand or the hem of his caftan, and flattered him with compliments and gifts because they knew what he meant to Napoleon, and that the general could not refuse him anything.

They said nothing all the way. The cart stopped outside the Citadel. Zeinab looked up to see a scaffold, with hang-man's nooses already in place. There were three of them. On each of them was a decapitated head, rotting in silence, mounted in that place as a reminder. She recognized the first head: it was Halim, who had kept a shop in the market that sold tobacco. He had supplied the men of the Campaign with tobacco and liquor. He had been a friend of her father's, and they had often spent the evening together. Her heart twisted, for now she knew the fate that awaited her. The man yanking her by the arm saw her looking up at the scaffolds. Spitting out his words, he said, "This is what happens to traitors, to everyone who had dealings with the infidel invaders."

He dragged her inside by the arm. They went down a long, dark corridor, lit only by pale candles in glass lanterns hanging on the sides of the high walls. Passages led onto passages like an endless labyrinth. Silence enshrouded it all, no sound but their footfall on the flagstones. At last they came to a great room with Ottoman couches. The judge sat upon one, a tray bearing fruit, dates, and sweets before him. He scrutinized her from beneath beetling black brows, asking, "Did Napoleon really take a fancy to this girl?"

Zeinab had grown dangerously thin since Alton's death. She was little more than a skeleton, pale and withered like an autumn leaf. "Were you Napoleon's lover?" he asked.

She gave no answer. The guard slapped her. The judge asked again, and the same thing happened. He repeated the question, again and again. Every time she refrained from answering, the guard slapped her until blood dripped from her mouth. Finally she slurred out, "I repent."

The judge asked her father, "What do you say to your daughter's confession?"

He stammered, "She is no daughter of mine. I had no hand in this. Do with her as you will." The man abandoned his daughter like a sacrificial lamb, as he had previously offered her to Napoleon.

The judge motioned to the guard, who took her away. The judge ordered her imprisoned in a cell in the Citadel until her execution.

The guard took her through a heavy wooden door, down a long winding staircase that seemed endless. They arrived at a locked door. He knocked at it and she heard the jangling of keys. The door opened to reveal a giant of a man with a thick mustache and a wild beard down to his chest. His eyes were unbearably cruel, the whole world's darkness in their black pupils. The guard tossed her to him. "Take good care of her. She was the general's mistress."

The man looked pitilessly at her and grasped her arm hard enough to hurt her. He dragged her past cell after cell, all locked, with a tiny window in them covered by an iron grate. Eyes appeared at the grates to look at the new arrival. She looked around. Massive, impenetrable walls with no way out; only corridors leading into corridors, locked cells on either side. The jailer opened a cell at the end of the passage with one of the massive keys on his ring. He shoved her inside, then locked the door again.

The cell was dark and cold, with a stinking pail in one corner of it as a toilet. Several women of different ages sat in the cell, each minding her own business, deep in thought. What was certain was that none of them was contemplating her future, for there was none, and their present was as dismal as it could be. They were all lost in their own pasts, perhaps remembering happier times, or looking back with regret, at sins committed, lost opportunities, roads not taken, wondering what they could have done, or not done.

Zeinab was dying in this place that resembled a tomb. Can one be buried before dying? The cell was opened once every morning. The jailer changed the dirty pail and put out a metal dish filled with murky water and a plate bearing some pieces of dry bread. Zeinab would not eat or drink. She could not remember how long she had been there in this place, nor could she know, for there was no daylight. It seemed like an age. She shriveled even more, until she appeared more dry and brittle than the crusts of bread they gave them. Her lips chapped; her sight dimmed; she could barely see or move.

One day, not much later, she heard the brutish footsteps of several men approaching, and knew that the moment had come when she would be free of her suffering. Their footsteps came closer and closer. She heard the shriek of the cell door opening. The men's mutterings increased in volume and the women cried out and screamed. She could not make out their faces or see how many of them there were. All she could see was a mass of humanity. Suddenly, she had an overwhelming need to see her mother, to hold her, to weep in her arms and say goodbye.

Her hands and feet were bound, along with the other women. They were tied at the ends of ropes behind a cart. The cart drove through the streets, the women dragged behind it over the ground, while a man beat on a brass tray so that everyone would come out and watch them. The cart drove all over the city, followed by little children, pelting the women with every piece of dirt they could get their hands on, while women let out ululations and men shouted insults. Her young once-beautiful body was dragged through the streets, cut and bruised and bleeding. It was sunset. The sun took on the color of parting. It was time for the final sentence to be carried out in a public square, to be seen and heard by everyone. Crowds poured in from everywhere, even from far-off villages and hamlets. It was time to gloat over the women who had surrendered their honor and their virtue to the French. Since Zeinab was the daughter of Sheikh al-Bakri, the gloating would be more extreme, the pleasure keener. Her body trembled in terror. The executioner, clasping his sword, took hold of her. She could see the whole world's cruelty in his eyes, and lost all hope for a merciful death. She whispered, "Please be merciful."

The man laughed mockingly, preparing his tools to send her to the afterlife. She did not know the method by which she would be executed. Would she be hanged? Would she be stoned to death? Would she be disemboweled? She did not know the fate planned for her. She did not know that he had planned to sever her head from her neck.

The man picked up a handful of dust, checking the texture. The dust should not be too moist or heavy. When the decisive moment came, he would throw dust in the eyes of the person to be executed, making them involuntarily blink and raise a hand to their eyes, at which point the sharp blade would cleave their head from their body. Her head was pounding with terror like an African drum, while every neck was craned, every eye trained on her. Everyone was running to get a better view, crowding in and jockeying for position and elbowing each other, those with a view telling those who could not see, the screams rising in one voice until the cries grew deafening: "Do it! Do it!"

Zeinab blinked. The noise faded and all was silence. All she could see was him. Alton was standing before her, as handsome as he had ever been, smiling at her. He stepped closer. He touched her hair. He reassured her in her extremity. He motioned to her to follow.

Her eyes fixed on the endless horizon. She never saw the man as he approached with the sharp blade, pulled her head back, and drew the sword across her neck, slitting her throat. In a few moments, her head was cleaved from her body. The head rolled across the ground with a dull thud, a fountain of blood spurting out. In seconds, the body collapsed, lying peacefully next to the head.

The crowd erupted. The women ululated, the men applauded, and the children cheered. The executioner lifted the head by the hair and held it out at arm's length, turning left and right to display it to the crowd, who shouted out in joy and kept cheering in the shadow of death. "The whore is dead! She lost her head!"

The bodies piled up, one on top of the other, still bleeding. A cart drawn by two horses carried them away to dump them on Muqattam Mountain, while the heads were gathered in a straw basket to be mounted on the walls of the Citadel.

Barefoot and bare of face and hair, Zeinab's mother ran after the cart, her features no longer visible now that she had smeared mud on her face, her *gallabiya* grey from where she had rolled in the dirt. She ran, crying in a barely audible rasp, "Zeinab! My girl!"

30

Yasmine's research had confirmed Zeinab's relationship to Napoleon and indicated that she had been executed after the Campaign left Egypt. A girl of sixteen, presented by her father as a gift to Napoleon, out of greed for a position as the head of the al-Azhar imams. The great historian al-Jabarti had described her in his chronicles as tall and dark, slim and fragrant. Napoleon had taken a fancy to her when he saw her. She took off her face veil and wore revealing clothes, and was seen getting into the imperial carriage to go to Napoleon's house.

The great historian had written in his diaries documenting the event,

> And on Tuesday, August 4, AD 1801, the daughter
> of Sheikh al-Bakri was brought in, having been one
> of the women who engaged in debauchery with the
> French, by two men appointed by the Vizier. They
> went to her mother's house in the district of Gudariya
> after sundown, and brought her and her father and
> asked her what she did, whereupon she repented.
> They asked her father what he said, and he said, "She
> is no daughter of mine," so they broke her neck.

Yasmine sat back, overcome with the injustice that had befallen this girl, her death to atone for a crime of which she was blameless. A girl of sixteen: what had she experienced of life or of seduction to make the emperor fall in love with her? He was a man of the world, a roué with a profound knowledge of women. Her father had offered her up to him like the sacrifices we make to the gods to appease them and make our wishes come true. She had been different from the other women he could choose from to take as lovers; she was beautiful and innocent.

Even stranger was that after all this research, all this testing and reading, she had found no information on Zeinab's relationship with the artist. There was no mention at all of her meeting him: how had he kept their relationship a secret, she wondered, from prying eyes, when everything had been so public?

She could not sleep that night. The end of Zeinab's tale kept her awake, the fate of a girl she had never known, who had passed away long centuries ago: why had she suddenly come to her, to look anew into her world, as though refusing to rest in peace after all these years?

The next morning, Yasmine was subdued. Sherif noticed over breakfast. "You look like you didn't get much rest."

"That's about right. You could say I didn't sleep at all."

"I didn't know I'd had that much of an effect on you," he joked.

Should she tell him that it was only one person, a girl, who had been giving her sleepless nights since she had been given the task of restoring that painting? "I was online," she said, "searching through books and al-Jabarti's diaries and other documents. I was researching Zeinab al-Bakri, the subject of Alton's paintings, but I couldn't find a single piece of information that said there was anything between them." She took a frustrated sip of her coffee. "The director of the Military Archives assured me that there was. And the book he gave me hinted that the artist was Napoleon's rival, and that when Napoleon found out, he wouldn't let his paintings be displayed in a museum or be included in *The Description of Egypt*. He wasn't just his rival, you see," she explained, "he was his opponent, against his policies, his injustice and oppression. That was why he painted Napoleon as a tyrant or a weakling."

"But what about the lock of human hair?" he asked. "Was it really her hair?"

"To find out," she said, "we'd have to find where she was buried and take a sample to compare. But she was beheaded and her head mounted on the Citadel, and no one knows where she went after, or what trash heap they threw it on." She shook her head. "What makes me so mad is that the people who set themselves up as judges to sentence her never lifted a finger to stop her doing it in the first place," she said, "much less stand up to Napoleon and try to stop him from taking up with her. According to their own code of honor, they ought to have done that, instead of waiting until the Campaign left. The only thing they were good for was standing around her on the scaffold cheering as she was executed. But not one of them could stand up to Napoleon's carriage when it picked her up. They were too cowardly."

She ate slowly, preoccupied. "I don't know whether to tell the secret or not," she said, "although it would be an exciting discovery. It could cause a stir. I could publish something saying 'Human Hair Found in Painting During Conservation,' or 'Why a French Artist from the Campaign Had His Paintings Removed from *The Description of Egypt*' or even 'Whom Did Zeinab al-Bakri Love? The Military Commander or the Painter?'"

"Maybe," he mused, "you should let the girl rest in peace. To society even today, her relationship with that artist would be considered a sin, and she would be doubly condemned, deemed once again a loose woman. A girl her age, and in that era, the lover of two men? What would people think of her?"

"But her love for the artist would mean it was never true that she was in love with Napoleon—that she was forced into a relationship with him, and that would mean she was unjustly executed."

"I think you should keep her secret." He looked at his watch. "I think I should go now if I want to be in time for my flight." He said goodbye with a warm hug. "I'll miss you."

She touched his cheek. "I'll be on the first flight back as soon as I'm done here."

She watched him go, pulling his carry-on bag behind him, until he was out of sight. She felt lighter, as if a heavy burden had lifted, a burden she had carried since she had found the painting.

It had been so much more than a painting to her: it had been a voice sent through the ether, bearing her a message.